GIRLS WHO LIE

A Mercy Harbor Thriller: Book Four

Melinda Woodhall

Melinda Woodhall
Visit my website at www.melindawoodhall.com

Printed in the United States of America

First Printing: November 2019
Creative Magnolia

For Tessa and David

Other books by Melinda Woodhall

The River Girls
Girl Eight
Catch the Girl
Her Last Summer
Her Final Fall
Her Winter of Darkness
Her Silent Spring
Her Day to Die

Sign up for the Melinda Woodhall Thrillers Newsletter
to receive bonus scenes and insider details at
www.melindawoodhall.com/newsletter

CHAPTER ONE

Burgundy liquid splashed into Jade Castillo's glass, sending blood-like spatters over the rim and onto the hardwood floor. The high-pitched ding of an incoming message sounded just as she stooped to wipe up the spill, a crumpled napkin clutched in one hand and an almost empty wine bottle in the other.

Stepping over to her laptop, Jade squinted at the screen. Her pulse quickened as she spied the flashing icon on the *Secret Fling* dashboard. A click on the icon produced a list of messages, all from the same sender.

The latest message from LonelyGuy10 sat unopened at the top of the list. Her dark eyes widened at the words in the subject line.

You Lied.

Resisting the urge to hit the *Delete* key without opening the message, Jade set down the glass and the wine bottle, her arms suddenly weak, her mind swirling with a mixture of fear and hope.

I guess I really blew it. But...he can't be that mad, can he?

The trembling of her hand as it hovered over the touchscreen belied the fleeting thought. She hesitated. Hadn't her mother often said that some things were best left unopened? Or had it been *unsaid*?

Chiding herself for her cowardice, she squared her shoulders.

I broke the rules and made a fool out of myself. Now the hottest guy in Willow Bay hates me and it's all my fault. Time to face the music.

Jade tapped on the screen, holding her breath as a new window popped open. The message was empty. There was nothing more he wanted to say.

You Lied.

The words echoed in Jade's head as she snapped the lid of her laptop shut. Her impulsive actions had violated *Secret Fling*'s strict confidentiality agreement, which was the core of the members-only website. The site boasted that it was the number one choice for consenting adults seeking discreet encounters.

I guess that's it then. No discreet encounter with LonelyGuy10 for me.

She closed her eyes, trying to block the image of his hard, handsome face. Trying to forget the scowl he'd worn when she'd approached him, eager to introduce herself.

A sudden rustling sound in the narrow hall behind her caused Jade to turn with a start. Wide yellow eyes stared out of the shadows, unblinking.

"Winston, what in the world are you staring at?"

The old cat cringed back against the wall, a low growl rumbling deep in his throat.

Jade frowned.

"Didn't I let you out when I got home from work?"

Moving across the room, Jade tried to recall what she'd done when she'd gotten home from her twelve-hour shift at the hospital. The long hours manning the ICU's busy nursing station, and the three glasses of wine that she'd quickly downed when she'd finally made it back to the rental house, clouded her mind and made it hard for her to remember much of anything.

A rush of fresh air greeted her as she entered the kitchen.

"What the hell?"

The heavy wooden door leading out to the backyard stood ajar, while the mild March wind sent the rickety screen door swinging back and forth in rusty protest. Shadow limbs from a nearby elm tree danced across the kitchen floor, sending a nervous shiver up Jade's back.

Padding across the hard tiles to the doorway, she peered out into the night, relishing the mild breeze on her alcohol-heated skin as she latched the screen and shouldered the backdoor shut.

The first faint notes of a song drifted in from the living room. Jade frowned and cocked her head. Was that Ray Orbison singing *Love Hurts*? Where was it coming from?

"You shouldn't have lied to me, Jade."

The deep voice growled in her ear as Jade twisted to face the man who had appeared behind her in the dark room.

"Who are you?"

The words were thick, sticking to the inside of her mouth like cotton candy. One rough hand covered her mouth while another wrapped around her waist, pulling her small frame against him in a suffocating embrace.

The music vibrated through her as did the words. Her stomach heaved as he bent to whisper in her ear, his breath hot and fetid.

"You wanted to meet me. Here I am. Or was that just a lie, too?"

A big fist made contact with the side of Jade's head, stunning her almost as much as his words had. He dragged her sagging body into the living room, stopping briefly to kick at Winston, who hissed and scurried under the sofa.

LonelyGuy10 stood over Jade's limp form, eyes gleaming behind a black ski mask. Jade stared up at him, willing herself not to blackout.

Karl has a ski mask like that. Only his is blue.

Her eyes watered as she thought of the sweet, pudgy man she'd left back in Minnesota. He'd been applying for jobs in Willow Bay but hadn't gotten lucky yet, and Jade had been secretly enjoying the single life for the first time since college.

Only she hadn't kept that particular secret from LonelyGuy10. She'd openly shared her fantasy with him. She'd admitted her intention to allow herself one last torrid affair before she settled down as Mrs. Karl Nickels.

"The single life isn't all it's cracked up to be, is it?"

Her attacker spit out the vicious words as he delivered a series of sharp kicks to Jade's ribs. She writhed on the floor, looking up at the man she had dreamed of meeting. The thought that he wasn't much taller than Karl floated through her throbbing head before he landed another kick. She wasn't the only one that had lied.

"Why are you–"

A hard fist stopped her mumbled words, and Jade teetered on the brink of consciousness, willing herself to fall into the blissful nothingness that threatened to overtake her. But a searing pain wrenched her back into the nightmare world of her living room.

The man in the black mask bellowed in anger above her, his hands clenching around a length of heavy wire. He wound the wire around her, trapping her arms at her sides, before moving down to her legs and ankles.

"Please, I'm sorry...I didn't mean..."

"You didn't mean to lie? You didn't mean to cheat?"

His angry laugh held something other than rage. What was it?

The sick bastard is getting off on this.

Fear rose in her chest as he dragged her toward the bedroom.

No, not like this. I didn't want this.

As he jerked her roughly forward, the wire around her caught against the edge of the sofa, sliding up to free one arm. Reaching up to claw at the hand that held her in an iron grip, her nails bent and snapped against stiff, unyielding leather. He was wearing gloves. He'd planned ahead, and he didn't intend to get caught.

But I know who he is. And he knows that I know...

The confused thought confirmed Jade's worst fear.

He's going to kill me. He won't let me live long enough to tell anyone who he is...and what he's done.

As the song started over, her stomach clenched in panic, forcing up a bitter mouthful of hot liquid. Turning her head to spit out the vile remains of her wine, she watched thick drops of blood fall from her battered face and quiver next to her on the hardwood floor.

"No use fighting," the man muttered, his deep voice muffled by the ski mask. "Now stop that whining. Time to take your punishment."

The man dropped to his knees beside her and wrapped his hands around her throat. He stared at her through the narrow slits of his ski mask as he tightened his grip.

"This is all your fault," he rasped, squeezing harder, his voice sounding far away. "You shouldn't have lied."

The telling ding of an incoming message sounded, penetrating the fog that had descended on Jade as the man's hands continued to tighten. Then the hands were gone, and the man was once again looming over her.

"Didn't waste any time now, did you?"

He emphasized his angry words with a forceful kick. Jade heard a sickening crack as pain radiated through her ribcage.

Forcing herself to keep her swollen eyes open, she watched the man stomp across the room to the computer and tap furiously on the keyboard. She used the reprieve to scan the room, hoping to see something, anything, that she could use to protect herself. She needed to find a weapon. Had to fight back.

Something moved in the shadows under the sofa. Winston's huge yellow eyes stared out at Jade as the frightened cat crouched beside a tattered wicker basket. The basket held a jumble of crafting supplies, but it was the dull gleam of a knitting needle that made Jade's heart jump with hope.

If I can just get my hand on the needle, maybe I'll have a chance.

Holding her breath, Jade stretched her arm out and felt the tips of her trembling fingers brush the rough basket. She'd need to get closer to get a firm grip on the long, slim needle.

A black boot appeared in front of her blurry eyes.

"What's your password, Jade?"

The man's voice shook with rage as he stared down at her, but her bruised throat constricted with fear, allowing only a tortured whimper to emerge.

"I asked you a question," the man hissed.

Jade shrank away as he raised his boot, but he lowered it again and strode back to the computer. Grabbing the thin laptop, he flung it against the wall with a hoarse yell.

"Now look what you've done!"

His harsh words reverberated around the tiny room as the scuffed black boots reappeared beside her.

Not waiting to see what he'd do next, Jade flung herself sideways, grabbing at the basket with her last bit of strength. Her hand closed around the smooth metal of the needle and pulled back in one swift movement.

Swinging her hand in a wild arc, Jade stabbed the needle into the back of the man's knee. The sharp point stuck into the thick fabric of his jeans, and he bellowed out in disbelieving fury, crashing to the ground like a wounded buffalo. He threw his head back in pain as he roared and thrashed against Jade.

Using her free hand to pull frantically at the wire around her, she squirmed backward but came up hard against the sofa. Steely hands seized her long, dark hair and wrenched her forward just as her other hand jerked free.

Before she could react, he lunged, throwing himself on top of her with a heavy grunt, forcing all the air out of her lungs. She gasped, feeling the room once again begin to fade away, and clawed up at him in a breathless, blind panic.

A jagged fingernail caught on a loose thread in his woolen ski mask. Suddenly the mask was in her hand and the man's face hovered over her, contorted and red with rage.

Her mind buckled in confusion and fear, but she held back a scream, forcing her lips to form the words.

"You're the one...who...lied."

The man jerked his head up at the whispered accusation, glaring at her in triumph. She stared back at him, a final spark of defiance flickering in her bruised and swollen eyes.

"You're not even..."

His arm moved with animal quickness to silence her words. She hadn't seen him pick up the empty wine bottle. She hadn't sensed the blow coming until it was too late.

As heavy glass smashed against fragile skin and bone, Jade's world, along with all her fantasies and plans, shattered into darkness.

CHAPTER TWO

Blue skies spread out in front of the white Expedition, setting an idyllic scene for another mild March day as Eden Winthrop steered the big SUV onto the winding road that led toward downtown Willow Bay.

Glancing in her rearview mirror, she saw Duke gazing out the window, his eyes bright with interest as they passed a woman walking a trio of tiny white poodles before swerving around a cyclist in yellow spandex.

"How about a little fresh air back there?"

Opening the back window far enough for the big golden retriever to stick his head out, she grinned, watching the wind blow his ears back and ruffle his soft fur. Feeling left out, she rolled down her own window, letting the cool breeze whip through her long blonde hair.

"Can't beat driving with the wind in our hair and blue skies ahead," she called back to Duke. "The only thing we're missing now, boy, is some feel-good music."

Eden switched on the radio and sat back in the driver's seat, her mind drifting immediately to her upcoming wedding and the long list of tasks she needed to get done before Saturday.

A few months ago, it seemed like the day would never come, and now it's almost here. Four more days and I'll be a married woman.

The thought of her future husband sent a thrill of anticipation through Eden, although it still seemed surreal that she was going to marry the tall, dark, and handsome defense attorney.

I'll be Mrs. Leo Steele, for better or for worse, 'til death do-.

Her musing was interrupted by an urgent voice on the radio. Channel Ten News had released a special bulletin. Eden raised both windows and turned up the volume.

"...the body was found this morning by a worried coworker when the woman failed to show up for her morning shift at Willow Bay General Hospital."

Straining to hear the rest of the report, Eden almost rear-ended a black Mercedes that had slowed down to turn onto Waterside Drive. She exhaled slowly, willing away the anxious ache that settled in her stomach just as a commercial for Willow Bay Auto Parts boomed from the car speakers.

Eden glanced once again at Duke's reflection in the rearview mirror, glad that he was with her. He'd been her emotional support animal for the last five years, helping her cope after the murder of her younger sister, Mercy, and supporting her as she'd struggled with the overwhelming anxiety that had followed.

While Eden had managed to get her anxiety under control, for the most part, it was nice to know Duke was still there for her if she needed him.

Turning the big vehicle into the parking garage beneath Riverview Tower, Eden navigated to the parking spaces reserved for the Mercy Harbor Foundation. The radio announcer's voice filled the car as Eden listened with dread.

"Now, back to our breaking story. What's the latest, Sabrina?"

The reporter's next words put an end to Eden's hope that the violence and killing in Willow Bay were over.

"Well, for those listeners and viewers just joining us, I'm standing outside a house on Juniper Circle where a woman's battered and mutilated body was found earlier this morning."

The reporter's high-pitched voice seemed to vibrate with excitement as she continued.

"The WBPD haven't released the identity of the victim yet, pending notification of next of kin, but neighbors tell me that the woman living here had recently moved to town and was an ICU nurse at Willow Bay General."

"Thank you for updating us, Sabrina." The words seemed strangely cheerful in light of the grisly report. "I'm sure all our listeners out there are wondering the same thing I am. Is this murder related to the recent attacks? I mean, two other women in the area have been assaulted. Could this be the same guy?"

Sudden voices rang out in the background, and loud sirens wailed shrilly, momentarily drowning out the reporter's response. By the time the siren had moved away, she was wrapping up.

"..reporting live from Willow Bay, this is Sabrina West."

Eden bit her lip, her mind echoing the announcer's suspicions that the murder was somehow connected to the previous attacks.

How will Bella and Olympia feel when they hear a third woman has been attacked...and that she didn't survive?

The two women who had both survived vicious attacks were still trying to heal, still broken and hurting from the brutal beating they'd each suffered. Closing her eyes, Eden tried to block out the images of the grisly injuries their assailant had inflicted.

Climbing out of the Expedition, Eden opened the door for Duke then hurried out of the sprawling concrete garage to the building's security entrance. She needed to get inside and talk to Reggie Horn.

She had to tell Mercy Harbor's director about the latest attack. Reggie would want to share the news with her two traumatized patients before they heard it from anyone else.

* * *

Eden's worry rose along with the elevator as she made her way up to the tenth floor. A stocky man wearing an expensive suit and an angry expression hovered in the doorway of Reggie's office, beads of sweat gleaming on his balding head. Turning as Eden approached, he surveyed her with small eyes that bulged behind designer glasses.

"Hello, Mr. Delancey, how are you?"

She braced herself for his response, reminding herself that Ian Delancey was suffering along with his wife.

It must be unbearable for him to know that Bella's attacker is still out there and there's nothing he can do but wait.

"Ms. Winthrop. Have you heard the news?"

Ian's lips pinched together in an accusatory line, and Eden felt her back stiffen in spite of herself.

"Yes, unfortunately, I did. I'm sure Bella must be very upset. How is she holding up?'"

"How do you think she's holding up? She woke up to the news that a killer's stalking Willow Bay. She's scared and...and the police are *useless*. They've done nothing to find the bastard that...that..."

His face suddenly fell, and for a minute Eden could see the fear and pain that lurked behind his belligerent attitude.

He's scared, too. And I can't say I blame him.

Reggie's small, thin frame appeared beside Ian in the doorway.

"Mr. Delancey wants to bring Bella in for an emergency session. I told him I have another patient scheduled this morning, and–"

"Who could possibly need help more than my Bella at a time like this?" Ian interrupted, his voice indignant. "I want you to see my wife this morning, Dr. Horn, or I'll be filing a complaint with the Department of Health for negligence and malpractice."

Holding up a placating hand to stop Ian's angry tirade, Reggie guided him firmly toward the elevator.

"I know you're upset, Mr. Delancey, and I understand your concern. How about I see Bella later this afternoon? If I juggle my schedule around I could see her around four o'clock. Will that work for you?"

The elevator doors opened and a willowy young woman with soft brown curls and wide, frightened eyes stepped out. An angry scar ran across one high cheekbone, and another trailed along her jawline.

Putting a small hand on Ian's back, Reggie prodded him into the open elevator and blocked the door to prevent him from stepping back into the hall.

"I'll see you and Bella at four o'clock, Mr. Delancey. Goodbye."

Eden breathed a sigh of relief as the door slid shut behind the man. She turned to Olympia Glass with a sympathetic smile.

"How are you, Olympia? I haven't seen you in a while."

The girl smiled back, revealing small, pearly white teeth.

"I'm okay, I guess. Everyone at the shelter has been so nice. I don't know what I'd do if I...if you hadn't..."

Letting her soft voice trail off, Olympia blushed and put a hand to her pink cheek as if to hide the scar.

"What I mean to say is...well...thank you."

The look of gratitude on Olympia's thin face caused Eden to blink back sudden tears. The young woman seemed so fragile, so childlike.

Olympia had been in shock when she'd arrived at Mercy Harbor two months ago, desperate for a safe place to hide. She'd been released from the hospital, her injuries having already started to heal but her psyche still reeling from the attack.

Without any family in town to turn to, Olympia had been too scared to stay on her own, so Eden had offered her a room at the foundation's main domestic abuse shelter for as long as she needed.

"I'm glad you're settling in." Eden tried to sound cheerful. "I believe Reggie is waiting for you."

Waving over at Reggie, Olympia walked toward the therapist's office. Eden felt a rush of anger as she noted the girl's uneven gait. The limp was a haunting reminder of the maniac who had attacked her, and Eden felt the familiar urge to hunt down the man who had inflicted it.

Walking down the hall to her own office, Eden sat at her desk, wondering how Olympia would take the news that a woman's body had been found. She felt too jumpy to start on any paperwork, so she pulled out her iPhone and read through her wedding to-do list.

She had gotten only halfway through the list when she heard raised voices down the hall. A loud crash and the sound of a door slamming brought Eden to her feet. She rushed into the hall to see Olympia standing by the elevator banging on the button.

"Olympia, what's going on? What's happened?"

Reggie appeared beside Eden.

"I explained that a woman's been found and there's no way of knowing if it's the same...person that attacked-"

"He's not a *person*," Olympia shouted. "That's just it. What person would do *this*?"

Olympia pulled the neckline of her shirt to the side, revealing a ring of red, angry-looking scars on her shoulder. The gruesome marks left by the vicious attack turned Eden's stomach, but she tried to conceal her revulsion.

"He's an *animal*. And he told me he'll come back for me."

The words stunned Eden.

"What? He threatened to come back? Why didn't you tell us, Olympia? Have you told the police?"

The doors to the elevator opened with a ding. Olympia spun around, scurrying inside. She turned back to Eden, a hunted expression on her face.

"I can't tell anyone," she moaned, her anger draining, morphing into stark fear. "He said he'd kill me, and...and I believe him."

Watching the doors close between them, Eden knew that chasing after the terrified woman would be futile. She was too upset to think clearly for the time being, and Eden could understand why.

Months had passed and the police had been unable to catch the man that had broken into the houses of two young women and brutalized them in their own homes.

Reggie clutched Eden's arm.

"I think you need to call the police and tell them what Olympia told us," she said, her big, brown eyes worried, but her voice firm. "I can't reveal anything Olympia's told me during our sessions without her permission, but..."

"But you want me to tell the police since I'm not Olympia's doctor?"

The sinking sensation in Eden's stomach was back.

"Well, if I believe a patient is in imminent danger I'm obligated to report my suspicions to the police," Reggie admitted, "but I'm not sure what I've just heard meets that requirement. Not yet...at least not officially."

Eden raised one smooth eyebrow in Reggie's direction.

"So, you think I should call the WBPD and tell them what Olympia said in an *unofficial* capacity?"

Reggie shrugged.

"I thought by now you'd have Detective Ainsley's phone number on speed dial. Maybe if you give her a call, she can assign someone to keep an eye on Olympia."

The thought of asking Detective Nessa Ainsley for help again tightened Eden's chest. The three previous times she'd called Willow Bay's only female detective to ask for help, they'd both ended up in perilous situations, barely managing to escape with their lives.

Memories of the violence and trauma she'd witnessed and suffered in the last year flooded in: the panicked chase to save her niece from serial killer, Vinny Lorenzo; the surreal horror of waking up in the barn where Chief Kramer was preparing to bury his next victim alive; the stark terror of being attacked by Jacob Albright in the vast Cottonmouth swamp at night.

Was she ready to get involved in a search for yet another violent predator? Eden winced at the thought of the nasty bite mark on Olympia's shoulder. She knew Bella Delancey had matching marks on her body as well. The angry scars turned Eden's stomach and made up her mind.

A monster is walking the streets of Willow Bay. What choice do I have?

If there was the slightest chance that the maniac who had attacked Olympia might return, Eden knew she'd have to let the police know.

But doubt lingered as she walked back to her office. The police had made a huge mistake by charging Oscar Hernandez with the attack on Bella Delancey. The wrongful arrest and prosecution of an innocent man had left the real attacker free to break into another woman's apartment.

The fact that Olympia Glass had been brutally assaulted in her own home while Oscar Hernandez sat in jail still infuriated Eden, along with everyone else in town. The entire community's faith in the WBPD to protect the public had been shaken.

So how can Olympia count on them to protect her now?

And Olympia wasn't the only one who'd gone through unnecessary anguish. Without Leo's help, Oscar Hernandez might still be in jail.

Luckily for Oscar, Leo had been there, working tirelessly to get the case dismissed, spending weeks going through the police files and talking to any and every witness that could shed light on the real attacker. Eventually, Leo had established that Oscar's alibi was airtight, and he was released.

But by then it had been too late to save Olympia from the horrific ordeal she'd suffered, and the real assailant had disappeared into the night.

The memory of Leo working night and day to prove Oscar's innocence brought a lump to Eden's throat. His obsession with that case had threatened their relationship, although, in the end, it had ended up bringing them closer together.

An idea began to form in Eden's mind.

Leo studied every detail of the attacks and combed through all the evidence. He probably knows as much about the case as the police do.

Her mood lightened at the thought of seeing Leo that evening. He would know what to say to make her feel better, and maybe he would be willing to share what he'd discovered during his defense of Oscar Hernandez.

Leo was absolutely convinced that Oscar was innocent; could he have some idea as to who the real culprit is?

Eden knew from experience that whoever had attacked Bella and Olympia would go on hurting women until he was caught and locked away. In fact, it seemed likely that he'd already escalated to murder.

And if he's the one that killed the woman over on Juniper Circle, it'll just be a matter of time before another woman is killed.

CHAPTER THREE

Pete Barker straightened the frame on the wall and stepped back to study it. The Class C Private Investigator license had arrived in the mail just that morning, and the mahogany frame lent the document a professional air that was sorely lacking throughout the rest of the shabby office. But Barker wasn't impressed.

His forehead creased into a deep frown as the door behind him opened. He didn't turn around at the sound of Leo Steele's voice.

"Congratulations are in order I see. You and Frankie are officially in business then?"

The words failed to remove Barker's frown. He swung around and pinned Leo with an accusatory stare. The innocent smile on Leo's face looked suspiciously like a smirk.

"The way I see it – this is pretty much your fault," Barker snapped, stepping around Leo to reach into a box on the floor.

He hadn't bothered to frame the document that he fished out and shoved at Leo.

"What's this?"

Leo took the paper. His mouth curled up in a smile as he read out loud.

"Class CC Private Investigator Intern license awarded to Peter Thomas Barker. I didn't know your middle name was Thomas."

Grabbing the license, Barker slapped it onto the desk and folded his arms across his substantial chest.

"You're the guy that helped Frankie earn his PI license, Leo." Barker cocked his head and raised his eyebrows. "So, that makes you partly responsible for the fact that I'm now Frankie's intern."

Leo's laugh filled the room, bringing Frankie in from the parking lot where he'd been unloading what looked like flat-packed office furniture from the back of a Chevy pickup.

"What's so damn funny in here?" Frankie asked, dropping the heavy IKEA box he'd been carrying with a loud huff.

Looking past Leo and Barker, his eyes found the newly hung frame. He scurried across the room, his fist pumping furiously into the air.

"Yessiree, Bob! That's me, Frankie Davis Dawson, Private Investigator!"

The glee in Frankie's voice caused Leo to laugh even louder, and soon Barker relented and joined in.

"Barker was just telling me how glad he is you were able to get this license, Frankie," Leo said, his voice thick with amusement. "I think he's looking forward to having you for a boss."

Barker smothered a pang of irritation as Frankie held up a skinny hand in protest.

"Don't start that crap, Leo. Barker and me are partners. Fifty-fifty and all that shit." Frankie grinned over at Barker with a conspiratorial wink. "Right, partner?"

Nodding in spite of himself, Barker gave a half-hearted thumbs up and bent to help Frankie lug the IKEA box further into the room.

"Let's get this desk set up so we're ready for the rush once we put up our *open for business* sign."

The Barker and Dawson Investigations sign they'd ordered wouldn't be delivered for several weeks, but Barker wasn't in any hurry. He was still recuperating, at least mentally, from the last case he and Frankie had tackled together.

They'd been trying to track down Taylor, Barker's estranged daughter, and he'd ended up collapsing from dehydration and exhaustion. In the end, Frankie had come to his rescue, overcoming an acute phobia of snakes and alligators to stay with Barker in the Cottonmouth swamp while waiting for help to arrive.

Wiseass, street-smart Frankie had proven to be a true friend more than once, and now his experience working as an investigator for Leo's law firm had secured the Class C license that he and Barker needed to open their own agency.

Like it or not, Barker owed Frankie.

Of course, that didn't mean he had to be happy about having to work under Frankie for a year as an intern to earn his own license.

But I guess there are worse guys I could be working for out there.

His mind flicked to Chief Kramer's surly face. The old police chief had run the department with an iron hand, all the while hiding a deadly secret. Barker had worked as a detective for the man for many years, never suspecting he was a serial predator.

Yeah, Frankie is definitely a step up from my last boss.

Barker's brooding was cut short when the office door swung open, revealing a stocky man in a crisp, expensive-looking suit. The tailored suit and designer glasses told Barker the man liked the finer things in life, and that he could afford to buy them.

Looks like this guy buys his clothes at the same place Leo shops.

The man looked around the dank office with obvious distaste.

"Is this Dawson and Barker Investigations?"

Opening his mouth to correct the man – it was Barker and Dawson after all – Frankie spoke up before he got the words out.

"Yes, sir, I'm Frankie Dawson and this is my partner, Pete Barker. How can we help you?"

Confused as to how the unpleasant man had found the office, Barker closed his mouth and listened, only vaguely interested in hearing what the man had to say.

Probably trying to sell insurance. Or maybe high-speed data.

"My name's Ian Delancey, and I'd like to hire a private detective," the man said, looking at Leo and Barker with suspicion.

"Let me guess," Frankie drawled. "It's about your wife. You think she might be foolin' around?"

Frankie's self-satisfied grin faded as he saw the anger rise in Ian Delancey's broad face.

"It's about my wife," Ian hissed, "but she's not *fooling around*. She was...attacked. *In our own home.*"

The man's eyes watered, but he held his composure as Frankie blinked and sputtered.

"Oh, man, I'm sorry. That was really shitty of-"

"Save the apologies, Mr. Dawson," Ian said, his words coming fast. "The police have done nothing, and now a woman has been killed. My wife is petrified; she's convinced the bastard that attacked her is going to come back, and that this time he'll finish the job."

Sucking in a deep breath, Ian spoke more slowly.

"So, I need someone who can track down the animal who did this. Your website said you were experienced in criminal investigations."

Barker glared over at Frankie.

"Website? What website?"

A guilty flush spread over Frankie's face as he turned to Barker.

"Uh, it was gonna be a surprise. You see, I kinda started this website and thought it'd be good-"

Ian's impatient voice stopped Frankie's hurried explanation.

"Is your agency capable of finding the man who attacked my wife or not?"

Barker stared at Frankie, trying to catch his eye. He wasn't sure he was ready to take on a highly emotional and demanding client like

Ian Delancey. They needed to talk it over before making a commitment, but his partner didn't look over or miss a beat.

"Sure we can." Frankie's voice was cheerful. "We kinda got a knack for tracking down and catching scumbags."

"Good," Ian said, closing his mouth abruptly as if momentarily taken aback at having accomplished his mission so quickly. "Then you'll start right away? Today?"

Clearing his throat discreetly, Leo stepped forward and placed a hand on Frankie's shoulder.

"I think you need to get an agreement in place first, right, Dawson?"

Frankie looked confused. It took him a minute to figure out that Leo was talking to him.

"Oh, right...Dawson. As in Barker and Dawson Investigations. I get it now. But I'm gonna just keep on using Frankie."

He turned to Ian Delancey with an earnest expression.

"Dawson is my last name, but everybody just calls me Frankie. I didn't think it would've sounded very professional if we named the company *Barker and Frankie.*"

Ian Delancey didn't smile at Frankie's attempt at humor. He just stared at Leo with a horrified expression.

"Why do you look familiar?"

Sticking out a big hand, Leo stepped forward.

"I'm Leo Steele, Mr. Delancey. I'm a lawyer. I believe we met when your wife gave her deposition in the Oscar Hernandez case."

Ian glared at Leo with bright, hard eyes, and Barker readied himself to jump between the two men if needed. After all, Leo had defended Oscar Hernandez, the man accused of attacking his wife; no telling what a distraught husband might do.

"I've been meaning to contact you, Mr. Steele."

Leo raised his eyebrows but remained quiet, giving Ian a chance to explain.

"You were very kind to my wife during the deposition," Ian said stiffly. "She was fragile and upset, and, well...I appreciate the fact that you treated her with...respect. And that you proved the police had gotten the wrong man."

"This is the best-damned lawyer in Willow Bay," Frankie said, slapping Leo on the back. "He's saved my ass more than once, that's for sure."

Ignoring Frankie's praise, Leo glanced at Barker, as if he wanted to say something, but was unsure he should. Barker shrugged and motioned for him to speak.

"Mr. Delancey, I'd be willing to share the background information I collected during the Hernandez case with Frankie and Barker if that would be of help. It'd save them quite a bit of legwork."

Ian narrowed his eyes in suspicion.

"Why would you do that? How much will it cost me?"

Barker saw Leo's back stiffen at the insulting tone, but the lawyer kept his face neutral.

"I want to get a violent offender off the street, Mr. Delancey. Your wife, and the other women in Willow Bay, deserve that much. There'll be no extra cost to you for my involvement."

Nodding in agreement, Ian turned to Frankie; both men ignored Barker's worried frown.

"Okay, Mr. Dawson, let's go ahead and get a contract signed. Then you and your partner can get out there and find the bastard."

* * *

Barker waited until Ian Delancey had left before he lit into Frankie.

"I thought we said we'd start off slow, *partner*," Barker fumed. "Maybe track down a few cheating husbands or help investigate bogus insurance claims. Nothing too dirty or dangerous."

Shaking his head in disbelief, Frankie turned to Leo.

"Can you believe this, man? I get us the biggest case in Willow Bay, a case that will make a name for us, and Barker's complaining."

"Yeah, it'll make a name for us all right. Our name will be mud with the WBPD after we start stepping all over their fucking toes."

The bewildered expression on Frankie's face made Barker even angrier. Did he really not understand how their involvement would be perceived by the department?

"You don't get it, do you, Frankie?"

"Oh, I get it, all right," Frankie responded, losing his jovial tone. "I get that you're wanting to play nice with the WBPD even if that means letting some loser run around killing women because they can't find jack."

Looking toward Leo for support, Barker was surprised to see the attorney's uncertain expression.

"He's right, Barker. The police have had months to find this perp and they've done nothing. Now a woman has been killed."

Leo shrugged his broad shoulders, but his voice hardened.

"I'd say somebody's got to try to find this guy before he decides to go hunting again."

"But working for the husband of one of the victims?"

Barker sunk into a folding chair and sighed.

"Maybe I'm still thinking like a cop, but isn't the husband always the number one person of interest? Does it make sense to work for a possible suspect?"

The words hung in the stuffy air of the dank office. All three men looked down at the threadbare carpet that had once been green but was now a mossy gray. Finally, Leo broke the silence.

"I'm pretty sure the cops are taking a close look at Ian Delancey. Once the charges against Oscar Hernandez were dismissed, the husband was bound to become a suspect again, but..."

"So, you think hubby could be the perp?" Frankie interrupted, eyes wide, "and that he could have attacked the other women to take the heat off himself?"

Shaking his head, Leo continued.

"No, what I was going to say is that I don't think it adds up. From what I can remember Ian Delancey was out of town the night his wife was attacked."

Barker rolled his eyes.

"That doesn't prove much. He could have hired someone to rough up his wife. Maybe he wanted to teach her a lesson. Or maybe the guy was supposed to kill her and he messes up."

Leo's face drained of color, and he closed his eyes. When he opened them again he stared at Barker with cold certainty.

"The man who attacked Bella Delancey was driven by pure rage and hate. He tried to tear her apart with his hands and...teeth."

He forced out the last word and swung to face Frankie.

"No, Ian Delancey didn't attack his own wife. I'd bet my career on it. The man who committed these attacks is extremely dangerous, and he's still out there."

Swallowing hard, Frankie looked down at the signed agreement and then over at Barker.

"And it looks like we're gonna be the lucky PIs trying to bring this guy in. So, when can we see your files on the case, Leo?"

He watched the attorney's dark eyes, sensing that Leo had something more to say.

"What is it, Steele? You know something we should know before we get started?"

Running a big hand through his dark hair, Leo grimaced.

"I hate to impugn a victim, I mean that's what a lot of defense attorneys do in court, and it always pisses me off, but..."

Frankie assumed his bewildered look again.

"What the hell are you talking about, Leo?"

"I'm saying I don't like implying that a victim's actions caused the crime...or justified the crime. So, what I'm going to tell you is in no way intended to tarnish Bella Delancey."

Barker nodded, pretty sure he knew where Leo was heading.

"It's just that, when I saw the photos, I wondered why Bella was wearing sexy lingerie the night she was attacked." Leo cleared his throat. "I mean, she was home alone, and Ian was nowhere to be found. It just struck me as odd, I guess."

Keeping his eyes on Leo, Barker frowned, not sure he understood.

"So, you think Bella was fooling around on her husband? That the perp knew her and that she invited him in?"

Leo hesitated, then nodded.

"Yeah, I guess that scenario crossed my mind."

"So, why didn't you ask her about it when you took her deposition?" Barker asked, scratching at the stubble on his chin he hadn't bothered shaving that morning.

"By the time I got a chance to talk to her several weeks had passed but she was still...fragile. I asked if she knew who her attacker was, but she insisted that she didn't. But something seemed...off."

"What do you mean?" Frankie asked. "You think she was lying?"

Doubt clouded Leo's face, and he shrugged again.

"I can't say for sure, but I got the impression she was hiding something, and that...that she was scared."

"Scared of who? You?" Barker asked.

"No, not scared of me. But she didn't want to talk, so maybe she was scared of...something, or someone. Maybe her husband. Maybe the attacker. I don't know."

Walking toward the door, Leo suddenly seemed anxious to leave. He turned with his hand on the doorknob.

"You guys can come by the office and look at the files this afternoon if you want. I'll tell Pat to get them ready for you."

Barker kept his eyes on the door after it closed behind Leo.

"That would really suck, you know."

Frankie's words were soft, almost thoughtful. Barker stared over at him in exasperation.

"What would suck?"

"If Bella Delancey held back information about what happened. If she didn't let the cops know how to find the guy. I mean, maybe she could have stopped him from attacking the other women."

Opening his mouth to disagree, Barker hesitated.

"Let's not get ahead of ourselves, Frankie. We don't even know if the attacks are connected to the body they found this morning. Could be two different perps."

"Yeah, sure, and I could win the fuckin' lottery tonight. I'd give both chances the same odds."

Barker rolled his eyes, but his gut was telling him that Frankie was right. The worst kind of killer was stalking Willow Bay, and it was now up to Barker and Dawson Investigations to find him.

"You finish setting up this desk," he told Frankie, pulling out his car keys. "I'm gonna try to talk to Nessa. See what she'll tell me about the body they found."

CHAPTER FOUR

The crime scene on Juniper Circle was less than a mile from Detective Nessa Ainsley's house on Cranberry Court. Earlier that morning she had kissed Jerry goodbye at the front door, yelled at the boys to get a move on before they missed the school bus, and then driven down several familiar streets toward the bloody scene that awaited nearby.

The whole morning had seemed surreal; like a nightmare that she couldn't escape, no matter how much she told herself to wake up.

"Hey, Nessa, I think you'll want to see this. Nessa...?"

Detective Simon Jankowski called to her from the depths of the little house. Turning her head toward her partner's persistent voice, Nessa hesitated.

She didn't want to go back inside. Not yet.

She preferred being outside, even with the reporters prowling at the edge of the crime scene perimeter like hungry beasts waiting to pounce on any scrap of information.

The morning air was cool and fresh, unlike the heavy, putrid air that filled the small living room behind her, and which had left a nauseating metallic taste in her mouth.

"What is it, Jankowski?" she called, stalling for time. "I'm kinda busy out here."

Jankowski appeared in the doorway, his handsome face set in an impatient frown as he glanced toward the throng of reporters and press, then glared over at Nessa.

She pushed back a red curl that had fallen over one eye and gestured toward the notebook in her hand, hoping the big detective wouldn't notice that most of the lines on the page were still empty.

"Stop slacking off and get in here," Jankowski growled as he spun and hurried back into the scene.

Taking one last gulp of fresh air, Nessa pulled up her face mask and checked that her protective overalls, gloves, and booties were still firmly in place.

"All right. Hold your horses, Jankowski. I'm coming."

The protective mask muffled her irritable reply but didn't quite hide her southern drawl.

"Back here, Nessa. In the bedroom."

Nessa walked carefully within the lines of tape that outlined the path of contamination across the hardwood floor.

Alma Garcia, Willow Bay's senior crime scene technician, had instructed everyone working the scene to use the path when moving between rooms. It helped to minimize unintended contact with forensic evidence, and Nessa had no intention of defying the order.

I'm just fine keeping my distance. In fact, I'd be even finer outside.

Keeping her eyes glued to the tape, Nessa avoided looking at the dead woman sprawled across the floor. She'd always hated leaving a dead body exposed and unattended at a scene while waiting for the medical examiner to arrive. But, as always, she had no choice.

I just hope Iris arrives soon. I'm starting to feel queasy.

The bedroom's window blinds were tightly closed against the blue sky beyond, but a portable LED light stood in the corner, illuminating every crack and crevice. Nessa stepped through the doorway, glad that the carnage had been restricted to the living room.

Jankowski stood next to a dresser against the far wall pointing down into the top drawer. Crossing to stand next to him, Nessa half expected to see a severed hand, or maybe a bloody weapon.

She looked down and saw with relief that the drawer held a stack of crisp white scrubs. The only other items in the drawer included a stainless-steel stethoscope and a laminated name badge.

"It's from Willow Bay General Hospital," Jankowski said, using a gloved hand to pick up the badge. "Jade Castillo, RN."

The photo on the badge showed a pretty woman with long, dark hair and a friendly smile. The resemblance to the body in the other room was unmistakable.

"So, now we know who the victim is," Nessa murmured, studying the photo. "All we have to do is find the perp."

Her eyes stayed on Jankowski as he bent to open the bottom drawer. He pulled out a framed photo that had been shoved facedown under a silky stack of lingerie.

"Women always hide something in their underwear drawer," he said, his voice uncharacteristically soft. "I guess they think no one will have the bad manners to look there."

Nessa watched as he propped the frame on the dresser, and she found herself swallowing a sudden lump in her throat.

A radiant Jade Castillo had been captured in time, her eyes sparkling as she held up a playful hand to admire a diamond solitaire ring on her finger. The heavyset man next to her had wrapped a thick arm around her shoulders as if he wanted to protect her.

Or, maybe he was holding on to her. Maybe he wanted to make sure she wouldn't leave.

"Does she still have that ring on her finger?"

Nessa raised her eyebrows at Jankowski's question. She hadn't noticed a big diamond ring, but then, there was a lot of blood.

"What ring is that?"

The soft voice made both Nessa and Jankowski jump.

A small figure in blue protective coveralls and a face mask stood in the doorway holding an enormous black bag.

"Thank goodness you're here, Iris."

Nessa rushed toward Willow Bay's chief medical examiner, relief flooding through her.

"Sorry, it took me a while." Iris gazed at Nessa through thick protective goggles. "I had arranged to take my father over to Tampa for a doctor's appointment this morning. We were almost there when the call came in."

Nodding in sympathy, Nessa couldn't help but admire Iris' dedication to her elderly father. He'd been suffering from Alzheimer's for a while now, and Iris had moved to Willow Bay a few years back to help her parents cope with the devastating effects of the disease.

"I'm sorry your trip was cut short, Iris." Jankowski's sincere tone surprised Nessa. "But I'm glad you're here now."

Nessa crossed her arms over her chest and raised an eyebrow in mock disapproval.

"So, you two are still dating, then?"

Iris ignored Nessa's question and turned back to face the blood-spattered living room. She squared her small shoulders and sighed.

"Let's get started."

* * *

Iris finished her examination of Jade Castillo's body just as Nessa ended her call with Jerry. She'd had to cancel their plans to meet for lunch at the new Indian restaurant on Bay Street. She didn't feel much like eating anyway. Not after the morning she'd had.

"I'll call Wesley and tell him to back the van up to the house." Iris pulled down her face mask, pushed back her goggles, and exhaled deeply. "We can try to get the body out before the press gets wind of what we're doing."

Noting the medical examiner's anxious expression, Nessa put a hand on her tense shoulder. Iris was usually so composed, especially at a scene.

"You okay, Iris?" Nessa asked, feeling oddly mature; normally she was the one being comforted by Iris.

Nodding weakly, Iris attempted a smile. She looked around to make sure none of the scene techs could overhear, then leaned closer.

"This is just so...disturbing." She seemed to search for the right words. "I mean, the bite marks...the blunt force trauma. It's just so vicious. Almost...*inhuman*."

Her words made Nessa's heart stop.

"Bite marks? On the body?"

Iris nodded, her face pale.

"I've seen bite marks before during my training, but this is the first time I've encountered them at a real scene."

Catching her breath, Nessa clutched Iris' arm tighter.

"I've seen bite marks recently. On a victim." She closed her eyes against the memory. "Two assault victims actually, only they were alive. I mean...they still are."

Iris raised delicate eyebrows.

"You mean the two assaults that have been in the news? The victims were *bitten*?"

Nessa nodded, anger simmering as her gaze rested on Jade Castillo's broken body.

"It must be the same nasty bastard."

Iris looked past Nessa, her eyes softening as Jankowski approached.

"You ready to bring out the body?"

Jankowski had once again assumed the gentle voice he reserved for Iris; Nessa rolled her eyes.

"Why didn't you tell your girlfriend here about the bite marks on the assault victims, Jankowski?"

Both Jankowski and Iris gasped at Nessa's blunt question.

"What? You two don't talk business?" Nessa sighed and looked toward the door. "Whatever happened to pillow talk?"

Before they could respond, Alma Garcia entered the room carrying a large evidence bag. She crouched next to the shattered wine bottle and began picking up shards of glass and placing them carefully in the bag. She called over as she worked.

"I've been thinking." Alma's forehead creased behind her protective glasses. "How come the reporters showed up here before my crime scene techs?"

"Maybe your techs were dragging their asses."

Jankowski's voice was hard again.

Alma wasn't put off that easily. She shook her head and stood up, putting one gloved hand on her hip. Nessa tried not to stare at the red smear that appeared on the blue Tyvek.

"My team arrived within minutes of getting the call from your first responders," Alma insisted, "but the Channel Ten van was already pulling up. The rest of the vultures weren't far behind."

A hulking figure knocked on the door, opened it, and stepped inside, pulling a metal gurney in after him.

"Hey, Wesley," Nessa called, glad to see the young man was back at work. "Were you able to back the van up close to the house?"

Nodding behind his protective hood, the forensic technician pushed the gurney between the lines of tape toward the body. He didn't look at Jankowski or offer a greeting.

Guess he's still pissed off about Jankowski's interrogation tactics.

When Wesley Knox had been deemed a person of interest in the murder of a young girl earlier in the year, Jankowski had mercilessly grilled the young forensics technician, refusing to take it easy on him just because he worked for the medical examiner's office.

Eventually, after missing several days of work, Wesley had been cleared of any wrongdoing and had returned to his job. But, based on his sullen attitude, Nessa figured Wesley still wasn't ready to forgive Jankowski for the whole upsetting ordeal.

Wanting to give Iris and Wesley time to load Jade's body onto the gurney, Nessa made her way into the kitchen. She tried not to touch anything as she pulled out her phone to check her messages.

Five missed calls. All from Pete Barker. She tapped the screen and waited for her old partner to pick up.

"Hey, Nessa. What's up? I hear there's a new homicide over near your neighborhood. Jerry and the kids all right?"

She relaxed at the familiar sound of Barker's voice.

"Yeah, the scene's just a stone's throw away, Barker. Scary shit."

She felt her skin crawl as she wondered if the man who had beaten Jade Castillo to death lived nearby.

Maybe he even passed my house on the way home from the scene.

Her eyes widened at Barker's next words.

"You think this new homicide could be related to the Bella Delancey assault? Could it be the same perp?"

Nessa hesitated, then looked over her shoulder to make sure Jankowski or Alma hadn't snuck up behind her.

"Yeah, actually, I think this perp is the same piece of shit."

Barker was silent for a long beat. Nessa wasn't the type to make snap judgments, and she didn't usually curse. She considered herself to be a southern lady. At least most of the time. Her foul-mouthed response took him by surprise.

"Wow, this guy has really got you all worked up."

She nodded, not caring that he couldn't see her over the phone. Finally, she cleared her throat to speak.

"I guess as you said, it's just a little too close to home. And, well...the killing and the assaults make it clear the perp is a sick bastard. And that he's escalating-"

She paused as Alma's raised voice sounded from the living room.

"I gotta go, Barker. We can talk later."

She hurried through the door to see that the body had already been removed, leaving behind a grisly pattern of bloody swirls and smears.

Alma stood by the sofa holding up an iPhone in a glittery pink case. A plump orange tabby cat slunk past Nessa's feet. Droplets of dark liquid glistened in the cat's fur.

"This phone was wedged under the sofa. Along with that cat."

Taking a deep breath, Alma dropped the phone into an evidence bag and then turned toward the computer that had been smashed against the wall.

"I'll send the phone and computer to my friend at the state lab. He'll be able to get me whatever's on the hard drive; he'll likely be able to hack into the phone as well."

Alma began to bag the remains of the laptop, then paused.

"What's going on outside?"

Nessa listened. The sounds of the crowd had grown louder. Sticking her head out the front door, Nessa immediately saw the cause of the commotion.

Gabby Jankowski, Willow Bay's media relations officer, stood on the sidewalk just past the crime scene perimeter wearing a tailored black dress and patent leather pumps. She flashed a flirtatious smile at Officer Andy Ford, who was manning the perimeter. The young cop's freckled cheeks turned bright pink as he allowed Gabby to slip past him.

Muttering another curse, Nessa opened her mouth to call out to the young uniformed officer, when Jankowski appeared next to his ex-wife, face tense.

"What do you want, Gabby?"

Nessa winced at the tremor of anger in his voice. He seemed precariously close to losing control and lashing out at the woman whose affair with a much-younger man had ended their ten-year marriage.

Jankowski's anger at her betrayal still simmered under the surface even though Gabby had already moved on from her first boy toy. In fact, if the rumors Nessa had heard were true, Jankowski's ex had moved on several times, with several different men.

Nessa watched as Gabby smiled coquettishly at her ex-husband, ignoring Wesley's attempt to steer the medical examiner's van out of the driveway.

Iris Nguyen's small face appeared in the van's passenger-side window as it accelerated toward downtown, but Jankowski didn't see her; he was too busy arguing with Gabby to notice Iris' crestfallen expression.

Rushing forward, Nessa put a hand on her partner's arm.

"Come on, Jankowski, she isn't worth making a scene over."

"Yeah, Simon, I just want to talk." Gabby let her eyes linger on his lips. "You could come by the house and *fill me in.*"

A small, blonde reporter pushed past Officer Ford, shoving a long microphone toward Nessa's face.

"Detective, have you identified the victim, yet? Is it true she was a nurse at Willow Bay General?"

Releasing an exasperated breath, Nessa shook her head.

"No information regarding the victim's identity will be released until we've notified next of kin."

The reporter opened her mouth to protest, then her eyes fell on Gabby.

"Hurry up, Boyd," she called out, waving over to a barrel-chested cameraman. "We might not get another chance."

Flipping a long strand of blonde hair over her shoulder, she thrust the microphone toward Gabby.

"This is Sabrina West with Channel Ten News. I'm outside the scene of a homicide on Juniper Circle with Gabriella Jankowski, the media relations officer for the city of Willow Bay."

Gabby glared at the reporter, then spun to face the camera.

"Thank you, Sabrina, for giving me the chance to reassure the citizens of Willow Bay that our police department has everything under control." She smiled over at Jankowski. "Isn't that correct, *Detective Jankowski?*"

Shooting a look of pure hatred at his ex, Jankowski turned on his heel and stormed back into the house. Nessa scurried after him.

Alma was brushing the tabby cat in search of trace evidence when Nessa entered the house. Forgetting to hold her breath in her haste, Nessa gagged as the putrid odor greeted her.

"The public is out for blood," she told Alma, who was stuffing a ball of orange fluff into an evidence collection bag. "The press are demanding an update."

Handing the heavy cat to Nessa, Alma reached for her camera and began to snap photos of the dazed feline. Nessa could feel the animal trembling in her arms, and she instinctively held him closer against her chest.

"It's okay, buddy. You're gonna be fine."

"His name's Winston," Alma said, nodding toward the tag that dangled from a blue velvet collar. "I think the poor thing is in shock."

Winston lifted his wide yellow eyes to Nessa's face, his expression unreadable. She wondered what would happen to the obviously well-loved pet once Alma was finished with her inspection.

The buzz of an incoming text message from city hall interrupted her thoughts. She thrust the phone back in her pocket without reading the message, knowing it would be the city's acting chief of police, Mayor Hadley, wanting an update. Reporting to the slick politician always set her teeth on edge, but she had no choice.

If I want to be the new chief of police, I have to play nice with Hadley.

Kissing up to the mayor and the good old boys on the city council was expected. Otherwise, they'd bring in someone else to run the department. Better not to risk it; the last chief of police they'd brought in had ended up being a serial killer.

Suddenly glad for an excuse to leave the smell of death behind, Nessa gave Winston one last hug, then handed him back to Alma. Slipping out the back door, she pulled off her coveralls and circled around to her Charger. She was well on her way to downtown Willow Bay before any of the reporters realized she was gone.

CHAPTER FIVE

C hannel Ten's newsroom buzzed with activity as Veronica Lee reviewed the data, already knowing what she would find. The mid-morning weather report would be just as boring as the breakfast report had been: mild temperatures, clear blue skies, and zero chance of rain.

The same weather pattern had been holding strong for over a week now; it was getting harder to come up with an opening teaser that would keep Willow Bay viewers watching, much less fill the full ninety-second weather segment with anything remotely interesting.

She scanned the data report again, hoping an idea for a fresh angle might strike. Something that would get the station manager's attention.

If I use more footage of smiling dog walkers and cheerful joggers, Hunter will slash my airtime for sure. Especially with everything else going on.

Releasing a defeated sigh, Veronica stared over at the busy news desk, her eyes lingering on Sabrina West's blonde head, surrounded as usual by the excited faces of the newsroom crew. She lowered her eyes to hide the jolt of envy that passed through her. Shame burned her cheeks as she scolded herself.

I should be happy for Sabrina. After all, I recommended her for the job.

Pushing her laptop away, Veronica stood and stretched her neck from side to side, trying to ease the stiffness. Several glossy strands of jet-black hair fell over one shoulder as she tucked her blouse into the waistband of a slim-fitting skirt.

Only ten minutes until she would be on the air, and she wanted to run through the report one more time using the green screen. She'd been reading the weather for over a year now, but she still got confused sometimes and pointed to the wrong spot on the screen.

"Can you believe this, Veronica?"

Sabrina had appeared beside her.

"I mean, can you believe I've caught such a big story?" Her roommate's big blue eyes filled with excitement as she clutched Veronica's arm. "And Hunter thinks some of the networks may even want to use my footage. Of course, I'm sure Nick Sargent at Channel Six will try to beat me to it."

Smiling with as much enthusiasm as she could muster, Veronica squeezed Sabrina's small hand and pushed back unkind thoughts about the blonde's lack of concern for the woman who had been killed, or the loved ones she may have left behind.

"It is a big story," Veronica agreed. "Although it's also scary."

Perplexed, Sabrina's smile faltered.

"What do you mean? I'm not scared. I'm ready for this."

Veronica shook her head.

"I don't mean that kind of scary. You do realize there's a killer on the loose in the city, don't you? You do realize what this is all about?"

But Sabrina's attention was already on the news van that had pulled up outside.

"Look, Boyd's ready with the van. We're going back out. I'll see you later."

Not waiting for a reply, Sabrina hurried out the door with Veronica staring after her in dismay.

"She's certainly enthusiastic."

The deep voice behind Veronica made her jump. She turned to see the station manager, Hunter Hadley, staring after Sabrina as well.

"Yes, and she's doing a great job," Veronica blurted automatically.

Hunter studied Veronica with a curious expression, and she felt her nerves begin to tingle. Something about the intense, brooding man made her feel like she was an awkward high school nerd again instead of a twenty-six-year-old college graduate with a degree in broadcast journalism.

"You did me a real favor by recommending Sabrina." Hunter sounded amused. "And I'm sure Tenley's relieved that we found someone to cover for her who's just as...well...*driven* as she is."

The cool eyes of Tenley Frost, Channel Ten's long-time senior reporter, flashed in Veronica's mind. She doubted the reigning diva of the news station was cheering on her young replacement, but her impending maternity leave hadn't given her a say in the matter.

And then I had to open my big mouth and mention that Sabrina was available. Way to go, Veronica!

Having Sabrina West, her best friend and college roommate, work with her at Channel Ten had seemed a perfect solution at the time. It wasn't until after Sabrina had been hired that Veronica realized she'd never even thought of asking to fill the position herself. But she only had herself to blame; it was her fault for being too timid to speak up.

"Better get over to the studio, Veronica. You're on in five."

She drew in a deep breath, determined to ask for a chance to report on a real story before the station manager walked away. She wanted to do more than read weather reports prepared by the meteorologist at Channel Ten's sister station in Tampa.

"Mr. Hadley? Um, I-"

"How many times do I have to tell you, Veronica? Mr. Hadley is my *father*. I'm Hunter, and you're going to miss your segment."

"But I want to report on the real news," she said quickly, needing to get the words out before she lost her nerve. "Not just the weather. I mean, I want to report on serious news, like this new homicide."

Hunter stepped closer and frowned down into her face.

"You have no idea how lucky you are to be reporting on sunny days in the safety of this studio."

He ran a big hand through his hair, pushing several unruly brown curls back from his forehead. His eyes blazed with a strange urgency.

"It's a dangerous world out there, Veronica. An ugly place...it can...damage you."

"Veronica, you're on in two minutes."

The producer's voice sounded over the buzz of the newsroom, causing Veronica to spin around in panic. When she looked back, Hunter Hadley was already striding toward his office, his shoulders tense and his fists clenched by his side.

Rushing toward the studio, she fixed a broad smile on her face, and she read the news report in a confident, cheerful voice that belied the insecurity Hunter's words had stirred up. She wrapped up her report with relief.

"...now, get out there and take advantage of the fine weather while it lasts. This is Veronica Lee, wishing you a wonderful weather day!"

Stepping away from the cameras, Veronica heard a lead-in to the next story.

"And now for today's breaking story..."

Needing a breath of fresh air, Veronica picked up her cell phone and headed back through the newsroom toward the exit. She didn't look up as she pushed through the door.

"Excuse me!"

The angry woman standing in the doorway was all too familiar. Veronica had seen the same tailored black dress on Sabrina's breaking news report just that morning.

"Sorry," Veronica muttered.

Stepping back to allow Gabby Jankowski to storm past her, Veronica saw Hunter open the door to his office with a scowl on his face. He didn't look at all happy to see the woman he'd been dating off and on for the last few months.

Looks like there's trouble in paradise...again.

Veronica had known Gabby was bad news from the first day she'd shown up flashing her plastic smile and putting her hand possessively on Hunter's arm every chance she got. But, of course, it wasn't Veronica's place to say anything. She was just the lowly weather girl and Hunter Hadley was the station manager and the mayor's son. He didn't need her advice on his love life.

Once outside, Veronica's mind returned to the angry look that had transformed Hunter's face when she'd asked to report on the real news.

Something's off with him lately, and I bet the wicked witch of Willow Bay has something to do with it.

Her phone buzzed and Veronica looked down to see her mother's number. Bracing herself with a deep cleansing breath, she tapped on the screen and again stretched her mouth into a smile.

Ling Lee could always tell when her daughter was smiling, even over the phone, and Veronica wasn't prepared to get into a conversation about why she was feeling down.

"Hi, Ma."

Veronica tried for a cheerful yet casual tone, hoping it would quell Ling Lee's incessant worry about her only daughter.

"You can stop the act, Ronnie. I know when something's bothering you."

Rolling her eyes, Veronica let her voice fall into a depressed monotone.

"Stop calling me that, Ma. I go by Veronica now. And are you trying to tell me you know how I feel by just hearing me say *hi*?"

"Am I wrong?"

A lump lodged in Veronica's throat. She coughed, then swallowed hard against the groan of frustration that threatened.

"No, you're never wrong, Ma. I'm just frustrated. It feels like I'll never be a real reporter."

She twisted around at the sound of the door opening behind her. Gabby Jankowski stomped past without a word. The look on her face was enough to let Veronica know that, for once, the media relations officer hadn't gotten her own way.

"You just keep doing your job, Ronnie. Something big is going to come your way soon. I can feel it."

"I hope so, Ma." Her voice softened at the thought of her mother's worried eyes. "I'm sure it'll work out, but I gotta go. See you later."

Ending the call, she kept her eyes on Gabby's sporty red car as it raced out of the station's parking lot, cutting into traffic without stopping. Horns blew as Gabby disappeared toward the city's modest skyline, and Veronica turned back toward the station, not ready to give up just yet.

There's a breaking story brewing out there for me, too. I've just got to find it before it's too late.

CHAPTER SIX

H unter held his breath as he saw the door to the news station open again. Exhaling in relief, he watched Veronica Lee cross to her little desk against the wall. Just as long as it wasn't Gabby coming back for round two. Their first round had already used up what little patience he had left.

Rubbing his eyes with a shaky hand, Hunter walked to his desk and collapsed into his chair. The nightmares had been worse than usual the night before, and it was all he could do to keep his eyes open. Gabby's surprise visit to tell him she was thinking of getting back with her ex-husband had only added to his bad mood.

Not that he cared what his father's manipulative media relations officer did, or who she dated. She'd lied to him once too often and he'd had enough. Time to move on. Again.

Trying not to think of the long list of women he'd dated since returning to Willow Bay, he closed his eyes and inhaled deeply. Bella Delancey's lovely face hovered, then faded into a scornful memory. Gabby's taunting had gotten under his skin.

"You still have the hots for Bella, don't you?" Her face had twisted into an ugly sneer. *"But she's moved on...and so should you."*

The voices in his head grew louder, mixing with the sounds of the past that refused to go away. He tried to push away the unwanted memories that Gabby's spiteful words had stirred.

I should never have opened up...never shared anything with her.

But Gabby had seemed so concerned, so sincerely interested in him, that he'd lowered his guard and admitted that he was still struggling to get over some things from his past.

Of course, his disastrous relationship with Bella Delancey was just one of the many past experiences he was trying so hard to forget. But the other things were impossible to explain to someone like Gabby. Someone who had never seen death close-up. Someone who had never experienced real fear.

So, he'd admitted that Bella had dumped him when he'd been at a low point and that her quick marriage to his old schoolmate, Ian Delancey, had felt like a betrayal.

What he hadn't told Gabby was that he'd realized long ago that he would never be able to commit himself to any woman. Bella had quickly figured that out, and she'd simply moved on. Hunter couldn't really blame her. It wasn't her fault he remained anchored to the past. Few women would be able to deal with the baggage he carried around.

Gabby was a perfect example. She'd soon lost interest in his brooding and mood swings, as well as his preference to stay at home, away from loud crowds and excitement. Gabby thrived on excitement, and it hadn't taken her long to get restless.

Just as well. Her true colors were beginning to show under all that polish.

Shaking the thought of Gabby and Bella from his mind, Hunter picked up his car keys and quietly opened the door to his office, hoping not to attract anyone's attention as he left the station. Only Veronica Lee looked up as he wordlessly slipped out into the dazzling blue day.

His Audi sedan was parked in the usual reserved spot, and he quickly climbed in and steered the sleek black car out of the parking lot, heading west on Townsend Boulevard. He wanted to get to the highway. He needed time to drive and think.

Stopping at a red light, his eyes automatically searched the surrounding area. He glanced in the rearview mirror, then checked out the cars on either side of him. He'd just decided it was safe to relax when the Oldsmobile in front of him backfired.

Pulse racing, Hunter unfastened his seatbelt and prepared to jump out of the car. It took only seconds for his mind to register that the only danger around him was the carbon monoxide spewing from the Oldsmobile's tailpipe.

But it was too late. He was already sweating, and his hands felt shaky. Adrenaline flooded through him, along with the disturbing memories that loud noises always conjured.

He drew in a deep breath and exhaled; it did no good.

Dr. Horn said the breathing exercises would calm my nerves. That eventually my flashbacks will start to fade. I guess she lied, too.

But then, nothing seemed to help lately. Hunter was starting to think he should never have stopped going to the therapy sessions his father had demanded he try.

"No son of mine's going to make a fool of himself in this town," his father had yelled after one of his more violent flashbacks. *"You go get some help before things go too far."*

Hunter stepped on the gas, accelerating past the offending Oldsmobile and moving into the fast lane that would take him toward the coast. Maybe a walk on the beach would stop the demons from taking over. Perhaps the fresh air and mild breeze would cleanse the images of blood and screams from his weary, aching mind.

* * *

The wet sand under Hunter's feet felt cold and unpleasantly rough. He rolled up his pant legs and let the tepid, salty water lap at his ankles as he held his face toward the sun, which was inching ever higher in the sky.

It was almost lunchtime, and his stomach was protesting his decision to limit his breakfast to a can of orange juice from the station's vending machine. He'd given up caffeine years ago, so the juice hadn't even been accompanied by a cup of coffee. Not much to go on for a man who stood six-foot-two and weighed a solid one-hundred eighty pounds.

My mind may be screwed up, but at least my body's still in shape.

Guilt pierced him at the thought. He'd known too many good people that couldn't say the same. Too many people that hadn't made it through.

"I'm whole, for Christ's sake." His voice disappeared into the wind over the water. "I'm in one fucking piece and yet I'm standing here whining like a damn baby."

Looking around in sudden fear that he was being watched, or even followed, he saw that the beach was still deserted. Tuesdays weren't busy days on the beach. At least not until Spring break started for the local schools.

He trudged back toward his car, stopping to stare again out into the horizon even though he felt the responsibility pulling on him. The Channel Ten team was handling a big story; they'd need his guidance to prepare the evening newscast. None of them had the type of experience he had.

Hunter's years spent as a foreign correspondent in the Middle East had exposed him to the kind of stories rarely encountered in a small town like Willow Bay. That was one of the main reasons he'd taken the job when his father had called to tell him that the previous station manager was going to retire.

"Come home and find yourself a wife." His father's voice had sounded lightyears away over the satellite phone. *"Get your act together and make me some grandbabies."*

But the last thing Hunter wanted was to bring an innocent child into the kind of world that produced suicide bombers and mass murderers. It was a dirty, ugly world, and he wanted no part in inflicting it on anyone else.

Forcing his sandy feet back into his work shoes, Hunter heard excited laughter and the exasperated call of a woman's voice. He twisted his head to see a small girl toddling across the sand, perhaps fifty yards down the beach.

"Bonnie? Wait right there!"

The girl raised a chubby hand to her mouth and giggled as she ran from her mother, who was loaded down with a beach bag, towels, and a cooler on wheels.

Hunter stared as the child, no more than two or three years old, darted toward the water, a mischievous smile on her face.

"Bonnie!"

The child splashed into the water, unprepared for the soft, sucking sand, immediately falling forward into the undulating surf. She rose with a frightened cry, then fell backward as a gentle wave washed over her.

A panicked scream from the girl's mother caused Hunter to jump into action. He pounded across the sand, heart thudding in his ears. Time seemed to slow down as he covered the space between them, his wet, sandy feet grinding painfully against the snug leather of his work shoes.

The pain faded and the sun seemed to set in the sky.

"Oh my god, my little girl!"

The voice sounded over Hunter, and he looked up in surprise. He was suddenly on the sand, holding the toddler against him in a tight grasp. He loosened his grip and the child pushed away, reaching for her mother.

"Thank you so much."

Standing over him, the woman stared down with shocked eyes. She wore the same look he'd seen many times on the faces of survivors. People who had glimpsed their worst nightmare as it had inexplicably passed them by while sweeping others away into the dark. It was a look that he always hoped never to see again.

"Are you okay?"

The woman was still staring at him as she used trembling hands to towel off her daughter. She wrapped the towel tightly around the little girl, who studied Hunter with wide eyes.

Nodding, Hunter stood and tried to wipe the sand off his pants. They were sopping wet and caked with sand. He thought distractedly that he'd have to swing by his house and change before going back to the studio.

"Yes, I'm fine." His voice was hoarse, but he managed to follow the words with a weak smile. "But you need to keep a close eye on this little one. The world's a scary place. You never know what can happen."

Turning to leave, he stopped long enough to help the woman gather the towels and bag she'd dropped in her panic.

"Thanks for...for saving Bonnie."

The woman's voice called after him as he plodded through the sand toward his car. He lifted a hand in response, not turning around, and continued to walk. He needed to get home and change, and then he needed to get to Reggie Horn's office.

He was losing time again, and he needed someone to help him figure out why.

CHAPTER SEVEN

Duke's eyes followed the pigeons as they fluttered onto the riverbank and jostled for position at Eden's feet. The veggie wraps she purchased from Bay Subs and Grub never failed to attract the birds to the wooden bench beside the Willow River. It was Eden's favorite spot to eat a quick lunch in peace, and she didn't have much time; the last fitting of her wedding dress was scheduled in less than an hour.

Watching the flock of pigeons with alert, curious eyes, Duke was careful to maintain a safe distance. He was almost six years old now, no longer a puppy, and much too dignified to chase after pigeons by the river.

Eden tossed bits of bread to the milling birds; the morning's events had ruined her appetite. Olympia's frightened words had stayed with her, and she couldn't push the image of the vicious bite marks on the poor girl's shoulder from her mind.

Who could commit such a heinous crime? And why Olympia?

The years she'd spent helping battered women at the Mercy Harbor Foundation had taught her that some men abused the ones they were supposed to love the most; her experience helping the Willow Bay Police Department solve a rash of kidnappings and murders had proven other men preyed on strangers, hurting or killing people they barely knew.

But nothing Eden had seen in the last five years had been able to numb her to the horror or anguish that filled her at the thought of the innocent victims and the lives that had been lost.

Her own sister, Mercy, had been taken from her by an abusive husband, leaving Eden to raise her niece and nephew in the devastating aftermath. The only thing that had saved Eden from disintegrating into her sadness was her mission to start a foundation that would help abused women.

Has it already been five years since Mercy Harbor opened its doors?

The thought prompted a wistful smile. The early days at the foundation had been so hard. Eden had still been sick with grief and suffering from anxiety, but the endless tasks of starting a new business had forced her to soldier on.

And then the women started coming. I thought I was saving them, but I guess the truth is, they saved me.

Throwing the last piece of bread to the nearest pigeon, Eden folded the wrapping paper and tucked it into her bag. She stood and led Duke back toward Riverview Tower, her mind still on the women that had turned to her for help.

Faces from the past hovered in her mind as if they weren't done with her yet, and a frustrating sense that she was forgetting something persisted as she walked along the flower-lined path. She let her mind wander through memories of the women that had passed through Mercy Harbor's doors.

She still knew some of them and saw them regularly around town, but most had moved on to start new lives. And then there were the women who'd never had the chance to start over.

The image of Celeste Reed's face, so young and achingly sad, surfaced above Eden's jumbled thoughts. Celeste had been one of the shelter's first residents. She'd turned to Mercy Harbor for refuge from her husband's drunken rages, and Eden had quickly offered the fragile young woman shelter.

Confident that Celeste would escape Mercy's fate, Eden had helped Celeste find a new job and move into her own apartment. Then, only weeks later, the police had shown up at the shelter asking questions, finally revealing the young woman's broken body had been found, and that her ex-husband had been arrested.

Eden stopped at the edge of the terrace, not ready to face anyone while her head was so full of the painful past. She knelt by Duke and hugged him to her, seeking the comfort of his soft fur and warm body, willing away the pain that had surfaced along with the dreadful memories.

Although Eden had been distraught over Celeste's death, in the end, it had hardened her resolve to help women like her sister. The senseless killing had made it clear to Eden that Mercy's death at her husband's hand wasn't unusual. That in fact, it was heartbreakingly common for women to be abused, stalked, and killed by their intimate partners.

And bitten.

The words flitted through Eden's mind. She frowned. Why was she confusing the bite marks Olympia and Bella had suffered with Celeste Reed's death?

But then...hadn't Celeste been bitten, too?

The troubling thought caused Eden to grip Duke even tighter. She willed herself to think back to the terrible weeks that had followed the discovery of Celeste's battered body.

Was she imagining that Celeste had been mutilated the same way Bella and Olympia had been? Or was she only now remembering horrifying details she had long buried away?

"Come on, Duke. I need to go back to my office before we leave for the fitting."

Giving the birds one last, longing look, Duke followed behind Eden as she hurried toward Riverview Tower and the answers that she hoped to find on her computer.

* * *

Eden read through Celeste Reed's file again. There was nothing inside that gave details about the injuries the young woman had sustained prior to her death. A note about the death had been added, as had a terse comment summing up the outcome of the trial.

Seth Reed (husband) convicted, voluntary manslaughter, 30-years.

Closing the window with a dissatisfied click of the mouse, Eden glanced at the clock. She'd need to leave within the next five minutes if she hoped to make the fitting at the dress shop over on Baymont.

Instead of standing up, she typed Celeste's name into the search engine, thought for a second, then impulsively added two words: bite mark. Her pulse picked up speed as the list of results appeared.

Seth Reed Sentenced to 30 Years for Killing Wife.

Clicking on the top story, Eden skimmed the report, stopping only when she saw the words she'd been dreading.

...died from blunt-force trauma to the head...multiple bite marks identified on the victim's body during the post-mortem...expert witness linked bite marks to suspect...

Eden read further down the article, wanting to assure herself that Seth Reed really had gone to prison. She relaxed as she confirmed he'd been sentenced to a thirty-year term in Raiford.

He couldn't have gotten released early for good behavior after only five years, could he?

Shaking her head against the thought, Eden enlarged the photo of the man that had brutally beaten his wife to death. She frowned at the blank, shell-shocked look in Seth Reed's eyes as he was led out of court by a uniformed officer.

Are those the eyes of a killer?

The shattered man looked more like a victim than a vicious killer. Eden had seen that same vacant stare on the faces of many women who arrived at Mercy Harbor struggling to understand what had happened to them. That empty look usually grew into expressions of disbelief and fear.

It often took time for the true horror to sink in. Just like with Bella and Olympia. Both women had come to Mercy Harbor's crisis counseling center following a brutal attack, looking for someone who could help them heal.

Reggie Horn was one of the only psychotherapists in the area that specialized in Post-Traumatic Stress Disorder, and Willow Bay General Hospital's ER and the Willow Bay Police Department made a habit of giving victims of assault Reggie's contact details.

But Reggie could only do so much. The women were just starting what was sure to be a long road to recovery. Picturing the raw emotion on Olympia Glass' face that morning, Eden thought she had seen both fear and guilt.

But what would Olympia feel guilty about? She was the victim.

The past and the present swirled through Eden's mind, and the clock ticked behind her as if to remind her she was running out of time.

I can't handle this on my own. I'll call Nessa. She'll take care of it.

Pulling her purse strap over her shoulder, Eden walked to the elevator, Duke close on her heels. She took out her phone and scrolled through her contact list. With only a slight hesitation, Eden tapped on Nessa's name.

"Eden, how are you?"

The detective's voice sounded just as tired and stressed as it had the last time Eden had seen her outside the CSL compound.

That night Eden had found two dead men in a roadside diner and had raced into the Cottonmouth swamp to save Pete Barker's daughter from the gun-wielding leader of a commune.

And Nessa's night had been just as harrowing, resulting in the arrest of an unlikely serial killer and her accomplice.

Now, months later and miles away from the events of that fateful night, they each had a new crisis to worry about. Some things it seemed never changed.

Holding the phone to her ear, Eden stepped off the elevator and made a beeline out the front door toward Baymont.

"I'm not so good, Nessa. Which is kind of why I'm calling. But first...how are you?"

"I'm on my way to view an autopsy." Nessa's words came out with a sigh. "But other than that? Well, I can't say I'm very peachy either."

Eden produced a weary laugh in spite of herself. Somehow just hearing Nessa's voice made her feel a little less frantic. She wasn't alone, and she wasn't the only woman in Willow Bay that was determined to make the city a safer place.

"So, now that we got that off our chests," Nessa said, "what can I do for you?"

"We've been helping Olympia Glass recover from her recent assault." Eden immediately felt guilty for sharing a resident's information with anyone else, even Nessa. "And she said something today that I thought you'd want to hear."

Looking both ways before crossing the street, Eden scurried toward the Bridal Bliss Boutique. She was already late, but with the outrageous amount of money she was spending on her dress, she hoped the shopkeeper wouldn't begrudge her a few extra minutes.

"I'm all ears."

Nessa's voice was suddenly alert.

"Olympia told me that her attacker threatened to come back and kill her if she told anyone about..." Eden paused, trying to remember exactly how Olympia had phrased it. "Well, about him I guess. It sounded like she knew something he didn't want her to tell."

After a beat of silence, Nessa cleared her throat.

"So, you think Olympia has information that could help us find the perp that attacked her?"

Eden stopped on the sidewalk and stared down at the phone.

"Nessa, I think the first priority is making sure you take action to protect Olympia." Her voice sounder harder than she'd intended. "The guy might follow through on his threat and come back."

"Of course, Eden, I agree. It's just that the best way to protect Olympia is to catch the man who is attacking and killing women as quickly as possible."

Eden froze with her hand on the door to the boutique. Stepping back into the middle of the sidewalk, she tried to speak, but her throat had closed up. Finally, she managed to force out the words.

"So, the homicide on the news this morning really is linked to the assaults on Olympia and Bella Delancey?"

Duke looked up at Eden with worried eyes. He could sense Eden's anxiety, and he was curious about her abrupt stop in the middle of the sidewalk.

"Yes, we think so," Nessa admitted. "Although it hasn't been confirmed yet for sure. I'll know more after I've attended this autopsy."

The door to the bridal shop opened and several women walked out carrying plush garment bags. They made their way around Eden, who still stood rooted to the same spot.

"Was she bitten, too?" Eden asked. "The woman that died?"

Another pause on the other end of the line, then Nessa's soft affirmation.

"Yes, she was. She was also beaten badly, like the other women."

Swallowing hard, Eden opened her mouth to share her concerns about the similarities to the Celeste Reed homicide, then closed it again. Celeste's killer was in jail. The cases couldn't be linked. Could they?

"Listen, Eden, I've got to go. But I'll need to talk to both Olympia Glass and Bella Delancey again. Once we confirm the attacks are related to this new homicide, we'll need to find out if they have any relationship or connection with the victim."

"And you'll need to protect them from the killer, right?"

Voices sounded in the background. Eden thought she heard Jankowski's deep voice.

"I've gotta run, Eden. I'll be in touch."

Putting her phone back in her purse, Eden walked again to the shop door. She needed to make sure she was ready for Saturday. Her dress fitting and all the other tasks on her list still needed to be done.

No matter what's going on in Willow Bay, I'm not going to let Leo down.

Pushing back her growing concern for Olympia and Bella, Eden forced herself to open the door and step inside.

CHAPTER EIGHT

Pat had stacked two thick files on Leo's desk, along with a cardboard box that held additional papers, notebooks, and documents. It looked like everything that Leo had compiled in Oscar Hernandez's defense case was there.

"I think that's all of it," Pat said in a satisfied voice. "Luckily I hadn't sent it off to the archives just yet."

Flipping through the files, Leo felt a hot wave of revulsion surge through him. It had only been a few months since he'd gone through the files, but his recollection of the injuries Oscar had been accused of inflicting on Bella Delancey had started to fade.

I thought it was over. Hoped I'd never have to see this stuff again.

Taking the lid off the box, Leo rifled through the contents until he found an envelope with the words *Bella Delancey Deposition* written on the outside. The envelope contained a slim, black memory stick.

Bella's frightened voice had been saved for later reference, and Leo pushed back another wave of disgust and anger at the remembered cruelty she had recounted. His jaw clenched in helpless frustration.

A man who tried to tear apart a woman with his hands and teeth must be insane. How could such a depraved person still be roaming the streets?

And why haven't the police found him, yet?

Voices from the lobby interrupted his frustrated thoughts as Pat and Frankie exchanged their usual, friendly insults.

"Hey, Leo, you ready for us?"

Frankie Dawson stood in the doorway; he shifted his lanky frame, revealing Barker's sturdier figure behind him.

"Yeah, come on in. I was just looking through this stuff."

The men shuffled in and regarded the files and the box with apprehension. With everything spread out on Leo's desk, it suddenly seemed overwhelming.

"You got time for this?" Barker asked, turning to stare at Leo. "Don't you have a case or something to prepare for?"

"Yeah, shouldn't you be in court or some shit?" Frankie added.

Leo shook his head as a self-conscious flush washed over his face.

"No, I'm not taking on any other cases until after the wedding."

Realization appeared in Barker's eyes as he absorbed Leo's words. He raised a big hand and slapped Leo on the back.

"That's right. You and Eden are tying the knot this weekend."

Barker's eyes were suspiciously bright. Leo wondered if the retired detective found it difficult to talk about weddings and marriage after losing his own wife several years before.

"I still say you're crazy, bro. Why tie yourself down unless you have to?" Frankie frowned. "You and Eden don't have to, do you? I mean, she isn't..."

"No, we don't have to, and this isn't a shotgun wedding."

Leo tried not to imagine Eden pregnant. They already had Hope and Devon to take care of, and they hadn't even discussed having their own kids yet, so he didn't want to get his hopes up.

"Well, you'll never find me walking down an aisle. Not unless there's a gun to my head."

Frankie stuck his hand into his pants pocket. He pulled out a single stick of gum, unwrapped it, and nervously shoved it into his mouth.

"Marriage is the best," Barker protested, throwing Frankie a dirty look. "You're going to love it, Leo. You and Eden are going to be real happy."

Swallowing the lump that had risen in his throat at Barker's quiet words, Leo put a hand on Barker's arm.

"You should put yourself out there again, Barker. You're still young. You could get married again."

Frankie snorted.

"If he's young, then I'm a damn baby."

"No, you're a damn idiot," Barker retorted. "But, thanks, Leo. I actually did have my eye on someone, but..."

Dropping his eyes, Barker shrugged.

"Well, I don't think it's appropriate."

"Why? Is she one of Taylor's friends or something?" Frankie asked, his eyes eager for gossip.

It was Barker's turn to snort.

"Hell, no. I'm not a pervert, and I'm not pathetic enough to try to date someone young enough to be my daughter."

"Then why's it inappropriate?"

Frankie assumed a familiar confused expression as a sneaking suspicion grew in Leo's mind. A snippet of the conversation he'd had with Eden months ago came back to him. He'd asked her if Reggie could help Barker with some counseling; the widower was still suffering from depression more than two years after his wife had died.

Eden had discouraged the idea.

"Reggie really likes Barker, but she's afraid it's unethical for her to treat him when she's...interested in him...personally."

Barker had never ended up pursuing the counseling for himself, but Reggie was now Taylor's therapist. Would Reggie consider it unethical to date a patient's father?

Leo winced at the idea of Barker being rejected. The older man had been through enough heartache.

"Let's just get back to the case," Leo said, ready to change the subject. "You two have a lot to learn if you're going to find the animal that attacked Bella Delancey."

Inserting the USB stick into his computer, Leo motioned for Barker and Frankie to take a seat.

"The best way to get started is to listen to Bella describe what happened during the assault." Leo waited for the computer to read the data. "I should warn you...it's hard to hear."

Both men nodded solemnly, and Barker pulled out a notebook and pen, ready to take notes. Leo prepared himself with a deep breath, then clicked on the file.

The recording was surprisingly sharp and clear as Leo could be heard stating the location, date, and witnesses in attendance. His voice softened as he addressed Bella, who answered each question in a hoarse, shaky whisper.

"Hello, Bella. I'm Leo Steele, the acting public defender for Oscar Hernandez."

"I know who you are."

"Okay, good. As you've requested, I'll be asking you some questions in this deposition instead of in the courtroom at the upcoming trial. The judge has given his approval, but there's still time to change your mind."

"No, I don't want to go to court and I...I haven't changed my mind. Just ask me what you want to know so I can go home."

"Of course. I'll go through the questions as quickly as possible. Let's start with where you were on the night you were attacked."

"I was at home."

"You were at your residence on Grand Isles Boulevard?"

"Yes."

"What time did you get home that evening?"

"Eight o'clock."

"Where had you been before that?"

"I'd gone to a spin class...after work. Then I went home."

"Was anyone at the house when you got there?'

"No. At least...I didn't think so. Ian...my husband...he was out of town, so I thought...I thought I was alone."

"The doors were all locked when you arrived?"

"Yes."

"Okay, so tell me what happened after you entered the house."

"I can't remember everything but I...I put my purse and gym bag down and went to the shower. Once I got out I put on my...my nightgown and...that's when I heard the music. I didn't have the radio on, so I thought it was strange. I turned off the water and listened."

"What did you hear?"

"It was an old song...one my dad used to listen to. It was coming from the bedroom."

"What did you–"

"I can still hear the words. Love hurts...that's what the song said...that it leaves scars..."

"After you heard the music...what did you do then?"

"I was confused...I didn't know what was happening. I thought maybe my alarm was going off or something. I went into the bedroom. My phone was on the bed and the song was playing. I shut it off and turned around and he was just...standing there."

"Did you see what the man looked like? Could you tell how tall he was, or how big?"

"He had a mask on. A black mask and gloves. I thought it must be a joke or something. But he moved so fast. All of a sudden he was beside me. He raised his hand and...he hit me. He wouldn't stop. I fell and then I screamed. But he just...laughed."

"Could you make out any identifying features?"

"It happened so...fast. I was trying to get away. Trying to stop him. I kicked out and he got really mad. He was yelling..."

"Did you recognize his voice? What was he saying?"

"I can't remember. I was scared. He fell on me and...and he had something in his hand. I couldn't see what it was but he...oh my god, he..."

"It's okay, Bella. Let's take a break. Let me-"

"I don't need a break. I just need to get out of here. That's all I can remember anyway. Next thing I knew I woke up in the hospital. I'd been in surgery to...fix the...the injuries."

"I'm sorry for what you've been through, Bella. I know it's-"

"You don't know anything about me, Mr. Steele. You have no idea what it feels like to be...torn apart."

"You're right, I don't know how you feel, Bella. But I know my client didn't do this to you, and I want to find the man who did before he can hurt anyone else."

"I need to go...I've told you everything I know."

"Just one more question, please. Do you have any idea who could have attacked you? Do you know of anyone that wanted to hurt you? Has anyone threatened you?"

"No...why would anyone want to hurt me? I haven't done anything wrong. It isn't my fault!"

"Of course, it isn't, Bella. Whoever did this to you committed a terrible crime. He needs to be stopped-"

"I'm done here. I've got to go. Now."

Leo stopped the recording, recoiling at the memory of the hunted expression on Bella's beautiful face. She'd been desperate to escape the little room, and he hadn't had the heart to ask her the questions that still bothered him.

If you were alone, and your husband was out of town, then why put on sexy lingerie? Were you expecting someone else?

Bella had been discovered that night after a neighbor called the police. A dark sedan had been seen casing the exclusive neighborhood; the suspicious vehicle had last been spotted speeding away from the Delancey's house.

Streaks of blood on the unlocked front door had convinced the responding officers to enter the house. They'd found Bella in the master bedroom unconscious, wearing the torn remnants of a white velvet corset. Despite the blood-spattered walls and obvious trauma, Bella was still alive.

After she'd been taken by ambulance to the hospital, and after the crime scene technicians had scoured the house searching for clues, photos of the ruined corset had been added to the boxes of evidence that Leo had collected during his defense of Oscar Hernandez.

The shock of the scarlet stains on the delicate white fabric had stayed with him, even after the charges against Oscar had been dismissed. He shook his head and cleared his throat.

"Those are the photos of the crime scene."

Leo motioned to a stack of pictures on his desk.

"Some of them show the injuries Bella suffered, too."

Turning toward the window, Leo waited in silence while Frankie and Barker sifted through the photos.

"This dude's a fucking freak."

Frankie's voice quivered with disgust. He'd been involved in investigations of violent crimes before, but Leo doubted he'd ever seen such disturbing images. The grisly aftermath of the attack that had left Bella Delancey with permanent scars, both the physical and the psychological kind, was hard to comprehend.

"Looks like he went ballistic," Barker growled, his forehead screwed into a tight frown. "This kind of rage seems *personal*."

Leo nodded in agreement.

"The doctor who treated Bella believes she sustained some type of blunt force trauma to her head that knocked her out cold. Based on a lack of defensive wounds he thinks the other injuries...the beating and the bite marks...were most likely inflicted when she was unconscious."

"Thank you, Jesus, for small mercies."

An embarrassed flush suffused Frankie's face as if he hadn't meant to let the words slip out, and he dug in his pocket for another stick of gum. Leo felt a surge of affection for the lanky man with the dirty mouth and the soft heart. There were still some good men in Willow Bay. Maybe the bastard that attacked Bella hadn't counted on that.

"Did the perp leave any evidence behind?" Barker's voice was hard. "Anything we can use to track him down?"

"No fingerprints, hair, or blood evidence was collected that didn't match Bella or her husband," Leo answered, his voice grim. "Unfortunately, the nurses at the hospital cleaned the bite wounds before the techs could try to collect DNA."

All three men closed their eyes in an attempt to block out the image Leo's words evoked.

"So, nothing we can use then," Barker said, already sounding defeated.

"Well, the neighbors gave a description of the car they saw in the area that night," Leo offered, wanting to give Barker some hope.

Barker raised his eyebrows, waiting for Leo to continue.

"Unfortunately, it was nighttime, and all they could see was a dark sedan. No make or model. No tag number available."

Sighing, Barker reached into a box and pulled out a file labeled *Evidence Log*. He opened the cover and ran a big finger down the list of items taken from the Delancey crime scene.

"What about her phone?"

Barker's finger paused over an item on the list.

"I see here they took her phone. Anything on it?"

"No, it was broken along with most of the other stuff in the room," Leo said. "But I requested a report on the calls made to and from the number, and there wasn't anything interesting. At least, not that I saw. Nothing unusual."

Biting his lip, Barker asked, "What about the computers in the house? They check the computers to see what websites she was visiting?"

"Bella's computer was collected as part of the crime scene," Leo confirmed. "But there was a backlog at the state's cybercrime lab. I still hadn't received any results by the time we went to court and the case against Oscar was dropped."

Chewing hard on his gum, Frankie pushed the pictures away and began pacing the room.

"So, basically we don't have jack shit to go on."

He ran a skinny hand through his limp, brown hair.

"What about that other girl? The other one that was attacked?"

Shrugging, Leo rifled through the stack of folders and pulled out a slim file labeled *Victim #2: Identity Withheld.*

"This is all I've got on the second victim." Leo dropped the file on the desk in front of Barker. "Her identity, like Bella's, hasn't been released to the public. Of course, lots of people in this town probably know who she is..."

Frankie cocked his head and raised an eyebrow.

"Quit messing around, Leo. Who is she? We need to talk to her."

Barker held up a hand to silence Frankie.

"Before we go down that rabbit hole, how do we know the two assaults are connected?" His eyes searched Leo. "What's the link?"

Forcing his voice to remain calm, Leo opened the slim file and tapped on a copy of the handwritten incident report, before reading a sentence he'd highlighted months before.

"Victim suffered serious head trauma and massive bruising to her limbs and torso, as well multiple injuries that appear to be human bite marks..." He looked up at Barker. "You get the idea. The description of the assailant, a man in a black ski-mask of average height, and the method of attack matched up, as did the bite marks."

Choking on his gum, Frankie coughed, then sputtered.

"You mean they matched up the dude's *teeth prints?*"

"Bite mark identification rarely holds up in court anymore," Leo admitted, "but initial analysis of the marks showed a strong match. It seems highly unlikely the first two attacks aren't connected, but without DNA..."

Leo was interrupted by the vibration of his phone. He looked down to see the reminder he'd set earlier.

"I've got to get to my tuxedo fitting," Leo said. "And you two better get to work. Ian Delancey doesn't seem the type to pay people to stand around talking."

Dropping his phone into his pocket, Leo headed toward the exit. Barker and Frankie trailed after him with worried expressions.

"I think I'll call Nessa," Barker said, waving to Pat as they hustled out the door. "See if she'll fill me in on the new homicide. She seemed sure it was related to the assaults."

Leo stopped and turned to look at Barker.

"What makes you think Willow Bay's next chief of police is going to share details of an ongoing investigation with an intern PI?"

A stubborn gleam entered Barker's eye, and his voice was suddenly sure and steady.

"There's an animal attacking women in Willow Bay. Nessa will want all the help she can get."

CHAPTER NINE

Nessa's nose twitched again; another sneeze was building behind her protective face mask. Turning away from the metal autopsy table, she pulled down the bulky mask and sneezed into her gloved hand.

"Sorry about that."

Readjusting the mask securely over her nose and mouth, Nessa stepped back into place beside Iris Nguyen.

"I've been sneezing all morning. I must be allergic to something."

Keeping her eyes on the bruised, battered body in front of her, Iris didn't seem to register Nessa's comment. With a small, steady hand, the medical examiner held a stainless-steel ruler next to an angry red gash across Jade Castillo's forehead.

She lifted her eyes to Wesley Knox and gave a curt nod. Pressing a big thumb down on the RECORD button of his handheld voice recorder, Wesley held the small device closer to Iris.

"Deceased has suffered blunt force trauma to the head resulting in a cranial vault fracture. The fracture radiates from a point of impact approximately three centimeters above the upper rim of the left orbital socket."

Iris' voice was calm, and her words clear, although her eyes looked troubled behind her face shield.

"Intracranial trauma is evident; multiple bone fragments are attached to the skull. Bone flakes are visible in the surrounding soft tissue indicative of a perimortem injury."

Wesley clicked off the recorder and Iris glanced up at Nessa.

"Sorry for the jargon. It's actually a pretty straightforward case."

Iris stepped back and crossed to a large sink. She pulled off thick latex gloves and began to scrub her hands with studied concentration. Following after Iris, Nessa leaned against the sink and waited until the medical examiner had turned off the steaming water and pulled down her face mask.

"Jade Castillo was killed by a violent blow to the head. The other wounds were inflicted around the time of death but don't appear to have directly contributed to her death."

A shadow flickered behind Iris' eyes as she looked back at Jade's alabaster face and thick tangle of dark curls. The rest of the body was concealed by a crisp white sheet.

"Based on my examination of the other injuries," Iris said, her voice grim, "I've noted that the contusions, abrasions, and bite marks are severe, but none can be considered life-threatening."

"Is there any way you can match the imprints of the bite...of the teeth...to one of the previous assault victims?"

Iris hesitated, as if considering the options, then shook her head.

"I'm not a forensic odontologist, but I know it's hard to get bite mark evidence to stand up in court," she admitted. "Quite a few high-profile cases have been overturned after experts testified that they'd matched bite marks to a perpetrator."

Before Nessa could reply, Iris held up a placating hand.

"But, we can match DNA found on the victim, so if the assault victims were tested..."

Sighing, Nessa shook her head, feeling another sneeze building.

"The paramedics were concentrating on saving the girls, not preserving evidence. They immediately cleaned and sterilized the wounds. Some of the injuries even required surgery..."

Grabbing a paper towel from the dispenser by the sink, Nessa blew her nose. The image of the big orange tabby cat in Jade Castillo's house flitted through her mind as she tossed the wad of paper into the trash and tried to focus on what Iris was saying.

"...and I've collected samples from Jade Castillo. So, if the perp has a record, we might get a hit."

Hope started to build in Nessa's chest.

"Or, if we find a suspect, we might be able to nail his ass using his own saliva."

The clatter of wheels on the tile floor sounded behind them. Nessa looked back to see Wesley pushing the metal gurney through the doorway. Jade Castillo's body would be kept in the mortuary cooler until she was officially released to her next of kin.

The thought made Nessa frown. She turned to Iris just as the medical examiner opened the door and hurried down the hall toward her office. Nessa scurried behind her, perplexed by Iris' strange behavior.

The medical examiner seemed distracted, if not downright worried. Could she still be upset over the violence of the crime? Or was she anxious about missing her father's appointment?

Maybe she's just upset about Gabby showing up at the crime scene to see Jankowski. After all, jealousy can consume the best of us.

Iris saw Nessa hovering in the doorway and motioned for her to come inside. Sinking into a chair across from Iris' desk, Nessa decided it would be best to save the personal questions for later. Right now, she had a murder to solve. The public and the mayor would want answers soon.

"Have you been able to notify her next of kin, yet?"

Iris nodded. She turned to her computer and typed something on the keyboard. After a short pause, she looked up.

"Jade Castillo listed next of kin on her employment application as Karl Nickels. He was her fiancé. Apparently, he still lives in Minnesota."

Iris clicked on her mouse and the printer whirred into life.

"Here are his details. I was able to reach him at the cell number provided this morning. He says he'll be here to ID the body as soon as he can find a flight."

Wincing at the thought of the bereaved man navigating through the impersonal bustle of the airport, Nessa picked up the printout and studied it. She would have to contact Jade Castillo's fiancé as well. He would need to be interviewed. Perhaps he would have information that could lead them to Jade's killer.

"At least we can release the name of the victim, now," Nessa murmured, thinking of the pack of reporters waiting outside the medical examiner's office for an update. "That should give them something to report on while we formulate an official statement."

Iris offered up a weak smile.

"Yes, I'm sure Gabby Jankowski is eager to hold a press conference. She seems to like the spotlight."

Nessa nodded, registering the hurt under the softly spoken words.

"She sure does, Iris. But don't worry, she's got nothing on you."

Confusion clouded Iris' face.

"What do you mean? She's got nothing on me?"

"I mean, that my partner may be thick-headed sometimes, but even Jankowski's not dumb enough to fall into that woman's trap again. And besides, he's smitten with you now, so there's nothing to worry about."

Doubt played behind Iris' kind, brown eyes, but she shook her head briskly, as if to clear her thoughts, and stood.

"I've got to write up the autopsy report now, and I'll need to consult with Wesley about the toxicology tests we need to arrange. I'll keep you updated as to our findings."

Realizing she'd been dismissed, Nessa snagged a tissue from the box on Iris' desk, then stood and moved toward the door.

"And I guess I better get over to city hall. Mayor Hadley's been texting me like a lovestruck teenager all morning. He seems desperate to see me."

Iris produced a real smile for the first time that day, and Nessa grinned back. But her mood soured as she made her way out the back entrance and hurried toward the mayor's office.

The mayor and the city council are gonna want answers, and I don't have any to give them.

* * *

Mayor Hadley sat behind his enormous mahogany desk, a stern look on his weathered, but still-handsome face as he considered Nessa's update.

"So, you're telling me you have no suspects, and no clue as to who might have killed this woman?"

Looking over at Gabby Jankowski with an incredulous expression, the mayor rubbed a well-manicured hand over his smoothly shaven chin, then stood and walked to the window.

"Those people out there are counting on us to keep them safe."

His melodramatic tone irked Nessa, but she managed to hold her tongue. She looked down and began shredding the tissue in her hand into tiny strips. The pretentious mayor might be irritating, but he wasn't wrong; it was her job to catch the man who had killed Jade Castillo.

"The press is getting impatient, Detective Ainsley." Gabby's eyes were hard. "I can go ahead and release a statement with the victim's name, but we'll need to hold a press conference soon."

"Exactly! I want to talk to my constituents. I need to reassure them that we are doing everything possible to find the man responsible for this crime."

Mayor Hadley held up a clenched fist as if trying to convey his passion and conviction to an enthusiastic crowd of supporters. Nessa had seen that same gesture in every speech she'd watched him give over the last five years, and it still failed to impress her.

Pinning his eyes on Nessa, the mayor frowned.

"How quickly do you think you'll have someone in custody? This could be the perfect opportunity to rebuild the community's trust in our police force."

Nessa bit her lip; she held back the words that threatened to spill out. It wouldn't help her chances of being appointed the next chief of police if she mentioned that the mayor's old crony Douglas Kramer was the main reason they'd lost the city's trust in the first place.

"We have no suspects at this time." Nessa decided to keep it simple. "So, it's impossible to say when we might be able to-"

"Nothing's impossible, Detective, if you have the right attitude. We need to give the people of this city some hope."

Mayor Hadley turned to Gabby.

"I want that press conference arranged for later today."

The thought of standing in front of the cameras and crowd admitting they had nothing to go on, and that the town was facing yet another serial predator, made Nessa's skin crawl.

The scornful smirk that appeared on Gabby's face melted Nessa's good intentions into outrage.

"Well, as the acting chief of police, *you* are the one that should be answering the questions at the press conference, *Mr. Mayor*."

Nessa held up her fist in a mock imitation of Hadley. The shreds of tissue fluttered down onto the carpet like soggy confetti.

"Your constituents have a right to know that you still haven't appointed a new chief of police and that *you* are thus responsible for finding the man who killed Jade Castillo and assaulted two other women so badly they needed surgery to repair the damage."

Lowering her voice to a hoarse growl, Nessa ignored Gabby's angry protests, keeping her eyes firmly on Mayor Hadley.

"He tried to rip them open with his teeth, Mayor. Maybe your constituents have a right to know that–"

"That's enough Detective Ainsley. You're out of line."

Straightening his red power tie, he held up a hand to silence Gabby. The media relations officer flushed with anger, keeping her bright, hostile eyes trained on Nessa.

"I guess we're all under a lot of pressure," Mayor Hadley conceded. "So, let's just focus on what we're going to tell the press."

Nessa shoved a file into Gabby's hands.

"Here's the information we have so far. Make whatever statement you want, but I've got to go. There's a murderer out there and we might not have much time before he attacks another innocent woman."

Nessa flung the door open and hurried back down the hall. She might not ever be Willow Bay's chief of police, but she still had a job to do. People were counting on her, and she wasn't about to let them down.

CHAPTER TEN

Preparations for the press conference were underway outside Willow Bay City Hall as the man pulled out his cell phone and tapped on the *Secret Fling* icon. Waiting for the app to load, he studied the crowd around him, noting fear on some faces and anticipation on others. Looking down, he saw the familiar profile picture appear above his username: LonelyGuy10.

Reporters and camera crews jockeyed for position, and the man let his eyes wander over the usual faces. Every station in town, and many from across the state, had come to hear gory details about the beautiful young nurse who had been slaughtered in her own home.

Catching a glimpse of glossy blonde hair, he watched as Sabrina West made her way through the crowd. Channel Ten's newest reporter claimed her spot close to the podium, then looked around with visible excitement.

It seems some of the women in Willow Bay aren't scared after all.

A fleeting smile turned up the corners of the man's mouth, revealing a row of sharp teeth as he imagined the look of fear that would cross Sabrina's pretty face if she saw him standing in her bedroom some dark night.

They're all cold and stuck-up until you get them alone. But then...

Watching as Sabrina took out a slim compact and patted powder onto her already flawless complexion, the man allowed himself to remember Jade Castillo's frightened eyes. But anger mixed with the excitement, and his jaws clenched at the thought of what could have happened. She'd almost ruined everything. Luckily he'd managed to take care of her before she could expose his secrets.

But not before I exposed her for the liar and cheat that she was.

Rage simmered under his skin, causing his face to redden and drops of perspiration to bead on his forehead. It was a mild day, but he suddenly felt sweaty and overheated.

"Excuse me...can I get through?"

A teenage girl pushed past him, dragging a reluctant boy after her.

"Come on, Devon, we're almost there."

"I want to go home, Hope," the boy whined, pulling away and refusing to move. "Aunt Eden won't like us going out without letting her know where we are."

The girl stopped and looked around in frustration.

"We need to buy a wedding present before Saturday, right? And it won't be much of a surprise if we tell her what we're doing."

A hush settled over the crowd as a slim woman in a tailored black dress approached the podium and leaned toward the microphone. The man's eyes flashed as the sun reflected off the highlights in Gabriella Jankowski's sleek bob.

After everything she's done, there she is acting like a pillar of the community. What kind of role model is she for the kids of this town?

He looked over at the girl named Hope, who was staring up at the podium with curious eyes. How young and pure she seemed next to the hard, brassy allure of the woman at the microphone.

Sure, she's innocent now. But just wait until she grows up.

The man figured the girl would end up just like Jade Castillo or Bella Delancey. Just another cheat. Just another liar that only cared about herself.

"What's going on, anyway?" the girl wondered out loud. "Why're all these people standing here?"

"This is a press conference about the recent homicide," the man said, using his most trustworthy, authoritative voice.

Hope stared back at him with wide, blue eyes.

She is a truly beautiful girl. And those clear, guileless eyes...

"Someone was murdered?"

The boy next to Hope grabbed her hand and began to pull.

"Come on, Hope, let's get out of here."

But Hope was too intrigued by the press and the crowds to leave yet. She glanced again at the man, flashing a shy smile, obviously impressed by his attention. Most girls tried to get his attention. Especially the young, pretty ones.

But then once I get them alone, it's a different story, isn't it?

"I can get you two closer to the front if you want," the man offered, adjusting his features into the helpful expression of a good Samaritan.

But the boy had already pulled his sister further into the crowd. After several seconds the man lost sight of her blonde ponytail. He turned his attention back to the conference just as Mayor Hadley joined his media relations officer at the podium.

Losing interest as the mayor began another one of his long-winded introductions, the man looked down at his phone and tapped on a heart icon. The screen displayed a collection of photos. These were the women he'd met using the app. The women who had hoped to become his secret fling.

Heat once again moved through him as he tapped on Jade Castillo's photo. She had been a beautiful woman, and the photo had been flattering, showing off her smooth tan skin and shiny black hair to perfection. Even her soft, lying lips looked inviting.

But underneath it all, deep down below the façade, she'd been ugly. And inquisitive. In fact, she'd almost seen past the rugged good looks displayed in his profile picture. She'd almost discovered the truth. She'd almost found out that he too had hidden his true self behind an attractive disguise. But he'd ripped away her mask, and she'd never have the chance to betray anyone again.

He took one last look at her photo, pushing away a trace of regret. *If things had been different, we might have been a good match.*

Gritting his teeth, he shook his head against the useless thought, then tapped on the *DELETE* icon. Jade Castillo was in the past now. She'd been an unrepentant cheater and a consummate liar. She'd treated her poor fiancé shamefully. The poor shmuck was undoubtedly better off without her.

No, Jade Castillo had gotten what she deserved, and the man had nothing to feel guilty about. It wasn't his fault that she'd ended up dead. She'd been foolish enough to try to follow him and even spy on him. She hadn't had any idea of who she had been messing with.

He'd learned long ago that girls who lie will only cause pain if given the chance. Just like his mother. Just like Bella and Olympia and the others. They were all lovely liars. Every last one.

"...and now our media relations officer Gabriella Jankowski will provide you with the latest update on the investigation."

The mayor's words broke into the man's dark thoughts, and he watched as Gabby again stepped to the podium. His eyes lingered on her red lips as she told the hungry crowd what they wanted to hear, but the roaring in his head allowed him to hear only bits and pieces of what she was saying.

"...was found yesterday at her residence on Juniper Circle...medical examiner is conducting an autopsy today...evidence recovered at the scene indicates the homicide may be linked to previous assaults...more information to follow as the WBPD continues its investigation..."

An electric thrill snaked through him as he realized the police had connected the previous attacks to Jade's death.

So, the police aren't complete idiots after all. But I didn't leave anything behind. They won't be able to link me to any of it.

The smug thought was replaced by a twinge of doubt as he remembered Jade's missing phone. He'd lost control of himself before he could make sure the phone had been destroyed, and he'd stayed too long in the house to waste more time searching for it.

At least he'd demolished the computer. Although he knew it was likely the police would be able to recover the hard drive.

Will they track Jade's activity back to Secret Fling? Will they be able to access her messages to LonelyGuy10?

Shrugging off the disturbing possibilities, the man closed the app and dropped the phone back in his pocket. He wasn't a computer genius, but he was savvy enough to know that eventually, his *Secret Fling* account was likely to be discovered.

Hopefully, the precautions he'd taken to hide his true identity would protect him, but he wouldn't allow himself to worry about it quite yet. There would be time for that later.

The end will come soon enough. And when it does, I'll be ready to go out with a bang. This shitty town might become famous for something after all.

With the prepared statement over, the reporters began shouting out questions, and the man allowed himself to be pushed along to the front of the crowd. The warm body of a young woman jostled up against him, and he turned to see Veronica Lee standing at his shoulder. Channel Ten's weather girl watched Sabrina West shout out a question, her eyes alert and her notepad out.

How long was she standing behind me? Did she see the photo of Jade Castillo on my phone?

Was this how he'd get caught? Wouldn't this young reporter, even if she was just the local weather girl, wonder why he had the dead woman's picture on his phone before the police released her image?

Allowing Veronica to slip in front of him, the man kept his eyes on her long, dark hair. Reaching out a finger, he touched one silky strand, before moving away. He'd need to keep an eye on the lovely young weather girl. He might even pay her a visit sometime soon.

CHAPTER ELEVEN

Veronica Lee inched closer to the front of the crowd, keeping her eyes on Sabrina West, who had managed to position herself directly in front of the podium. Sabrina waved her small hand in the air, signaling to Gabby Jankowski that she had another question to ask. But Gabby was pointing to a tall, handsome reporter further back in the crowd.

"So, you're telling us this guy is a suspect in other cases?"

Veronica recognized Nick Sargent, a reporter with Channel Six News. Gabby nodded, clearly prepared for the question.

"Yes, the WBPD has reason to believe the perpetrator that killed Jade Castillo has been involved in multiple other crimes."

"What other crimes?" Nick cleared his throat, speaking above the other voices shouting for attention. "Are you saying this man has killed before? That we have a serial killer in Willow Bay?"

The confident look on Gabby's face faltered. She looked toward Mayor Hadley, who was busy typing in a message on his phone. She dropped her eyes to her notes as she spoke.

"Well, at this point we're not able to say for sure. We believe he's attacked at least two other women, but this is the first homicide we've been able to-"

"What can you tell us about his victims?" Sabrina's high-pitched voice quivered through the air. "How are they connected?"

The question caused a buzz in the crowd. Gabby hesitated, then opened the folder in front of her, shuffling through the papers inside.

"Well, there was no sign of forced entry in any of the cases, which likely means that the victims knew their attacker and let him in."

Veronica frowned, realizing for the first time that no one from the Willow Bay police department had shown up to answer questions about the investigation. Gabby Jankowski was obviously trying to wing it on her own.

"Have any witnesses come forward?" Sabrina again shouted, ignoring the protests from the other reporters. "Is there a police sketch of the suspect we can circulate?"

Holding up a hand to quiet the crowd, Gabby shook her head.

"We don't have a sketch, but witnesses have come forward to report seeing the same vehicle in the vicinity of each crime. We believe the perpetrator may drive a black, late model sedan."

A stocky man with tired eyes pushed his way through the crowd, stopping beside Veronica to look back. She recognized Pete Barker. The retired WBPD detective had recently been involved in several high-profile cases, and his picture had been in all the papers.

"Where the hell are Nessa and Jankowski?" Barker muttered to a tall, lanky man behind him. "Sounds like Gabby's making this shit up as she goes along."

He looked over at Veronica with an apologetic smile, then raised a beefy hand, but Gabby had lost control of the crowd. She flipped through the pages in the folder again with nervous hands, her cheeks flushed pink and her lips pursed in frustration.

A large man emerged from the crowd, his broad shoulders tense underneath a white linen shirt, and his face tight with anger. Gabby retreated as the man stepped behind the podium and pulled the microphone toward him.

"I'm Detective Simon Jankowski of the Willow Bay Police Department. I'm working the Jade Castillo homicide along with my partner, Detective Nessa Ainsley. We advised against holding this press conference until more information becomes available since the investigation is still in the early phases."

Jankowski scowled over at Gabby and the mayor as if he wanted to throttle them both, then exhaled loudly and leaned toward the microphone again.

"However, since you're all here now, I'll try to answer any questions I can. But as I said, there's not much to tell just yet."

Studying Gabby's ruggedly handsome ex-husband, Veronica wondered how the self-centered woman managed to snare such interesting men.

First, she'd married this hunky detective, then she'd had a torrid affair with Hunter Hadley, arguably the most eligible bachelor in town. Perhaps Gabriella Jankowski wasn't all bad despite the cold-hearted exterior she'd displayed to Veronica.

There must be something that attracts men to her like bees to honey.

Distracted by her thoughts, Veronica almost missed the words Pete Barker's lanky companion shouted out above the crowd.

"Hey, Jankowski, good to see you finally showed up, man. I got a question for you."

The detective turned his head toward the booming voice, then rolled his eyes when he saw who had spoken.

"Yeah, Frankie, what do you want to know?"

"This black car that's been seen hanging around...you think it means this guy cases the victims before he attacks? That he's some kind of obsessed stalker?"

Jankowski shrugged thick shoulders. Before he could open his mouth to respond, a deep voice rang out.

"The *Willow Bay Stalker*. Catchy name for a killer."

Veronica looked over to see who had spoken as Jankowski tried to quiet several people in the crowd who began repeating the name in agitated whispers. The usual reporters and crew were all there. Even Hunter Hadley had finally made an appearance.

She watched as Hunter greeted Nick Sergeant, who was typing something into his phone. Was it the attractive reporter that had coined the killer's press name? Or had it been Hunter's deep voice?

Looking past the men, she saw Sabrina and Boyd preparing to film another segment. The ambitious reporter was obviously eager to have plenty of footage for the evening news. Perhaps she wanted to be the first one on air to use the Willow Bay Stalker moniker.

Veronica stuck her notepad and pen back into her purse, feeling suffocated by the growing throng of spectators. It seemed like everyone in Willow Bay had shown up to hear about the murder.

"Funny how all of a sudden the whole fucking town is upset about a woman getting killed. Nobody gave a damn when runaways from the wrong side of the tracks were turning up dead in the river."

The bitter words made Veronica turn her head. The tall man named Frankie stared around him with a scornful grimace.

"I guess it's different when *respectable* women in middle-class neighborhoods are being attacked...and when the next victim might be anyone's sister, mother, or next-door neighbor."

A shiver ran down Veronica's back at the image Frankie's words conjured up. Her mind turned to her own mother, who was home alone in a house only a few miles from Jade Castillo's rental.

"You're probably right," Veronica said, watching Sabrina talking into the camera, one hand clutching a microphone, the other gesturing to the scene behind her. "These attacks have struck a nerve with the community. It's as if they're all taking this personally."

Realizing that Frankie was now staring at her with narrowed, curious eyes, she smiled self-consciously and looked away.

"You're the weather girl on Channel Ten, right?"

Veronica nodded, ignoring the urge to tell him she was a reporter.

"Yes, that's me. Veronica Lee, *weather girl*."

"You don't sound too excited about it."

Shrugging with a casualness she didn't feel, Veronica sighed.

"Not much to report on when the weather's this nice. I'd rather report on real news anyway...like the Jade Castillo homicide."

Pete Barker appeared behind Frankie just as the skinny man scowled and waved a long finger in her face.

"If you know what's good for you, you'll stay clear of this whole thing. You have no idea what kind of animal this guy is-"

Barker put a big hand on Frankie's shoulder.

"Leave the nice weather girl alone, Frankie. She doesn't need you reading her the riot act. Now, come on, I want to find Nessa. See what she knows and why she isn't here."

Veronica watched as Frankie and Barker worked their way through the growing mass of bodies, her spirits sinking.

I guess it's official. Nobody thinks I'm capable of being a real reporter. To them, I'm just some feeble girl who's only fit to read the weather report.

She flashed resentful eyes at Hunter. The one man who had the power to give her a shot at her dream wanted to protect her from...what? From making a fool of herself?

Moving toward the edge of the crowd, Veronica noticed Gabby Jankowski standing in the background, her gaze inscrutable as it rested first on Detective Jankowski and then shifted to Hunter Hadley.

Sidling over to Hunter, Gabby placed a possessive hand on his arm. He jerked away as if her touch burned, then spun on his heels to push past a camera crew standing behind him.

Hunter's clearly been under a lot of stress lately. If I want him to give me a chance, I'm going to have to make it impossible for him to ignore me.

An idea began to take shape in Veronica's mind. Maybe she wouldn't wait for Hunter to give her an assignment.

Maybe I should show him that I'm not scared and that I'm capable of chasing down a big story on my own. Maybe that's my only chance.

CHAPTER TWELVE

Bella Delancey's delicate hand trembled as she lifted the tissue and dabbed under her eyes, wiping away an inky streak of mascara. Unshed tears made her grey eyes appear luminous under Reggie's sympathetic gaze.

"Is there anything else you wanted to discuss, Bella?"

Glancing at the clock, Reggie was surprised to see they'd already exceeded the usual fifty-minute session. But something about the way Bella huddled against the back of the big armchair told Reggie the young woman wasn't ready to leave.

"I just feel really bad about...well, about what happened to..."

Bella's voice faded, but Reggie remained silent, knowing the distraught woman was struggling to understand and explain her intense reaction to the reported murder.

The morning's news had hit Bella hard, and she'd quickly lapsed back into the state of extreme fear and confusion she'd suffered in the aftermath of her attack.

"I just feel so bad that a woman...died. I mean, it doesn't seem fair, you know...that I'm still here, and she's..."

After a long pause, Reggie's reassuring voice broke the silence.

"It's normal to feel that way when you've survived a life-threatening event and someone else didn't. It's aptly called *survivor's guilt,* and it'll very likely lessen with time if you allow yourself to come to terms with it."

Throwing the soggy tissue into the trash can, Bella stood up and moved to the big window that looked out over Willow Bay. The view from the tenth floor was impressive, especially on clear, cloudless days, and Reggie thought she saw Bella's shoulders relax as she looked toward the river.

"How can I ever come to terms with something so terrible?"

Reggie crossed to stand next to Bella, her voice soft.

"You can remind yourself that none of this is your fault and that you are not responsible for what anyone else has done. The man who attacked you is the only one to blame for his actions."

"But, what if I *am* to blame? What if it *is* my fault?"

Shaken by the desperation in Bella's voice, Reggie shook her head.

"You can't let yourself think like that, Bella. You have to realize there was nothing you could have done to prevent this."

A flash in the street below the window drew Reggie's eyes. A sleek black sedan had pulled next to the curb. It looked like Ian Delancey had arrived to pick up his wife.

"I think your ride is here."

Bella followed Reggie's gaze to the street and to the black car idling at the curb. Her back stiffened, and she whimpered low in her throat.

"Bella? Are you okay?"

Putting a hand on Bella's shoulder, Reggie gave a gentle squeeze. Bella jerked away, her long chestnut curls spilling over her shoulder.

"No...don't, that hurts."

Too late Reggie remembered the tender scars on Bella's shoulder. Although some time had passed, the site of the injury was still healing, and any reminder of the wound would surely be psychologically painful.

"I'm so sorry, Bella," Reggie soothed, following the agitated woman toward the door. "Please try to get some rest this evening. I can give you another prescription for diazepam if you think it would help."

But Bella wasn't listening. She hurried to the elevator and jabbed at the *DOWN* button. Reggie tried again.

"Bella, promise me you'll try to relax. Perhaps some breathing exercises will help."

Ignoring Reggie's words, Bella rushed toward the stairwell and banged through the door with a loud clatter. Reggie called after her in a worried shout.

"Bella, it's ten floors down. Please, wait for the..."

Just then the elevator door dinged open. Reggie impulsively stepped in and pushed the button.

She shouldn't be alone right now. No telling what she'll do in this state.

As the door to the elevator slid open to reveal the ground floor, Hunter Hadley barreled into the lobby. His worried expression turned to relief when he spied Reggie getting off the elevator. Rushing toward her, he didn't see Bella burst through the stairwell door until she was directly in front of him.

"Hunter? What are you doing here?"

Bella's voice was shaky, and for a minute Reggie thought the young woman was going to throw herself into Hunter's arms.

"I'm here to see Dr. Horn. I need to...to book an appointment. Why are you here?"

Bella looked at the therapist with a stricken expression, then turned back to Hunter.

"I'm a patient now, too. I'm-"

A loud curse sounded behind them. Reggie turned to see Ian Delancey standing in the lobby, his face red, his eyes trained on Hunter Hadley.

"Just what the hell is going on her, Dr. Horn?"

Reggie bristled at his accusatory tone. This was her office, and she had every right to see whatever patients she wanted. She turned to Hunter with a stern look.

"Please go up to my office and wait for me there."

Only after Hunter had disappeared behind the elevator doors did she turn back to face Ian.

"Mr. Delancey, please control yourself. Your wife's session is over, and she's ready to go, although I am worried about her. The last thing she needs is more stress."

"What do you expect when I left her in your care and then come in and find my wife meeting with her ex-boyfriend behind my back?"

Reggie opened her mouth in shock, then counted to ten. This man was getting on her nerves, but Bella needed her to remain calm and in control.

"No one was doing anything behind your back, Mr. Delancey, and frankly it's none of your business who comes to this office. My services are provided with the assurance of complete discretion."

A flutter of guilt played in Reggie's stomach as she thought of Olympia Glass. By now Eden would have already talked to Nessa and told her what Olympia had said. A light switched on in Reggie's mind.

Maybe Bella was threatened by her attacker, just like Olympia had been. Maybe she didn't tell the police what she knows. Maybe that's why she feels so guilty now that a woman has been killed.

Wanting to ask Bella more, but knowing she couldn't do so in front of Ian, Reggie watched in frustration as he pulled Bella to the door. His wife offered no resistance. Her violent need to escape had fizzled out as abruptly as it had erupted.

Bella has kept whatever she knows about her attacker from her husband, as well as the police. She won't appreciate me asking about it in front of him now.

"Come on, Bella. Let's go home."

Ian opened the door and guided Bella outside. He threw a last piercing stare at Reggie before crossing to his black sedan and helping Bella inside. As the car roared away from the curb, Reggie turned back to the elevator and stepped inside.

Leaning against the wall of the elevator, she folded both arms over her chest and sighed. Hunter Hadley had been one of her most disturbing cases before he'd ended their therapy sessions over two years ago. He'd insisted his PTSD was under control, but Reggie had known the truth, and she'd known that sooner or later he'd be back.

CHAPTER THIRTEEN

The nightmares and panic attacks had begun to fade the last time Hunter had been in Reggie's office. He'd been sure back then that the worst was behind him and had impulsively stopped the medication and quit coming to his weekly sessions.

Looking around the familiar office, he wondered how he could have been so naive. The medicine and the therapy had quieted the demons, but they'd only been sleeping. Lately, they'd been stirring again; they were getting restless.

"Why are you here, Hunter?" Reggie stood in the doorway, her eyes wary. "I haven't seen you as a patient for years and now you show up and expect me to-"

"I'm losing time again, Reggie."

The words were harsh, as if they'd been torn out of his throat.

"I need...help. More pills maybe. I don't know what...but I need something to...to quiet my head."

Crossing to the window, he looked down at the curb ten floors below. His sleek, black Audi was still there.

Reggie remained in the doorway as if she were deciding if she would let him stay. He expected her to tell him to leave. He deserved no less after the way he'd abruptly ended treatment two years before.

"How do you know Bella Delancey?"

The quiet words shocked him. He frowned over at Reggie, immediately defensive. Had Bella mentioned their past? What had she told the therapist?

"Maybe this is a bad idea," Hunter said, dropping his eyes. "If Bella's your patient now, too, it could be...awkward."

"Why's that?" Keeping her tone level, Reggie moved toward her desk. "Are you in a relationship with Bella?"

The anger that always accompanied thoughts of Bella's betrayal surged through him.

"Not anymore," he admitted. "She moved on after she found out about my *issues*. I guess Ian was a better bet. More stable and dependable. And his father was loaded, too, so no loss in that area."

The words tasted stale and bitter in his mouth. It was time to move on. Time to stop whining about the past and accept that his split with Bella wasn't all her fault. Who could blame her for swapping him for a more reliable meal ticket?

"I'm sorry that happened to you," Reggie said, her eyes softening. "I didn't know you two knew each other."

"I started dating Bella right about the time I stopped seeing you. Everything had been looking up. Then...well, after I quit the pills the nightmares came back. And the anxiety..."

Pain radiated through him at the remembered fear and revulsion on Bella's face as he confessed to suffering from PTSD.

"She couldn't handle the stress, and good old Ian offered her a shoulder to cry on. Not hard to figure out the rest of the sordid story."

Reggie nodded, but her face remained neutral. She wasn't the type to offer opinions or judgments, and Hunter felt himself relax a little.

"Was today the first time you've seen Bella since your break-up?"

Hunter shook his head and sank into a chair.

"No. We've seen each other here and there. Our families...or at least Ian's family and mine...are in the same social circle. In fact, Ian and I grew up together in Willow Bay. Same schools, same classmates. Just very different career paths."

Picking up a pen, Reggie leaned forward over the desk and jotted a few words on a notepad. Hunter couldn't see what she'd written.

"A few months back Bella approached me at a holiday party. She'd been drinking. Said she wasn't happy. That she was bored and wanted to...well, she wanted to see me."

"How did that make you feel?"

Swallowing hard, Hunter tried to keep his tone calm.

"It hurt. Made me feel about two feet tall. Like I was damaged goods only fit for a casual fling while Ian was husband material. I was offended, to say the least."

"How did you respond to Bella?"

Closing his eyes, Hunter pictured Bella's flushed face. She'd been so beautiful. And so angry. She usually got whatever she wanted.

"I told her I wasn't interested. That I'd moved on with someone else. Which was partially true. But she didn't take it well."

Her cruel response had shredded his delusion that he would ever be able to live a normal life or have a healthy relationship.

"She laughed...said whoever I was seeing would eventually wise up and leave me, too. That no woman wants to be with a crazy man."

"I hope you didn't believe her."

Reggie's brusque response startled him. He looked up to see anger lighting her bright brown eyes and felt suddenly ashamed that he had let Bella's bitter words wound him.

Or maybe it just hurt so badly because Bella finally said what I've been thinking.

Reggie bent to scribble notes on her paper. Hunter nodded toward the words she'd written.

"Does that mean you'll take me back as a patient?"

Reggie raised an eyebrow and shrugged.

"Are you giving me another option?"

Contemplating the patch of blue sky beyond the window, Hunter felt an unexpected sense of release flow through him. Maybe he could let the past go. Perhaps with therapy and help from Reggie, he wasn't a lost cause after all.

The buzz of his phone disturbed the peaceful moment. He ignored the call but knew he'd have to get back to the station soon. The press conference had been a disorganized mess and he'd need to decide what footage they could use.

The Willow Bay Stalker story was bound to be the top headline on every broadcast and in every paper in the state. The story may even go national if it was a slow news day. He'd have to make sure the crew didn't go overboard and embellish the little information they had. And Sabrina West had grown increasingly aggressive; she may need to be reined in.

"Let's make an appointment for next week to continue our discussion," Reggie suggested, opening her laptop and tapping on the keyboard. "I have a session open on Wednesday at ten if that works for you."

Nodding agreement, Hunter took out his phone and added the appointment to his calendar. His eyes were drawn to the missed call; Gabby had left a message.

"And I'll go ahead and call in a prescription for the same Benzodiazepine you were taking before,' Reggie murmured, her long red fingernails again clicking over the keys. "That should help you sleep more soundly."

Impatient to get back to work, Hunter jogged down the stairs and climbed back into his Audi. He took out his phone and stared at the missed call, resisting the urge to delete the message. In his position, there was no way to avoid the city's media relations officer. If he wanted to receive updates on the Stalker case for his viewers he'd just have to find a way to deal with Gabby Jankowski.

CHAPTER FOURTEEN

E den stared at her reflection in the floor-length mirror. The lighting in the well-appointed fitting room was soft and flattering, illuminating the happy glow on her face and the soft shine of the white satin dress. Glancing toward the mirror behind her, Eden caught sight of Duke's sleepy face.

"Well, how do I look?"

Grinning at the golden retriever's reflection, Eden spun around, letting the silky hem of her skirt skim Duke's paws. The big dog shifted positions, seemingly unimpressed by the luxurious swirl of white fabric. Now that Eden's mood had shifted from anxious to excited, Duke had settled into a comfortable position on the plush pink carpet, content to watch as Eden modeled her wedding dress.

"Maybe it's too much, Duke."

Eden bit her lip and twisted from side to side.

"I think it's divine."

The boutique owner bustled into the room carrying an armful of diaphanous material. She dropped the fabric onto a chaise lounge and tuned to Eden.

"You make a beautiful bride." The woman's kind eyes twinkled. "You're going to have one very happy husband at the end of all this."

Blushing, Eden stepped back from the mirror and reached back to tug at the zipper.

"I wasn't fishing for a compliment, Martha, but I'll take it."

"That's good. Granny always said a lady should accept compliments graciously. Although come to think of it, she rarely gave any out."

Giggling like a schoolgirl, Martha Bevins helped Eden pull off the heavy dress and put it back on the hanger. Her cheerful mood was contagious, and Eden found herself laughing along with the older woman.

"Thank you for everything." Eden dragged her eyes away from the dress. "I'll be back to pick it up on Friday."

"Don't be silly, dear. I'll make the final alterations and have it delivered out to the venue first thing Saturday morning." Martha's tone was firm. "You're having the wedding out at Beaumont Plantation, right?"

A nervous flutter twisted Eden's stomach as she nodded. The renovated plantation house had been the only venue within a hundred miles that still had availability for a Spring wedding. While the isolated location may have discouraged some brides, Eden had fallen in love with the grand old house and well-tended gardens at first sight. She'd immediately pictured herself walking down the rose bordered path in a flowing white dress and fresh flowers in her hair.

She hadn't thought about how inconvenient it might prove to have to drive an hour out into the countryside. And there would be no nipping back home if she forgot something on her wedding day. But it was too late to back out now, even if she'd wanted to. Beaumont Plantation was the place, and Saturday was the day.

Waving goodbye to Martha, Eden clipped on Duke's leash and led him out into the street, hating to leave the safe cocoon of the bridal shop. She'd been able to forget everything else for the last blissful hour, but now she was back in the real world where a dangerous predator might be lurking around any corner.

She'd just reached the corner of Baymont and Townsend when she saw a familiar figure taping a cardboard sign onto the window of a vacant building. Or at least the building had been vacant the last time she'd walked by.

"What are you doing, Frankie?"

Her words startled the man. He whirled around, his wide eyes covered by wispy locks of lank brown hair, his overlarge shirt hanging loose around his tall, thin frame. At the moment, Frankie Dawson didn't look much like a hero, but he'd helped save Eden's life on more than one occasion.

"Our new sign won't be ready for a few weeks," Frankie told her, his surprise morphing into a childish excitement. "So, I made one to hang up for now. That way we don't lose out on any business."

Eden considered the handwritten words on the poster board.

"Barker and Dawson Investigations. I like the sound of that." She noted Frankie's expectant expression. "And your sign is very...neat."

Nodding with obvious pride, Frankie waved her into the little office, which was full of cardboard boxes and what looked like the bottom half of a desk.

"Almost done setting up in here," he said, offering her the one chair in the room. "Gotta hurry because we've already got us a big case to work on."

Duke situated himself at Eden's feet and stared up warily at Frankie. Eden suppressed a smile, wondering if the golden retriever was remembering the trouble that always seemed to appear whenever the lanky man was around.

"Congratulations are in order, then." Eden glanced around the room. "I'm guessing your partner is out working your big case?"

"Yeah, we went over to your boyfriend's office earlier to get some background info," Frankie said, dropping to his knees and picking up a screwdriver, "and now he's out trying to find Nessa."

Raising her eyebrows at Frankie's bowed head, Eden couldn't resist asking the question.

"So, what were you guys talking about with Leo?"

She smothered the spark of indignation that had ignited at the thought of Leo taking on another case right before their wedding. After all, it'd been his idea to hold off until after they'd gotten back from the honeymoon.

"It's kinda confidential," Frankie said, straining against a resistant screw. "But seeing how you're gonna marry Leo on Saturday, I guess you'll find out anyway."

Shaking her head at the remark, Eden opened her mouth to tell Frankie that Leo wouldn't share his client's secrets with anyone, but he spoke again as he dug through a big box for more screws.

"Bella Delancey's hubby hired me and Barker to find the scumbag who attacked her."

Eden closed her mouth and blinked.

"He hired you to find the guy..."

"Yep. And I don't blame him. If some maniac tore up my wife I'd want to find him, too. And the cops around here have done fuck-all."

Flicking his eyes up to Eden, Frankie blushed.

"Sorry about that. I better start watching my mouth. Clients won't like me talking like that, will they?"

Eden ignored the comment, her heart beating an erratic rhythm at the thought of Leo helping to track down the man who had assaulted Bella and Olympia. Fear and pride mingled inside her.

"Was Leo able to help?"

"Hell, yeah," Frankie sputtered, flipping the desk over onto its four wobbly legs. "Your man had all these pictures and files."

The expression on Frankie's face hardened as he spoke.

"I'll tell you one thing for sure. The man that attacked Bella is one jacked-up mother-"

"I get the idea, Frankie," Eden said, not ready to hear more gloom and doom when she had been feeling so happy only moments before.

"You know what the press are calling him now?" Frankie asked.

Eden shook her head, which was beginning to ache. Lunchtime had come and gone, and she hadn't eaten anything. Duke was probably hungry, too.

"The Willow Bay Stalker." Frankie's mouth stretched into a sarcastic grin. "Can you believe it? Some genius at the press conference came up with that beauty. They said the same guy who killed the lady over on Juniper Circle has attacked other women."

"The Willow Bay Stalker?" Eden tried not to shiver as she spoke the words. "Sounds like something out of a horror movie."

The thought of food vanished. Eden's head spun as she thought of poor Bella and Olympia. The two women would be terrified at the headlines that were sure to fill the evening news.

"You know, this case reminds me of another woman I knew." Eden spoke slowly, not sure why she was telling Frankie about Celeste Reed. "A woman who was killed by her husband. Beaten and mutilated, like Bella and...well, like the other women."

"You think Ian Delancey attacked his own wife?"

Eden stood and shook her head.

"No, I don't think that. But I am wondering if there's someone out there who did this before. If maybe Celeste Reed's husband wasn't guilty after all."

Dropping the screwdriver, Frankie frowned up at Eden.

"You think this other woman was killed by the same guy that attacked Bella Delancey?"

Eden shrugged, not ready to commit herself to the idea just yet. She needed to find out more about Seth Reed, the man who had been locked away for Celeste's murder. The man who had sworn to love, honor, and protect the young woman, but instead had beaten her and betrayed her trust. But had he killed her as well? Or had it been someone else?

"Celeste Reed was a resident at Mercy Harbor about five years ago. She was trying to escape an abusive relationship but ended up going back to her husband. Her body was found only a few weeks later."

Eden instinctively knelt down by Duke and put a hand on his back. The warmth of his fur, and the soft rise and fall of his breathing, made the words easier to say.

"The police arrested her husband, and he was convicted."

"So, what's the problem?"

Frankie's voice was more curious than contentious. He leaned back against the slightly lopsided desk.

"Well, Celeste was beaten and bitten, just like Bella. I'm just thinking it's strange that her husband would do that. I mean...would change the way he..."

Swallowing hard, Eden felt her voice give way. It never got easier to talk about abuse or think about the women that turned to Mercy Harbor in desperation. Sometimes just saying the words hurt.

The furrow deepened on Frankie's forehead as he watched Eden struggling to explain. He reached into his pocket and retrieved a stick of gum. He pulled off the shiny wrapper and wadded it into a ball between his fingers. The gum disappeared into his mouth.

"You gotta tell Barker and Nessa about this other woman," Frankie said, getting to his feet. "If it's even a possibility..."

Eden nodded. She knew he was right. Frankie and Barker were working the Bella Delancey case, but they had just gotten started. And Nessa would be bogged down with the new murder. They needed all the clues and leads they could get. Another thought flitted through her mind.

"I also know the woman who was assaulted after Bella. She may have information as well." Wondering if she was doing the right thing, Eden continued. "I can ask her if she'll meet with you and Barker. No guarantees she'll say yes, of course."

Frankie's eyes lit up and he chewed faster on his gum.

"That'd be swell." Digging back into his pocket, he pulled out a cell phone and began thumbing in a number. "I gotta let Barker know we got a couple of hot leads to follow up with."

As she listened to Frankie's side of the conversation, Eden hoped she was doing the right thing. Would Olympia even agree to talk to the two private investigators? Would Nessa be mad at her for bringing Frankie and Barker further into the investigation? All she knew for sure was that there was a maniac on the loose in Willow Bay.

And if the people in this town don't start working together, more innocent women might die.

CHAPTER FIFTEEN

T he sprawling building on Waterside Drive nestled up against the Willow River; Barker watched the light sparkle off the water as the sun drifted west in the bright blue sky. He glanced at Frankie, who was nervously pacing back and forth on the shelter's wide terrace. The Stalker's second victim had agreed to meet them, but she wanted to do so on her own terms, and on her own turf. All they could do now was wait.

Checking his watch, Barker began to worry.

Did she have a last-minute change of heart? Was she too scared to talk?

Just then the back door swung open. Barker recognized Eden Winthrop's honey blonde hair and tall graceful figure as she stepped outside. A willowy girl with wavy brown hair walked beside her and a slim black woman in a silky red dress brought up the rear. Barker's heart jumped when he recognized Reggie Horn.

"Oh yeah, somebody's got a *crush...*"

Frankie's high-pitched, sing-song voice caused Barker's face to flush a deep red. He turned furious eyes on his partner.

"Shut your mouth, Frankie. We're here on serious business."

Standing to greet the approaching women, Barker tried to arrange his features into a casual smile.

"Eden...Dr. Horn...good to see you. And this is?"

He looked down at the wisp of a girl, careful to keep his voice soft and relaxed. The tense set to her narrow shoulders told him she might turn and flee at any minute.

"Hello, Detective Barker." Eden looked toward Frankie and nodded. "Frankie, thanks for coming. I'd like to introduce you both to Olympia Glass. She's a resident here at the shelter. She's agreed to talk to you."

Keeping his eyes on Olympia, Barker noted the defiant tilt to her chin.

She may have agreed to talk to us, but I won't count on her sharing anything useful. Not with that stubborn look on her face.

Before Barker could ask Olympia to sit down, Frankie stepped around the table and stood in front of her.

"It's good to meet you, Olympia. My name's Frankie Dawson. Barker and me are private investigators." Barker smiled at the girl, but she kept her eyes on Frankie. "We're hoping to ask you a few questions about the creep that assaulted you. We're tryin' to track him down."

Olympia stared at Frankie with wide, glassy eyes, then turned toward Reggie.

"I can't do this." Her voice shook. "I wanna go back inside."

Taking Olympia's trembling hands in hers, Reggie stared into the young woman's frightened eyes.

"These people are trying to help you, dear." Reggie's voice was low and calm. "They just need to know what you know about the man who attacked you so that they can find him before he hurts anyone else."

"But he already hurt someone else. He *killed* someone else."

Reggie nodded slowly.

"Yes, he did. He killed an innocent woman." Her voice was gentle, but her tone was resolute. "And that means it's even more urgent now to tell the police and these investigators whatever you know."

Barker gestured toward a small patio table. He pulled out a metal chair and motioned for Olympia to take a seat.

"Let's all just sit down and get to know each other first."

Olympia lowered her frail body into the chair and immediately folded thin arms protectively over her chest. Barker turned to Reggie.

"Dr. Horn?"

Barker felt the blush starting to creep back up his neck as he offered Reggie the chair next to him.

"Please call me Reggie, Detective. And may I call you Peter?"

Warmth spread through Barker as he nodded. He couldn't resist giving Reggie a quick smile as he waited for Eden to sit across from him. Frankie pulled over a chair from another table and wedged it next to Olympia. They all sat in silence for a long beat, then Barker cleared his throat.

"I know it's tough for you to talk about what happened, so we won't get into any details that make you uncomfortable."

Barker waited, but Olympia kept her mouth closed, her lips drawn into a thin, tight line across her face.

"Let's start with an easy question. How long have you lived in Willow Bay?"

"I moved here from Miami about ten years ago." Olympia's voice was sullen. "After my parents split, my mom wanted a fresh start. Somewhere away from the dangers of the big city."

An angry smirk pulled up the sides of her mouth.

"Guess she was wrong about that, too, like everything else."

Barker resisted the impulse to ask Olympia what else her mother had been wrong about. It wouldn't be wise to let her lead them down into the rabbit hole of her dysfunctional childhood. That would only be a distraction.

She was too quick to share the information for it to be useful.

Whatever it was that Olympia Glass was afraid to tell them, it wasn't something she would offer up so easily.

"And where have you been living?"

"You mean before here, at the shelter?"

Her brown eyes softened as she looked past Barker toward the charming building that had once been a boutique hotel but now served as the main shelter for Mercy Harbor's residents.

"I was living in an apartment over on Channel Drive. On my own."

Barker pulled out a little notepad and pen.

"You planning to go back there once you leave the shelter?"

Shaking her head, Olympia dropped her eyes.

"No. I never want to go back there. I'm not sure where I'll go. My best friend Zoey wants me to come live with her and...and with Milo. That's her...her husband. I mean, they've got a big place and all, but I'm not sure what I'm gonna do."

Noting the stutter in Olympia's voice, Barker frowned and paused. His hesitation gave Frankie a chance to jump in.

"You know anybody that drives a black car?"

Confusion clouded Olympia's face, but she also seemed relieved by the change of direction in the questioning.

"Of course. I know lots of people that have black cars. Why?"

Frankie shrugged and looked toward Barker. When Barker didn't protest, he continued.

"Witnesses have seen an unknown black sedan in the vicinity of each crime. Not much to go on, but if you've seen a car that matches the description, or know of someone that has a black car, we could check it out."

Standing abruptly and pushing back her chair, Olympia glared down at Frankie.

"That's bullshit. Lots of men in Willow Bay drive fancy black cars. That doesn't mean anything."

Reggie jumped to her feet as if preparing to chase after the girl if she decided to run.

"They're just trying to figure out who could have done this, Olympia. Every clue or piece of information could help."

Barker stood up as well, feeling awkward as he towered over Reggie. His instinct was telling him that Olympia wasn't mad. She was scared. But why?

"Please, Olympia. If you know who attacked you...if you know anything that could help us...we need to know. Lives might depend on it."

"Yeah...*my life!*" Olympia shouted, her words echoing over the water, prompting a flock of pigeons to scatter up and into the air. "You have no idea what you're talking about. If I say anything *mine will be the next body found.*"

All heads turned to follow Olympia as she scurried back toward the safety of the shelter. Reggie's worried eyes met Barker's, then she spun around and hurried away. Barker waited until the heavy door closed behind her before turning back to Eden and Frankie.

"She definitely knows more than she's saying."

Barker replayed Olympia's words in his mind.

Lots of men in Willow Bay drive fancy black cars.

Why had she panicked after Frankie asked if she knew anyone who had a black car? And had they said anything about the black car being *fancy?*

"The poor girl is fucking petrified." Frankie stopped chomping on his gum to speak. "Believe me, I know just how she feels."

"I can't believe this is happening again," Eden murmured, looking out over the water. "When will it all end?"

Barker's phone buzzed. He looked down to see Nessa's name and number. Frankie and Eden turned to him with curious eyes as he answered.

"Hey, Nessa, what's up?"

Nessa spoke in an artificially cheerful voice.

"I've been summoned to an emergency City Council meeting by Mayor Hadley. He's either going to fire me or promote me."

Barker sighed and shook his head.

"Sit tight, Nessa. I'm on my way."

CHAPTER SIXTEEN

The scene outside City Hall was chaotic as Nessa approached. Several news vans had pulled onto the bricked-paved courtyard amidst a frenzied swarm of reporters, camera crews, and the usual onlookers. Spotting Detective Marc Ingram walking toward her, Nessa ducked into the corner shop across the street. She stared out through the window at the man who had once been the top candidate for the vacant chief of police position, her mind whirring.

What the hell is Marc Ingram doing here? Did Mayor Hadley ask him to come to speak to the city council members as well?

The elderly clerk behind the counter coughed, and Nessa looked over with an embarrassed smile.

"Just need a bottle of water."

The little man nodded toward the glass cooler on the back wall where bottled drinks were on display before turning back to the tiny television mounted on the wall. Nessa followed his gaze. She froze in place as she took in the headline splashed across the screen.

Fear Spreads as Willow Bay Stalker Strikes Again.

Stepping closer to the screen, Nessa pointed to the television.

"Can you please turn up the sound?"

The clerk picked up a battered remote and jabbed at it. Suddenly the strident voice of a young, blonde reporter filled the quiet store.

"This is Sabrina West, reporting live outside City Hall."

Nessa was tempted to look out the window again, but her feet refused to move. She kept her eyes on the screen as the reporter spoke into a long microphone.

"City officials held a press conference earlier today where they confirmed that last night's murder of Willow Bay resident, Jade Castillo, is in fact connected to two other attacks on women in Willow Bay in the last few months."

Nessa felt a hot rush of anger.

I hope Gabby Jankowski has evidence that can confirm the connection between the cases because I sure as hell don't.

Although Nessa was convinced the same perp had committed the crimes, at this stage only circumstantial evidence connected the attacks on the three women. No physical evidence had been obtained yet. No NDA. No fingerprints. No hair or bodily fluids.

"The citizens of Willow Bay are showing up in force this afternoon, insisting that the mayor and the city council do something to find the killer."

The reporter gestured to the people milling in front of the big building. She turned and stepped toward a teenager standing on the edge of the crowd.

"What do you think about the Willow Bay Stalker? Are you afraid?"

Startled, the girl stared at the microphone, her big, blue eyes wide and her cheeks pink. Nessa immediately recognized Eden Winthrop's niece, Hope.

"I'm...not sure, really."

The girl's stuttered answer seemed to frustrate the reporter, but Nessa didn't wait to hear the next question. She banged out of the door and sprinted across the street, her heart pounding.

Searching for the Channel Ten van, Nessa spotted Sabrina West's blonde hair and charged across the courtyard, stopping at the edge of the shot just as Sabrina raised the microphone.

"Now that we know a serial killer is on the loose in Willow Bay, aren't you worried you could be next?"

Nessa pulled her badge out and held it up toward the reporter, but Sabrina West was looking only at Hope, waiting for a reply.

Moving rapidly toward the stocky man holding the camera, Nessa again held out her badge. This time she decided to use her big girl voice.

"I need you to stop filming, now. I'm with the Willow Bay Police Department and I need to talk to you."

The cameraman hesitated as her words sunk in, then turned his head to gape at Nessa. She thrust out her badge and repeated her demand that he stop filming. The cameraman shrugged and motioned to the reporter. He held up five fingers, then began the countdown. Five, four, three...

"That's all we have time for now...this is Sabrina West, now back to the studio."

The camera lowered, and Sabrina West stomped toward them, her eyes blazing, Hope already forgotten.

"Boyd, what's going on? Why'd you stop filming?"

The cameraman shrugged again and shifted his camera.

"When the police tell me to do something, I do it."

Sabrina turned on Nessa.

"You ruined my segment–"

Nessa pushed past her to where Hope stood. The girl's face was flushed a soft pink and her small hand trembled as Nessa took it.

"Come with me, Hope."

Wrapping a protective arm around the teenager's shoulders, Nessa led her toward the steps of City Hall.

"I'll call your aunt. You shouldn't be out here alone. Not with everything going on and not after...well, after what you've been through."

An angry hand grabbed at Nessa's shoulder, and she swung around to face Sabrina West.

"What do you think you're doing?" the reporter squealed in outrage. "You ever hear of freedom of the press?"

Leaning toward the younger woman, Nessa kept her voice low.

"You ever hear of common decency? Don't you know that girl has been through enough without you scaring her half to death? Now move back before I take you downtown for harassing a minor."

A deep voice spoke behind her.

"Come on, Nessa. You need to get inside. The mayor is waiting."

Pete Barker stepped between Nessa and Sabrina, his solid body effectively stopping the heated conversation. Nessa guided Hope up the stairs into the cool lobby of the building as Barker followed close behind. When she turned to face her old partner, he wore a disapproving scowl.

Leaning toward her, he hissed in her ear.

"You missed a major press conference earlier today and then violated the First Amendment by interfering with the press. I'd say that's two strikes against you. Try not to strike out when you go in to talk to Mayor Hadley."

* * *

The City Council sat behind a long table at the front of the meeting room. Mayor Hadley stood up as Nessa and Barker entered the room, his eyes guarded and his words somber.

"Please have a seat, Detective Ainsley."

Nessa looked at the rows of folding chairs that faced the council members. Several of the chairs were occupied. Marc Ingram sat in one chair with his arms firmly crossed over his chest, his pale crewcut translucent in the harsh overhead light, his eyes narrowed in her direction.

Moving further into the room, Nessa regarded the council members behind the table. They were all men. Most of them were old enough to be her father. None of them offered up a smile.

"Afternoon, everyone." Nessa kept her head held high. "Thanks for inviting me to this little meeting, Mayor. You mind telling me what's this all about?"

Her legs wobbly, Nessa decided to take Mayor Hadley up on his offer. She perched on the edge of an empty chair at the end of the front row and took a deep breath, her eyes trained on the mayor.

"It's been called to my attention that I need to appoint a new chief of police." Mayor Hadley cleared his throat and straightened his tie. "Although I've been filling in as acting chief for the last few months, the recent series of violent crimes calls for more aggressive measures, and my duties as mayor preclude me from continuing on in this role."

Nessa's stomach tightened as she saw Hadley glance nervously toward the man sitting to his left. Archibald Faraday was the longest-serving member on the city council, and his wealth and position in the town guaranteed that Hadley would seek the old man's approval before appointing a new chief of police.

Sensing movement in the row behind her, Nessa looked back to see Barker and Jankowski. Barker held up a thumb, but Jankowski remained stony-faced as Nessa turned back to the mayor.

"I've asked Detective Nessa Ainsley to join us since she's an applicant for the open position." Mayor Hadley looked over the rest of the faces staring back from the chairs. "I'm guessing these other folks are here to support you, Detective Ainsley?"

Before Nessa could respond, Archibald Faraday spoke up in a raspy voice that made Nessa's back stiffen.

"Now Hadley, we can't make a decision like this without a proper search for the right kind of person," the old man said, a nasty smile pushing up the fleshy skin on his face. "In fact, I have a few suitable candidates in mind that we could talk to if we take our time and do this right."

"I agree with Archie."

Nessa swung her head to where Judge Eldredge sat, his brow furrowed, and his lips pursed in consternation.

"After everything that's happened lately we need to be sure we have the right man for the job."

Jumping to her feet, Nessa opened her mouth to protest but realized that someone had beaten her to it. A striking woman with thick black hair and the trim, athletic build of a runner stood in the back row. She wore red-rimmed glasses and held a slim black briefcase in one hand. Her voice was ice-cold.

"Mayor Hadley, the city council has no say-so in this appointment, and frankly their input is offensive and obstructive."

Archie Faraday gasped in outrage as the words sunk in. Judge Eldredge banged his fist on the table as if he held a gavel.

"How dare you-"

Walking toward the row of men, the woman held up her hand.

"Please, gentlemen, your objections have been heard and registered, but the decision about the chief of police falls squarely on the shoulders of the city's chief executive. I believe that's Mayor Hadley."

Angry mutters followed her words, but no one contradicted the statement. Mayor Hadley turned miserable eyes toward the disgruntled men.

"I guess I should introduce Riley Odell. She's the new prosecutor assigned to the Willow Bay circuit. Apparently, there's been some concerns raised at the state level about the goings-on in our little town, so the state attorney sent her down here to...to help us."

Suppressing a smile at the look of shock on Archie Faraday's face, Nessa watched Riley Odell approach the mayor.

"As your judicial circuit's new prosecutor, I'm responsible for charging and prosecuting offenders who commit serious crimes in Willow Bay. It's imperative that I have a point person to work with on the police force. I imagine that'll be the chief of police."

Nessa's inner smile faded as she imagined working with hard-edged Riley Odell. The woman wasn't the type to suffer fools or mistakes.

She's sharp enough to cut our department down to size pretty darn fast.

Riley ignored everyone but Mayor Hadley.

"I highly recommend that you appoint someone other than yourself as interim chief of police, Mayor. There's a serial predator in this town and you need a professional to run the investigation."

Mayor Hadley swallowed hard, his eyes darting toward Archie Faraday before turning to Nessa.

"Well, I was going to ask Detective Nessa Ainsley to take on the interim role-"

Marc Ingram shot out of his chair like an angry jack-in-the-box.

"What ever happened to a fair recruitment process? I applied for the job, too, and I haven't even been interviewed, and I've got seniority over Detective Ainsley."

Nessa glared at Ingram, but his outburst didn't faze Riley. She kept her eyes on the mayor.

"You need to make a decision, Mayor. From what I've heard, Detective Ainsley would be acceptable. Once she's officially in place as the interim chief, you can decide what sort of selection process you'll implement for the permanent assignment."

Heart falling at the prosecutor's last words, Nessa turned worried eyes toward Barker and Jankowski, glad to have the support of both her old partner and her new partner.

"Okay, fine."

Mayor Hadley sighed and faced Nessa.

"Detective Ainsley, if you're willing, I'll appoint you as interim chief, with all the authority and responsibilities of the permanent chief."

He ignored the grumbling from the city council.

"But I will conduct a formal recruitment process to fill the permanent position. It's only fair."

Resisting the temptation to throw the reluctant offer back in Mayor Hadley's face, Nessa nodded. This wasn't the time and place to give in to her pride. Lives might depend on her keeping her head straight and her ego in check

"Okay, I understand. I only ask that you wait until we bring in the perp that killed Jade Castillo before you make a decision. Give me a chance to find the bastard."

She didn't wait for a response from the mayor, but instead spun on her heel and walked toward the door. She was surprised to see that Hope stood just inside the big room, next to Eden Winthrop and Frankie Dawson. She hadn't realized she'd had such a big audience.

"I'm glad you're going to be the chief of police," Hope said in a solemn voice.

"Yeah, those old guys don't know their ass from a hole-"

"All right, Frankie," Eden scolded, shaking her head.

She regarded Nessa with worried eyes, then smiled.

"Let's all just congratulate Nessa on her new role."

A lump rose in Nessa's throat at the words of support. She wasn't sure how long she'd be the chief of police, but she had to stay strong as long as she was. The town deserved that much.

"Come on, everybody, the show's over for now."

She'd already wasted too much time, and now it was officially her job to find Jade Castillo's killer.

CHAPTER SEVENTEEN

T he steps of City Hall swarmed with people coming and going. The whole town seemed to buzz with the latest news about the Willow Bay Stalker. The man smiled with satisfaction. He'd chosen the name himself, and the idiots had picked up on it just like he'd planned. Now every television and radio station in town was blaring headlines about him.

Keeping an eye on the big doors, the man reached for his phone. He was tempted to check his messages on *Secret Fling*. Had his new fling responded to his latest message? She already seemed eager to meet, but he needed time to prepare.

He wasn't ready to rush into anything and risk getting caught. Not yet. No, for now, he would be patient and sit tight.

Glancing up, he caught Veronica Lee staring at him. She offered him a half-hearted smile and waved. He nodded curtly, then held the phone to his ear as if engaged on a call. When he looked up, he saw with relief that the weather girl was gone. Now he could wait for the new prosecutor to emerge in peace.

He wanted to see where she was staying. It would be smart to keep an eye on her since she was the one that would build the case against the Willow Bay Stalker.

An image of Riley Odell's cold eyes stuck in his mind. Those eyes told him that the new prosecutor wasn't like the other small-time officials in Willow Bay. She was smart and ruthless. She was big-time, and she was aiming for him.

Pushing back the anxiety that began to gnaw at his stomach, the man wondered how he'd lost sight of his original goal. Why had he allowed himself to kill Jade Castillo? That hadn't been his intention.

I just wanted to punish her. To teach her a lesson that she would spend a whole lifetime remembering.

That was how love worked, wasn't it? You loved someone and they hurt you. Then you suffered. And you kept on suffering until you finally died.

Wasn't that what his mother had taught him when she left? She was still out there somewhere. Was she suffering, too?

Fury and pain rose in a terrible crescendo as he tried to block the hurt that always accompanied such useless thoughts. Sometimes the hurt caused him to act out. Like with Jade. Like with Celeste Reed. Turning his face away from the crowd, the man tried to block the memory that the woman's name conjured, but it surged up and pulled him back into the past.

Celeste stared at the flowers he held with sad, pitying eyes. The eyes that had seen him at his most vulnerable. The eyes that had looked away when he'd begged her to stay.

"I'm sorry, Junior, but I told you. I love my husband."

She tried to close the door, pushing against the vase, causing a few petals to fall to the ground at his feet. He stepped forward without thought, crushing the petals under his shoe and wedging his thick shoulder against the door. He was too big, too heavy for her to hold him back.

"Please leave...I don't want you to..."

Bringing his fist down hard on her arm, he shoved past her, kicking the door closed behind him.

"What are you-"

Intense rage erupted inside him, blurring his vision and causing his jaws to clench. The pain and the hurt were unbearable. He'd thought she loved him. Thought they'd be together forever. But she'd lied.

"How could you leave me and go back to him?"

He lifted a heavy foot and smashed it into her knee, causing her to collapse onto the floor. As she writhed on the ground, he kicked out again, this time connecting with the side of her head.

A soft grunt escaped from her lips as her head crashed back against the tiled floor. Blood seeped into the strands of her mousy brown hair as he fell to his knees beside her. He lifted his fist and brought it down hard, wanting to close the girl's lying eyes. Needing to know that she could never look on him with pity again.

When his hands grew tired he began tearing at her with his teeth, heedless of her cries, mindless in his fury. Slowly he became aware that Celeste had stopped moving.

He paused, panting over her while she lay limp beneath him. A pool of bright red blood surrounded them, coating her clothes and hair, smearing his face and hands.

"Why..."

The whispered word of rebuke stirred his tortured mind, and the answer to her question simmered inside him.

"Because you're a liar," he bellowed, throwing his head back in fury. "Because you left me. Because you don't love me like..."

His words faded into an incoherent roar as he grabbed the discarded vase and smashed it downward, shattering his pain into a million pieces.

Sharp words brought the man back to the steps of City Hall. He blinked and turned toward the disdainful voice.

"What the hell are you doing out here, Junior?"

Staring at the familiar face, the man swallowed hard and cleared his throat. He tried to explain, but his father held up a hand. The man flinched as if he were a little boy again. As if his father was still twice his size. Still capable of doling out a swift, harsh punishment.

"Sorry. I haven't been getting enough sleep lately, I guess."

His father looked at him with narrowed eyes, then glanced around, worried someone might see them.

Yes, that's my father. More concerned about what strangers think than what his own son feels. Good old Dad.

Looking over his father's shoulder, the man saw Riley Odell exit the building. Her thick black hair bounced around her shoulders as she took the steps two at a time. His eyes stayed with her as she made her way across the courtyard.

"Junior? Are you even listening to me?"

His father's voice grated on the man's nerves, but he knew better than to cause a scene. He didn't need to draw attention to himself. Especially with the new prosecutor nearby.

"Don't call me that. I'm not a kid. Now I've got to go to work."

He also needed to figure out who to pick as his next fling. He was still weighing his options and he needed time to think. Without waiting for a reply, the man slipped past his father's disapproving stare and fell into step behind Riley. It looked like she was heading for the big parking garage on the corner. It would be good to get a look at the car she was driving.

But the prosecutor unexpectedly turned into the little shop on the corner; the man had no choice but to keep on walking. He couldn't risk being seen following attractive young women around.

People in this town know me, and they all like to gossip and spread rumors. Best to keep my distance for now.

Continuing down the sidewalk, the man's mind turned unwillingly back to his father, then darkened with thoughts of his mother. He clenched both hands into fists.

I can't blame her for leaving and never coming back. What woman in her right mind would stay with such a cold and selfish man?

But he did blame her. She'd known the type of man his father was, and yet she'd left her young son alone with him. Left her only child to suffer the abuse on his own.

She said she'd never leave. No matter how bad things had gotten, she shouldn't have gone. She shouldn't have lied.

Gritting his teeth against the painful memories, he managed to keep his composure as he entered the garage and pressed a big thumb on the key fob to unlock the doors of the expensive black sedan. Sliding onto the soft leather seat, he shut the door and started the engine. The first sweet strains of the song filled the car, sending waves of exquisite pain crashing through him.

Love hurts. It hurts and hurts until...

A figure passed in front of his car. Riley Odell was heading toward a big Dodge double cab pick-up. He watched as she opened the door and swung up and into the driver's seat. The truck rumbled to life and then pulled slowly out of the parking space and rolled toward the exit ramp. Moments later the man's sleek black car nosed out onto the street and turned toward the highway.

He'd need to make a decision tonight. He couldn't hold back much longer. But which girl would it be? It needed to be someone that would make everyone in Willow Bay sit up and take notice. He was getting tired of playing it safe, already getting bored.

Jerking to a stop at a red light, the man looked over at the now dispersing crowd. A familiar face passed through the crosswalk. Was she the one? He turned his head to watch the graceful figure disappear into the crowd, wondering if fate was telling him something.

Maybe this isn't just a coincidence. Maybe I was meant to see her here. Maybe she's supposed to be the next one to die.

The light turned green and the man accelerated. He began to lay out the plan as the city skyline disappeared in his rearview mirror.

CHAPTER EIGHTEEN

Veronica Lee had already inserted her key in the lock before she realized the door was slightly ajar. Sudden fear coursed through her as she leaned forward and peered through the crack into the little apartment. She paused, listening for suspicious sounds, then clawed through her purse to find her phone. If someone had broken in she wouldn't hesitate to run back to her car and call 911. She'd watched too many scary movies to just go in and start looking around.

The clicking of fingernails on a keyboard, along with a sprinkling of soft curses, let Veronica know that her roommate was at home; she must have left the door open. Leave it to Sabrina West to forget to secure her own apartment when she'd just reported on a killer who was stalking women in her neighborhood.

"Can anyone come in and join you?" Veronica asked. "Or did you leave the door open for someone in particular?"

Snapping the lid of her laptop shut, Sabrina spun around in her chair, her expression guarded.

"I came home to work in *private*."

Sabrina picked up the stack of papers beside the computer and nervously shoved them into her computer bag. A handwritten note fluttered to the floor, prompting her to grab for it and crumple it in her fist.

"Okay, what are you up to?"

Raising her eyebrows, Veronica moved closer to the table, searching her roommate's face; the ambitious reporter was obviously hiding something. The computer bag next to Sabrina started to buzz.

"You gonna get that?" Veronica asked when Sabrina made no move to pick up her phone.

"No, I'm not, actually. I'm busy working on a story if you must know." A secretive smile played around Sabrina's lips. "I found a source inside the WBPD and he's provided some very interesting information."

"He? Who is this guy?" Veronica's imagination sprang into action. "One of the detectives? Someone on the crime scene team?"

Shaking her head in protest, Sabrina stood up.

"Oh, no. I'm not betraying my source, and I'm not letting anyone steal my story."

A flush spread over Veronica's pale cheeks as she realized what Sabrina was implying.

"You think I'd try to take credit for your story?"

Picking up her laptop and sliding into the computer bag, Sabrina shrugged. Her baby blue eyes took on a suspicious gleam.

"I'm breaking real news and you're stuck on the weather desk. You think I don't know how that makes you feel?"

The air left Veronica's lungs in one long breath as she stared at her friend in silence. Sabrina huffed and rolled her eyes.

"Don't act like it isn't true. It's written all over your face every time you look at me in the newsroom. You're pissed that I'm doing so well. Why wouldn't you try to-"

"That's ridiculous," Veronica sputtered, finding her voice. "I'm your *friend*, and I'm *glad* you're doing well. Sure, I'd like to move up at the station, but if you think I'd try to do that at your expense, you obviously don't know me at all."

Dropping her eyes, Sabrina pushed the computer bag under the table and turned toward her bedroom. She paused in the doorway to look back at Veronica.

"I'm sorry, Ronnie, that was a shitty thing to say. I didn't mean it." A shine of tears brightened her eyes. "Lately, I've just been feeling a lot of pressure and it's making me act...well, act like a bitch. Just ignore me for the next few days, okay?"

Veronica nodded, but Sabrina had already closed the door behind her. Her indignation turned to concern as Veronica considered her roommate's words. Who was feeding Sabrina information? Could her source at the WBPD be trusted?

Doubt hovered as she thought of the recent downfall of the previous chief of police, Douglas Kramer, and Kirk Reinhardt, a long-term police detective. Both men had been proven to be dangerous predators. Could Sabrina's source be dangerous as well? Could someone be trying to lure the attractive, young reporter to her doom?

Scolding herself for being overly dramatic, Veronica stared down at Sabrina's computer bag under the table. She glanced at the door to the bedroom; it was firmly closed.

Not giving herself the chance to chicken out, she scurried forward, crouched by the table, and slid the computer bag out. Propping it on her knee, she opened the lid, relieved to see that Sabrina hadn't logged off or shut the computer down. Staring at the icons on the cluttered desktop, Veronica debated what to look at first.

Her source may have sent an email...or maybe I should check recent docs.

A notification popped up on the screen before she could decide.

You Got Lucky! There's a New Message in Your Secret Fling Inbox!

Veronica automatically clicked on the box and waited as an app began to load. She stared at the list of messages in the inbox, noting the last one had come in from someone calling himself LonelyGuy10 only minutes before.

What's Secret Fling? And why is Sabrina trying to hook up with someone online? She always told me online dating creeped her out.

Moving the cursor over the unread message, Veronica hesitated. If she opened the message Sabrina would be able to tell that someone had read it. And if her friend really was just trying to find a date, she had no justification for snooping.

I want to protect her from getting into trouble, not pry into her love life.

Sabrina suddenly called to her from the bedroom.

"Ronnie? You still out there?"

Slamming the lid shut, Veronica shoved the laptop back into the bag and pushed it under the table just as the bedroom door swung open. Sabrina had changed into a fire-engine red jacket and slim black pants. Her long blonde hair was pulled into a low ponytail.

"Hey, can you loan me some cash? Boyd's outside in the van to pick me up, so I won't have time to stop at the ATM."

Swallowing hard, Veronica nodded and reached for her purse.

"Sure, I think I have a twenty tucked away."

Sabrina waited while she searched through the contents of her purse for the money. Veronica's hand closed over the wrinkled twenty-dollar bill just as her phone chirped. It was the ringtone she'd set for her mother.

"Hi, Ma, what's up."

Switching her phone to her other hand, Veronica held out the bill. Sabrina snatched the twenty, then bent to pick up the computer bag. Slinging it over her shoulder, she strode to the door and wrenched it open, hurrying outside without a word of thanks or goodbye. The door slammed shut behind her.

"What was that?" Ling Lee asked, worry thick in her voice.

"That was just Sabrina leaving." Veronica tried not to sound as annoyed as she felt. "She's in a hurry to get to work."

She resisted the urge to add a few choice words about her roommate's insensitive behavior. Her mother already harbored enough resentment toward Sabrina. No use adding fuel to the fire.

"You're not in that apartment all alone, are you? With the Willow Bay Stalker on the loose?" Her mother sounded incredulous that Veronica would be so reckless. "You come home and stay with me."

Rolling her eyes at her mother's alarm, Veronica stifled a sigh.

"Ma, there's no reason to panic. The doors are all locked," she lied, crossing to the door to turn the deadbolt. "And there are plenty of neighbors around. Nothing's going to happen to me. I'll be fine."

"It's not good for you to be on your own, Ronnie."

Veronica braced herself for what she knew would come next.

"Have you been dating anyone lately? Met anyone interesting?"

She tried to think up a new answer to the same old question her mother always asked.

"First you tell me to be careful, and then you ask if I'm out meeting new men?" Veronica warmed to her theme, letting her voice rise in mock dismay. "Ma...don't you think it's best that I keep away from strangers until this stalker is caught and locked up?"

Ling inhaled sharply at her daughter's words.

"Very true. You can't be too careful, can you? There are a lot of bad men out there."

The edge of fear in her mother's voice brought a hot flush of shame to Veronica's cheeks. Although Ling Lee's concern for her sometimes verged on hysteria, Veronica knew it stemmed from Ling's own traumatic past. A past that she refused to talk about, but which still seemed to have a terrible hold on her.

"Not all men are bad, Ma," Veronica soothed, "but I'm focusing on other things now, anyway. Like work and-"

"Well then, what about Hunter Hadley? You work with him, and he's so handsome..."

The concern and worry left Ling's voice as quickly as they'd come. Now she sounded almost girlish.

"He's my boss, Ma. It wouldn't be right for him to date me even if he wanted to. Which he doesn't."

"How do you know? Maybe he's just too shy to say anything."

Veronica groaned. How could she explain to her fiercely protective mother that Hunter Hadley was out of her league?

"I know because he's dating someone else, Ma." She thought of Gabby Jankowski's icy stare. "Someone who's beautiful and successful and...sophisticated."

Ling huffed, and Veronica could imagine the look of outrage on her mother's small face.

"I know everyone in town, and there's not a single girl more beautiful than my girl."

"But Hunter Hadley is older and..."

Veronica tried to think of the right words. Words her mother would understand.

"He's a player, I guess. I mean, he's always got women hanging around, and he doesn't seem to care too much about them one way or the other. It's like he doesn't care about anything but work."

"You know I taught Hunter back when he was at Willow Bay High," Ling said as if she'd only just remembered the fact. "He was a good boy. Very smart. And he had a good heart. Not like those other boys that hung around him."

The pause that followed made Veronica suspect her mother was thinking back to the years she'd taught at the local high school before Ling had been promoted to her current position as principal. The small woman had a large personality, and she'd taught many of the people in town, most of whom she still remembered.

"Well, maybe he's changed, Ma. People do sometimes, you know."

"The heart doesn't change." Ling's voice was soft but firm. "If his heart is good, it stays good. And if it's bad...well, it stays that way."

Veronica sensed that her mother wasn't talking about Hunter Hadley anymore. Could she be talking about Veronica's father, the man whose memory had haunted Veronica's childhood home like an unnamed ghost? Did her father have a bad heart? Is that why her mother would never speak of him?

Opening her mouth to ask about her father for the thousandth time, Veronica closed it again. She didn't have time to get distracted now. She needed to find out what Sabrina was doing on *Secret Fling*. And she needed to think of a breaking story that would get Hunter's attention. The chance to find out the details behind her own sad story would just have to wait for another day.

"If you don't like Hunter, what about that cute reporter on Channel Six. You know, the tall one with dark hair...Nick something."

"I've gotta go now, Ma," Veronica said, refusing to be drawn into a conversation about hunky Nick Sargent, the star reporter for Channel Ten's rival network. "But I'll stop by and see you soon. And don't worry, I won't let the Willow Bay Stalker get me."

But as she ended the call, Veronica's mind turned to the man who had killed Jade Castillo and attacked two other women.

Is he out looking for another victim right now? What will he do if he finds out that Sabrina's on his trail? The stalker won't come after her...will he?

CHAPTER NINETEEN

Olympia Glass sat at the table by the window, staring down at the blank sheet of paper in front of her. Eden Winthrop had brought her a sketch pad and drawing pencils weeks ago when she'd learned that Olympia was an artist, but all the pages were still empty. Constant fear and regret had suffocated any hint of creativity or inspiration.

Turning her face toward the window, Olympia's eyes felt heavy under the warm rays of the morning sun. Sleep had been elusive since the attack, and she allowed her eyes to close, enjoying the drowsy comfort of the quiet room. Seconds later she jerked awake, roused by a persistent knocking on the door.

"Olympia? Are you awake?"

It was Reggie Horn. The therapist stopped by her room for a visit most days, although usually not so early in the morning.

"Coming!"

Olympia stood and hurried toward the door. She turned the deadbolt and peeked out.

"Sorry, Reggie. I was up, but then I sort of dozed off again."

"No, I'm sorry for showing up so early. But the police are here, and they're asking to speak with you."

When Olympia didn't respond, Reggie's voice softened.

"They said they just need to ask a few more questions. I'm sure it won't take long."

Dread settled in Olympia's stomach, but she forced herself to nod. "Let me throw on some clothes and I'll be right out."

She pushed the door closed, and leaned against it, wishing she could bolt it from the inside and never open it again. How was she going to get through another interview with the police without breaking down and telling them the truth?

After pulling on a faded pair of jeans and a long sleeve t-shirt, Olympia went into the bathroom. She ran a brush through her wispy brown curls and studied her face in the mirror over the sink. She traced her scars with the tip of her finger, already getting used to them.

Dark shadows circled her eyes, making her look older than her twenty-six years. It wasn't hard for her to see her mother's worn face staring back at her.

I always said I'd never be like you, Mom. Guess I lied.

Suddenly the words her attacker had screamed at her began to echo again and again inside her head.

You shouldn't have cheated. You shouldn't have lied....

Grabbing for the handle, Olympia yanked open the door and stumbled back out in the sitting room. She couldn't let herself fall apart now. She had to get through the next hour and stick to her story. If she kept her mouth shut everything would be okay.

Reggie was waiting for her in the hall, and Olympia followed the therapist into the shelter's dining room, self-conscious about her uneven gait. The smell of coffee and toasted bread hung in the air. Two people sat at one of the little wooden tables. Olympia swallowed hard and kept her eyes on the tiled floor as Reggie closed the door behind her, then turned to make introductions.

"Olympia, this is Detective Ainsley and Detective Jankowski. They're with the Willow Bay Police Department."

Reggie gestured toward the table.

"Go on and sit down. The detectives have agreed to let me sit in while they ask you some questions...if that's what you'd like."

Nodding in agreement, Olympia sank onto the chair and crossed her arms around her body. She raised her eyes warily, recognizing the woman right away.

"You were the one that came to the hospital," Olympia said, hating the way her voice trembled. "I already told you everything."

"That's right. I'm Detective Ainsley...well, actually Chief Ainsley for the time being...but you can just call me Nessa."

Nessa offered a sympathetic smile, and Olympia felt a momentary impulse to blurt out everything she knew. Maybe this kind woman would take care of her. Perhaps she'd be able to protect her. But the fear was too big, and the risk was too great.

"I'm Detective Jankowski." The big man next to Nessa spoke softly, but he didn't smile. "I'm sorry to bother you this morning with more questions, but another woman has been attacked, and we think the man who attacked you was responsible."

The detective waited for a reaction, but Olympia looked away, uncomfortable with his searching gaze. She put a hand over the scar on her cheek.

"Have you ever met a woman named Jade Castillo?" Nessa asked. "She worked as a nurse at Willow Bay General Hospital."

Shaking her head, Olympia forced herself to speak.

"No, I never met her. I did hear her name on the news yesterday, but I've never heard of her before that."

Jankowski shifted in his chair as if he wanted to say something, but Nessa spoke again.

"What about a woman named Bella Delancey? Have you met her?"

An image of a glamorous young woman with long, dark hair came to mind; she'd often seen her on the society pages of the Willow Bay Gazette. Olympia frowned and shrugged.

"I know who she is, but I don't think we've actually met. At least, not that I can remember. Why?"

Ignoring her question, Jankowski leaned forward.

"How about her husband, Ian Delancey? You know him?"

Olympia bristled at his tone. The question had sounded like an accusation. She looked to Reggie for help, but the therapist just nodded.

"Go ahead, Olympia. Tell the detectives everything you know. They just want to find the man who hurt you."

Jankowski tried again.

"Is there something you aren't telling us?"

The words sent a bolt of fear down Olympia's spine, and she stiffened and sat up straighter in her chair.

"I've already told you everything I know, Detective. I've never met Jade Castillo or Bella Delancey. And I don't know what you're trying to imply, but I've certainly never met her husband."

Cocking his head, Jankowski frowned.

"What would I be implying, Olympia? I'm simply asking you a question. Why are you getting defensive? Is there something you're trying to hide from us? Something you don't want us to know?"

Blood rushed to Olympia's head; she closed her eyes against the wave of dizziness that crashed over her.

I can't faint now. I have to keep it together.

Shaking her head firmly, Olympia opened her eyes and forced out a bitter laugh.

"I'm the victim, Detective, in case you've forgotten. I'm not the one with something to hide."

Jankowski opened his mouth to reply, but then fell silent as a phone vibrated on the table in front of them. Nessa's eyes dropped to the display, and she raised a finger.

"Sorry, but I've got to take this."

Turning away from the table, Nessa answered in a low voice.

"Hey, Alma, what's up?"

Nessa listened to the caller, then pulled out a pad of paper to take notes. Olympia tried to see what the detective had written but couldn't make out the words before Nessa stood up and circled around the table.

"Okay, got it. Thanks for the update, Alma. I'll take it from here."

Sinking into the chair beside Olympia, Nessa leaned forward.

"Olympia, have you ever used an app called *Secret Fling*?"

Panic blossomed in Olympia's chest at the softly spoken question. Did they really know she'd been using the dating app, or were they only fishing for information?

"No! I don't know what you're talking about."

She stood and backed away from the table, her legs shaking underneath her. Whatever happened she couldn't admit she'd met LonelyGuy10 on *Secret Fling*. She couldn't tell them anything about him. If she did, he'd promised to come back and find her. And this time she was sure he'd finish the job.

He'll kill me just like he killed Jade Castillo.

Another thought sent a fresh wave of panic through her.

And if I admit I used Secret Fling, Zoey might find out the truth as well. She might find out about me and Milo.

She shuddered at the thought of Zoey finding out her husband had been cheating on her with her best friend. The imagined hurt on Zoey's face scared Olympia almost as much as the thought of facing her attacker again.

Shame and regret filled her eyes with tears as she rushed awkwardly toward the door. She twisted the knob and pulled, but Jankowski was suddenly beside her, his big hand holding the door shut.

His voice was cold and hard as he spoke next to her ear.

"You're gonna have to tell the truth soon. A woman has died. There's a killer on the loose. We need to know what you're hiding."

"Back off, Jankowski."

Reggie wedged her small body between them, and the big detective stepped back as Reggie guided Olympia back toward the table.

"You can't run away anymore, dear." Reggie's eyes were full of sympathy as she took Olympia's hands in hers. "No matter what it is you're afraid of, you have to be honest with the police so that they can help you."

But Olympia was no longer listening. She was back in her apartment the night of the attack. The pain was unbearable, and as she looked up into the man's merciless eyes, she knew she was going to die. Then the darkness closed in, and his hateful words penetrated the pain and the terror.

"If you tell anyone how we met, I'll find you and I'll kill you."

The words resounded in her mind, bringing back the horror and shame. Dropping her head onto the table, Olympia began to cry. If only she hadn't betrayed Zoey. If only she hadn't been so selfish. This was all her fault, and she could never tell anyone what she'd done.

When Olympia finally looked up, Reggie and the detectives were gone. But Detective Jankowski's suspicious eyes stayed with her, and she knew it wasn't over. The big man would be back, and next time he just might break her.

CHAPTER TWENTY

Frustration quickened Jankowski's steps as he hurried out of the Mercy Harbor shelter and climbed into the black Dodge Charger. The department's standard-issue vehicle was built for speed, and the angry detective allowed himself to put his foot on the floor as he headed back to the station. The roar of the engine competed with the noise inside his head.

Why is Olympia Glass lying? What is she hiding...and why?

His impulse to grab the fragile girl and shake the answers out of her had scared him. He needed to get control of his emotions before he did something stupid.

Tapping on the breaks as he neared the station's parking lot, Jankowski tried to clear his mind of anything but the case. He needed to find the connection between the women chosen by the perpetrator.

Why these women? What did they do to piss him off?

He knew Nessa would tell him not to blame the victims, but that wasn't his intention. To catch the guy, he'd have to think like him. And in the perp's mind, Jankowski knew there was a reason he'd beaten the victims so viciously. The fact that the attacker had used his hands and teeth meant he'd had to get up close and personal. He'd wanted the women to see him; to feel him inflicting the pain.

And why did he leave Bella Delancey and Olympia Glass alive, but kill Jade Castillo? Was it an accident, or was Jade special in some way?

Glancing toward the station, Jankowski saw that Nessa was waiting for him outside the building. She waved to get his attention and then watched as he stepped out of the car and made his way across the lot.

"Hurry up, Jankowski, Alma is waiting for us."

Her words spurred him to move faster. Alma's connection at the state lab had uncovered an app called *Secret Fling* on Jade Castillo's phone and computer hard drive.

Did the Willow Bay Stalker find his victims online?

He frowned at the thought. Had the perp stalked Jade Castillo through some sleazy online dating site? He hurried toward the building, anxious to hear more about *Secret Fling*.

Alma and Nessa were waiting for him inside the lobby when he banged through the door.

"I've reserved the briefing room," Nessa said, already heading down the hall. "The computer analyst is on standby to talk to us."

Following the women into the big room, Jankowski closed the door and turned to Alma.

"So, what did they find exactly?"

Alma held up a finger and punched several buttons on the bulky phone she'd set up on the table in front of her.

"I've got the analyst on the line now." Alma raised her voice and leaned forward. "You there, Jaime?"

"Yep, I'm here."

The analyst sounded too cheerful for Jankowski's liking. What was there to be so happy about when investigating a dead woman's computer? Jankowski rolled his eyes as Alma made the introductions.

The guy must be a real geek...or a total freak.

"Jaime, can you go over what you found on the hard drive again?" Alma asked. "The detectives have some questions."

"Everything seemed pretty standard at first. She was using a standard email app that I was able to access. I've copied the existing messages onto a server, along with the documents and files she had stored on her hard drive. I've sent you the instructions for getting in and reviewing all the files."

A hint of excitement entered his voice as he continued.

"The only unusual find was the *Secret Fling* app. I saw that it was installed on the hard drive and that–"

Irritation pushed Jankowski to interrupt.

"What is this *Secret Fling* exactly?"

Ignoring Alma's glare, Jankowski paced in front of the speaker phone, his fists clenching and unclenching at his side as he listened.

"It's an application...and a web portal. The victim's computer had the application installed on the hard drive but most likely the messages were being stored in the cloud on the system's data–"

Jankowski turned to Nessa with an exasperated stare. She grimaced and stepped toward the phone.

"Jaime, are we able to see who Jade Castillo interacted with through the app? Is there a way to track that?"

The analyst's excitement faded.

"Not yet," he admitted. "I've tried to hack into her account, but the site requires the use of strong passwords and I haven't been able to get in yet."

"Call the damn company that makes the app and tell them we need in," Jankowski barked toward the phone. "We need to know if Jade Castillo's killer found her on *Secret Fling*."

A low throbbing started up in Jankowski's head as he spoke, the likely result of too much tension and not enough sleep.

"I've contacted the company and was informed we'd need an ECPA court order to access the account since the account owner is no longer able to give her consent," the analyst replied. "Apparently they have a strict privacy policy, which isn't surprising since the site is geared toward users wanting *discreet encounters*."

"Refresh me...what the hell is an ECPA court order?" Jankowski asked. "And how long will it take?"

The analyst chuckled as if he'd anticipate the question.

"ECPA is the Electronic Communications Privacy Act. It protects user data from being shared except under specific legal circumstances. Most big tech companies require an ECPA court order to release a user's associated email account or IP address."

"So, the law protects people who want to remain anonymous online?" Nessa asked.

"Right," Jankowski growled in disgust, "but what it really means is that people using the app can cheat on their spouses and no one will be able to prove they're screwing around. And if they end up getting killed, well, that's too bad."

Sending Jankowski a warning look, Nessa raised her voice.

"Sit down and get control of yourself, Jankowski."

Her stern tone allowed no argument. Reluctantly he sank into an empty chair, noting that the throbbing in his head was getting worse.

"So, we need to work on getting this court order, then," Nessa said, biting her lip. "Maybe Riley Odell can help us."

Alma looked confused.

"You know, that new prosecutor. Otherwise, I'll have to go begging to Judge Eldredge myself, and you know how that'll go."

Nodding in sympathy, Alma's eyes flicked nervously to Jankowski as if she expected him to erupt again. He dropped his head into his hands and tried to think. An idea pushed past the ache.

"If this guy met Jade Castillo through this app, maybe that's how he met Olympia Glass and Bella Delancey."

Nessa raised her eyebrows, waiting for Jankowski to finish his thought. Alma leaned forward to listen.

"We already asked Olympia about *Secret Fling* and she reacted badly, which makes me think she knows something about it. But we haven't asked Bella Delancey. Maybe she can tell us what's really going on. Or maybe we should just check her computer, too."

Jumping to his feet, Jankowski looked toward the phone.

"You still there, Jaime?"

"Yep, I'm here."

The analyst sounded wary.

"You say that the company behind *Secret Fling* needs the user's consent to access the account, right? So, if Bella Delancey used the app, and she gives her consent, we can look through the app and track down anyone who contacted her?"

There was a pause, and the analyst cleared his throat.

"Theoretically, yes, but most likely the guy would've used a fake name and credentials to open his account."

Jankowski's heart sank. Of course, the guy who did this would try to use a fake identity. Unless he was an idiot. Or unless he wanted to get caught.

"But maybe there's something in his messages that'll review his real identity," Nessa said. "If she'll let us look through them."

"We can sure the hell ask," Jankowski agreed, heading toward the door.

"Where are you going?" Nessa called.

He didn't look back.

"To speak to Bella Delancey."

"Wait, Jankowski!" Nessa scurried after him, chasing him out into the hall. "Before you go to the Delancey's there's something you need to know."

The urgency in Nessa's voice made him stop and turn around.

"Ian Delancey hired Pete Barker and Frankie Dawson to find the man who attacked his wife. They've been working on the case for the last few days."

Jankowski tried to make sense of what Nessa was telling him.

"Working the case? What...how?"

"They've opened up a private investigation business. Ian Delancey has retained their services since, according to him, we haven't been able to find the man who attacked his wife."

Anger boiled under his skin as he realized what she was saying.

"And you're okay with two civilians poking around and confusing the investigation?"

Nessa recoiled at the venom in his voice.

"It's not up to me, and you know it. Ian Delancey can hire whoever he wants. All we can do is try to find the perp as quickly as we can."

She lowered her voice as two uniformed officers passed by.

"I just wanted you to know before you get over there and hear it from Mr. Delancey or Bella. I don't want you to do anything to get the department in more trouble."

Softening her words with a wry smile, Nessa sighed.

"We're all frustrated, you know. But we've got to stay calm and follow the clues. It won't help to go off all half-cocked and piss off the victim's husband. That'll just stir up a lawsuit."

Jankowski's anger dissolved into gloomy pessimism. How would they ever be able to find the Willow Bay Stalker in time to save the next woman? His phone buzzed in his pocket; he looked up at Nessa as he reached for it.

"Don't worry. I won't embarrass the department."

He read the message and scowled. Gabby again.

"Bad news?" Nessa asked.

"Is there any other kind?"

Dropping his phone back in his pocket, Jankowski pushed through the door to the parking lot. If Gabby wanted to talk, he was ready.

After the day I've had, it'll be a relief to give her a piece of my mind.

Minutes later the Charger was speeding through his old neighborhood. He'd driven the same route home every day before his marriage had ended. A wave of sadness threatened to descend.

There's no going back, Jankowski. All that's over now.

He looked down at Gabby's message again, paying little attention to the black sedan that roared past him in the opposite direction.

He saw Gabby's sporty red car as soon as he turned onto the street. He swallowed the bitter lump that rose in his throat at the sight.

After everything she's done, it still hurts like hell just to be near her.

Parking in his old spot, Jankowski stomped up the path and knocked on the big wooden door. He arranged his face in a mask of indifference. He raised his fist to knock again, then saw the thick, wet splotches on the black welcome mat.

He crouched and reached out a hand. The blood clung to his finger before dripping back to the ground with a soft splash. Heart thudding in his chest, he reached for the doorknob and turned.

The door swung open easily, revealing a sticky crimson trail along the white marble floor. Feeling as if he'd fallen into a terrible dream, Jankowski stumbled forward, already knowing what he would find.

Gabby's bruised and battered body lay motionless in a pool of blood on the floor. Running to her, Jankowski dropped to his knees, checking desperately for a pulse.

"Please, please don't be dead. Dear God, don't let her be dead."

Resting his head against her chest, he held his breath, hoping to hear the beating of her heart. Slowly he detected a sound. But it wasn't his ex-wife's heartbeat. It was the sound of sirens, and they were coming closer.

Jankowski sat up, his hands and face covered in Gabby's blood, and looked toward the door. He didn't know if minutes had passed, or if it had been hours, but suddenly Andy Ford was next to him.

The young, uniformed officer stared at him with wide, disbelieving eyes. Jankowski looked past him as harsh voices sounded in the hall. Detective Marc Ingram appeared in the doorway, closely followed by Detective Ruben Ortiz.

Ingram moved toward him, his thin lips set in a grim line of satisfaction. Looking down at Jankowski with pitiless eyes, Ingram opened a notepad and started to read.

"You have the right to remain silent..."

Jankowski ignored Ingram's words as the reality of what was happening started to sink in.

"Andy!" Jankowski suddenly bellowed. "Officer Ford!"

Andy's freckled face appeared in the doorway again.

"Call Nessa!" Jankowski shouted over Ingram's protests. "Tell her to meet me at the station. We need to find out who did this. We need to find the bastard that killed Gabby!"

CHAPTER TWENTY-ONE

Eden looked around Nessa's office with interest. Although she'd visited the police station several times in the last year, this was the first time she'd been allowed past the interrogation rooms and into the station's inner sanctum.

The large office Nessa had inherited from the previous chief of police was exactly how Eden would have envisioned it. The big desk was covered in piles of folders and stacks of papers. A long whiteboard hung on one wall and a huge map of the city hung on another. A small motivational poster had been stuck on the wall behind Nessa's desk. It looked slightly out of place in the otherwise stark surroundings.

"Hang in there."

Eden read the words on the poster with amusement, liking the determined look on the tiny kitten's face as it clung desperately to a shredded curtain.

Nessa looked back at the poster with a tired grimace.

"A little too close to home right now," she said, pushing aside a tottering stack of files and opening her laptop.

Wishing she had something reassuring to say, Eden decided she'd better just get on with the task at hand.

"I know you must be swamped right now with everything going on," Eden began, feeling slightly flustered. "But I thought you might want to know about a past homicide that appears very similar to the recent murder."

Nessa cocked her head to the side, reminding Eden of Duke. The golden retriever often stared at her in just the same way. She suddenly wished she'd brought the dog with her instead of leaving him at home with Barb and the kids. She might need him to get through the grisly details of Celeste Reed's tragic death.

"Go on," Nessa encouraged, her eyes curious.

"Well, right after I opened Mercy Harbor, a young woman named Celeste Reed was referred to one of our shelters."

Eden tried to keep the emotion out of her voice. She didn't want Nessa to think she was being overly dramatic or paranoid. She just needed to explain what she knew about Celeste Reed, and then the interim police chief could decide what to do about it.

"Celeste had only been married a few months when she realized her husband had a drinking problem. She confronted him about it and he ended up hitting her, so she left him. She had no family to speak of, so we helped her get into a new apartment and find a new job. I thought I'd...saved her."

Eden's voice wavered, but she continued, determined to get the story out.

"I guess I was pretty naïve back then. I thought it would be simple to *save* people. But I was wrong, of course. Celeste went back to her husband. She swore he had gotten sober. She was sure he had changed. It was a fatal mistake. Or at least I thought it was."

Nessa's fingers had been moving over the keyboard as Eden was speaking. When Eden paused, the police chief looked up with a grim expression.

"I see the file here on Celeste Reed's death. Her husband was charged with voluntary manslaughter."

Nessa's eyes scanned the file as Eden watched her. She felt her stomach tighten as Nessa's eyes grew wide.

143

The phone on Nessa's desk vibrated, but the police chief ignored it; her eyes remained glued to her computer screen.

"The injuries to Celeste Reed..."

Eden nodded sadly as their eyes met over the desk.

"They're very similar to the injuries Olympia Glass and Bella Delancey suffered," Eden murmured, wincing at the images that came to mind.

"And very similar to those suffered by Jade Castillo," Nessa added.

Resisting the urge to apologize for being the bearer of bad news, Eden stood and picked up her purse.

"Well, that's all I wanted to tell you. Just in case there is a connection. But I'll leave you to it. I've got errands to run. Lots of stuff to do before Saturday."

Nessa looked at her blankly.

"My wedding's on Saturday," Eden reminded her with an embarrassed smile. "I hope you and Jerry can still come...with everything that's going on I understand if you can't."

The door swung open before Nessa could answer. A uniformed officer was halfway through the door before he saw Eden standing behind it.

"Sorry to interrupt, Chief."

"That's okay, Officer Eddings. What's going on?"

Eddings hesitated, looking at Eden as if unsure he should say what needed to be said in front of a civilian. Finally, the words spilled out.

"There's been another homicide. It's...well, it's bad."

Rushing through the door, Nessa headed toward the front of the building. Eden followed close behind, all thoughts of her impending wedding gone.

Nessa burst into the lobby just as the front doors opened and Detective Jankowski stumbled through the door. It took a minute for Eden to realize the big man had his hands cuffed behind his back.

"What the hell is going on?"

Nessa sounded as confused as Eden felt.

Two men held Jankowski's arms. One was well-built and handsome, with thick black hair and dark eyes, while the other was thin and pale, with the small, furtive features of a rodent.

"Gabby Jankowski was murdered in her home this morning," the pale man said. "We found Jankowski at the scene covered in blood."

A soft gasp sounded behind Eden, and she turned to see that Riley Odell was standing in the lobby. The new prosecutor's cool, calm demeanor had slipped momentarily as she took in the scene. Quickly recovering, she opened the door to the back and motioned for the men to bring Jankowski through.

Eden watched in dismay as the door shut firmly behind them.

* * *

Twenty minutes later Leo charged into the lobby. Eden watched as he scanned the room then crossed to where she sat by the window.

"I came as soon as Pat gave me your message."

He sat in the chair next to her and took her hands in his.

"What's happened? Pat said someone's been arrested?"

Eden leaned forward and rested her head on Leo's broad shoulder, her mind still spinning with the image of Jankowski in handcuffs and the news that Gabby Jankowski was dead.

Breathing in the familiar scent of Leo's cologne, and feeling the solid strength of his body beside her, Eden felt her anxiety subside.

"It's Detective Jankowski," Eden said, raising her face to look into Leo's worried eyes. "His wife's...dead and he's been arrested for her murder."

Surprise flashed in Leo's eyes, but he accepted her words without question, and Eden was grateful that he didn't voice doubts about

Jankowski's innocence. They both knew Jankowski was a good man. He'd proven it again and again during the previous year.

"I'm not sure why they think Jankowski could have done this..."

Leo put a finger to Eden's lips and shook his head.

"Don't you worry about that now. I'll find out all the details soon enough. For now, I just want to make sure you're okay and see to it that you get home safely."

Eden wanted to protest, but she knew it would do no good. Leo could always tell when she was upset. He could see how badly she'd been shaken by the morning's events, and there was no way to hide it. The tremor in her hands and the strain in her eyes proved it.

Besides, she hadn't had a panic attack in months, and she wasn't about to take any chances of relapsing only days before their wedding. The Willow Bay Stalker might be terrorizing Willow Bay, but she couldn't let him ruin her wedding, too.

"I guess I'd better go home and check on the kids," Eden said, getting to her feet. "Now that you're here to help Jankowski I can leave without feeling so guilty."

"Why would you feel guilty?"

Shrugging, Eden tried to explain.

"Jankowski has done so much for us," Eden said slowly, trying to organize her jumbled thoughts. "It just feels wrong not to try to help him now that he's the one in trouble. Besides, it's not fair to just arrest him before they've done a proper investigation."

Leo smiled and pulled her to him.

"You're starting to sound a lot like me."

Pushing against his chest, Eden feigned outrage.

"Maybe it's *you* who's starting to sound like *me*!"

Leo bent to kiss Eden's pouting lips, then guided her toward the exit. They hadn't gotten far when Riley Odell stepped into the lobby.

"Ms. Odell?" Eden called out impulsively. "May we have a word?"

The prosecutor studied Eden, her eyes guarded.

"Yes? How can I help you?"

Leo stepped forward, his voice suddenly cool and crisp.

"I'm Leo Steele, Detective Simon Jankowski's lawyer, and I'd like to understand why my client has been taken into custody."

The prosecutor's dark eyes flashed as she studied Leo, and Eden felt a flutter of unease as she watched the woman that would be prosecuting most of the felony cases in Willow Bay going forward.

"Mr. Steele, good to meet you," Riley responded smoothly. "I've heard a lot about you from my predecessor. Sounds like we may be working together in the future."

Leo ignored the comment and repeated his question.

"Why has my client been arrested, Ms. Odell?"

Riley looked around the room as if she was afraid of being overheard. Her eyes rested briefly on Eden, who stared back defiantly, then returned to Leo.

"Let's go into one of the interrogation rooms and I'll fill you in."

Nodding curtly, Leo tuned to Eden and squeezed her hand.

"You go on home, Eden. I'll come by as soon as I'm done here."

Eden watched Leo follow Riley's slim figure into the back as an unfamiliar emotion settled into her chest. She turned on her heel and forced herself to head for the exit, scolding herself for being foolish.

Now's not the time to start being jealous and possessive.

But as she walked back to her big SUV, a sense of impending doom threatened. Happiness had seemed so close. Saturday was only two days away. Now everything was starting to spiral out of her control.

Refusing to give in to her growing anxiety, Eden steered the car toward home. Barb and Duke and the kids would cheer her up.

And whatever happens, I won't let anyone, or anything, stop me from marrying Leo on Saturday.

CHAPTER TWENTY-TWO

B arker had suggested they start out early for the three-hour drive north. He'd hoped to make it to the Florida State Prison at Raiford before lunchtime and be back home in time to have dinner with Taylor. But Frankie wasn't exactly a morning person, and in the end, they'd agreed Barker would pick Frankie up outside his house at ten o'clock. When the blue Prius pulled up to the curb, Frankie was still yawning.

"Early bird catches the worm," Barker called out as Frankie climbed in. "You've already missed out on half the day."

"Nothing interesting happens before lunchtime," Frankie insisted, reclining the passenger seat and stretching out. "And besides, I need a solid eight hours every night or I get cranky."

Steering the little car toward the highway, Barker looked over at Frankie with raised eyebrows but decided to drop the subject. They had more important things to discuss in any case.

"Well, while you were catching up on your beauty sleep I went to the Delancey house to talk to Bella."

Frankie sat up in his seat, his eyes suddenly alert.

"Why'd you go without me?" Frankie complained. "What'd you find out?"

Wishing he had something useful to share, Barker shrugged.

"I found out that Bella is just as scared as Olympia Glass. Both women refuse to say anything about the man who attacked them."

Frankie scratched at a patch of stubble on his chin.

"It kinda makes sense. I mean, they must be scared stiff if they think the piece of shit who beat them up is gonna come back and finish the fucking job. I'd be freaking out, too."

"But the only reason the guy might come back is if they can identify him somehow, right?" Barker asked, confident he already knew the answer. "They must know who he is."

Barker felt his frustration growing into anger.

If Bella or Olympia would say who had attacked them, the whole thing could be over. No one else would have to get hurt.

Pushing his foot down harder on the gas pedal, the Prius hummed along, swerving in and out of the traffic at an ever-increasing speed. They needed to get to Raiford and talk to Seth Reed. If he was an innocent man as Eden Winthrop suspected, then maybe he would have something useful to tell them.

Barker knew it was a longshot, but at this point, they couldn't afford to pass up any lead, no matter how unlikely.

* * *

Raiford looked just the same as it had the last time Barker had visited, but Frankie seemed awed by the silver razor wire fence and intimidating concrete building.

"This place is fucking big, man," Frankie whispered to Barker as they went through the heavy security gates. "Maybe I shoulda' done my time here."

Rolling his eyes, Barker looked around the crowded visiting room for Seth Reed. Inmates sat at long tables with their families or stood by the concrete walls waiting for their visitors to make it past the security check.

A muscular man in a prison jumpsuit hovered near the door. He'd gained weight since being incarcerated, and his hairline had receded, but Barker recognized Seth Reed from his mugshot.

Barker approached cautiously. The inmate stared at him with dull, defeated eyes. Were they the eyes of an innocent man given a thirty-year sentence?

"Seth Reed?"

"Yeah?" The man's voice was hoarse as if he wasn't used to talking. "Who are you?"

"I'm Pete Barker, and this is my partner, Frankie Dawson. We're private investigators from Willow Bay."

Seth's eyes widened at the name of his hometown.

"What do you want with me?"

Moving toward an empty spot at one of the long tables, Barker motioned for Seth to follow him.

"Let's sit down, Mr. Reed. This won't take long."

"I got all day if you do," Seth replied, slouching onto the bench and propping his elbows on the table in front of him. "Got nothing else to do for about twenty-five years."

Frankie laughed loudly at the words, but Seth didn't crack a smile.

"Good one, man," Frankie said, slapping the table and looking around the room nervously. "Glad to see you still got a sense of humor in here. When I was locked up I was always as serious as a fucking heart attack."

Glancing at Barker, Frankie winced.

"Sorry, man, I didn't mean to imply heart attacks are funny..."

Seth looked confused, but Barker figured he might as well use Frankie's gaffe to try to build a connection with the man.

"You'll have to excuse my partner, Mr. Reed. You see Frankie has a habit of putting his foot in his mouth."

Resting his hand over his chest, Barker sighed.

"You see, I had a heart attack last year. That's when I retired from the police force."

Seth's eyes darted to Barker's face, and he looked ready to panic.

"Of course, I was getting sick of the corruption at the WBPD as well, which I'm sure you've heard all about."

Shaking his head, Seth looked even more confused.

"Well, I can tell you personally that some of those cops put people in jail that were innocent," Frankie said, assuming a self-righteous tone. "They even had me up in prison before I got a lawyer to get my sentence overturned."

A spark of interest lit up Seth's eyes at Frankie's words.

"I'm innocent, too," Seth said, his voice low as if he feared being overheard. "But nobody believed me. They railroaded me and–"

A guard walked past, and Seth froze. As the guard moved on, Seth turned to Barker.

"I didn't kill my wife," he muttered, his voice shaking. "But I know who did."

Keeping his voice casual, Barker raised an eyebrow.

"You know who killed her? Why didn't you tell the cops?"

"I did tell them...but they wouldn't believe me," Seth moaned. "And I bet you don't believe me either."

Frankie leaned forward so that he was only inches from Seth's flushed face.

"Why should we believe a man who beat up his own wife?"

Recoiling from the disgust in Frankie's voice, Seth swallowed hard and stood up. His Adam's apple bobbed wildly in his throat.

"Yeah, I hit Celeste that one time, and I regret it. Hell, I've paid for it for the last five years. But that was because I was drinking. I had a problem. But I got help and we were getting back together. I was making it up to her. I loved her..."

Barker stood and faced Seth, his face somber.

"How did she die then, Mr. Reed? If you didn't kill her, who did?"

"It was that rich guy she started seeing after she moved out," Seth's voice deepened with anger. "She was always talking about him. Saying he was buying her stuff and helping her out. She thought he was a real friend. But then once we got back together, he wouldn't go away."

"Did you tell the cops about him?" Frankie asked. "Do you remember his name?"

Crumpling back onto the bench, Seth shook his head.

"Celeste just called him Junior. She didn't tell me his last name. The cops thought I was making it all up."

"You told the police about Junior? You told them what you knew?"

Barker's heart sank at the thought that the WBPD may have screwed up another case.

"Yeah, I told them. But they wouldn't listen. Said some fancy expert told them my teeth matched the marks on...on her skin."

Dropping his head into his hands, Seth's shoulders started shaking. Barker leaned forward and put an awkward hand on the man's arm. A sudden thought filled him with guilt and pity.

If Seth Reed really is innocent, he must still be grieving his wife's death.

"I'm sorry for your loss, Mr. Reed." Barker kept his voice low. "My wife died a few years ago, so I know how it feels. It sucks."

Raising his head to stare at Barker with red-rimmed eyes, Seth nodded and wiped his nose on the back of his hand.

"You know, you're the first person who ever said that to me."

The man's quiet words stayed with Barker as he and Frankie left the prison and started the long drive home.

"I believe him," he said to Frankie. "Seth Reed is telling the truth. And that means someone else has gotten away with murder for the last five years."

CHAPTER TWENTY-THREE

Nessa decided to walk the few blocks from the police station over to City Hall. No matter how badly things had been going at the WBPD, the weather in Willow Bay was still flawless, and it seemed wrong not to take advantage of the cool blue day while the mild weather lasted.

The morning had been difficult, to say the least. Karl Nickels had finally arrived to view Jade Castillo's body. He'd taken one look at his fiancé's ruined face and promptly threw up the plane food he'd eaten on the flight down from Minneapolis. Nessa could still see the horror and grief in his red, watery eyes as she reached the courtyard.

Inhaling a last gulp of fresh air, Nessa pulled open the heavy door and stepped into the lobby. It took a minute for her eyes to adjust to the dim lighting, and she didn't notice Archie Faraday posting something on the notice board until she almost bumped into him.

"Oh, sorry about that Mr. Faraday, I didn't see you there."

She glanced toward the board, curious as to what the old man was up to. He wasn't the type to perform his own administrative tasks, so whatever he was doing must be something he considered important enough to take care of himself.

"You better watch where you're going, Detective," Archie said in the disapproving tone that always made Nessa's nerves stand on end. "I'd hate for you to get hurt."

"I think you meant to say chief, Mr. Faraday," Nessa heard herself reply. "I'm the interim chief of police now, not a detective."

Pointing to the document he'd posted on the board, Archie produced a malicious smile.

"Not for long, dear," he murmured in mock sympathy. "But do enjoy it while you can."

Nessa read the words with a sinking heart.

Open Position: Willow Bay Chief of Police

Not giving Archie the satisfaction of a reaction, Nessa continued down the hall to the executive conference room. Mayor Hadley had called an emergency meeting, and he was already sitting at the big table. Riley Odell was on his left and Archie Faraday quickly took a seat on his right.

Nessa sat across from the mayor and pulled out her notes, bracing herself for what she was sure would be a full-scale attack on the department's handling of the case. She didn't realize anyone else had entered the room until Mayor Hadley called out a greeting.

"Detective Ingram, Detective Ortiz, come in and take a seat."

Spinning around in her chair, Nessa watched Ingram and Ortiz hurry forward to sit next to her. Ortiz offered her an apologetic smile, but Ingram ignored her, keeping his eyes straight ahead as Mayor Hadley began to speak.

"I'm sure you all know how devastated I am by the death of Gabriella Jankowski. She and I worked closely together, and I'm in utter shock that she's gone."

Archie Faraday made sympathetic noises, but everyone else remained awkwardly quiet. Gabby Jankowski had been Willow Bay's media relations officer for several years, but she hadn't endeared herself to many of the officials or government employees. As terrible as her murder was, Nessa knew that few people would be genuinely heartbroken that she was gone.

Except for Jankowski, of course. I think he loved her just as much as he hated her. Gabby wasn't an easy person to love, but then, neither is he.

Riley Odell met Nessa's eyes and offered her a quick smile before clearing her throat.

"I'm sure you must be very upset, Mayor Hadley. We certainly appreciate you calling us together so we can discuss the plan to move forward with the investigation into Gabriella Jankowski's homicide."

Nodding gravely at Riley's words, the mayor straightened his tie and glanced surreptitiously at his watch, as if he had another appointment to get to.

"Luckily I hear that we already have a suspect in custody?"

Ingram raised his hand as if he was a student that had the answer to a particularly hard question. Riley ignored him.

"Detective Simon Jankowski claims he discovered his ex-wife's body after receiving a text from her phone asking him to come by her house," Riley said, jumping straight into the case without preamble. "And then Detective Ingram arrived on the scene and made the decision to arrest Detective Jankowski."

Mayor Hadley's mouth dropped open at the words. Nessa could see he hadn't known Jankowski was the man they had in custody.

"We won't be able to decide if we have enough evidence to actually charge Detective Jankowski until we get the results of the autopsy and the crime scene techs submit their findings."

Ingram shot out of his chair, slapping both his palms on the table.

"You've gotta be kidding me! The man was found rolling in his ex-wife's blood. He had it on his hands, his face...it was everywhere."

Shifting in her chair to glare up at Ingram, Nessa was tempted to tell the little weasel just what she thought of him. Before she had the chance, Riley spoke up in a cool, dismissive tone.

"Exactly. With a violent serial predator active in this area, and based on the heinous nature of the crime, it's possible Gabriella Jankowski was a victim of the Willow Bay Stalker."

"That's exactly what Jankowski hoped we would think," Ingram sputtered in outrage. "Only I caught him red-handed."

"Proving someone was at a crime scene is not the same as proving they committed the crime, Detective."

Riley's patronizing tone left a flush of color on Ingram's pale face.

"I'm the one who will have to stand up in court and convince a jury that Detective Jankowski was hurting his ex-wife and not trying to help her," she continued. "If I'm not convinced, a jury won't be either."

Mayor Hadley looked back and forth between Ingram and Riley.

"What are you saying, Ms. Odell? Is Jankowski a suspect or not?"

"I'm telling you that your police department will need to complete a comprehensive, objective investigation before we can determine who is a suspect and who, if anyone, we have enough evidence against to charge with a crime."

Nodding in agreement, Nessa stood to face Mayor Hadley.

"Ms. Odell is exactly right, Mayor. My team is just starting to investigate Gabby's murder. Detective Ingram acted impulsively when he arrested Jankowski at the scene. We have no grounds to hold him in custody at this point."

Archie emitted a derisive laugh, then shook his head in disgust.

"And we're expected to believe that you, Detective Ainsley, are going to perform an objective investigation of your own partner? How stupid do you think we are?"

"Out of respect for your advanced age, Mr. Faraday, I won't answer that last question," Nessa replied, her voice dripping with southern honey. "But I certainly would appreciate you calling me by my proper title. I'm the chief of police, at least for now, and I expect to be called Chief Ainsley, or, if that's too much for you, just plain old Nessa."

Not giving Archie a chance to respond, Nessa again addressed Mayor Hadley and Riley.

"I agree that it would be a conflict of interest for me to investigate Jankowski, seeing that he was my partner up until yesterday when I hired in a new detective to fill my old spot."

Enjoying the look of surprise on the mayor's face, Nessa resisted the urge to turn and stick her tongue out at Ingram.

"Therefore, I suggest we assign the new detective coming in to take on the investigation into Gabby Jankowski's homicide. That way there will be no chance of bias either way."

Riley was already nodding her head in agreement as both Archie and Ingram shouted out objections.

"Everyone quiet down," Mayor Hadley roared, his face turning almost as red as his tie. "The decision's been made. The new detective will handle the investigation into Gabriella Jankowski's homicide, and will work closely with Riley Odell to make sure we pull together a solid case before any official charges are filed."

Leaning forward in his chair, Archie whispered furiously into Mayor Hadley's ear. After a moment's pause, the mayor looked over at Nessa in disbelief.

"Is it true that our chief medical examiner is dating the victim's ex-husband?"

Stunned by the unexpected question, Nessa briefly considered lying about Iris and Jankowski's relationship. It all seemed much too complicated and confusing.

"Well, yes, Iris Nguyen has gone out with Detective Jankowski, but it's nothing serious..."

Even Riley Odell looked taken aback by the shift in the conversation. Archie turned to Nessa with a triumphant sneer.

"We can't allow Iris Nguyen to perform an autopsy on her boyfriend's ex-wife, now can we? Or have we all given up any pretense of following proper procedures in this town?"

Shocked silence followed Archie's words. Finally, Mayor Hadley spoke in a numb voice.

"Archie, you used to be the medical examiner. You can perform the autopsy. That way we don't have to embarrass our town by calling in an outsider."

"But he's no longer qualified," Nessa responded, stopping herself from adding that he never really had been. "If he doesn't have the proper credentials the autopsy results won't hold up in court, will they?"

Riley shrugged, clearly stumped by the web of relationships at play in the small town. Hadley tried again.

"Well, maybe Iris can still perform the autopsy, but with Archie's supervision. That way there will be a witness to validate that it was all done according to protocol."

Nessa whirled around at the sound of the conference room door banging open, then closed. The chair beside her was empty. She caught Riley's eye and shrugged.

"Looks like Detective Ingram has left the building."

* * *

When Nessa left City Hall half an hour later, a man with a red crewcut and freckles was waiting for her. He leaned casually against a black Harley Low Rider, wearing faded jeans and a plain white t-shirt that showcased his thick arms and washboard abs.

"What's the verdict?"

His voice was husky, with just a hint of a backwoods twang.

"It's all set, Detective, and I hope you're ready to hit the ground sprinting. Let's get back to the station and I'll fill you in."

Tucker Vanzinger smiled, his blue eyes crinkling at the corners and ruining the tough-guy routine he'd had going.

"Glad to hear it, Chief. I thought they'd throw a shit fit when they found out you wanted to bring me back."

Nessa quickly decided Vanzinger didn't need to know that she hadn't actually told anyone his name yet and that she hadn't revealed to the mayor that the new detective she'd hired had worked for the city years before, or that he'd left under mysterious circumstances.

It'll come out soon enough. All that matters is that Vanzinger's a good detective and a good man. He's exactly what the WBPD needs right now.

Vanzinger had jumped in to help her and Jankowski more than once in the last year, and he'd been the first person she'd thought of when she realized she'd have to back fill her own position after she moved into the chief's office. She'd need someone with the type of criminal justice and military background Vanzinger had. And she wanted someone who would have her back no matter what.

"Meet me back at the station," Nessa said, turning to see Riley Odell coming down the steps. "Oh, wait a minute, Vanzinger. I'd like to introduce you to the prosecutor you'll be working with on the case."

Turning away from the Harley, Vanzinger looked back with a smile. The smile faded as he met Riley Odell's cool gaze.

"Hello, Tucker," Riley said, her voice strained. "It's been a while."

Vanzinger froze, and for the first time since Nessa had met him, he didn't seem to know what to say.

"Do you two know each other?" Nessa asked, feeling awkward as Riley and Vanzinger faced each other, both seemingly unable to break eye contact.

"I thought we did," Riley finally answered, her voice cold. "But it turned out I never knew him at all."

Moving past Vanzinger toward the sidewalk, Riley called over her shoulder.

"I'll see you back at the station, Nessa."

Nessa watched as the prosecutor made her way down the block, then she turned to face Vanzinger.

"Don't tell me I've hired in a detective that has bad blood with the new state prosecutor..."

"It was a long time ago," Vanzinger murmured. "And a lot has changed since then. I'm sure she's moved on by now."

The longing in Vanzinger's eyes was plain, and Nessa sighed.

"Yes, she probably has, my friend. But have you?"

The brawny detective didn't answer. He swung a long leg over the Low Rider, pulled on his helmet, and steered the bike onto the road.

Nessa stared after him, knowing that whatever had happened between Riley and Vanzinger in the past, they'd have to put the past behind them and figure out a way to work together. They needed to find out if Jankowski had finally lost it and killed his ex-wife in a fit of rage, or if Gabby had been another victim of the Willow Bay Stalker.

"My money's on the Stalker," Nessa muttered to herself as she trudged toward the station. "And I'd bet a million bucks that Gabby won't be his last victim."

CHAPTER TWENTY-FOUR

The man watched as Sabrina West stared into the camera, her wide blue eyes shining with a strange satisfaction. She wasn't scared like the other women in town who were locking their doors and setting their alarms. No, Sabrina wasn't hiding from him; she was trying to track him down.

"Another woman has been found murdered in her own home this morning, this time in the upscale Bayside subdivision."

Motioning to the busy crime scene behind her, Sabrina's voice practically vibrated with excitement.

"Officials have yet to confirm the identity of the latest victim, but an anonymous source had revealed exclusively to Channel Ten that the home where the body was discovered is owned by Gabriella Jankowski, Willow Bay's media relations officer."

The man sneered at the thought of the reporter's mysterious anonymous source. He'd seen the man that was feeding her information. Do doubt she was leading the poor schmuck on.

She's probably pretending she likes him. Telling him what he wants to hear. Then once she gets what she wants, she'll leave him high and dry.

He almost felt sorry for the cop. He knew what it was like to believe in someone that ended up being a liar and a fraud. Too many women had hurt him, or someone like him. He thought of the women he'd known.

Celeste Reed, Bella Delancey, and Jade Castillo had all lied to the men they were supposed to love. Olympia Glass had lied to her own best friend. It seemed that no relationship was sacred.

And Gabby Jankowski? Well, she'd been one of the biggest liars of all. She'd actually told her ex-husband she was thinking of getting back together with him when in reality she was coming on to every man in town. It was women like Gabby that gave love a bad name.

Dragging his eyes away from Sabrina West's lying lips, he looked around at the people in the crowd. Everyone wore a somber expression. A few of the women were even crying. The fear and dread that hung in the air filled the man with bitter pride.

He was finally getting the attention and respect he'd always wanted. Even if no one knew who he really was, they knew enough to fear what he could do, and he enjoyed their fear.

His father must have felt the same sense of power when he'd terrorized his family, always keeping them in a state of dread, never letting them know what might happen next.

Of course, his father no longer had the power to hurt him, at least not physically, and his mother had escaped long ago. She said she'd never leave him, but that had been a lie. Then she'd promised to come back for him, but she never had returned.

After she'd gone, the years of loneliness and pain had seemed endless. Until he'd met Celeste. She'd been damaged just like him. She'd been hurt and abandoned, too. And she'd said she cared about him. She'd listened to his sad story and even let him cry on her shoulder. But in the end, it had all been an act. She'd gone back to her husband. Had probably even told her husband all the secrets he'd shared with her. They'd probably laughed together at his weakness and his tears.

Only they aren't laughing now, are they?

The man hadn't intended to kill Celeste, but rage had taken over. He'd been possessed by a frenzied need to destroy the source of his pain before it consumed him.

He'd thought for sure he'd be caught after he'd killed Celeste. There was so much blood. So much evidence. Even his father had suspected him, although he'd never been sure.

"Junior, you didn't do anything to that girl they found, did you?"

But the cops had gone after the husband. They always did; it was the easiest answer, and so he'd somehow gotten away with it. Perhaps his father had helped. Maybe the old man had known after all.

In any case, the fear that he'd be caught had stopped him from acting out again. He'd bottled up his rage for years, even as the urge to seek vengeance festered inside him.

Then last year he'd happened upon *Secret Fling*. The fact that an app existed solely to enable liars and cheaters to deceive the ones they were supposed to love sickened him. An idea began to grow. He could use the app for his own purposes.

It seemed somehow fitting that women who used the app became the victims of their own deception, and that they'd suffer tenfold the hurt that they had been willing to inflict on others.

A commotion in the crowd of spectators brought the man's attention back to the scene. A metal gurney was being wheeled down the driveway to the big, white medical examiner's van. People strained their necks to catch a glimpse of the white sheet that covered the figure underneath.

Running toward the van, Sabrina West kept speaking into the microphone, determined to get footage for the evening news.

"As you can see the body of the victim is being taken away to the medical examiner's office for autopsy. The police will try to determine if this is the latest victim of the Willow Bay Stalker."

Once the van had pulled out of view, Sabrina took a break. She fished her cellphone out of her pocket and began tapping on the screen. The man knew what she was doing.

Back to her snooping and prying.

She was trying to find LonelyGuy10. She was just as determined as Jade Castillo had been to meet him. Of course, Jade had thought she knew who he was. She'd even gone so far as to show up at his job and try to talk to him. She'd almost ruined everything. Luckily, he'd gotten to her house in time to stop her.

And while he'd only meant to teach her a lesson, it had all gotten out of control. He didn't think he'd left any evidence, but then, he couldn't be sure. Hopefully, Gabby Jankowski's death would confuse the cops and take the pressure off him. The police would probably jump on Gabby's ex-husband as the main suspect.

That'll give me time to line up my next fling.

The man let his eyes linger on Sabrina West's flushed face.

And I think this one just might be my grand finale.

CHAPTER TWENTY-FIVE

Veronica read over her notes with a critical eye and then slumped back into her chair. She'd been waiting for the chance to pitch a new story idea to Hunter Hadley, but he'd been locked in his office with the blinds drawn most of the day, coming out only to bark orders at the crew before retreating once again behind the closed door.

She stared at the door with a mixture of sympathy and impatience, telling herself her story would just have to wait until the station manager was in a better frame of mind.

The poor man must be torn up by Gabby's murder. Even if they had been fighting lately, it must be a terrible shock.

Dropping her notes onto the desk, she looked up to see two men charge through the newsroom door. Stepping out from behind her desk, she greeted them with a quizzical smile.

"How can I help you gentlemen?"

The thin man with pale hair and close-set eyes held up a badge. He looked familiar.

"I'm Detective Ingram from the Willow Bay Police Department and this is my partner, Detective Ortiz."

Ortiz nodded at Veronica, his dark, handsome features breaking into a friendly smile that made Veronica blush.

Bet I can guess which one gets to play the good cop.

"We're looking for the station manager, Hunter Hadley," Ingram said, his small, suspicious eyes scanning the room.

"What do you want with Mr. Hadley?"

Startled to hear Sabrina's voice behind her, Veronica twisted around to see that her roommate had returned. She also noticed that almost everyone on the news crew had heard the detective's request and had gathered around.

"We just need to ask him a few questions," Detective Ortiz reassured Sabrina. "It shouldn't take very long."

"It'll take as long as it takes," Ingram snapped, throwing his partner an irritable scowl. "We're investigating the murder of Gabriella Jankowski. From what we've heard Mr. Hadley was in a relationship with the victim, but they'd recently had a falling out."

"Are you implying that Hunter Hadley is a suspect in Gabby's murder?" Sabrina asked, her blue eyes wide and eager.

"Of course not," Veronica protested automatically. "Mr. Hadley would never hurt anyone."

Several people in the crew voiced their agreement, but Ingram only smirked at the circle of worried faces.

"According to Mayor Hadley and our new chief of police, we can't rule anyone out yet. I'd say that goes for the mayor's son as well."

Veronica saw Ortiz roll his eyes at Ingram's remark. What exactly was going on? Did Ingram have some sort of grudge against the mayor and his son?"

"You really consider the mayor's son a suspect?" Boyd asked skeptically. "Isn't that career suicide for a man in your position?"

Several crew members laughed, and Ingram glowered at them.

"If doesn't matter if Hunter is the mayor's son; no one is above the law in this town," he growled. "His big-shot daddy might have gotten him this job, but he can't save him from the long arm of the law if he committed a crime."

Veronica suddenly remembered where she'd seen the offensive little man. He'd been the detective involved in the Oscar Hernandez scandal only months before. Ingram had arrested the young man for assault and battery and was later accused of misconduct when Oscar was proven to be innocent of the crime. Rumor had it that the man's blunder had cost him a promotion to chief of police.

And now Detective Ingram's at it again, but this time he's trying to make up false charges against Hunter.

"You going after Hunter wouldn't have anything to do with his father rejecting your application for the open chief of police job, would it?" Veronica asked, forcing herself to meet Ingram's beady little eyes as she spoke. "I'd have thought you would've learned your lesson after you falsely accused Oscar Hernandez of assault."

Pushing Veronica to the side, Sabrina West raised her microphone and shoved it toward Ingram. His face twisted with disdain.

"No comment," he sneered, putting a hand over the camera Boyd had lifted in his direction. "Tell Hunter Hadley we need to speak to him now."

"You can tell me yourself."

Hunter's voice was icy as he loomed over the little detective.

"What's this all about?"

Stepping between Ingram and Hunter, Detective Ortiz attempted to diffuse the situation.

"We're sorry to bother you, Mr. Hadley." The detective kept his voice low and deferential. "I'm sure you're very upset right now, but we do need to ask you a few questions as part of our investigation. Is there somewhere we can speak privately?"

Hunter considered the words, then nodded. He turned and led the two detectives into his office, firmly shutting the door behind them.

"That man really has it in for Mr. Hadley," Veronica murmured to Sabrina as most of the crew dispersed. "What a jerk."

"Well, he does have a point."

Veronica frowned at Sabrina.

"What are you trying to say?"

"I'm saying that the old men in this town run things, and people like you and me and Ingram, well, we don't get much of a say."

Pushing back a long strand of blonde hair, Sabrina glanced around the room, as if fearful someone was eavesdropping.

"That's why we can't rely on the WBPD to find the real Willow Bay Stalker. At least not if turns out to be Hunter Hadley or some other privileged man with the right connections."

Gasping at Sabrina's words, Veronica shook her head.

"Hunter's *not* the Stalker! And anyway, that's not always true. We just had a new woman prosecutor assigned to our district...and the mayor appointed a woman as chief of police. Nessa Ainsley's family's not from Willow Bay."

Sabrina raised a hand in triumph.

"That's exactly why she won't be chief of police for long," Sabrina crowed. "You just wait. They'll bring in some crony of the mayor. Or maybe hire the son of one of the council members."

Putting a finger to her lips, Veronica motioned for her roommate to lower her voice.

"You're going to make people mad around here if you talk like that." Veronica dropped her own voice to a whisper. "But do you really think the police won't be able to find the Stalker?"

A gleam came into Sabrina's blue eyes. It was a familiar look that meant her roommate was plotting something outrageous.

"They might not have to," Sabrina said with a smile. "Not if my special investigation goes the way I think it will."

Veronica watched Sabrina walk away with a puzzled frown. But an idea for a new story was already taking shape in her head. She just might have an idea for a story that would shake up the town and change everything. It might even help catch the Willow Bay Stalker.

Of course, she'd need to do a little more digging, and make sure her facts were straight, but then she could pitch her idea to Hunter.

A thrill shot through Veronica at the thought of breaking a story that would change Willow Bay forever. She'd finally be seen as a real reporter, and her mother would be so proud.

And maybe Hunter will finally see me as something more than just the weather girl. He'll have to start taking me seriously when he sees my story.

The thought of Hunter's reaction prompted a pang of anxiety. He might not appreciate her digging into the city's dark secrets. He and his family may not want their past revealed. For the first time, Veronica worried that Hunter Hadley may have something to hide.

CHAPTER TWENTY-SIX

The prescription bottle of diazepam felt heavy in Hunter's pocket as he led Ingram and Ortiz back to his office. He'd picked up the pills the previous afternoon and had taken a double dose as soon as he'd gotten home. He'd fallen asleep by ten but had woken up in the middle of the night, his nightmares proving stronger than the drugs.

"Let's just cut right to the chase, shall we, Mr. Hadley?" Ingram snapped as soon as the door had closed behind them. "We need to know every move you've made during the last twelve hours, and who you've been with."

Assuming a look of shocked surprise, Hunter took a seat behind his desk and motioned for the two detectives to sit down.

"I was always told that I shouldn't speak to the police without my lawyer present." Hunter looked into Ingram's bitter eyes. "Are you suggesting that I forgo legal counsel?"

Ortiz responded before Ingram had the chance.

"Mr. Hadley, a woman that you knew intimately has been viciously killed. My partner and I were called to the scene." Ortiz swallowed hard on the words. "It was a...a terrible sight."

Ingram leaned forward and banged his fist on the desk.

"There was blood all over, Mr. Hadley. Your girlfriend was torn-"

"Ingram, that's enough," Ortiz interjected, his eyes blazing. "I'm sure Mr. Hadley wants to help us find the person responsible."

Impatient with Ortiz's good cop routine, Hunter turned to Ingram. The look of raw hatred in the man's small eyes shocked him.

"Fine, let's just get this over with,' Hunter said, suddenly too tired to play games. "I was at home last night from eight o'clock on. I slept in until almost ten this morning when I got a call from the station telling me that another woman had been killed."

He didn't mention driving around in the early hours of the morning trying to escape the demons. And the fact that he'd been loaded up on benzos wasn't any of their business.

"When was the last time you saw Gabriella Jankowski?" Ortiz asked, opening a little notepad.

"Yesterday afternoon," Hunter replied, picturing his angry confrontation with Gabby in that very same office only twenty-four hours earlier. "She stopped by to see me here. She only stayed a few minutes before leaving."

"You didn't see her after that?" Ortiz asked. "You didn't go to her place last night or this morning?"

"No, I didn't."

He resisted the urge to take the pill bottle out of his pocket. The detectives might misunderstand his need for anxiety medicine. Most people didn't understand PTSD. They just thought it meant he was unstable or even dangerous.

"A black car was reported in the victim's neighborhood, Mr. Hadley. It matches the description of a car we passed out there in the station's parking lot. A shiny black luxury sedan."

Hunter dropped his eyes to his desk, trying to think back to where he'd driven. Had he gone past Gabby's house? Could he even have stopped by to see her?

"I know from many years reporting out in the field that most witnesses are unreliable. What's a black sedan to one witness might be a blue crossover to another witness."

Leaning back in his chair, Hunter looked at his watch.

"Now, if you don't have any more questions..."

Ingram jumped up, and for a minute Hunter thought the high-strung detective was going to come at him over the desk. Instead, he paced to the window and looked out at the parking lot beyond.

"You mind if we have a look at your car, Mr. Hadley? If you have nothing to hide, it shouldn't be a big deal."

"Look at my car all you want, Detective. Just do it at a distance," Hunter replied as he too stood up. "There's no justification for you to perform a search of my vehicle, and it would only waste time that should be spent finding Gabby's killer."

Ortiz looked at the two men standing over him and sighed.

"Can you both please just sit down so we can get through this?"

"I thought we were through here," Hunter said, but he sank back down in the chair. "There's nothing else I can tell you about Gabby."

"How about telling us about Jade Castillo then," Ingram said, taking out a photograph of an attractive woman and slapping it onto the desk in front of Hunter. "When did you first meet her?"

Glancing at the photo, Hunter lifted his eyes to Ingram. He knew the name of the woman killed only days before. Everyone knew her name now that she'd been linked to the Willow Bay Stalker. But this was the first photo he'd seen.

"Are you kidding me?" He sputtered. "You're really going to try to pin the Willow Bay Stalker crimes on *me*? That's ridiculous."

His eyes dropped back to the photo; an uneasy sensation worked its way up his spine. The woman in the picture looked familiar.

Flipping through his notepad, Ortiz stopped on a page filled with handwritten notes. He ran a long finger down the paper, stopping on an underlined sentence.

"An anonymous tip was called in after the press conference about Jade Castillo's murder. The caller witnessed Jade Castillo talking to a man outside the Channel Ten news station the day before. The man described by the caller meets your description."

Hunter shook his head emphatically.

"That's impossible."

But a muddled memory stirred. A few days earlier he'd pulled into the station's parking lot and a dark-haired, attractive woman had appeared out of nowhere. They'd only spoken for a few seconds before he'd realized she'd mistaken him for someone else. He'd been in a hurry to get inside and she'd gone away, red-faced.

Could that have been Jade Castillo? Why would she want to see me?

Ingram folded his arms over his narrow chest and smiled.

"Okay, so you don't know Jade Castillo. How about the Stalker's first victim, Bella Delancey? You know her, right?"

The words were like a punch to Hunter's stomach.

"Bella was a victim of the Stalker? She was the woman that-"

"Don't play dumb with me, Hadley. You knew all along that your old girlfriend had been attacked, didn't you? Do you expect us to believe that it's just some kind of crazy coincidence that several of the women who were attacked by the Willow Bay Stalker are women you know?"

Hunter's head began to ache as he tried to make sense of what the detectives were saying.

"It's not true. I never even knew Jade Castillo, and I would never hurt Bella or Gabby. I may have made some mistakes...I admit I have my issues...but I would never hurt anyone."

"Unfortunately, that's not what your record tells us, Mr. Hadley." Ortiz looked down at his notepad again. "From what I see you have a record of acting out violently."

Bolting up from his chair, Hunter crossed to the door.

"I'm done with this conversation. If you want to talk to me further, then arrest me and let me call my lawyer."

Motioning for Ingram to follow, Ortiz stood and walked to the door. Hunter leaned forward and stared into Ingram's eyes.

"Go look for the person who really killed Gabby." Hunter's voice was hard. "Start with her ex-husband. She was scared of him. Always said he had a bad temper. Or are you not looking at cops?"

"I'm looking at everyone," Ingram said. "Especially Jankowski."

Hunter opened the door and waited for the two detectives to leave. He was about to close the door again when he saw Veronica Lee. She raised a hesitant hand at him.

"Mr. Hadley? Do you have a minute?"

"Call me *Hunter* for Christ's sake," Hunter barked before he could stop himself.

Recoiling as if she'd been struck, Veronica stared at him with wide, green eyes.

"Are you okay?"

"A woman I've been seeing has just been killed," Hunter exploded, reaching for his pill bottle, "and I'm the number one suspect, so, no, actually, I'm not okay!"

Twisting open the cap, Hunter shook two pills into his palm and looked around for something to wash them down. His eyes fell on Veronica's distraught face, and his rage deflated.

"I'm sorry, Veronica," he mumbled, moving toward her, his big hands still clenched into fists. "I didn't mean-"

But Veronica had already turned and fled back toward her desk.

Hunter stared out at the newsroom, seeing that all eyes were on him. Sabrina West was even taking notes. He'd made a fool of himself again, and he wasn't getting any better.

Maybe I should go see Reggie Horn. Or maybe talk to my father.

But the thought of admitting to anyone just how bad things had gotten stopped him. He was alone, which was for the best. He couldn't risk hurting anyone else.

CHAPTER TWENTY-SEVEN

The Delancey's house on Grand Isles Boulevard nestled behind an ancient row of moss-covered oak trees. Sunlight filtered through the stooping branches, throwing lacey shadows on the road ahead as the Channel Ten News van stopped at the end of a long, winding driveway.

"Wait out here with the van," Sabrina West commanded, pulling the strap of her bag over her shoulder and pushing open the door.

"That's private property." Boyd checked the rearview mirror as if he suspected they were being followed. "They could call the police on you. Say that you're trespassing."

Rolling her eyes at the cameraman's warning, Sabrina climbed down from the van and looked back with an amused laugh.

"Don't be a ninny. I'm just going to ask a few questions. If Bella Delancey doesn't want to talk to me, then I'll leave." A determined gleam entered her eyes. "But if I can convince her to give me an interview, I'll call you in to film it."

Without waiting for Boyd's response, she slammed the door shut and scurried up the driveway. No need to get the uptight cameraman's approval in any case. He would just try to convince her to give up her plan. Especially if she told him the real reason she wanted to talk to Ian Delancey's young wife.

The identity of the Willow Bay Stalker's first two victims hadn't been made public, and thus far the media had respected the women's wish to remain anonymous. But that hadn't stopped Sabrina from using her source inside the WBPD to find out who they were and to get all the gory details about the investigation thus far.

Tucking a wayward strand of hair behind her ear, Sabrina took a deep breath, exhaled fully, then put a tentative foot on the wide step leading up to the front door.

She hadn't made it to the second step when the door swung open. A young woman in a pink track suit glared out at her with red-rimmed eyes. She wore no make-up, and her mass of long dark hair had been twisted up into a messy bun.

"What do you want?"

Sabrina produced a wide smile, concealing her surprise at Bella's rough appearance and belligerent manner.

I guess Mrs. High Society isn't feeling so high and mighty right now.

Sticking out a small hand, Sabrina reached the top step.

"I'm Sabrina West with Channel Ten News. I'd like to talk to you about a story I'm working on."

"What kind of story?"

Bella's eyes narrowed as she took in Sabrina's fixed smile.

"A story about the Willow Bay Stalker." Sabrina watched for a reaction. "I want to find the man who's terrorizing this town, since the Willow Bay Police Department doesn't have a clue."

Panic flashed behind Bella's tired, gray eyes. She gripped the edge of the door with a trembling hand, and Sabrina thought the distressed woman was going to slam it shut in her face. Instead, she opened it and motioned for Sabrina to step inside.

As Sabrina moved past her into the dim foyer, Bella stared out the door, surveying the driveway and lawn. Apparently satisfied that no one was lurking in the bushes listening to their conversation, she closed the door and turned to Sabrina.

"What does a story on the Willow Bay Stalker have to do with me?"

Deciding the truth would be the fastest way to get her story, Sabrina arranged her face into a sympathetic expression.

"I know you were the Stalker's first victim, Bella." Her voice was gentle. "And I think you know more about the man who hurt you than you've told the police."

Bella flinched, shaking her head in mute denial.

"What do you know about *Secret Fling*?" Sabrina asked, suddenly sure that Bella wanted to tell her the truth.

If her suspicions were correct, the woman had met her attacker on the hook-up app. That was the only link the police had been able to find between all three women, and Sabrina's own recent activity on the app convinced her she was on the right track.

"I don't know what you're talking about," Bella insisted.

"You're trying to tell me you've never used *Secret Fling*?"

Sabrina stepped closer to Bella, almost quivering in anticipation of the answer she so badly wanted to hear.

"Are you saying that you didn't meet the man who attacked you through the app?"

"Who the hell are you?"

Jumping as a deep, angry voice boomed behind her, Sabrina swung around to face Ian Delancey. Instinctively, she stepped back; her shoe caught on the edge of the doormat and she tumbled backward onto the marble floor.

"I know you."

The big man towered over her, his hands fisted at his side, his jaw clenched in anger.

"You're the reporter that's always getting in people's faces, aren't you? Samantha something or other."

Scrambling to her feet, Sabrina straightened her dress and pulled her bag over her shoulder. The phone inside the bag began to ring.

"Sabrina West," she corrected Ian, "I'm a reporter with Channel Ten and I was just asking your wife some-"

"She knows I was...attacked, Ian. Someone told her."

Bella's voice trembled on the words, and Ian turned and wrapped a protective arm around his wife's shoulders. He glared back at Sabrina, pure loathing in his eyes.

"Who've you been talking to?" he snarled. "Who gave you confidential information about my wife?"

Straightening her shoulders and lifting her chin, Sabrina reminded herself of the women that might end up being killed if Bella continued to lie to everyone about what had happened.

"I have an obligation to protect my sources," she said, her voice calm and low. "And your wife has an obligation to help the police find out who attacked her so that he can't go on terrorizing this town."

Sabrina's phone rang again but she ignored it.

"What are you implying?" Ian's eyes grew narrow.

"I think your wife knows more than what she's saying about the man who attacked her. I think-"

Emitting a high-pitched scream, Bella collapsed onto the hard floor. Ian fell to his knees next to his wife's limp body just as someone pounded loudly on the door.

"Sabrina?"

Boyd had come to look for her. Sabrina wrenched open the door and stared out at the stocky cameraman with wide, startled eyes.

"She's fainted," she told him weakly.

She looked back to see that Bella was already stirring and that Ian was helping her sit up. He turned to face Sabrina.

"Get out now," he roared, "before I call the police!"

Scurrying down the steps after Boyd, Sabrina raced down the driveway and jumped back into the news van. As Boyd started the engine, Sabrina looked back to see Ian staring after them, his face a mask of rage.

"Boy, you really pissed him off," Boyd muttered, navigating the van out of the exclusive neighborhood and heading back toward the station.

"The truth hurts sometimes," Sabrina murmured, her heart still thudding inside her chest. "But it's still the truth."

Boyd glanced over, a question on his lips, then sighed and sat back in his seat. He'd learned not to ask too many questions around her.

Replaying the encounter with Bella in her mind, Sabrina settled back into the seat and congratulated herself. Her story would be bigger than anything Tenley Frost or Nick Sargent had ever done. She'd followed her gut and it had been dead on.

Bella definitely met her attacker on Secret Fling...and she knows way more than what she's saying. I'd bet my life on it.

CHAPTER TWENTY-EIGHT

The sun was starting to set as Eden entered the warm, fragrant kitchen. She'd spent the last hour sitting on the terrace trying to finalize the vows she would make to Leo on Saturday. Her mind, still full of the terrible events of the week, had refused to cooperate. The rumbling in her stomach had finally convinced her to push the pen and paper away.

Inhaling the savory scent that hung in the air, Eden crossed to the covered pot on the stove. She lifted the lid, releasing a swirl of the curry's spicy aroma.

"Dinner's not ready yet," Barbara Sweeny scolded as she pushed through the door carrying a basket of towels fresh from the dryer. "But you might as well call the kids down to set the table."

"Smells wonderful, Barb." Eden's stomach protested as she put the lid back on the pot. "Come on, Duke, let's see what Hope and Devon are up to."

The golden retriever followed Eden out of the kitchen and up the stairs. Stopping abruptly in Hope's doorway, Eden felt Duke's soft body close behind her.

"Dinner's almost ready, Hope."

Her niece didn't look up from the brightly lit screen.

"Okay, Aunt Eden," she murmured. "Just give me a few more minutes and I'll be right down."

"You've been working on that computer an awful lot lately."

Stepping into the room, Eden glanced toward the monitor, suddenly worried that Hope was spending too much time online.

"You aren't chatting with any strangers on that thing are you?"

She kept her tone light despite the niggle of anxiety that had awakened in the pit of her stomach. The thought of some creepy cyber predator targeting her vulnerable niece triggered Eden's mama bear instincts.

"You know better than to let anyone know where you live, right? And you'd never send anyone pictures..."

Raising one delicate eyebrow, Hope finally looked up at her aunt.

"I'm not an idiot, Aunt Eden. I know how to take care of myself."

The defiant tone in the teenager's voice worried Eden, as did Hope's naive belief that she could take care of herself in a world where stalkers hunted down women like prey.

Although Hope wasn't even sixteen yet, she'd already been through so much: witnessing the death of both her mother and her father, and then, just as she'd been settling into her new life with her aunt, being kidnapped by a gang of traffickers.

"Just don't get too cocky, Hope. It's a dangerous world out there. You and I should know that better than most people."

Hope's stubborn look faded, and she graced Eden with a sad smile.

"I haven't forgotten anything, Aunt Eden. I never could." Her eyes returned to the monitor. "So, no need to worry about me."

Detecting a note of sadness in her niece's voice, Eden wondered what could be troubling her. Luke Adams hadn't been hanging around lately; could they have had a falling out? For the last few months, Hope's boyfriend had been coming to the house several times each week. Eden had worried they may be getting too serious. Now she wondered if they were still an item.

Seeing that Hope was no longer listening but was once again typing on the keyboard with avid concentration, Eden decided not to pry. Hope would confide in her when she was ready.

Eden moved further down the hall to see that Devon's door was closed. She knocked and waited to be granted permission to enter. Her ten-year-old nephew had recently complained about her walking in unannounced; since then she'd made a special effort to respect his need for privacy.

"Devon, dinner's going to be ready soon. Why don't you come downstairs and help me and Duke set the table?"

"Sure thing, Aunt Eden." He jumped up from his desk, scattering an array of papers and schoolbooks on the floor. "Anything to get out of doing this homework."

He flashed her a wiseass grin, then darted past her and down the stairs. She looked down at Duke and shook her head, trying not to think about anything other than her nephew's cheerful voice as he called out to Barb.

"Whatever you're cooking... it smells awesome."

Descending the stairs, Eden heard the security system announce that movement had been detected at the front door. Her heart jumped. Not waiting for Leo to knock, she hurried to the door and swung it wide open.

"What happened?" she demanded, pulling him inside and planting a quick kiss on his mouth. "Did you get Detective Jankowski out on bail?"

"Actually, Riley decided not to press charges. Said they didn't have enough evidence. And least not yet."

Eden felt a pang at Leo's familiar use of the attractive new prosecutor's name and chided herself for being insecure. She was being foolish.

Leo and I are getting married in two days. He isn't looking for a fling. Although, of course, Riley Odell might be...

"Dinner's ready," Barb called out from the kitchen.

She bustled down the hall and saw Devon setting the table.

"Where's Hope?"

Catching sight of Leo, Barb insisted that he stay and taste the vegetable korma she'd made.

"It smells too good in here to pass up," Leo agreed. "But then I'll need to get back to the office."

Eden waited for Barb and Devon to go back into the kitchen before she turned toward Leo. He could read the question on her face.

"I told Jankowski I'd meet with him tonight to go over the case. Just so we're ready to fight any charges they may come up with."

Dropping her eyes to hide her anxiety, she nodded and turned away, pretending to straighten the plates on the table. Leo reached for her hand and squeezed.

"Hey, what's wrong? What've I done now?"

Eden allowed herself to be drawn back into his arms. She rested her head on his shoulder, liking the solid feel of his body against hers. How could she admit she was worried about him getting caught up in the new case with Jankowski after she'd been the one that had called him and begged him to take it on?

She knew she was being irrational and unfair, but that didn't lessen the doubt that was starting to consume her as she wondered how she could go ahead with the wedding

How can we enjoy a celebration of love when the town is filled with fear?

Looking up into Leo's worried eyes, Eden forced herself to ask the question she knew she could no longer avoid.

"Do you think we should postpone the wedding?"

She felt Leo's whole body stiffen against her.

"I mean, because of the attacks, and the Stalker still being out there, and Jankowski and...well, everything going on right now. Do you want to wait for things to calm down?"

Leo stared down into Eden's miserable green eyes and smiled.

"That's the worst idea I've ever heard."

He shook his head in disbelief.

"Don't you know that marrying you and becoming an official part of this family is the most important thing in the world to me?"

Eden felt a tear trickle down her cheek. Leo lifted a thumb to wipe it away, his smile fading into a look of concern.

"That's still what you want, isn't it?"

Nodding through her tears, Eden pulled his head down for a kiss.

"Yes, of course, it is. I just didn't want you to feel pressured, and with everything-"

"Don't worry about everything. You can't control everything so there's no use worrying about it."

Eden wished she could be as practical as Leo. If only she could take his advice and stop worrying about things outside of her control.

"But the Stalker..."

"That's Nessa's problem to deal with," Leo said, his eyes taking on a satisfied shine. "Willow Bay is in safer hands now that Nessa is the chief of police."

Still doubtful, Eden wondered what one woman could do to stop the kind of monster they were dealing with.

"But, Leo, she can't do it on her own, and now that Jankowski is out of the picture..."

"She's not on her own,' Leo reassured her. "Nessa's hired in Tucker Vanzinger as well. And soon Jankowski will be back on the case."

Eden shrugged, wanting to let herself be convinced.

"And don't forget Barker and Frankie," Leo added. "They're looking for the bastard that's attacking women, too."

A creak on the stairs made them both look around. Hope stood on the bottom step, her eyes wide and fearful. Eden wondered how long she'd been listening.

"What's wrong, Hope?" Eden asked. "I'm sure you're scared about the things you've been hearing on the news, but-"

"What if Nessa isn't the chief of police anymore?" Hope asked, stepping down into the room. "What if they bring in someone else? Someone bad, like Chief Kramer or Detective Reinhardt?"

The words startled Eden. It was a very good question. Her niece had witnessed the evil that the two policemen had done, and she'd barely lived to tell about it. How could the town ever feel safe if they couldn't even trust their own police department?

"That won't happen," Eden assured her, masking her own reservations about Mayor Hadley's judgment. "I'm sure the mayor will make the right decision and keep Nessa on."

Exchanging a worried look with Leo, Eden called out to Barb and Devon to bring out the food. As plates were piled high with the savory curry, Eden tried not to let her anxiety take over. But Hope's question lingered in her mind.

The mayor won't let the old men on the council get rid of Nessa, will he?

She thought of the meeting where Archie Faraday and Judge Eldredge had protested that they needed to find the right kind of man to be chief of police.

Is that what they thought Douglas Kramer had been?

Eden doubted they'd ever accept their responsibility for supporting a man who had turned out to be a serial killer, and she couldn't shake the conviction that Willow Bay's future was perilously at stake and that its wellbeing rested on Mayor Hadley's decision.

As long as the same old men are in charge, Willow Bay will never change. And it will never be safe.

CHAPTER TWENTY-NINE

The smell of fresh coffee wafted into Barker's room, prompting him to open one bleary eye and direct it at the battered clock radio. It was pushing eight, and he had a full day ahead of him. It wasn't a good day to lounge around in bed. Not when the Willow Bay Stalker was still on the loose.

Pulling on a robe and sliding his feet into slippers, Barker walked down the hall to the kitchen.

"I thought the smell of coffee might lure you out of your cave."

Taylor poured the steaming brew into two big mugs, then added a splash of almond milk to each. She set one cup on the table in front of her father and cradled the other cup in her hands.

"I'm getting used to this," Barker said, taking a sip of the sharp, sweet liquid. "Definitely perks me up more than tea ever did."

Setting the cup on the table, Taylor nodded in agreement. They'd both been tea drinkers before Taylor's recent experience at the CSL compound where one of the residents had been growing devil's weed to add to her toxic blend of tea.

Once Barker had gotten Taylor safely back at home, they'd switch to coffee without discussion. The almond milk was Taylor's attempt to help Barker stick to his post-heart attack diet.

"Don't forget we're going to Eden and Leo's wedding tomorrow."

Taylor nodded as she sat down across from him. She picked out a banana from the fruit bowl on the table, unpeeled it, and took a bite.

"Will Reggie be there, too?"

Barker swallowed another mouthful of coffee and grimaced.

"Don't talk with your mouth full."

He dropped his eyes to his cup, trying to hide the excitement that surged through him at the thought of seeing Reggie the next day. He wondered what he should wear. The usual black suit he wore to special events was still serviceable, but it wasn't anything special.

Thinking through his schedule for the day, he reluctantly vetoed a last-minute shopping trip, then silently berated himself for being an old fool. No one would care what he was wearing anyway.

"Any progress on your big case?" Taylor asked, her bright blue eyes inquisitive. "Can't you tell me what it is?"

"No, I can't," Barker said, mortified at the thought of Taylor hearing the gory details about Bella Delancey's attack and the related crimes attributed to the Willow Bay Stalker. "It's confidential."

Taylor sat forward in her chair and glared at her father.

"You don't have to protect me from the truth you know." She shook her head in exasperation. "I might even be able to help you."

Reaching in the bowl and plucking out a shiny green apple, Barker used a napkin to polish it before taking a huge bite.

"Just be careful, Dad." Taylor's eyes grew serious. "Remember that bad people sometimes blend in and appear harmless...and their motives aren't always obvious."

Barker felt his throat tighten and he had a hard time swallowing the remains of the bite. He sometimes forgot just how traumatized his daughter must be after her ordeal. She'd learned the hard way how bad people could hide in plain sight.

"I'll keep that in mind, Taylor," Barker said, trying to keep his tone light. "And I promise to be careful if you will."

A faint buzzing down the hall brought Barker to his feet. He shuffled back to his room and grabbed the phone by his bed.

"Mr. Delancey, how are you?"

"I'm frustrated, Mr. Barker, as I'm sure you can understand. And I'm hoping you can give me an update on your progress tracking down my wife's attacker."

Barker looked over his shoulder, not wanting Taylor to overhear his conversation.

"Yes, Frankie and I have made some progress. I'll give you a full report next time we meet. How about we set up time Monday morning to discuss?"

"It's only Friday," Ian spluttered. "Why wait until Monday? Don't tell me you're planning to take the weekend off?"

Lowering his voice, Barker closed his bedroom door and paced to the window. The day was shaping up to be as blue and sunny as the day before.

"I can assure you we will be doing everything possible over the weekend, Mr. Delancey. But we won't have a meaningful report ready for you until Monday. Can we plan to meet around ten?"

"Fine, if that's the best you can do." Ian's voice was cold. "But I have some additional information to share with you."

Barker watched as a blood-red cardinal landed on his backyard fence. The tiny bird fluttered away as Ian spoke.

"My wife dated Hunter Hadley before we met. He never got over her. At least, that's what I've heard."

A frown creased Barker's forehead as he listened.

"Now the woman he's been dating more recently, Gabriella Jankowski, has been violently killed," Ian continued. "It certainly is a morbid coincidence. I suggest you look into him as soon as possible."

Barker digested the information. The mayor's son hadn't been on his list of suspects, but his connection to two of the victims was certainly intriguing.

"Why do you say that Hunter Hadley never got over Bella?"

"We live in a small town, Detective. And Hunter and I socialize in the same circles. Everyone knows everything that's going on."

The statement didn't impress Barker. During his long career as a police detective, he'd found that small-town gossip rarely reflected reality and that it should never be confused with reliable evidence.

"But you've known Mr. Hadley for years...has he ever done anything to make you think he would be capable of such violence?"

"Hunter doesn't like being rejected, so maybe he decided to do something about it," Ian snapped, his voice bitter. "He's a head case, you know. Came back from the Middle East damaged."

Barker ended the call, knowing that his growing dislike of Ian Delancey shouldn't stop him from following up on the information the man had provided. But as he started to get dressed, Barker resolved not to jump to any conclusions until he'd had the chance to talk to Hunter Hadley for himself.

* * *

The newsroom was busy when Barker opened the door. He walked slowly into the cavernous room, his eyes searching for Hunter Hadley's tall figure. He'd encountered the station manager a few times over the years, and he figured he'd know him if he saw him.

"Detective Barker?" Veronica Lee stood next to him, her pretty eyes wary. "Are you here to interrogate Mr. Hadley, too?"

Barker smiled down at the weather girl, surprised she remembered him, and unsure how to best answer the question.

"Well, I really just want to talk to him. I have a few questions about a case I'm working on, but I wouldn't call it an interrogation."

Returning his smile, Veronica pointed to a glass-walled office. Barker could see Hunter's wavy brown hair as he bent over a desk.

"You can ask if he'll talk to you," Veronica suggested, although she didn't sound optimistic. "He's been a little preoccupied today."

Barker walked toward the office, taking in the crew and equipment as he went. He'd never been inside the station before, and he was fascinated as he saw the news desk in the studio beyond a big glass wall. If he opened the studio door and slipped inside, he'd be only a few yards away from the lights and cameras.

"Detective Barker?"

Turning at the sound of his voice, Barker saw Hunter standing at the door of his office. He looked resigned as he waved Barker over.

"I'm assuming you're here to talk to me?"

Barker nodded, noting the dark circles under Hunter's eyes, and the slight tremor in his hands.

"If it wouldn't be too much of an imposition," Barker replied, following the station manager into the office. "I guess I should have called ahead to ask for an appointment."

"But then I might have said no." Hunter's voice was weary. "And you weren't about to take no for an answer, were you, Detective?"

Grinning sheepishly, Barker shrugged.

"You may have me on that one, Mr. Hadley. But I promise not to take up too much of your time."

Hunter leaned back in his chair looking puzzled.

"I thought you'd retired from the force, Detective. When we covered your involvement in the take down of Chief Kramer you said you were done with law enforcement. So, what happened?"

The smooth tactic the seasoned newsman had used to turn the tables on Barker was impressive. Suddenly Barker was the one on the hot seat being questioned. He felt a spark of admiration.

"I've been retired from the force for close to a year," Barker admitted. "But I'm a private investigator now, Mr. Hadley, and I'm working on a case for one of my clients."

"Which client would that be?"

Offering an apologetic smile, Barker shrugged.

"I'm not at liberty to say at this time, due to the sensitive nature of the investigation."

Barker opened his notebook and took a pen from his coat pocket. He kept his eyes on the paper and his voice low.

"Can you tell me the last time you saw Bella Delancey?"

The following sigh of frustration made Barker look up. Hunter sat with his head in his hands, his shoulders hunched over his desk.

"Are you okay, Mr. Hadley?"

"Not really," Hunter muttered, lifting his head and sighing again. "It seems I'm on everyone's list as a monster who attacks women."

Leaning back in his chair, Barker digested the statement. So, Hunter already knew that Bella had been one of the Stalker's victims. He waited to hear what the man would say next. Silence and patience were often his most effective weapons when questioning a suspect.

"I'm not a bad guy, Detective," Hunter finally said. "I'm just a little...damaged. Although Dr. Horn wouldn't like to hear me say that. She tells me that I'm just *working through my issues.*"

Barker's ears perked up at the mention of Reggie, but Hunter didn't seem to notice.

"But then my dad tells me to just *buck up and get on with things.*"

A sad tone entered Hunter's voice at the mention of his father, and Barker wondered what it would be like to have Willow Bay's smarmy mayor for a father. He'd always thought Mayor Hadley must be made out of plastic. Nothing about the mam seemed genuine.

"Why do you think you're damaged?"

The question came out of Barker's mouth before he knew what he was going to say. He suddenly wanted to know what had caused the haunted look in the station manager's eyes.

"That's an easy one." Hunter's voice took on a brittle edge. "I spent a few years covering news in the Middle East. I got into some...trouble. I saw some things I couldn't *un-see*. I thought if I came home, then I could forget about it. That it would all just go away."

Swallowing hard, Hunter shook his head and took a deep breath.

"But it didn't. It just followed me home, and now I have *anger issues*." He grimaced at the words. "I guess the official diagnosis is Post-Traumatic Stress Disorder, but it really just means that sometimes my brain confuses the past with the present."

He looked straight into Barker's eyes.

"But I would never hurt anyone. Especially not a woman, and definitely not Bella."

The way he said Bella's name made Barker pause.

"You loved her?"

Hunter smiled, but his eyes were bright with pain.

"No, Detective. Not really. But I thought she might be my chance to find out what it felt like. To love someone that is."

He stood and paced to the window.

"But it didn't work out. She needed something...else. And I'm not relationship material, as I'm sure you've already discovered."

"Is that what Dr. Horn said?" The therapist's name felt awkward on Barker's lips. "That you're not ready for a relationship?"

Gazing out into the parking lot, Hunter didn't seem to register Barker's question. Perhaps it was time to move on before Hunter decided to end their impromptu heart-to-heart.

"What about Gabriella Jankowski? You were in a relationship with her, weren't you?"

Barker held his breath, waiting for Hunter's reaction, preparing for his rage or indignation. But he only shrugged.

"If it was a relationship, it was a dysfunctional one," Hunter said, turning to look at Barker. "Gabby had been recently divorced. She'd been married for a long time and was determined to enjoy her freedom...no matter what anyone else wanted."

"You don't sound happy about that," Barker observed, trying to keep his voice neutral. "Did she upset you?"

Hunter nodded his head, but he didn't seem angry, only tired.

"Gabby upset a lot of people." Hunter ran a distracted hand through his hair. "I think she got off on making people angry. But I got tired of it. I wasn't into her mind games, so I ended it."

"And she didn't like that?"

Ignoring Barker's comment, Hunter reached for his phone, which had started buzzing on the desk.

"Yeah, I'm almost done here," he assured the caller. "Just give me a few more minutes and I'll head over."

Worried that his time was running short, Barker stood and blocked Hunter's path to the door.

"It seems odd that you dated two women who were attacked..."

He let the words hang in the air.

"Willow Bay's a small town, Detective. The fact that I dated both Bella and Gabby isn't so unusual around here. We were all part of the same social circle."

"What circle is that?" Barker asked, his forehead creasing into a frown. "Is Ian Delancey part of this *circle*?"

"My father is the mayor, as I'm sure you know, and Ian's dad runs the local bank. Our fathers are friends. Their friends are the town leaders. City Councilmen, businessmen. I grew up with all their kids. It's a small group really."

"Sounds very chummy."

Barker's voice hardened as he thought of the old men on the city council. The same men who had allowed Chief Kramer and Detective Reinhardt to use Willow Bay as a stalking ground. Men like Archie Faraday and Judge Eldredge who were fighting Nessa's appointment as chief of police.

The man in front of him had all the perks and privileges associated with the old men who ran the town, and yet he seemed miserable.

"I'm sure it seems that way from the outside."

Hunter picked up his phone and car keys.

"But when you've seen the things I've seen and then come back here to live among people who don't know what true horror is...it can be hard." He pushed past Barker to open the door. "It might not be obvious, Detective, but I'm actually a pretty lonely guy."

Barker watched Hunter hurry toward the exit. He wasn't sure what he thought about the mayor's son yet. He hadn't made up his mind. All he knew for sure was that Hunter Hadley was a very complicated man.

CHAPTER THIRTY

I ris Nguyen took the stairs two at a time and emerged from the parking garage at a steady jog. Her father's appointment with his neurologist had taken longer than she'd expected, and she was running late. Wesley Knox would already be in the autopsy suite by now, and Archie Faraday was scheduled to arrive at the medical examiner's office at any minute.

A sign taped to the outside of the bulky concrete building caught her attention. She smiled as she read the words.

Make Willow Bay Safe Again! Nessa Ainsley for Chief of Police.

She thought of the email she'd received that morning. She hadn't had time to read it, but the title indicated there was an online petition circulating that urged Mayor Hadley to make Nessa chief of police.

Glad someone's finally putting pressure on Mayor Hadley. And if anybody deserves that job, it's got to be Nessa.

Pushing through the heavy doors, Iris' mind turned to the task ahead of her. Wesley would already be prepping the body and setting up the tray of tools she'd use to cut Simon Jankowski's ex-wife open. A wave of panic rushed through her, and she had to stop and put a small, trembling hand on the wall to steady herself.

"Are you all right, Chief?"

Maddie Simpson looked over the reception counter with a frown, pushing her wire-framed glasses up further on her nose to get a better look at Willow Bay's chief medical examiner.

"Yes, Maddie, thank you," Iris answered, forcing herself to stand up straight and walk forward. "Is Mr. Faraday here yet?"

Raising her thin eyebrows dramatically, Maddie nodded; her heavily sprayed cap of jet-black hair moved stiffly back and forth.

"Oh, yes, that man is certainly an early bird," she gushed approvingly. "He's been here for ages. Wesley's looking after him since you were running late."

Iris ignored the hint of reproach in the woman's voice. Maddie had been a government employee for decades, and she was quick to point out any of her fellow employees' failure to adhere to the City's many rules and regulations. Some people might call her a busybody, but Iris knew the older woman didn't mean any harm.

Hurrying through the reception area and into the back, Iris dropped her purse and keys on the desk in her office, then proceeded down the hall to the small changing room adjacent to the autopsy suite. She pulled on protective coveralls and booties, layered on two sets of gloves, and positioned a plastic face shield so that it securely covered her eyes, nose, and mouth.

Wesley Knox was ready for her when she entered the room. She recognized his bulky frame under the coveralls and his earnest brown eyes behind the face shield. A smaller figure stood next to Wesley, protected only by a lab coat, gloves, and disposable face mask.

"Mr. Faraday, did we not have coveralls for you or a face shield?"

Iris glanced at Wesley in surprise, but Archie Faraday waved her concerns away with a thin hand.

"I don't need all that." He pointed a shaky finger at Iris' face shield. "I never had all that fancy equipment and I managed just fine for years."

Biting her lip, Iris tried to think of a diplomatic way to insist that the retired medical examiner wear the proper protective gear.

"It may seem unnecessary to you, Mr. Faraday, but the new regulations that we follow-"

"Spare me the lecture, Miss Nguyen," Archie sneered. "Nothing we're doing here today fits your precious regulations I'm sure. The very fact that you're allowed in this room proves that this town has done away with all sense of propriety and decorum."

Gasping at the old man's rudeness, Iris turned to Wesley, who was glaring at Archie from behind his clear plastic shield.

"Have you taken the initial photos, Wesley?"

She kept the anger out of her voice as she spoke, not wanting to give Archie the satisfaction of knowing he'd rattled her.

"Yes, I have, *Chief*," Wesley answered, earning an amused look from Iris, who appreciated the young forensics technician's efforts to show Archie that she was the chief now. "I've also washed and prepped the body as usual."

"Then let's get started with the external examination," she said. "Mr. Faraday, I'm assuming you will observe and ask questions as needed?"

Without waiting for an answer, she moved to the dissecting table, allowing her eyes to rest on Gabby's dead body for the first time. Her stomach twisted at the sight of the bruised, discolored face and the savage wounds visible on the upper torso.

For one dreadful moment, Iris thought she wouldn't be able to hold down the bagel and coffee she'd eaten in the car. Swallowing hard, she forced herself to turn to the tray of cutting instruments Wesley had arranged, pretending to inspect them as she regained her composure.

She would have to be strong if she was going to make it through the complete autopsy. Steeling her nerves, Iris let her training take over. As if on autopilot, she began to describe Gabby's pitiful remains. The injuries to the head were significant, and Iris noted that blunt force trauma to the head was the likely cause of death.

As she performed a thorough external examination of the body, Wesley held up the handheld voice recorder, allowing her to note each scar, surgical incision, and identifying mark.

Her breath caught in her throat as she saw the small tattoo, but she forced herself to continue speaking in a calm, impassive tone.

"The initials S.J. are tattooed onto the decedent's front, right hip."

Avoiding the look of sympathy Wesley gave her, Iris picked up a stainless-steel ruler and held it against an oval-shaped laceration on Gabby's shoulder. She waited for Wesley to take a close-up photo, then moved to a ring of angry red lacerations on the right upper arm. The last mark consisted of two opposing U-shaped contusions on her forearm.

"Three distinct bite marks are visible on the decedent-"

A gasp sounded behind her. She turned to Archie, surprised to see him looking pale and weak. Her anger melted into concern.

"Are you all right, Mr. Faraday?"

The old man's eyes were fixed on the gruesome wounds; he didn't seem to hear Iris as he stared in horrified silence.

"Mr. Faraday? Did you want to inspect the body before I make the Y incision?" Iris glanced at Wesley, unsure what to do. "Mr. Faraday?"

"Those injuries," Archie croaked in a weak voice, "are you...sure...that they are bite marks?"

Nodding behind the face shield, Iris wondered if she'd misjudged the older man. She hadn't pegged the cold-eyed ex-medical examiner as squeamish.

"I'm not a forensic odontologist, of course, but it's quite clear that the person who inflicted the injuries left three distinct bite marks."

She met Wesley's eyes as the older man staggered backward. He found a stool and leaned against it, his pale skin wet and sweaty. He certainly didn't seem to be in any shape to continue with the rest of the procedure. Her worry grew as she noticed his dilated pupils.

If seeing the external injuries has this effect on him, what will happen when I cut the Y-incision in Gabby's chest? Or when I remove the chest plate and open up the thoracic and abdominal cavities?

"Maybe we should take a break while Wesley collects the toxicology specimens and obtains fingerprints," Iris suggested. "And then I can finish up with the neck and head."

Acting as if she hadn't spoken, Archie shook his head and muttered to himself. Iris couldn't quite make out what he was saying. Could he be suffering from some type of dementia? Or maybe Alzheimer's, like her father?

But his next words sounded lucid. And they sent an unwelcome shiver down her spine.

"The other women that have been attacked...did they suffer the same type of injuries? Did they have bite marks, too?"

"Yes," Iris said, puzzled. "Why? Have you seen these types of injuries before?"

He hesitated, his eyes suddenly guarded, then shook his head.

"No, I haven't." The unpleasant frown was back on his face. "Now, let's get back to the autopsy."

* * *

Two hours later Iris slipped out the side door and walked the ten blocks to the Blue-Ribbon Diner. The weather was mild, but the sun was bright, and she wiped a thin sheen of sweat off her forehead as she opened the door and stepped inside.

Jankowski was already there, settled into an old-fashioned booth. Iris sat across from him, noticing at once that his face was drawn and that his eyes were bloodshot.

"I guess you didn't get much sleep," she said, putting a small hand on his and squeezing. "But at least they saw sense and didn't try to hold you overnight."

The bell on the door tinkled behind her, and Iris glanced nervously over her shoulder. She suddenly felt guilty, knowing that Jankowski would surely ask her about the autopsy findings and that ethically she wasn't allowed to reveal anything to a man that the police still considered a person of interest. Even if that man was a police detective.

"No, I didn't get much sleep," Jankowski replied, his voice hoarse. "I kept seeing Gabby the way...well, the way I found her. I can't stop thinking about all the blood."

Dropping her eyes, Iris tried not to think about the traumatic injuries she'd just witnessed. She also tried not to wonder how Jankowski could have gotten covered in his ex-wife's blood.

"So, you found her like that? I mean, she was already gone?"

Jankowski stopped moving. He cocked his head and stared across the Formica table as if he couldn't believe what he was hearing.

"I don't fucking believe this," he finally said, banging a big fist down between them, rattling the empty coffee cup beside him. "You think I might be the one who killed Gabby. Don't you?"

Iris shook her head, but her mouth felt dry, and she cleared her throat, stalling for time.

"I just want to understand. I mean, the report said you were covered in the victim's blood, and-"

"The victim happens to have a name. And her last name used to be the same as mine," Jankowski choked out. "We may have gotten divorced, and we may have had our differences, but she wasn't just a victim to me."

Picking up the bundle of silverware beside her, Iris unwrapped the napkin and held it out toward Jankowski. He ignored it.

"And as for why I was covered in Gabby's blood, it was because I tried to save her...tried to listen to see if she had a...a heartbeat."

The image of Jankowski holding Gabby's dead body against him sent a stab of pain through Iris. She tried to take his hand again, but Jankowski was already on his feet.

"If you could even remotely think that I could do...*that*...to anyone, then you don't know me at all."

Jankowski charged past Iris, his wide shoulders knocking her small frame backward as he slammed out of the door.

Running after him, Iris called out, her voice desperate.

"Wait, Simon! Please, I didn't mean..."

But Jankowski had already disappeared around the corner.

CHAPTER THIRTY-ONE

The briefing room door was open as Nessa approached. She'd called a meeting to discuss the cases attributed to the Willow Bay Stalker so they could come up with a game plan for moving the investigation forward. It looked like the attendees had already gotten started without her.

"Nessa, I didn't think you'd be joining us."

Tucker Vanzinger stood at the front of the room. He held a marker up to the whiteboard as Iris Nguyen and Alma Garcia looked on. Nessa felt as if she'd interrupted a brainstorming session.

"Of course, I'm here, Vanzinger," Nessa said, confused. "I'm the one who requested the meeting."

A flush spread across Vanzinger's cheeks, camouflaging the freckles on his face. He scratched at his ear awkwardly.

"Sorry, I guess I misunderstood, Chief." Vanzinger dropped the marker and stepped away from the board. "I thought you wanted me to meet with Iris and Alma about the Jankowski crime scene and autopsy results so I could come up with a game plan."

"I did," Nessa agreed, beginning to understand what was going on. "But I didn't mean on your own. I may be the chief, but I plan to be very involved, and very hands-on. I don't plan on sitting around barking orders while everybody else solves the crimes."

Vanzinger picked up the marker again and held it out to Nessa.

"That works for me," he said, a grin pushing up the sides of his mouth. "I never liked Kramer's style anyway."

Closing the door behind her, Nessa turned to the whiteboard, continuing where Vanzinger had left off. He'd written Gabriella Jankowski's name on the left side of the board and had posted a recent photo of her beneath her name.

Nessa added three more names across the top of the board: Bella Delancey, Olympia Glass, and Jade Castillo.

"So, you're convinced Gabby was killed by the Willow Bay Stalker?" Alma nodded slowly. "She does seem to fit the pattern."

Iris stared down at her hands, her shoulders slumped. Nessa was about to ask if she was feeling okay when she heard a persistent scratching on the door. Crossing the room, she swung open the door to reveal an empty hallway. Before she could shut the door, an orange blur darted past her feet.

"Winston," Alma groaned. "How did you escape my office again?"

A violent sneeze stopped Nessa from responding. She searched the room for a box of tissues, then swung around to face Alma.

"What is that cat doing here? Isn't that the cat from the Jade Castillo crime scene?"

Bending down to scoop up the plump tabby cat, Alma nodded.

"Yep, this is Winston. He's an orphan now, so I thought I'd try to find him a good home." A mischievous gleam entered Alma's eyes. "Your boys might like to have a pet, huh, Nessa?"

Vanzinger cleared his throat and pointed toward the whiteboard as Alma plopped Winston into her lap.

"Anyway," Nessa said, giving Alma a dirty look before resuming her place at the board, "I think we need to consider the theory that the same man attacked all four women."

"Okay, I get it," Vanzinger said, "but if we're saying the Stalker may have killed Gabby, doesn't that mean we have to bring Ingram and Ortiz into the discussion? I mean, they have been assisting on the Stalker case, right?"

A ripple of irritation rolled down Nessa's back at the mention of Ingram and his partner.

"We need them in the field collecting more information right now," Nessa said, trying to sound practical. "But we can bring them in as the situation allows. Now let's add what we know about each victim to our board so we can look for links."

"They all had the same case of death," Iris volunteered, speaking for the first time. "And the same pattern of injuries."

Jotting *cause of death* under each name, Nessa waited.

"The method of entry and condition of the crime scenes were very similar," Alma said. "But we haven't gotten anything to test for DNA yet, although Iris should have samples to us soon."

Iris looked up and grimaced.

"Yes, we took a DNA sample and then excised the bite marks from Gabby Jankowski's skin. We'll use that to make a dental mold of what the perpetrator's teeth might look like. Although we'd need a suspect to compare them with."

Nessa cringed at the grisly images Iris' words conjured. She looked at the board, wondering what they were missing.

"Alma, have you heard back from your cybercrime buddy over at the state lab? Was he able to find anything on Bella's computer?"

Stroking Winston's soft fur, Alma looked up in surprise.

"It was all in my report, Nessa," Alma said. "I gave it to Ingram and Ortiz yesterday. Didn't you get a chance to read it?"

Resentment flooded through Nessa as she realized Ingram must have kept the report from her. But she knew that she had to play it cool. It was her fault for not asking about it sooner. She was to blame for not following up on Ingram and Ortiz's activities.

"Sorry, Alma, it's been pretty hectic around here," she said, using a smooth as silk voice that belied her irritation. "Can you update all of us now that we're together?"

"Sure, it's actually really interesting."

Alma stood and moved to the front of the room next to Nessa.

"We examined Bella's computer, as well as phones from the other two victims. They'd all recently used an app called *Secret Fling*."

Nessa's heartbeat quickened as Alma confirmed the link.

"What the hell is *Secret Fling*?" Vanzinger asked. "I never even heard of that."

Alma raised her eyebrows and smirked.

"Good try, Vanzinger, but do you expect us to believe that a man like you doesn't know about all the latest dating apps?"

Ignoring Alma's remark, Vanzinger turned to Nessa.

"It's an app for people looking to cheat on their partners," Nessa said bluntly. "Or people just looking for anonymous sex."

"And you think the victims met their attacker on that app?"

Vanzinger ran a big hand through the short red bristles of his crewcut as he watched Nessa nod and add the words *Secret Fling* under three of the names.

"What about Gabby?" he asked, his eyes still on the board. "Have we found a link to the app on her phone or computer?"

Nessa turned to Alma, who just shrugged.

"It's too early to have gotten anything back, but I'll put a rush on it. I've also asked my cybercrime buddy to try to get a list of all the users that had contact with the women through the app. He said we'd need an ECPA court order, and that the company that develops the app would likely fight it even if we do get one."

A somber silence settled over the room at her words.

"I can ask Riley Odell to start the paperwork," Nessa said, feeling dejected. "Although it takes ages to get anything through the court."

"I can talk to her about it if you want," Vanzinger offered, not meeting Nessa's eyes.

She only shrugged, feeling sure she was missing something vital.

"There's got to be something else that links them," she muttered, pacing in front of the board. "I mean, even if they met online initially, they also met in person. How else would the Stalker have killed them? So, there has to be a physical connection as well."

They all stared at the whiteboard as if new clues might suddenly appear. Finally, Iris spoke up.

"Eventually we'll have the bite mark DNA and dental mold to match up," she offered. "So, if we can identify a suspect, or if someone who committed a past crime is a match..."

Another name popped into Nessa's head. She lifted her hand to the board again and wrote a fifth name: Celeste Reed.

"Who's Celeste Reed?" Vanzinger asked.

"She's a woman who was killed in Willow Bay five years ago. Her husband was convicted, and he's serving thirty years in Raiford for manslaughter."

Alma sat back down, but she looked excited.

"I remember the case. It was a nasty scene."

Nessa used the marker to write *same cause of death* and *similar crime scene* under Celeste's name.

"But the *Secret Fling* app was only released a few years ago," Alma said. "So, she hadn't been using the app."

Iris reached in her bag and pulled out a slim laptop.

"I can pull up the autopsy report on Celeste Reed," she offered. "Maybe we can see something that links her to the other women."

After a few minutes of typing, Iris gasped.

"Celeste Reed died from blunt force trauma to the head," she said, her eyes wide. "Injuries included a series of bite marks, and the autopsy was performed by Archie Faraday."

Her voice faltered as she looked up.

"During Gabby's autopsy today, Mr. Faraday seemed very upset by the bite marks on Gabby. He said he'd never seen anything like it before."

Alma frowned over at Iris.

"That's strange, I remember Archie testifying in court against the husband. He claimed to be able to match the bite marks on the victim's body to the husband's teeth."

"Why would Archie lie?" Iris wondered.

Nessa thought of the crabby old man's cold eyes.

"Maybe he's just old," she said, not believing her own words. "Maybe he just forgot."

But somehow Nessa couldn't convince herself that the old crony of Chief Kramer and Detective Reinhardt had forgotten anything.

He's hiding something behind those cruel eyes. And I'm going to find out just what it is.

Dropping the marker on the table, Nessa turned to Vanzinger.

"I'm going to give Mayor Hadley an update. And maybe I'll ask him a few questions about his buddy Faraday while I'm there."

"And I'll follow up with Riley Odell about the court order," Vanzinger said, falling in step beside Nessa as she left the room.

He held the door open as she exited the building, then watched as she headed toward the mayor's office. She heard him call after her in a confidential voice.

"By the way, Chief, I've already signed the petition. Great idea!"

Nessa looked back in confusion, but the door had already closed and Vanzinger was gone.

* * *

The courtyard outside City Hall was quiet as Nessa approached. She'd expected to encounter angry citizens demanding for something to be done to find the Willow Bay Stalker. Instead, only a few senior citizens sat by the fountain throwing bits of bread to a scattering of pigeons.

A sign beside the fountain caught her eye.

Make Willow Bay Safe Again! Nessa Ainsley for Chief of Police.

Looking around as if the sign might be somebody's idea of a joke, Nessa saw that no one appeared to notice her or the sign. She proceeded into the building with the growing conviction that Archie Faraday had purposely misled Iris and that he may have information about Celeste Reed's death.

Seeing that Mayor Hadley's assistant wasn't at her usual post, Nessa strode straight into his office. The mayor looked up in surprise, quickly clicking on the computer screen to close the window he'd been working in.

"Detective Ainsley? What are you doing here? Shouldn't you be out looking for the Willow Bay Stalker? Or are you too busy trying to get people to sign your petition?"

Nessa stared at him with a blank expression, wondering if the whole town had gone mad.

"What petition?" She didn't bother trying to hide her southern drawl. "What in the world are you talking about?"

"There's a petition circulating online." His voice dripped with indignation. "Apparently they're trying to pressure me to appoint you as the permanent chief of police."

Trying to make sense of what he was saying, she took out her phone and typed her name into the search engine. Within minutes she'd found the online petition; thousands of people had already signed it. She blinked back tears at the realization that she wasn't alone. The people in Willow Bay were with her, even if the mayor wasn't.

She lifted her chin and squared her shoulders. The town was counting on her and she couldn't let Mayor Hadley's disapproval keep her from doing her job.

"We're confident Gabby Jankowski's murder is connected to the Jade Castillo killing and the other assaults."

Hadley's mouth dropped open.

"Gabby was killed by the Willow Bay Stalker?"

"We believe so." Taking a deep breath, Nessa forced herself to tell him the rest of it. "We also suspect the killings might be connected to an old homicide case."

"A cold case?"

The mayor watched Nessa with suspicious eyes as if he sensed she was trying to tell him something he wasn't going to like.

"No, not a cold case. It's a solved homicide. The victim was a woman named Celeste Reed. Her husband was convicted and he's currently in Raiford."

Hadley's unnaturally smooth forehead suddenly creased into a deep frown as he absorbed her words.

"But then it can't be the same man..."

Nessa hesitated, then decided there was no way to avoid upsetting him. An innocent man may have been sent to prison, and a man the mayor trusted might have been involved in the wrongful conviction.

"Mayor Hadley, the Celeste Reed case closely matches the Jade Castillo murder. We can't be sure, but it's possible the same man who killed Celeste Reed is the man we're looking for now. The man we're calling the Willow Bay Stalker."

Shaking his head, Mayor Hadley stood up and glared at Nessa. Before he could say anything Nessa raised her hand to silence him.

"That's not all, Mayor. I have reason to believe that Archie Faraday misled Iris Nguyen about his role in the Reed case. He knows something he's not telling us."

A shadow behind her made Nessa spin around. Hunter Hadley stood by the door, the expression on his face inscrutable. The mayor turned to Nessa, a look of relief on his face.

"I'm sorry, Detective Ainsley, but I need to speak with my son."

"It's *Chief* Ainsley," Nessa corrected. "And I'm sorry to have barged in uninvited. I figured you'd want an update."

Nessa met and held Hunter's eyes as she left the office. Hearing the soft click of the door closing behind her, she wondered just how long the mayor's son had been listening, and if he had ever met Celeste Reed.

CHAPTER THIRTY-TWO

The assessing look in Nessa's eyes stayed with Hunter as he watched her leave his father's office. He wondered if she, too, thought he could be the man mutilating and killing women in Willow Bay. The thought depressed him.

"That woman loves to stir up trouble."

His father's words made his mood sink even lower. When would the old man ever learn that the *good old days* were over? It was time to evolve and move on to the twenty-first century, only his wooden-headed father didn't seem to understand.

"I think Nessa Ainsley will be a good chief of police."

Hunter crossed to the window and looked into the courtyard beyond.

"Willow Bay needs new blood. The same old men have run this town for too long. They've run it into the ground if you ask me."

"I didn't ask you."

Returning to his chair, the mayor collapsed into it as if he'd run a marathon. Hunter almost felt sorry for him.

"The police paid me a visit earlier."

Hunter turned away from the view and looked down at his father. From this angle, he could see that the older man's hair was thinning and that there was more than a little gray scattered in what was left.

"What could they want with you?"

Shrugging, Hunter paced restlessly to the far side of the office and leaned against the side table.

"I'm not sure I care," he said, folding his arms across his chest. "But I am interested in the fact that Archie Faraday was caught lying to the medical examiner about an official case."

His father slapped a hand on the desk and snorted.

"Do you believe everything Nessa Ainsley says? She's just paranoid after that business with Kramer and Reinhardt."

"Yes, I do believe Nessa, father. She's done nothing to make me doubt her." Hunter raised an eyebrow. "I can't say the same for Archie Faraday."

The mayor stiffened at his son's words.

"Archie Faraday has been a good friend to our family. He's a pillar of the community and–"

"Right, just like your old buddy, Chief Kramer?"

"That's not fair. Archie's no more to blame than I am for what Kramer did."

Hunter pictured the hard, cold eyes of the old medical examiner.

"I never liked him, you know?"

He stood up straight and moved toward the door, feeling suffocated by his father's refusal to acknowledge the reality that surrounded them.

"Archie Faraday is a mean old bastard. At least he is to everyone in town that's not on the city council. Hell, he's a bastard to his own son. Men like that shouldn't be held up in admiration. They should be run out of town."

Sputtering in anger, the mayor stood to face his son, eyes blazing.

"And I suppose I've been a terrible father as well? You boys grew up with everything. You had the run of the town and everything you could ask for, and yet all you can do is blame your daddies for anything that goes wrong."

Hunter watched his father raise a clenched fist as he spoke, thinking that the old man had made too many speeches.

He doesn't know what's real and what's just bullshit anymore.

Hunter gripped the doorknob as his father continued to rant.

"Is it my fault you decided to go off to a fucking war zone and get messed up? I begged you not to go if you remember. So, I'm not gonna sit here and let you bad-mouth me or one of my oldest friends for being a bad father. Archie did the best he could just like me."

Opening the door, Hunter slipped through without another word.

* * *

Nessa Ainsley was sitting by the fountain when Hunter walked out of City Hall. He sat down beside her, squinted into the sunny blue sky, and waited for her to say whatever it was she wanted to say. The benzos had drained his energy and taken away his anxiety, at least for the time being.

"What medication are you on, Mr. Hadley?"

"Call me Hunter, why don't you? And I'll call you Nessa."

He waited for her to respond, but she didn't. She just sat there staring at the water and waiting. It was a trick he liked to use as well when interviewing a subject for a news story. Give someone enough time and opportunity, and soon they'd be spilling all their darkest secrets.

"Diazepam," he finally said, tiring of the waiting game. "And I have a prescription from Dr. Regina Horn if you'd like to see it."

"No, that's not what I meant," Nessa said, her blue eyes matching the clear sky behind her. "It's just...well, I've seen your record. I'm glad you're getting help."

Keeping his face impassive, Hunter leaned toward the fountain and let the cool water run over his outstretched hand. Nessa Ainsley

213

hadn't stayed around to ask him about his treatment. At least, that wasn't her main concern. She had something else on her mind, and he might as well get it over with now. She wasn't the type to let anything go.

"So, now that you've assured yourself I'm getting proper medical attention, go ahead and ask me what you really want to know."

"Okay." Nessa didn't bother protesting. "What do you know about a woman named Celeste Reed?"

The question surprised him, but the name was familiar.

"I remember the basic story," he said, trying to recall the details. "She was killed by her husband. I ran the story not long after I started working at Channel Ten."

Reaching into the computer bag at her feet, Nessa rifled through the papers within before pulling out a slim file folder. She slid out a photo of a young woman.

"She wasn't just a story, you know. She was a real person. And she died a horrible death at the hands of a monster."

Hunter studied the photo, his mind playing tricks on him as he watched the girl's face faded in and out. Where had he seen her before? He closed his eyes, trying to think.

When he opened them again Nessa was holding a picture of a blood-spattered living room. Celeste's body was splayed on the floor like a broken doll.

"This is what he left behind."

Hunter turned his head from the blood and carnage; he swayed as the world began to tilt.

"Mr. Hadley, are you okay?" Nessa's voice sounded far away. "Hunter, can you hear me?"

Panic fluttered in his chest. He stood abruptly, suddenly scared that he was falling back into those dark days. Days when time had seemed to fade in and out and he never knew where his tortured mind might take him. He'd just gotten back to Willow Bay, and his psyche had been so fragile. The PTSD had taken over for a time. It was still hard for him to remember everything that had happened.

I remember that face. I've seen her before. And not on some news story.

Celeste Reed's plain, tear-stained face had stared up at him with so much worry and regret. She'd begged him to...what? To help her? To save her? He couldn't remember.

Or maybe I don't want to remember. Maybe it's better that way.

"Look, Nessa, that's all I know. It was a news story....an old story. What does it matter now, anyway? The husband was convicted, right? As sad as it is, Celeste Reed got the only kind of justice we can give."

Standing to face him, Nessa shook her head, prompting a red curl to fall over one eye. She smoothed it back with an impatient hand.

"I'm not sure we did give her justice, Hunter. That's the problem. I think we may have gotten it all wrong."

Hunter suddenly needed to get away from Nessa and her questions and her searching gaze.

"I've gotta go," he said, not meeting her eyes. "I hope you catch the Stalker. I really do. Those women deserve...justice."

His words quivered between them in the fresh afternoon air. He turned to walk back toward the parking garage, feeling the weight of her eyes on him the whole way.

CHAPTER THIRTY-THREE

The man sat in the big, black sedan, waiting for the woman to appear. Turning up the volume, he let the music roll through him, each note an excruciating reminder of all that he'd suffered, and all the women he'd made suffer.

Love hurts...love hurts...

The words echoed deep inside him as he watched the spot where the lovers would meet. Jealousy stirred in his gut, making his jaws clench. This one was different. He actually wanted this one. Even though she was a liar and a cheat. Even though he knew it was impossible. He wanted to possess her.

Shame heated his checks at the thought of how she would laugh if she knew. And she would try to use it against him, just as she was using the cop's lust to get the confidential information she needed for her big story. The poor fool would learn soon enough that she had no loyalty: liars never do.

She pretends she wants to meet me, tries to lure me on Secret Fling; then she meets up with another man. She doesn't know who she's messing with.

Banging his fist against the black leather steering wheel, he tried to think through his plan again. He glanced at the little backpack in the back seat, wondering if he'd have the nerve to actually go through with it. Or was it too late, anyway? Had she already learned too much about him? Had she told anyone what she was doing?

The door to the news station opened and Sabrina West slipped outside. She looked around the parking lot, her eyes lighting up when she saw the black Dodge Charger. The man kept his eyes glued to her slim figure as she hurried toward the car and climbed into the passenger seat. He prepared to follow them, but the Dodge didn't move.

Taking out a big pair of binoculars, he trained the lenses on the Charger's side window. Sabrina's blonde hair shimmered behind the glass, and he watched as she lifted a graceful hand to her mouth, as if covering a laugh. He clutched the binoculars in an iron grip, tempted to stomp across the parking lot and wrench open the door.

He'd love to see her beautiful face when she realized that he was the Willow Bay Stalker and that she was his next victim. Her shock and fear would make all his skulking and sneaking around worth it.

Straining to get a better view, he didn't notice that the news station door had opened again. He looked over to see Veronica Lee standing on the sidewalk, phone in hand.

Panic fluttered inside his chest. The little weather girl was going to ruin his big chance. It was only a matter of time before the police brought in a cybercrime analyst who would find out that LonelyGuy10 had been messaging the three known Stalker victims.

Eventually, they'd be able to link his *Secret Fling* account back to him. Or at least to the credit card he'd used. He'd known all along that it couldn't last forever. Nothing ever did. And he'd had no illusions that he was some kind of computer genius.

He had come to accept that eventually they'd work it out and he'd be caught. But he didn't intend to go down without taking Sabrina with him. And if everything went to plan, she wouldn't be the only one. He put a reassuring hand on the backpack. The whole town was going to get a shock.

Veronica looked in his direction with a curious expression, then lifted her hand in a half-hearted wave when she saw him looking back. After a few minutes, she ended her call and went back inside. His eyes immediately returned to the Dodge. Before he could lift the binoculars again, the car door opened.

Sabrina stepped out, then bent to look back inside. The man caught a glimpse of the detective's handsome face and dark hair before she closed the door. She was smiling when the Charger pulled away. What inside information had the small-town Don Juan shared with her this time? And what had she told him about her own attempt to catch the Stalker?

Sabrina's messages on *Secret Fling* were becoming more aggressive. She'd been practically begging to meet him, and he had the feeling she was planning to set up some kind of trap. As the reporter headed back toward the station doors, the man felt a jolt of adrenaline surge through him.

Time for me to stop Sabrina from playing Nancy Drew once and for all.

The ambitious young woman had thought she could lie to him. She thought she'd lure him into her trap and catch one hell of a scoop. But he'd been playing the game too long to be fooled by someone so eager and so obvious.

Starting the car's engine, the man took a final look around the parking lot before driving toward Sabrina's approaching figure. She didn't seem to recognize him until he was right next to her.

"I think I have some information you might want to hear," he called out as she bent to stare in at him. "Get in for a minute."

His heart thudded heavily in his chest as she opened the door and slid into the plush leather passenger seat.

"Who were you just talking to back there?" he asked, accelerating toward the exit. "Looked like a cop car."

She dropped her eyes and offered him a coy smile.

"Oh, it was just that nice Detective Ortiz."

When he didn't respond, she looked out the window, noticing how far away from the station he'd already driven.

"Where are we going?" she asked, a faint frown appearing between her eyes. "I've got to be back in the studio now."

"I just wanted to show you something I don't think you'll want to miss," he said, keeping his tone casual. "Won't take long."

Sitting back against the seat, Sabrina studied him, her blue eyes narrowed. Her gaze dropped to the stereo as the song started to play again. He'd set it on repeat.

Love hurts...love hurts

"What kind of song is this?" she complained. "It sounds like something my grandfather used to listen to."

When he still didn't speak, she huffed and turned toward him.

"So, what is it you want to show me exactly?"

He steered the car onto a narrow, overgrown side road and turned off the engine.

"Here we are."

Confused, Sabrina stared out the window at the empty dirt road ahead. As if sensing she'd made a terrible mistake, she stiffened and turned toward him just in time to see the heavy metal binoculars in his hand. She screamed as his big fist came down again and again.

Finally, the screams turned into whimpers, but it was the sight of the blood that made him stop. He didn't want it to end too soon. This time he planned to take his time. This would be his last chance for vengeance, so he might as well enjoy it.

CHAPTER THIRTY-FOUR

S canning the Channel Ten newsroom, Veronica didn't see Sabrina's blonde head anywhere. Her roommate had said she was only going outside for a few minutes. But that had been more than an hour ago and she still hadn't returned.

Veronica looked at her watch. Sabrina's special report on the Willow Bay Stalker was scheduled for the six o'clock broadcast. Her roommate had less than ten minutes to get on set.

Fidgeting with the corner of her report, Veronica wondered if she should ask for Sabrina's input on her story before she showed it to Hunter Hadley. Although her roommate was unapologetically self-centered, she did know a good story hook when she heard it. And she wasn't the type to sugarcoat her opinion.

"Where's Sabrina?"

She looked up to see Hunter standing over her. He repeated his question, sounding annoyed. Veronica glanced toward the door, hoping to see Sabrina charging through it.

"I think she just stepped outside for a minute." Veronica felt Hunter's eyes drop to the report on her desk. "Um, I'll go check outside and see if I can find her."

Glad for an excuse to escape Hunter's impatient gaze, she hurried outside and surveyed the parking lot. No sign of Sabrina anywhere. They'd ridden to work together in Veronica's big red Jeep, and it was still sitting right where she'd parked it.

She looked toward the fenced-in lot where the station's two news vans were kept. Both vehicles were parked and accounted for; Sabrina hadn't rushed out with a crew to cover a story.

Dragging her feet, Veronica walked back inside. Hunter still stood by her desk. He was holding her report in one big hand while his eyes skimmed the text. Fighting the urge to flee, she forced herself to walk toward him.

"Petition for chief of police candidate goes viral as Willow Bay's mayor is on the hot seat," Hunter read out loud when he saw that Veronica had returned. "This doesn't sound like a weather report to me, although the word *hot* is used."

He dropped the papers back on her desk and crossed his arms over his chest as if waiting for a response.

"Well, the weather's been uneventful lately," Veronica said, not quite meeting his eyes. "So, I thought I'd try to come up with something a little more interesting."

Raising his eyebrows, Hunter pointed to the report.

"Okay, so sell me on it then. What's your hook?"

Flustered, she hesitated, then inhaled deeply.

You can do this, Veronica. It's a good story. And a good hook.

Exhaling slowly, she picked up the report and cradled it against her chest as she recited the opening words from memory.

"Detective Nessa Ainsley is well-known throughout Willow Bay for saving lives, catching criminals, and exposing the former chief of police as a serial killer. Now the citizens of Willow Bay are banding together to demand that Nessa Ainsley is named as the city's next chief of police. In an attempt to block the mayor and the city council from installing another candidate in this key position-"

"Okay, I get the idea."

Hunter held up his hand to stop her, but he didn't appear to be angry. In fact, he looked amused.

"That'll piss off my father, the entire city council, and the delightful Detective Ingram," he said, his mouth curling into a sarcastic grin. "I love it. Maybe we can squeeze a live feed into the first half-hour tomorrow morning. That is if you can be outside City Hall at dawn. See if Boyd will meet you."

"Really?" Veronica gaped at him, her green eyes wide and scared. "You'll let me report it live...like...tomorrow morning?"

"Why not?" Hunter said, looking around for Sabrina in vain. "Let's give it a try and see how you do."

Checking his watch, Hunter shook his head.

"Sabrina has five minutes, otherwise I have to cut her segment."

As he hurried toward the studio, Veronica took out her phone and tapped on Sabrina's name in her favorites list.

She waited as the phone rang again and again without answer. She was just about to give up when she heard the annoying duck ringtone Sabrina had assigned to her. Following the quacking sound to Sabrina's desk, she reached into Sabrina's work bag and pulled out her roommate's phone.

Carrying the phone back to her own desk, she entered the password Sabrina had used since college and viewed the call log. There were seven missed calls and a dozen unread text messages. Veronica tried to think. It just didn't make sense.

She wouldn't have left her phone unless she thought she'd be right back.

Scrolling through the calls and text messages, Veronica didn't see anything unusual. An unfamiliar icon caught her eye. It was the *Secret Fling* app that she'd seen on Sabrina's computer. Dread settled in the pit of her stomach, but Hunter's voice boomed out behind her before she could click on the icon.

"I just cut Sabrina's Willow Bay Stalker segment. Most of our viewers are now switching to Nick Sargent's update on Channel Six."

She spun around to see Hunter hovering behind her, suddenly feeling guilty that she'd been snooping through Sabrina's personal messages. Could her roommate have simply gotten ill and gone home? The idea took the edge off her mounting anxiety, and she held on to it, trying to convince herself that she was overreacting.

"I'm going to go home and see if she's there."

Veronica adopted a casual tone she didn't feel.

"If she's not there you'd better call the police." Hunter's voice was grim. "Let's not forget someone has already killed two local women in the last week. If Sabrina is missing we'll have to assume the worst."

Swallowing the lump that had risen in her throat, Veronica nodded and gathered her purse and keys. She trudged to her battered Jeep on legs heavy with dread. A terrible possibility hovered in her mind.

Sabrina was trying to find the Stalker, but what if he found her instead?

* * *

The sunlight blazed relentlessly through a gap in the blinds, finally driving Veronica to open one eye, then the other. She wasn't sure where she was or what time it was. The last thing she remembered was huddling on the sofa after calling the police to report Sabrina as missing.

She bolted upright and looked frantically around the living room. Had Sabrina come home in the night? Was she even now sleeping in the Ikea platform bed Veronica had helped her assemble only months before?

Springing off the sofa, Veronica lunged toward Sabrina's door, already knowing what she would find. The bed was empty. There were no discarded clothes on the floor, no half-empty Evian bottles, or wadded-up protein bar wrappers on the bedside table.

The room was untouched from the night before when Veronica had straightened the room and made the bed as she'd waited for

Sabrina to call or come home. She'd needed something to keep her busy. Anything to keep her from wondering what could have happened to her roommate.

Grabbing for her phone, she saw three missed calls. One was from her mother, the other two were from Hunter Hadley. He'd also sent a text message.

Update on Sabrina? Nessa for chief story?

Veronica stared at the words in stunned dismay; her heart dropped. She'd blown her first chance to report her own story live.

She checked the time and groaned. It was almost eight, and the morning news ended in little more than an hour. There was no hope of getting to City Hall with a cameraman on time, even if she had the will to try. But with Sabrina missing her goal of reporting real news didn't seem so important anymore.

Walking back into the living room, Veronica typed her response to Hunter's text with numb fingers.

No Sabrina yet...no story...I overslept...sorry.

She stared glumly at the phone, waiting for his angry reply, but it remained still and silent. After a few long minutes, she realized he wasn't going to respond. She was on her own, and it was up to her to figure out what to do. She considered her options.

If Sabrina really had been taken by a crazed killer, she'd need the police to form some sort of task force, or maybe even a search party. But the officer she'd talked to last night had already taken her report, and he'd promised to pass it on to the detectives that worked on missing person cases and advised her to let them know if Sabrina hadn't shown up by the morning.

But in the cold light of day, Veronica realized that Sabrina wasn't simply a missing person. She was the likely victim of an abduction. Raising the phone, she considered the *Emergency* option on the call screen. Would a call to 911 make any difference now? Wasn't there something more she could do?

Her hand buzzed with Hunter's text reply.
Come down to the station now. I have an idea.

* * *

Veronica noted the dark shadows under Hunter's eyes and unshaved stubble on his face. It was obvious the station manager hadn't gotten much sleep, and she knew she didn't look much better.

After reading his text she hadn't taken time to do anything other than throw on a change of clothes, brush her teeth, and splash cold water on her face before jumping in her Jeep and racing to the station. She ran a self-conscious hand through her long dark hair as she waited for Hunter to tell her his idea.

"You're going to give a live report this morning after all," Hunter said, guiding her toward the studio. "You're going to make an appeal to our viewers for Sabrina's safe return."

Veronica stared at him with an open mouth.

"You don't want to get the public's help in finding her?" he asked in a hard voice.

"Of course, I do. It's just, we aren't sure–"

He shook his head in exasperation.

"It's that kind of thinking that paralyzes people so they can't take action," he exploded. "I've seen it too many times. I've made that mistake myself, and...now I have to live with it. *Every single day.*"

Hunter's face twisted with pain, and he squeezed his eyes shut as if trying to block out a terrible sight. Veronica held out a hand to steady him, worried he might collapse on the floor in front of her.

"People died because of me...women...girls..."

Veronica stared at him in horror. What was he saying? She tried to back away, but the station crew had overheard Hunter's raised voice and were gathering around. She was pushed forward. She could see a vein throbbing in Hunter's temple. She could see the gleam of sweat on his skin as his voice rang out over the buzzing of the crew.

"Sabrina West is missing. We think she might have been abducted. Maybe even by the Willow Bay Stalker."

A collective gasp filled the room as his words sunk in.

"We're going to broadcast an appeal to the public. Ask for them to help us find her. See if we can find her in time."

Heads nodded and several people murmured approval.

"You really think the Willow Bay Stalker could've gotten her?" Boyd asked, his eyes wide.

Hunter turned to him with a haunted expression.

"I think anything's possible in this fucked-up world."

His eyes moved to rest on Veronica's frightened face.

"Now come on, Veronica, let's get you on the air. I have a bad feeling we might already be too late."

CHAPTER THIRTY-FIVE

Eden stared out her bedroom window at the crystal-clear sky beyond. It was a lovely day for a wedding. The forecast last night had predicted sunshine and mild temperatures, which meant the outdoor venue she'd chosen would be perfect. Making her way downstairs, she decided to check the latest weather report, just to be safe.

Switching on the television in the kitchen, she took out a mug and filled a small kettle with water. A cup of green tea would help relax her nerves before the big event. She ignored a series of commercials as she prepared the tea, looking up only when Channel Ten's familiar breaking news music filled the room. Her eyes widened as she read the headline across the bottom of the screen.

Local Reporter Missing: Sabrina West Possible Willow Bay Stalker Victim.

Setting down her mug, Eden moved closer to the television screen. She recognized the reporter that stood in front of the camera as Veronica Lee, the station's weather girl.

"This news bulletin strikes close to home for the Channel Ten News crew," Veronica said, her eyes bright and earnest. "Our local reporter, Sabrina West, is missing. She was last seen outside the Channel Ten station on Townsend Road yesterday at approximately five o'clock in the afternoon."

A picture of a young, blonde woman appeared on the screen. Eden recognized the missing reporter from the live reports she'd seen recently about the Willow Bay Stalker. The woman's blonde hair and blue eyes reminded her a little of Hope. A ripple of unease made its way up her spine at the thought of her niece, and an irrational fear seized Eden. What if Hope had gone missing, too?

Racing back up the stairs, Eden made herself stop and take a deep breath. No need to wake her niece up early over her silly, irrational fears. After all, it was Saturday, and they all had a long day ahead. She would check on Hope just to reassure herself, and she'd be careful not to wake her up.

Inching the door open just a crack, Eden peered into the room. Her breath caught in her throat at the sight of the empty bed. Flinging back the door, she gasped in relief as she saw Hope already awake and sitting at her computer.

Hope jumped to her feet with a terrified scream. When she saw Eden in the doorway, she sagged with relief.

"You scared me to death, Aunt Eden," Hope moaned, slumping back into the chair in front of the computer. "What are you doing?"

"I should ask you the same thing," Eden replied, her relief turning to concern. "Why are you up so early and already on your computer? You've been spending way too much time on that thing."

Shrugging her thin shoulders, Hope turned back to the screen.

"And where did you go before school yesterday morning?" Eden demanded, her intuition telling her that Hope was hiding something. "I got a call from the school saying you missed first period, but you left here on time. What happened?"

"Your phone's ringing, Aunt Eden."

A faint trill echoed up the stairs. Eden hesitated.

"Go on, Aunt Eden, it might be the venue calling. It could be something about the wedding," Hope urged. "I promise I'm not doing anything bad. I'll tell you everything later, after the wedding."

"I'll hold you to that," Eden said, her voice reproachful as she turned and hurried down the stairs.

The news report had finished, and another commercial blared loudly as she entered the kitchen. The ringing had already stopped as she reached for her phone. Within seconds, a text message popped up. It was from Reggie Horn.

Sorry to bother you today, but Bella Delancey just called. She's hysterical and wants to talk. I think you'd better come.

* * *

"I'll meet you all over at Beaumont Plantation by noon," Eden told Barb. "That'll still give us a few hours to get ready since the ceremony isn't scheduled to start until two."

Aghast, Barb followed Eden into the garage.

"But what about your dress? How will you get ready?"

"Martha over at Bliss Bridal insisted on delivering the dress this morning. It'll arrive before I do."

She opened the back door to her big white Expedition and Duke climbed in. Seeing the concern on Barb's face, Eden hesitated.

"Don't worry, I won't miss my own wedding," she assured Barb. "But they need me at the shelter this morning, so I've got to go."

Reaching out, Barb grabbed Eden's hand before she could get into the car. The nanny wore a somber expression.

"I know how much you want to help the women in this town, Eden, but Hope and Devon need you, too."

She gave Eden's hand a tight squeeze, before slowly letting go.

"So please...be careful. Those kids would be lost without you."

Tears welled in Eden's eyes at the kind words. She'd almost forgotten how good it felt to be fussed over. But Barb was now a vital part of their household, acting as a protective mother hen to them all, and Eden suddenly felt very lucky.

"And we'd all be lost without you, Barb."

Eden gave the older woman a quick hug and climbed into the SUV. "Now no worrying. I'll see you all at the plantation at noon."

Wiping her eyes, Eden hoped that would be the last time she cried all day. She wanted her wedding day to be full of joy, not tears.

* * *

The weekend traffic was light, and before she knew it Eden was stepping off the elevator outside Reggie's office. The therapist met her at the door, her face tense and her eyes worried.

"She's in here," Reggie said, waving Eden inside. "Apparently she saw the morning news and...well, I'll let her tell you."

Bella Delancey huddled in one of Reggie's big armchairs. Her head drooped, and her thin arms were wrapped tightly around her body. Eden's heart squeezed at the sight of the once vibrant woman.

Taking a seat in the chair next to Bella, Eden knew she would have to be patient. Whatever Bella wanted to say, it wasn't going to be easy for her. She'd held it inside for months, but now it would finally come out, and hopefully, Bella would then be able to start the healing process.

"I saw the news this morning," Bella said, her teeth chattering despite the warmth of the room. "The reporter that came to see me is missing. *He's* got her."

The hair on the back of Eden's neck stood up at Bella's words.

"Who's got her?" Eden asked. "Bella, do you know who might have taken Sabrina West?"

Bella nodded as a tear slid down her cheek.

"I should have told them before," she moaned, beginning to rock back and forth. "I should have told the police what I knew."

Reggie met Eden's eyes over Bella's bowed head. They needed to proceed with caution. If Bella knew who the Stalker was, then they'd have to alert the police right away.

"But I was too scared."

Offering Bella a tissue, Reggie pulled up a chair next to her.

"What were you scared of, dear?" Reggie asked.

Bella took the tissue and looked at the therapist with haunted eyes.

"I was scared that Ian would find out that...that I was cheating on him," Bella choked out, dabbing at her streaming eyes with the tissue. "I didn't want him to know that I'd been using a dating app called *Secret Fling* to meet other men."

"And you met the man who attacked you on this app?"

Eden tried to keep the judgment out of her voice, but she struggled to ignore the questions that rose in her mind.

Why didn't you tell us before? Did Jade Castillo die because you didn't tell? Will Sabrina West die next because of your silence?

"Yes, but I thought he was...someone else," Bella said, looking down at her hands. "I downloaded the app just for a laugh. Ian's always working and I was lonely I guess. A man contacted me..."

Bella's voice cracked then, and Reggie moved swiftly to get her a cup of water. After a few sips, Bella continued in a raw voice.

"I got a message from someone called LonelyGuy10. He said he wanted to meet. I couldn't believe it when I looked at his profile..."

Taking another small sip of water, Bella looked up at Eden.

"I recognized the profile picture," she said softly. "He had on sunglasses and a cap, but I'd...I'd know him anywhere."

"Who was it?" Eden asked, needing to hear the answer.

Bella swallowed hard as if it hurt to say the words.

"Hunter Hadley."

The words came out in a whisper. Bella cleared her throat and turned to Reggie.

"You know, the man who was here the last time. The man I dated before I married Ian."

Reggie looked stunned.

"Hunter Hadley attacked you? He's the one that..."

Bella shook her head, trying to explain.

"No, he's not the one that...that hurt me. I thought I was meeting Hunter, but the man who showed up wasn't him. It was..."

Terror filled Bella's face. Her chest began to heave in and out with deep, gasping sobs as she tried to speak.

"It was a man in a mask. He yelled at me. Called me a liar and a cheat. He said Hunter didn't want me anymore. That nobody wanted a liar. He knew things about us...about me and Hunter."

Her voice was thick with tears and pain.

"He hit me...again and again. He was so angry, so full of rage. I thought I was going to die. I thought he was going to kill me."

Leaning forward, Eden grasped Bella's trembling hands in hers.

"You're okay now. He can't hurt you anymore," Eden soothed. "We won't let anything happen to you. We'll tell the police and–"

Bella shook her head and raised red, tear-filled eyes to Eden.

"That's just it, though. He said he would come back, and that if I told anyone how we met, that he would come back and finish the job." Eden had to strain to hear the next words. "I don't want him to come back and kill me. That's why I didn't tell anyone."

A heavy silence filled the room as Eden digested the information Bella had shared. The attacker was someone she'd been in contact with on a dating app. A man that claimed to know Hunter Hadley and had used his profile picture to meet women online.

Surely the police would be able to track this man down through his computer or IP address or whatever. Once they had all the details, they would be able to find him and stop him, wouldn't they? All she had to do was find Nessa and tell her everything Bella had said.

Eden looked at her watch. She still had time to update Nessa and drive out to Beaumont Plantation in time to walk down the aisle.

CHAPTER THIRTY-SIX

In the dream, Nessa was running through heavy fog trying to find something. Or was it someone? She knew she couldn't stop running or it would be too late. But her legs felt so heavy. She couldn't lift them, couldn't move them.

"Mom! Wake up!"

The sound of Cole's voice in her ear brought Nessa up and out of the dream. The heavy weight on her legs was Cooper's warm body, still clothed in his Star Wars pajamas.

"I want pancakes," Cole insisted, his mouth only inches from her ear. "Daddy said to let you sleep, but I want pancakes!"

Cooper jumped up and down with excitement, his knees digging into Nessa's legs with boyish abandon.

Grabbing both boys around their waists, Jerry pulled them off the bed and dropped them unceremoniously on the floor.

"I told you boys to let your mother sleep. She's had a tough week."

Jerry sat on the bed next to Nessa and ran his hand through her soft, red curls. He'd been asleep when she'd come home the night before, and it felt as if they hadn't seen each other in days.

"You've gone viral you know."

Nessa thought she detected a touch of pride in Jerry's voice.

"Over five thousand signatures so far and the petition's only been circulating for two days. People are threatening to vote out the mayor and all the current council members in the next election if they appoint anyone else."

"Who do you think is behind it?" Nessa asked, racking her brain for the likely culprit. "I don't know anyone that seems like the *online petition* type, do you? And what about all those signs?"

Shrugging, Jerry stood and moved toward the door.

"You've helped a lot of people, Nessa. And I can think of quite a few who would be willing to do a lot more than add their signature to a petition for you."

He raised his eyebrows as she slipped out of bed.

"If you're sending me a message, I'm hearing it loud and clear."

Looking down at the slinky black nightgown she normally reserved for special occasions, she offered him a wry smile.

"Great, then I guess you'll be washing our clothes today, honey, cause this is the only nightgown I have that's clean."

Rolling his eyes in mock disappointment, Jerry disappeared through the door. Seconds later she heard the boys whooping in the kitchen.

"Hooray, daddy's gonna make pancakes!"

She knew they weren't going to be quite so happy when they found out she'd promised to meet Riley Odell down at the police station before she headed out to Eden's wedding. The prosecutor wanted to discuss the evidence they'd collected so far in the Willow Bay Stalker investigation.

Picking up her phone, she was surprised to find the battery was dead. She'd put it on charge before she'd fallen into bed the night before, but when she followed the charging cable back toward the wall, she saw the plug on the floor.

"Crap!" Nessa grabbed the plug and stuck the prongs back into the socket. "Jerry, what time is it?"

Her shout was drowned out by the boys' bickering over who would get to help Jerry pour the mix into the skillet.

Dashing to the bathroom, Nessa brushed her teeth and took a cold, five-minute shower. Still damp, she pulled on the same pants she'd worn the day before. She was relieved to see a clean blouse hanging in the closet. Fastening the buttons, she promised herself she'd take care of the laundry as soon as she got home.

Nessa checked the time on her phone and cringed. She'd promised to meet Riley at nine o'clock sharp, and she was already a few minutes late. She'd be lucky to be there by nine-thirty.

Her eyes fell to the missed call notifications. She'd missed half a dozen calls while her phone had been dead. Tension hardened in her shoulders as she wondered what might have happened in the eight hours she'd been asleep.

Relax, Nessa. The world won't end just because you're incommunicado for a few hours. You can check your messages on the way to the station.

Fifteen minutes later she was halfway to the station, having left Jerry and the boys quarreling at the kitchen table over the last pancake. She took out her phone and pressed the voicemail button with a sense of foreboding. The first message was from Officer Dave Eddings.

"Sorry to bother you at home, Chief, but we got a report of another missing woman and I thought you'd want to know about it. She's a reporter over at Channel Ten and her roommate claims she left work without her phone or bag and never came back. Let me know how you'd like us to handle this. I mean, she is an adult, and there's no evidence of foul play, but with the Stalker situation..."

Nessa listened to the rest of the messages with growing apprehension. Sabrina West was missing. She'd disappeared outside Channel Ten the previous afternoon and still hadn't returned.

The final message was from Tucker Vanzinger.

"Where are you, Chief? Another woman's missing and the news stations have already picked it up. The shit's hitting the fan. Call me as soon as you can."

Before she could dial Vanzinger's number her phone vibrated with an incoming call. It was Eden Winthrop.

Oh hell. There's no way I can go to a wedding with everything going on.

Tempted to let the call go to voicemail, Nessa wavered. She could always apologize after the crisis had passed. Or she could just bite the bullet now and explain there was no way she could go to a wedding in the middle of the current crisis.

"Eden? I'm sorry but something's come up-"

"This is an emergency, Nessa," Eden interrupted in a grim tone that let Nessa know she wasn't calling about the wedding. "I have information about Bella's attacker that may help you find him."

Pulling into the parking garage, Nessa found the first available spot and cut her engine.

"I'm listening, Eden."

"Bella Delancey met her attacker on a dating app called *Secret Fling*. She didn't tell you because she didn't want her husband to find out what she'd been doing."

Nessa felt her hope fading.

"We already knew she was using the app. We suspect the Stalker may have used *Secret Fling* to meet all or some of his victims."

"But Bella said the man who contacted her went by the username LonelyGuy10, and that she recognized the profile picture he used. It was a man she used to date. They arranged to meet and-"

"Who is this man?"

Nessa's pulse quickened with anticipation. Was she finally going to hear the name of the Willow Bay Stalker?

"Hunter Hadley, the mayor's son," Eden said, then quickly added, "but Bella insisted he wasn't the one who attacked her. She said the attacker mentioned Hunter's name, and that he seemed to know a lot about him. She's sure it's someone he knows."

"And why is she only coming out with this information now?" Nessa asked. "Bella has sworn up and down for months that she doesn't know anything about the man. Now she comes up with this?"

Frustration entered Eden's voice.

"The man threatened her, Nessa. He told her he would come back and kill her if she told anyone how they met or anything about him. The poor woman was scared for her life."

Suppressing her skepticism, Nessa tried to remain objective.

"Okay, she was scared," Nessa conceded. "But why come forward now? What makes her think he won't come after her now?"

"Two women have died, and another is missing," Eden said. "I think Sabrina West's disappearance was the final straw. Bella's still scared. Hell, she's *petrified.* But she's trying to do the right thing."

An image of Hunter Hadley's guarded eyes flashed through Nessa's head. Could the mayor's son know the Stalker? She wondered if he could somehow be involved with the attacks.

Chief Kramer had an accomplice for his murders. Who says Hunter Hadley couldn't be in cahoots with the Willow Bay Stalker?

Maybe that was why Hunter's alibi for the night of Bella's attack had checked out. He could have planned the whole thing as a way to get revenge for being dumped.

"Listen, Nessa, I'm sure you're busy today, and I've got to get out to Beaumont Plantation soon, but I'd like to hear what Hunter Hadley has to say. I'm outside the station now and I'm going to have a word with him."

Nessa's eyes bulged as she digested Eden's words.

"Oh, no you're not!" Nessa started the car and jerked the gear into reverse. "You stay right where you are. Don't do anything until I get there."

* * *

Eden's white Ford Expedition was sitting in the Channel Ten parking lot when Nessa's Dodge Charger roared in. She'd managed to get Vanzinger on the phone and he'd agreed to meet with Riley while she followed up on information she'd received about Hunter Hadley.

Relieved to see Eden's blonde head in the car, she parked and climbed out of the Charger. She smiled despite herself as Duke's face appeared at the back window.

"Thank goodness you didn't do anything stupid," Nessa said when Eden stepped out. "You can't know that Hunter isn't involved in all of this. He could be dangerous."

"That's why I need to speak to him," Eden insisted as she lowered the back window to give Duke some fresh air. "If he's the man that hurt Bella and Olympia, I need to know. Besides, what can he do in public? There are loads of witnesses in there...and cameras."

Skirting around Nessa, Eden charged toward the station door. Nessa followed behind at a trot, feeling the holster under her jacket to make sure her Glock was secure.

The atmosphere inside the station was tense as they entered. A young woman with long, dark hair approached them, her face was familiar.

"Hi, Chief Ainsley, I'm Veronica Lee. I'm the one who reported Sabrina missing. She's my roommate."

Nessa nodded and forced a smile.

"Thank you for calling us in so quickly, Veronica. I need to see Hunter Hadley. I have a few urgent questions for him. Is he here?"

A look of dismay entered Veronica's green eyes, but she nodded and pointed to a glass-walled office in the back corner. By the time they'd reached the office, Hunter was on his feet. Nessa's hand hovered near her gun, her nerves jumping.

"Have you found Sabrina West?"

She wasn't prepared for the question. She'd come to interview him, not the other way around.

"Mr. Hadley, I'd like you to come down to the station with me and answer a few questions."

Nessa used her most authoritative voice, but Hunter just raised his eyebrows and sat back down in his chair.

"I've got a newsroom to run," he said. "And one of my best reporters is missing. I don't have time for more inane questions."

"Have you ever used the *Secret Fling* dating app?" Eden blurted out, stepping up beside Nessa. "Have you used it to meet women?"

Hunter cocked his head and stared at Eden.

"Who are you? You look familiar..."

"I'm Eden Winthrop. I'm the founder of the Mercy Harbor Foundation. Your station has run a few stories about the work we do to make this community a safer place for the women who live here."

"How very noble of you, Ms. Winthrop," Hunter said, his eyes inscrutable. "And to answer your question: no, I have no interest in using *dating apps*."

Stepping in front of Eden, Nessa leaned over Hunter's desk, infuriated by his high-handed response.

"We have reason to believe that your picture is being used on the *Secret Fling* dating app to lure women. Women who are attacked or even killed. Does that interest you?"

Hunter glared up at Nessa, then slumped back in his chair without responding.

"Now, can you come down to the station so-"

"That would just waste your time and mine," Hunter said, his voice soft but firm. "I have never used a dating app in my life. Whoever used my picture did it without my permission."

Picking up his phone and his laptop, he held them out to Nessa.

"Take these or whatever else you want. Do whatever you need to do to check them out. Just don't waste any more time on me."

His eyes pleaded with Nessa over the desk.

"Just go find Sabrina before it's too late. She's out there and...I don't know how to find her."

Nessa held his gaze for a long beat, then she picked up the laptop and phone and turned to Eden. She saw that the fury had drained from Eden's eyes, and she knew it was time for them to go.

Exiting the newsroom, they stood in the lot next to Eden's SUV.

"I guess today's not the day we find the Stalker after all."

Nessa reached out and ruffled the fur on Duke's head as he leaned out the window to greet her.

"I'll get these back to the station for now, and you need to get out to Beaumont Plantation, where you have a very handsome man waiting to marry you."

Eden smiled and nodded, but her eyes returned to the station door.

"I guess the Stalker wouldn't use Hunter's photo to create a fake profile if they were working together, would he?"

"Hunter Hadley doesn't really seem stupid enough to use his own picture," Nessa agreed. "But we'll have to consider him a person of interest until we can eliminate him or find a reason to charge him."

The door to the station swung open and Veronica Lee slipped out. She hurried across the lot, looking over her shoulder as if she feared being followed.

"Chief Ainsley?" Veronica called. "Can I talk to you?"

Preparing herself to fend off Veronica's questions about their search for her roommate, Nessa nodded reluctantly.

"I overheard what you asked Mr. Hadley," Veronica said, a guilty flush tinting her cheeks. "And I wanted to let you know that Sabrina has been using the *Secret Fling* app. She was investigating the Willow Bay Stalker. She wanted a scoop...I think she was trying to track him down on the app."

"How did she know about the app?" Nessa asked.

Veronica shrugged.

"I'm not sure, but she mentioned having friends in the WBPD. Maybe someone there told her."

Outrage bubbled in Nessa's veins at the thought of someone in her department sharing information with the press. If it was true, whoever had leaked the information might have cost Sabrina West her life.

"Do you think Hunter Hadley could be the Willow Bay Stalker?"

Eden's voice cut through the fog of Nessa's rage. She turned to see Veronica once again shaking her head.

"No, I'm sure it isn't Mr. Hadley." Her face was earnest as she spoke. "He's a bit messed up, of course. He's been through some bad times from what I gather, but he's a good man."

The door opened behind them. Two men appeared and walked toward the news van. Veronica seemed suddenly nervous.

"I think I might know who the Stalker is," she said under her breath. "But I can't talk here. My apartment's over on Hammer Street. I can meet you there in ten minutes."

Struck by the intensity in Veronica's eyes, Nessa nodded.

Maybe today will be the day we find the Stalker after all.

CHAPTER THIRTY-SEVEN

B arker's suit jacket hung loosely around his shoulders as he waited in the shelter's lobby for Reggie Horn. The healthy eating regime he'd adopted after his heart attack last year had taken fifty pounds off his six-foot frame, and he belatedly wished he'd taken the time to buy a new suit before the wedding.

"Why are you so nervous, man?" Frankie asked, tugging at the knot in his tie. "And how the hell is anybody supposed to breathe with one of these fucking things wrapped around his neck?"

Hearing the faint sound of voices, Barker turned to the big picture window that looked onto the terrace. A young woman with wispy brown hair sat at one of the tables. She wore a strained smile.

"Hey, Frankie. Isn't that Olympia Glass?"

Frankie followed his gaze.

"Yeah, that's her."

Barker tried to see who she was sitting with, but whoever it was had their backs to the window.

"She doesn't look any happier than the last time we were here."

Barker's words seemed to irritate Frankie. He lifted a distracted hand to scratch his freshly shaved chin.

"What should she be happy about? Some idiot attacked her, remember? I doubt you'd be dancing in the streets if that happened to you...or to Taylor."

"You leave Taylor out of it," Barker snapped. "And don't say anything to embarrass me in front of Reggie."

Just then the lobby door opened. Barker's breath caught in his throat as Reggie stepped inside. She wore a form-fitting dress of pale pink silk. Seeing Barker, she smiled and held out a thin folder.

"This is all we have I'm afraid," Reggie said. "Celeste Reed wasn't with us very long, and it was early days for the shelter, so we didn't have the computer system up and running yet. Which is why everything in her file is handwritten."

Barker tucked the file under his arm.

"I really appreciate this. I'm sure you've been busy today getting ready for Eden and Leo's wedding."

Clearing his throat awkwardly, Barker summoned his courage.

"You look great by the way. That dress really suits you."

"Why, this old thing?"

Reggie flashed a brilliant smile, her eyes dropping to Barker's suit. He detected a slight widening of her eyes, but she recovered her composure quickly.

"And your suit looks very...spacious."

She caught his eye and winked, and suddenly they were both laughing. Barker knew his face must be as pink as her dress.

"He looks like he got that suit out of his daddy's closet," Frankie said, pulling at his tie. "And he's trying to kill me with this thing."

"Here, let me fix that." Reggie brushed away Frankie's hand and began adjusting his tie. "This should feel better. My Wayne always hated wearing a tie, so I learned how to knot it nice and loose so he wouldn't even notice he had it on."

Barker liked the easy way Reggie talked about her late husband. It sounded like she really enjoyed her memories, and it didn't seem to make her sad to think about him. He wondered if he'd be able to talk about Caroline like that one day.

"Well, I'd better let you gentlemen get on your way." Reggie's eyes rested on Barker's face. "I'll hope to see you both over at Beaumont Plantation later on."

Watching Reggie's departing figure, Barker hoped the morning would pass quickly. He glanced back to see Frankie push through the back door onto the terrace.

"Hey, Olympia, how's it going?" Frankie called. "Remember us?"

Barker rushed out just as Olympia looked up. Her eyes darted nervously between Frankie and the couple sitting across from her at the table.

"I'm *Frankie*," he said as if he couldn't believe she'd forgotten him. "And that's my partner, Barker. We talked just a few days ago."

A small, pretty woman at the table twisted around to face them.

"Hi, Frankie, I'm Olympia's friend, Zoey Eldredge."

She produced a smile and gestured toward the man next to her.

"That's my husband, Milo."

Barker tried not to stare, but he couldn't help noticing Zoey's extremely pregnant stomach. She appeared to be almost as round as she was tall. He raised a hand in greeting.

"Nice to meet you both," he said, then turned to Olympia and offered an apologetic smile. "Sorry for the interruption, Olympia. We stopped by to see Reggie and...well, Frankie just wanted to say hello."

Milo Eldredge turned unfriendly eyes toward Frankie. In contrast to his wife, his face was narrow and his expression sour. Barker noted with distaste that the man had scraped his hair back into a man bun.

"Eldredge? You any relation to Judge Eldredge?" Frankie asked with a curious frown. "The old guy on the city council?"

Giving her husband an anxious glance, Zoey nodded.

"That old guy's his dad."

Although her voice was light, Barker saw tension stiffen her shoulders. Milo ignored the exchange and pulled out his phone, obviously indifferent to the conversation.

"So how do you know Olympia?" Zoey asked. "She never tells me about anyone she's met here. I've been worried she'll get lonely, which is why I've been begging her to come to stay with us. And now another woman is missing..."

Zoey absently rubbed her stomach as she spoke. Barker signaled Frankie to keep his mouth shut, but he was too late.

"We're private investigators," Frankie offered, not even looking in Barker's direction. "We're here working on a case."

"You mean...on Olympia's case?" Zoey sounded hopeful. "Are you helping to find the man who attacked her?"

Milo abruptly jumped to his feet and turned impatient eyes on Zoey. She stared up at him in surprise.

"We've got to get going," he muttered. "I told my father we'd stop by this afternoon."

Reluctantly Zoey stood to follow her husband. She stopped on the way out to give Olympia a long hug, although her enormous bump made it impossible to get too close.

"Take care of yourself," she whispered in her friend's ear.

Nodding in numb silence, Olympia waited until Milo and Zoey were out of sight, then dropped her head onto the table, letting her fluffy brown curls cover her face.

"So, how are you really doing, Olympia?" Frankie asked, falling into the chair next to her. "I hope I didn't spoil the party."

Olympia didn't move or respond.

"It's just...well, you kind of looked like you wanted to be rescued from that guy," Frankie said. "If I was wrong then I apologize."

"You weren't wrong," Olympia murmured from underneath the cloud of silky hair. "I don't ever want to see him again."

Barker frowned, unsure what was going on.

"He's a terrible person."

Lifting her head, she wiped away a tear. Barker tried not to look at the scars on her cheek and jaw.

"But then, so am I."

Frankie scoffed and shook his head. Barker was surprised to see him take a small pack of tissues out of his pocket. He handed one to Olympia and waited for her to blow her nose.

"I slept with Milo," she sniffled, keeping her eyes on the desk." I actually slept with my best friend's husband. How shitty is that?"

"Pretty shitty,' Frankie said quietly. "Why'd you do it?"

With a heavy sigh, Olympia shrugged.

"I'd say it's because I'm stupid and self-destructive," Olympia said. "But Dr. Horn tells me I have *commitment issues*. She thinks I sleep with married men because I know it'll never get too serious."

"But what do you think?" Frankie asked. "You think you sleep with douche bags like Milo because you can't have a normal relationship?"

Cringing at Frankie's callous words, Barker tugged on his sleeve.

"Come on, Frankie. We'd better get going."

But Frankie held out a rigid hand, motioning for Barker to wait. After a long pause, Olympia cleared her throat.

"I ended it when I found out Zoey was pregnant," she croaked. "Milo and I had only slept together a few times and...well, I was looking for an excuse to stop the whole fucked up thing anyway."

She raised bitter eyes to Frankie.

"I would have ended it sooner, but Milo doesn't play well with others. Especially when someone is trying to take his toys away."

A lightbulb went off in Barker's head.

"Is Milo Eldredge the man who attacked you?"

Shaking her head, Olympia's eyes filled with fear.

"No, it wasn't him...but...it...was..."

A shudder rippled through her thin body, and she hugged herself tighter. Barker felt sure she was ready to tell them the truth. As long as Frankie didn't scare her away first.

"Who attacked you, Olympia?" Barker asked, his voice gentle. "It's important that we know, so we can catch him before anyone else gets hurt."

Olympia's head dropped like a wilted flower.

"So, what? You're just gonna let Sabrina West die?"

Frankie's voice pierced the air, and Olympia stiffened in her chair.

"You're all scared and shit, so you can just forget about all the other poor women this jackass is going to kill? Is that it?"

Shaking her head, Olympia tried to stand, but her legs buckled underneath her. She raised a trembling hand to cover her eyes.

"You think just because you're scared of this creep it makes it okay for you to hide away in this shelter instead of hunting his ass down?"

"Frankie, that's enough," Barker shouted, his heart hammering hard in his chest. "Just leave her alone."

Staring down at Olympia's quivering shoulders, Frankie sighed.

"All right, Barker. Let's get out of here."

They were already at the door when she lifted her head.

"I met him through a dating app called *Secret Fling*."

Wiping her eyes with the tissue, she looked over at Frankie.

"At first he seemed really nice in his messages and...I was stupid enough to admit I'd just ended a relationship with my best friend's husband. He wanted to meet up, but I told him I wasn't ready yet. That's when he got nasty...and then ...he showed up in the mask..."

Frankie pulled out his phone and tapped on the browser icon. Within seconds he was on the *Secret Fling* login screen.

"Log in to your account."

"What?" She looked horrified. "I don't want to ever–"

"Do it, Olympia...so we can go find the fucker."

But Frankie's voice had lost its rough edge; he sounded drained.

With trembling hands, Olympia took the phone and began to type. When she handed back the phone, Barker stared at the screen with wide, disbelieving eyes.

The profile of LonelyGuy10 included a small photo of a man in glasses and a baseball cap. Barker immediately recognized the strong jawline and broad shoulders of the mayor's son.

"That's him," Olympia said in a shaking voice. "That's the man who attacked me."

*　*　*

Frankie sat in the passenger seat of Barker's Prius. He'd been unusually quiet since they'd left Olympia at the shelter.

"You believe her?" Barker asked, keeping his eyes on the road.

"Yeah, I do." Frankie stopped chewing on his gum and looked over at Barker. "Why the fuck would she lie? The poor girl hasn't got anything left to lose."

"Only her life," Barker said.

"Sometimes, after you've screwed up everything good, that doesn't seem like a lot."

Barker wondered if Frankie was talking about Olympia Glass or himself. It seemed like the traumatized woman had really gotten under Frankie's skin.

The fact that Frankie wasn't married, and never talked about a special someone in his life, made Barker suspect his partner suffered from the same type of commitment issues Olympia had mentioned. Perhaps Frankie could see his own lonely reflection in her wounded eyes. Maybe that was why Frankie was overlooking the obvious flaw in her story.

"It just doesn't seem likely that Hunter Hadley would upload a photo of himself if he was trolling for victims on *Secret Fling*," Barker said, although his reasons for doubting Olympia went deeper than just the photo.

"Maybe he thought he could scare her into silence," Frankie insisted. "Or that she wouldn't live long enough to tell anyone."

Changing lanes to pass a slow-rolling tractor in front of them, Barker shrugged. He just didn't buy Hunter Hadley as the Willow Bay Stalker. His recent conversation with the mayor's son had revealed a damaged man, but a sensitive one. He didn't strike Barker as a violent man. Not the kind of man who would beat a woman to death.

"How far out is this place?" Frankie moaned, ignoring the view as they flew past an idyllic pasture dotted with grazing cows.

"We're almost there," Barker assured him, checking his watch.

It was only noon, and the wedding wasn't scheduled to start until two, but he'd agreed to act as an usher and had promised to get there before the other guests started to arrive. But he could see when he pulled up that another car was already parked in the guest lot.

Climbing out of the Prius, Barker recognized a blonde man standing by the entrance talking on his phone. The man put his phone away and smiled as Frankie and Barker approached.

"Hello, again," the man called out in a jovial tone. "Looks like I'm not the only early bird around here, although I was hoping there'd be a few drinks and hors d'oeuvres available. The food on my red-eye flight from San Fran was horrendous."

Frankie rubbed his chin and cocked his head.

"You're that guy that Eden knows, right? The one that was with her out in the Cottonmouth swamp?"

The big man grimaced dramatically.

"Yes, unfortunately, that was me. I'm Nathan Rush, Eden's business partner. I flew in from the West Coast for her big day."

"It's great to see you," Barker said, suddenly remembering that Nathan had been with Eden the night they found Taylor. "I can't thank you enough for trying to save my girl."

Nathan shook his head and put both hands up.

"That was all Eden's doing. She insisted that we go to the diner."

Nathan looked around as if someone might be listening, even though they were completely alone.

"Of course, my contact was able to hack into the phone company's system and find the diner's address for us, so that made it possible."

Frankie suddenly looked interested.

"You know somebody that can hack into computer systems?" He shot Barker an excited look. "Can they find out who might be behind a user account on *Secret Fling*?"

"What's that?" Nathan asked, a slight frown forming between his eyes. "And what are you trying to find out?"

By the time Barker had filled Nathan in on what had been going on in Willow Bay, his frown had turned to a deep scowl, and other guests had started to arrive.

"How does Eden always get herself involved in this kind of stuff?" Nathan fumed. "She's got the kids to think about, and now she has Leo to consider as well."

Leaving Nathan venting to Frankie, Barker led a guest inside. When he turned around he saw Leo Steele hurrying toward him. The groom was handsomely dressed in a black tuxedo; his black curls had been brushed back into a formal style that suited him.

"You clean up nice," Barker boomed out, slapping Leo on the back. "Eden is a lucky lady."

"I hope she thinks so," Leo said, looking around as if she might be standing behind him. "We agreed not to see each other or talk this morning, so I better keep out of the way."

"I don't think she's arrived yet, so no need to worry," Barker said. "But her ex-business partner is outside if you wanted to say hello."

Leo's face lit up.

"Nathan's here? That's great. Eden will be so glad he made it."

Making their way toward the front, Barker filled Leo in on what they'd learned from Olympia Glass. When they stepped outside they saw Frankie and Nathan deep in conversation. Barker didn't like the eager look on Frankie's face.

"Hey Leo, you ready to walk down the plank? I mean *the aisle?*"

Leo rolled his eyes at Frankie's bad joke and greeted Nathan with a hearty handshake.

"Thanks for coming all this way," Leo said. "And I'm sorry I didn't get to see you before you left last time. I wanted to thank you."

Inserting himself between Leo and Nathan, Frankie held up his phone. Barker could see that the *Secret Fling* app was open.

"I hate to interrupt this touching reunion," Frankie said, "but Nathan was just offering to help me with our investigation."

Leo raised his eyebrows and looked at Nathan.

"Apparently they need information about a user account on some dating app," Nathan said, keeping his voice low. "They said it was a case you all were working on together, so I said I'd help by getting my contact to do a little digging and see what he can find out."

Nathan smiled at the doubt on Leo's face.

"Don't worry, you and Eden won't be involved at all," Nathan assured him. "It'll be all on me."

"You mean you can find out who set up the account?" Leo asked.

Nathan shrugged.

"Probably. Might even be able to track back the activity on the account to a specific IP address."

"Which could be traced to a physical address." Leo sounded excited. "It could end up leading us straight to our guy."

Holding up a cautionary hand, Nathan clarified.

"This isn't a guarantee. I can't promise it'll work."

"Right," Leo said, "but whatever happens, I owe you one."

Nathan tapped a number into his phone and grinned.

"No worries," he said. "Consider it a wedding present."

CHAPTER THIRTY-EIGHT

Sabrina had finally regained consciousness and was struggling against the ropes by the time the man returned to the guest house on his father's property. He'd left the reporter trussed up on the bedroom floor that morning, confident that no one would come by and find her. His father's estate was located on a lightly traveled road more than thirty minutes outside town, and the old man was rarely willing to receive visitors, even if they were willing to make the drive.

"Everyone's looking for you, Sabrina," he said, tugging the gag from her mouth. "You've been on the news all morning."

"Why are you doing this to me?" she gasped out, her voice raw.

Staring down with cruel, calculating eyes, the man wondered how long she could last. She hadn't had any water since he'd dragged her into the house, so he imagined her throat must be getting pretty dry.

How long can a person survive without food or water? It's a shame I can't let her live long enough to find out.

He knelt beside Sabrina and searched again through her blood-stained clothes. There was nothing in any of her pockets.

"Where'd you leave your phone?" he demanded.

Tears trickled from her swollen eyes as she tried to think.

"It's in my bag, back in the newsroom," she whispered.

"That was stupid of you," he growled, sitting back on his heels.

He'd been planning to search through her emails and text messages to see who she'd been talking to. He wanted to know what she'd learned during her investigation into the Willow Bay Stalker.

"What did your boyfriend, Detective Ortiz, tell you about the investigation?" he asked in a dangerous voice. "What do the police know about me?"

Shrinking back against the floor, Sabrina shook her head.

"He didn't tell me...anything," she whimpered. "They don't know anything about you."

He saw the lie in her scared, blue eyes. The urge to smash his fist down on her deceitful face flooded through him. But he forced himself to hold back. At least for now. She'd been unconscious for hours, and her eyes still looked dazed. If he allowed himself to give in to his anger, he might go too far. He might end everything before he had a chance to carry out his plan.

"If it wasn't Ortiz, then who told you about *Secret Fling*?"

He watched her pupils dilate with fear as she tried to think up something to say.

"What, you can't think up any more lies?"

His hand shot out and grabbed a fistful of blonde hair. The roots were stiff and sticky with blood, but the ends felt soft and silky in his palm. He brought his lips within inches of her ear, his breath escaping in hot puffs of excitement. The fear vibrating off her was intoxicating.

"You thought you were so smart. Sending me messages. Pretending you wanted to meet me. It was all lies, wasn't it?"

Sabrina shook her head as she began to sob.

"No, I wasn't lying. I just wanted...I wanted..."

But she was crying too hard to speak as she saw the unbridled fury on his face, and her words faded into muffled cries.

A heady sense of power washed over him at her show of weakness, and he pulled her head back and stared into her terrified face.

"Junior!"

Jerking at the sound of his father's voice, the man cupped an iron hand over Sabrina's mouth and squeezed.

"Junior, are you in there?"

A glimmer of hope flashed into Sabrina's eyes and the man had to fight back the temptation to squelch that hope forever.

Silence throbbed around them as they both listened for another shout, expecting a knock on the door or the sound of a key in the lock. But all was still. After a full minute of quiet listening, the man hefted himself up and wrenched the gag back over Sabrina's mouth. He tied it firmly in place and took a deep, cleansing breath.

"That was close," he murmured, wiping sweat off his forehead with a big hand. "But I'm not quite ready to introduce you to my father yet. I've got other plans for you first."

Slipping out the back door, the man circled around the guest house and made his way up to the main building. He climbed the steps to the veranda and sank into the big porch swing. It was the same swing his mother used to sit on every night as the sun went down.

Suddenly he was very tired. He hadn't allowed himself to fully sleep for days. Closing his eyes, he listened to the soft whoosh of air as he glided back and forth and wondered if his mother had missed the old swing once she'd gone.

Did she miss anything about this place? Did she want to come home?

A sharp voice brought him out of his stupor.

"Junior, what in the world are you doing on that swing?"

His father stood at the big door with a newspaper in his hand.

"You look like an imbecile. Now, have you read about this woman that wants to be the new chief of police? This whole town's going to hell in a handbasket. I don't know what's going to happen next."

"I think you're right, father. This town is full of crooks and liars, and it's about time everyone in it got a wake-up call."

Frowning over at him, the old man paused and stared down at the newspaper again.

"There's also a lot of fuss about this Willow Bay Stalker in the paper. You wouldn't…"

His father's voice wavered and died out.

"What, Father?" the man urged. "Go on, say it. I wouldn't what?"

"You wouldn't know anything about that, would you, Junior?"

But the man wasn't listening anymore. He just swung back and forth until his father went back into the house. The old man would be leaving for his townhouse in the city soon. And once he was gone, the fun could begin.

CHAPTER THIRTY-NINE

Jankowski perched on the only stool still available at the lunch counter and ordered a black coffee. The Blue-Ribbon Diner was filling up with its lunch hour crowd; none of the booths were empty. He looked over at the booth he'd shared with Iris the day before and wished he hadn't lost his temper. It wasn't fair for him to be hurt that Iris had questions about the scene. She had a scientific mind and thrived on logic. He couldn't expect her to start operating on faith alone, could he?

Taking out his phone, Jankowski pressed Leo Steele's number. He needed to make sure they had a game plan ready in the event Riley Odell decided she had enough evidence to bring him back in for questioning.

"Jankowski?" Leo sounded worried. "Everything okay?"

"Yeah, I'm still a free man, if that's what you mean," Jankowski replied, straining to hear Leo's voice over the din of the diner. "But I was hoping we could talk if you have time."

The harried counter server slid a mug of steaming coffee in front of him along with the check.

"It's not a good time for me, Jankowski," Leo said, sounding distracted. "I'm out at Beaumont Plantation getting ready to take my vows. It's the big day for me and Eden."

"Oh shit, I'm sorry, Leo, I completely forgot."

The woman on the stool next to him frowned and Jankowski turned away, lowering his voice as he spoke into the phone.

"Well, I'm sure you have more on your mind than my wedding," Leo said. "And try not to worry about Riley Odell filing official charges. I have a feeling there will be a break in the case very soon and Nessa will find the real perp."

"I hope you're right," Jankowski muttered.

"In the meantime, just take care of yourself," Leo said, sounding concerned. "Gabby's death has got to be hitting you pretty hard."

Swallowing the lump that had suddenly risen in his throat, Jankowski tried to make his voice sound as normal as possible.

"Thanks, Leo. I hope you and Eden enjoy your wedding day."

"We will, and I'll let Eden know you said so."

A sudden vision of Gabby on their long-ago wedding day, so young and pretty, hit him in the gut. How had he gotten from that day to this one so quickly? Could he ever have imagined the tragic end for the beautiful bride he'd married that day? The sense of loss and grief for everything they'd once been staggered him.

"Leo, you got lucky, you know that, right?" Jankowski said, feeling awkward, but needing to say it. "Eden's a good woman. Make sure you appreciate her."

There was a brief silence on the other end before Leo responded.

"I will, Jankowski," Leo agreed in a soft voice. "I definitely will."

Draining his coffee in two hot gulps, Jankowski threw a five-dollar bill on the counter and headed for the door. His phone buzzed in his hand as he stepped back onto the sidewalk.

His heart beat faster when he saw the familiar number. Iris didn't waste time on pleasantries. Her words were crisp, and they got Jankowski's attention right away.

"We were able to get viable DNA samples from the bite wounds we excised from Jade Castillo and Gabby. Alma ran them through her new rapid DNA machine and confirmed the DNA samples collected from the two bodies are a match. So, we now know for sure that the same perp killed both women."

A bolt of relief shot through him. The DNA would prove he was innocent. He wasn't going to go to prison. His relief was followed by a burst of outrage. Someone had killed his ex-wife, and he had almost been framed for her murder. He could have been in a cage for the next twenty or thirty years.

"Why are you telling me this?" Jankowski asked. "Even if the DNA results exonerate me, couldn't you get in trouble for sharing them with me at this stage of the investigation?"

"Yes, I suppose I could," Iris agreed. "But I thought you'd want to know as soon as possible. I would if I was the one being accused of murder."

Dropping onto a bench outside the diner, Jankowski tried to decide what he should do next. A killer was on the loose and a young woman was missing. If he was in the clear for Gabby's murder, Nessa would need him back on the job.

"Has Alma run the DNA through the state and national databases...or through CODIS yet?

"She's in the process now, but it's the weekend, and there could be a delay in getting the results back. Of course, if the perp isn't in any of the databases, we'll be back at square one."

"How fast could you run the results against someone already in the database? I mean, if I gave you a name, could you see if they're a match?"

Iris hesitated before she answered.

"I'll have to check with Alma. But who would you want to try to match? Do you have a suspect in mind?

"Hunter Hadley," Jankowski replied. "He was dating Gabby and they had a falling out. We need to eliminate him at the very least. Or if he's the one, then we need to stop him."

Thinking back to the background check he'd done on Hunter when he'd found out Gabby had started seeing him, Jankowski recalled that the mayor's son had an arrest record. It was possible the police collected a DNA sample at the time.

"Ask Alma to check if Hadley's DNA is on file. I know he has a record; it's worth a shot."

"Okay," Iris agreed. "And one more thing...Alma and I haven't passed the results of the DNA tests to Nessa yet. We tried to call her but she's not picking up. Her phone goes right to voicemail."

Jankowski felt a stab of unease. Why would Nessa be missing in action with everything going on?

"We could always give Ingram or Ortiz the results," she continued in a disapproving tone, "but they never passed on the cyber analyst's results from Bella's computer, so we weren't sure they could be trusted to get this info to her either."

The mention of the cybercrime analyst spurred Jankowski's memory. They needed a court order to see who owned the account that had communicated with Jade Castillo and the other women. Last he'd heard Riley Odell had been trying to track down Judge Eldredge.

"Any update on the court order? Has our new hotshot prosecutor been able to talk to old man Eldredge?"

"I don't know," Iris said. "I haven't talked to her today, but I did see her talking to your buddy Tucker Vanzinger earlier."

"What's he doing in town?" Jankowski asked, then answered his own question. "Oh, he must have heard Riley was back."

Smiling at the thought of Tucker and Riley back together again, he wondered how the news had traveled so fast.

"You haven't heard? Nessa's hired him in as a detective to fill her spot now that she's chief."

Stunned by the news, he tried to control his excitement. He had to make sure this was a permanent thing before he allowed himself to celebrate. Having a good man like Tucker back on the force and Nessa leading the department would be a dream come true. All he'd have to do would be to get rid of Ingram and it would be perfect.

"I'm glad to hear it," Jankowski said, impatient now to call Nessa. "And thanks for sharing the news about the DNA results. I really appreciate it."

"No problem." Her voice was cool. "Talk to you later."

Then she was gone. He kept the phone pressed to his ear, listening to the silence as regret and self-loathing filled him.

I guess I've lost Iris as well as Gabby thanks to the Willow Bay Stalker.

He shook himself, refusing to give in to the negative voice in his head, and tapped on Nessa's number. Her voicemail picked up right away. He left a message, then debated calling her house. He hated to worry Jerry and the boys unnecessarily.

Maybe I should call an old friend instead.

Vanzinger picked up on the first ring.

"I was wondering when you'd call to welcome me back, Jank."

Grinning at the sound of Vanzinger's voice, Jankowski leaned back and let himself relax against the bench.

"I just heard the good news, although I'd thought you must have come back to town sniffing after your old flame. I mean, Riley's back here for a day or two and then you suddenly show up?"

"That's just a coincidence," Vanzinger protested. "I had no idea she was back in Willow Bay when I got the call from Nessa. And that's old news anyway. She and I are all business now. Unfortunately."

Jankowski laughed at the dejection in Vanzinger's voice.

"Sounds like you've still got it pretty bad for her."

"Did you call to talk about my love life Jank, or do you want to maybe try to catch a killer?"

Sitting up straight, Jankowski saw two men approach the diner. They were deep in conversation and didn't notice him on the bench as they pushed through the door.

"I think I'll take you up on the second option," Jankowski said. "I'm outside the Blue-Ribbon Diner. I'll wait for you here."

CHAPTER FORTY

Veronica Lee's apartment was farther away than Eden had expected, and she was starting to get worried about making it out to Beaumont Plantation on time. Pulling out her phone, she typed in a quick text to Barb assuring her that she was on the way.

"Thanks for coming here," Veronica said, ushering Nessa, Eden, and Duke into the apartment before closing and locking the door. "It's just that if my suspicions are correct, it isn't safe for us to talk at the station."

Eden met Nessa's eyes, seeing that Willow Bay's new chief of police was just as anxious as she was to hear what Veronica had to say. Could Veronica really know who had abducted her roommate? If she did, the Willow Bay Stalker's campaign of terror might be over.

"I thought you said you were sure Hunter wasn't the Stalker," Nessa said. "So, why not talk at the station?"

"I am sure it isn't Hunter," Veronica agreed. "But I think the man who abducted Sabrina is someone he's close to. Someone who knows everything about him."

Pulling out a slim iPhone, Veronica tapped on the *Secret Fling* app and handed it to Nessa.

"This is Sabrina's phone." Her eyes flicked nervously to Nessa. "I guess I should've turned it over sooner. But I didn't want to get her into any trouble."

"Why would she be in trouble?" Nessa asked.

Veronica grimaced and held out the phone.

"Because she got her information about the Stalker using *Secret Fling* through a source in the police department. He's a detective. The text messages are all there."

Anger flashed in Nessa's eyes as she grabbed the phone. She scanned the text messages with growing rage, then tapped on the *Secret Fling* icon. After a few more taps she was studying LonelyGuy10's profile picture.

"Sabrina had been messaging LonelyGuy10 pretending to be someone else," Veronica explained. "She thought she was hiding her true identity, but I think he knew who she was all along. I think he targeted her."

Shaking her head in confusion, Eden tried to make sense of what Veronica was saying. She rubbed Duke's soft, furry head as she spoke.

"So, you think Sabrina was communicating with someone on this *Secret Fling* app because she suspected he was the Stalker? She was trying to catch him herself?"

Veronica nodded, her face tense.

"I'm pretty sure she was planning to set a trap for whoever is behind the profile."

"But he caught her first," Nessa whispered as she read through the message. "*See you soon...*that's the last message he sent her."

Eden felt the skin on the back of her neck begin to crawl. Was LonelyGuy10 really the Willow Bay Stalker? Was Sabrina West with him now? Or were they already too late to save her?

"So, you said you think you know who this is?" Nessa turned to Veronica. "You think it's someone who knows Hunter?"

"I'd been trying to figure out where I'd seen the app's icon," Veronica said. "The first time I saw it on Sabrina's phone I knew I'd seen it somewhere before. Then this morning, I remembered."

Both Nessa and Eden listened in rapt silence.

"It was at the press conference about Jade Castillo's murder. Sabrina was reporting live and her cameraman, Boyd Faraday, had the app open on his phone. When he saw me looking at him he got all nervous. I didn't think about it much at the time but now I think...I think he's the one who's been messaging Sabrina. I think he's the one that...that took her."

Choking up on the words, Veronica grabbed a tissue and blotted her eyes. When she looked up, her eyes were red-rimmed but dry.

"Boyd Faraday?" Nessa sputtered. "You mean Archie Faraday's son? The sullen one Archie always calls *Junior*?"

"Yes, that's him. He's known Hunter since they were boys. I think they grew up together." Veronica's distaste for the man was obvious. "I always thought that must be why Hunter gave him the job. I mean, he's a bit...weird. But he knows everything about Hunter, and he was obsessed with Sabrina. Wouldn't let anyone else on the crew near them when they were working the Stalker story."

Nessa stared at Veronica as if assessing her mental state.

"You really think Junior Faraday is the Willow Bay Stalker?"

Nodding slowly, Veronica's voice trembled.

"Yes, I think Boyd's the Stalker. And I think he has Sabrina."

Eden tried to picture the man she'd seen in town on occasion with his father. He hadn't left much of an impression, although she remembered thinking he looked just as miserable as his father.

"Is he working today?" Nessa asked. "If he is, I can go back to Channel Ten. Bring him downtown for an interview."

Taking out her phone, Nessa moaned.

"Shoot, it's dead." She shoved the phone back in her pocket with a frustrated sigh. "I didn't get a full charge last night."

Eden held out her phone, panic setting in as she saw the time.

"Here, use mine, then I've got to go. My wedding is scheduled to start in little more than an hour."

"What?" Veronica gaped at Eden. "It's your wedding day and you're here trying to...to catch the Stalker?"

Eden nodded miserably as Nessa told someone on the other end of the call that she was heading back to Channel Ten to check out a lead.

"Is Vanzinger at his desk?" Nessa paused to listen. "All right, I'll try to reach him on the radio when I'm back in my car."

She turned to Eden.

"You ready to go?"

With a sinking sensation, Eden remembered she and Duke had ridden over to Veronica's apartment in Nessa's Charger. The weather girl had said she lived nearby, but it was a twenty-minute drive back to the news station. And Beaumont Plantation lay thirty minutes away in the opposite direction.

"I'm not going to make it to my own wedding," Eden said in a numb voice. "I've screwed it up. After all the planning and everything, I've...ruined it."

"What time is the ceremony scheduled to start?" Veronica asked, checking her watch, which was inching toward one.

"At two o'clock sharp," Eden said. "But the venue's thirty minutes away, and my car's back in the Channel Ten lot."

Staring at Eden's jeans and sweater, Veronica frowned.

"And your dress?"

"Oh, it's already at the venue," Eden said, "only...I'm not."

Veronica pulled out her keys and waved them in the air.

"I'll drive you there," she said, sounding vaguely hysterical. "I can have you there with thirty minutes to spare."

Nessa nodded in agreement.

"It's probably best for you not to go back to Channel Ten anyway. At least until I have a chance to talk to Boyd Faraday. It'll be safer if you both stay away until we find out more."

A bright flame of hope flickered in Eden's chest. Maybe she hadn't messed up her big day after all. Maybe she could still make it on time.

The thought of Leo's handsome face waiting for her at the end of the aisle made her determined to at least try.

But as Eden hurried outside and waited for Duke to climb into the back of Veronica's big, red jeep, she couldn't stop herself from wondering if Sabrina West was still alive.

CHAPTER FORTY-ONE

Leo stood on the big veranda of Beaumont Plantation's manor house and checked his watch again. Although Barb had been worried when Eden didn't show up at noon as arranged, Leo had promised himself he wouldn't start panicking until at least one o'clock. It was now a few minutes after one.

"Any sign of her?" Barker asked, coming up behind him.

Checking the plantation's winding driveway in hopes of seeing the big white SUV, Leo shook his head.

"She's allowed to take her time on her wedding day," Leo said, knowing he sounded defensive. "She's probably decided on a last-minute hair appointment. Or maybe she...broke a nail."

Reaching into his pocket he checked the status of the text message he'd sent to Eden at twelve-thirty when Barb had started to worry.

Can't wait to see my bride. Checking in to make sure everything is okay?

The message was still unread.

"I better call her," he muttered, feeling vaguely foolish in front of Barker. "Just to keep Barb happy."

The phone rang again and again. Leo was about to end the call when an unexpected voice answered.

"Hey, Leo, this is Nessa."

Leo's heart dropped into his stomach, and his blood turned cold. Something must have happened to Eden for the chief of police to be answering her phone. Had she been in an accident? Had she been attacked? A tidal wave of terrible possibilities flooded through him.

"What's happened, Nessa?" Leo managed to say. "What's happened to Eden?"

Barker inhaled sharply behind him and put a hand on Leo's arm.

"Calm down, Leo," Nessa quickly responded. "Eden's fine. She just got a bit delayed and ended up leaving her phone behind when she rushed out."

Sagging with relief, Leo turned to Barker with a shaky thumbs-up.

"Why was Eden with you in the first place, Nessa?" Leo asked, his mind starting to function again as the surge of fear dissipated. "Has something happened to one of the women at the shelter?"

"It's related to the recent murders, but I don't have time to get into much detail. I'm on my way to the Channel Ten station to question a suspect."

Leo could hear the urgency in Nessa's voice.

"A suspect? You think you may have found the Stalker?"

Listening to Leo's side of the conversation, Barker began to pace back and forth, his baggy suit jacket billowing around him.

"It's a long story, Leo, but a reporter at Channel Ten believes she knows who abducted Sabrina West. She says she saw him using the dating app that Sabrina used. She also said that he's been obsessed with Sabrina and that he had the opportunity to abduct her."

"So, who is this guy?"

Barker stopped in front of Leo and waited.

"Boyd Faraday," Nessa said. "He's part of the Channel Ten crew."

The name sounded familiar. Suddenly it clicked.

"Archie Faraday's son?" Leo tried to picture the man. "He's a cameraman, right?"

"Yeah, apparently he worked closely with Sabrina on the Willow Bay Stalker story. Her roommate, Veronica Lee, says she saw Boyd Faraday using the *Secret Fling* app and acting strange."

Voices sounded behind him, and Leo turned to see Nathan Rush waving a piece of paper in the air triumphantly.

"Hold on just a sec, Nessa."

Taking the paper from Nathan, Leo read the name and address with growing excitement.

"Are you sure?" he asked Nathan, who displayed a satisfied smile.

"My contact's never been wrong before," Nathan assured him.

Raising the phone again, Leo wondered if Nessa would even believe him. How could he explain how he'd gotten the information without going through the proper legal channels?

"Nessa? You won't believe this, but I just got an update from a...a contact who was able to track down the IP address used to send messages to Olympia Glass through *Secret Fling*."

"You what?" The new chief of police sounded confused. "How'd you know who messaged Olympia? She wouldn't tell us anything."

"Frankie and Barker worked their magic I guess," Leo said. "And it's paid off because my contact traced the IP address back to the ISP; we now have a name and address."

By this time Frankie had joined the little group on the veranda. His face hardened as he looked at the name Nathan had written on the sheet of paper. And as he relayed the information to Nessa, Leo was suddenly sure that they had their man.

"The address is for property owned by Archibald B. Faraday."

Nessa's responding curse was loud enough for the other men on the porch to hear even though the call wasn't on speaker.

"Veronica was right. Junior really is the Stalker," Nessa said after she'd calmed down. "I'm almost at the news station, and I'll radio Vanzinger now and ask him to go out and check the address you got from the ISP. We don't have a warrant to search the place, but

Veronica Lee reported Faraday acting suspiciously so we have a justifiable reason to question him."

Leo glanced up at Barker, already knowing what the ex-police detective would want him to say.

"Make sure you have back-up before you talk to Boyd Faraday, Nessa. Don't approach him on your own."

"Yep, I'll radio in a request. I think Ingram and Ortiz are on duty and in the area," Nessa agreed. "Shouldn't take long for them to get here. And hopefully, Veronica will be dropping off Eden there soon. They left almost thirty minutes ago."

The words made Leo pause.

"Why is Veronica driving Eden out here?"

"Eden went with me to Veronica's. That's how we found out about Boyd. But she didn't have time to go back to pick up her car and still make it to the venue on time, so Veronica offered to drive her. Eden was desperate to get to you, Leo. I'm sure she'll be there soon."

After Leo disconnected the call, he saw Barb hurrying across the front lawn. Her eyes squinted against the glare of the afternoon sun. Reggie Horn was with her, resplendent in pink silk.

"Eden's still not answering her phone," Barb called out as she approached. "And Reggie verified she's not at the shelter."

"Perhaps someone needed her help and she lost track of time," Reggie soothed. "She has been known to do that from time to time."

A terrible suspicion began to grow in Leo's mind.

"That address for Archie Faraday isn't far from here," Leo murmured, trying to convince himself he was wrong. But looking down the empty driveway, he couldn't take the chance.

"Come on, Barker and Dawson, we need to investigate a missing person." Leo moved toward the guest parking lot.

"Who's missing now?" Frankie asked, following Leo and Barker off the veranda.

"My future wife," Leo called over his shoulder, accelerating into a jog. "I hope I'm wrong, but I think I might know where she is."

CHAPTER FORTY-TWO

The drive out to Beaumont Plantation took them through the kind of bucolic countryside Veronica normally loved to see, but with Sabrina missing she barely noticed the scenery whipping by. The possibility of Sabrina suffering the same fate as Jade Castillo and Gabriella Jankowski made Veronica sick to her stomach.

"Do think he'll hurt her?' Veronica asked Eden, who was staring out the window of the big red jeep with impatient eyes. "Or kill her?"

Checking first to make sure Duke was still comfortable in the back seat, Eden looked over at Veronica and sighed.

"The man who has been attacking women is a very disturbed individual," Eden said. "I can't pretend to understand his motives or predict what he might do next. But if he has abducted Sabrina, then he's already deviated from his previous pattern of behavior. It could mean that Sabrina is different to him in some way, so perhaps he'll treat her differently."

Eden's words weren't entirely comforting, but Veronica thought that maybe Eden was right. Maybe Boyd hadn't taken Sabrina to kill her. Maybe he just wanted to be with her.

Of course, the idea of beautiful, vibrant, self-centered Sabrina ever being interested in a man like Boyd Faraday was hard to imagine. The councilman's son was short, stocky, and balding, with a wide face and bad teeth. Veronica knew that he was the sort of man

Sabrina would never look at twice. Then again, few men could live up to her roommate's high standards or tolerate her inflated ego.

While Sabrina had taken advantage of the cameraman's obvious interest in her, expecting him to shoot footage for her reports at a moment's notice, Veronica knew that the ambitious reporter never intended to give Boyd anything in return. And she now realized that Boyd had been manipulating Sabrina all along. It had all been part of his plan.

Sabrina thought she was using Boyd, but he was actually using her.

Thinking back through the last week, Veronica could see that Boyd had stayed close to Sabrina to get information about the case against him. She'd sweet-talked Detective Ortiz into sharing the details of the case with her. That definitely wasn't something Boyd could have done on his own.

And she gave Boyd a legitimate reason to be front and center at all the crime scenes and press conferences.

Without Sabrina as his front, his constant presence might have raised questions, but as her sidekick, he had blended in. Veronica felt stupid for not seeing through his scheme. But she was naturally trusting, unlike her mother, who would have smelled a rat like Boyd from a mile away. The thought of her mother made her wince.

"You okay?" Eden asked, noticing Veronica's dismay.

"My mother's going to flip when she finds out Sabrina is missing, and I've been working in the same room as the Willow Bay Stalker."

A faint smile lifted the corner of Eden's mouth.

"I don't blame her," Eden said. "It's a mother's right to be protective of her children."

"Well, my mother definitely got that memo." Veronica snorted as she thought of the usual string of warnings Ling Lee issued every time Veronica left her house.

"My mother's a real pro at being overly protective. All her students think she's so cool and laid back, but they don't know how she nags me and is always paranoid that something bad is going to happen to me."

Pushing the seat back to give herself more legroom, Eden turned toward Veronica and cocked her head.

"Students? Is your mother a teacher?"

"She used to be a history teacher. Now she's the principal at Willow Bay High."

Eden gasped and clapped her hands, causing Duke to look around in surprise.

"Your mother must be Ms. Lee, my old history teacher."

Veronica didn't respond. She was staring ahead at a big house set back from the road. A wrought-iron sign announced that they were passing Faraday Manor.

"Maybe that's where he took Sabrina," Veronica said, slowing down. "She could be in there right now."

Glancing over at Eden's anxious face, Veronica offered her an apologetic smile, then wrenched hard on the Jeep's steering wheel. As they skidded onto the driveway leading up to the property, Veronica saw a sleek black sedan parked in front of the main house.

"You know, Boyd drives his father's Mercedes to work sometimes." Veronica nodded toward the sedan. "That's it there."

"And Gabriella Jankowski said at the press conference that the Stalker had been seen driving a black sedan," Eden added.

They both kept their eyes glued to the big house that lay ahead as the Jeep rolled up the driveway.

"If we call for help..." Veronica said, feeling her courage starting to desert her.

"Then it might be too late to save Sabrina," Eden finished for her in a miserable voice. "We can't just drive away and leave her if she is here."

Resisting the urge to fling the Jeep into reverse and back up the same way they came, Veronica opened the door and stepped outside.

She jumped at the sudden drumming of a woodpecker's beak on a nearby tree, then flinched as a squirrel scampered down the trunk of a huge oak.

Spinning around, she saw Eden standing next to the Jeep. Duke stared forlornly out of the back window. An unnerving silence descended as Veronica and Eden crept wordlessly up the walkway leading from the driveway to a wide veranda that encircled the house.

Eden reached out and put a restraining hand on Veronica's arm at the bottom of the wooden stairs.

"This is crazy," Eden whispered, her eyes bright with fear. "We need to go for help...or wait for Nessa to send someone."

The practicality of Eden's words registered, but they didn't change Veronica's conviction that Sabrina was in danger. Any delay might mean the difference between life and death for her roommate.

"I'm sorry, Eden. I just...have this feeling that Sabrina is here somewhere...and that she needs help."

Exhaling deeply, Eden nodded and began to ascend the short flight of stairs. Veronica followed closely behind, her legs growing weak as she stepped onto the veranda.

The house was much less grand close up than it had looked from the street. The wood floor was dried and cracked, and the red paint of the front door was faded and chipped. Silvery spiderwebs crisscrossed the rafters overhead as Veronica crossed to the window by the door and peered in. She screamed as a withered faced stared back at her.

Seconds later the door was flung open to reveal Archie Faraday, his face twisted into an indignant scowl.

"Who are you, young lady? And why on earth are you sneaking around and peeking in my window?"

"I'm...I'm looking for my friend..."

Veronica felt a spark of anger at the scorn she saw in Archie's sour face. She suddenly felt foolish for sneaking around like a common criminal. She had a right to be there searching for a missing friend. But before she could give him a piece of her mind, Eden stepped forward and addressed Archie with an icy authority that Veronica envied.

"Mr. Faraday, a woman is missing, and we have reason to believe she may be here with your son. We need to speak to him right away."

"Junior? You want to speak to Junior about a missing woman?" The old man laughed derisively, his yellowed eyes narrowing in his pale, thin face. "Then you better go look for him at the Channel Ten station. He's working today."

Anticipating the old man's move, Veronica lunged forward and braced her shoulder against the door before he could slam it shut.

"We need to look around, Mr. Faraday. To make sure Sabrina isn't here," Veronica muttered, pushing against the man's feeble attempt to close it. "We just need to make sure she's okay."

"I'm going to call the police if you don't leave."

His shrill voice vibrated with outrage.

"Go ahead, Mr. Faraday. I think that's exactly what we need to do," Eden shot back. "In fact, they're probably already on the way."

Fear replaced the indignation in Archie's eyes. He darted a furtive look at the black car on the driveway, then over at the gravel path leading around the back of the house.

"Is your son back there, Mr. Faraday?" Eden asked, turning to stare at the lawn and trees surrounding the path.

"I'm here on my own," Archie said, his tone less defiant. "Come on in and look around. See for yourself."

The old man stepped back and opened the door wider, lifting a skinny arm to wave them inside. Veronica took a step forward, wincing at the smell of mold and decay that greeted her, but Eden reached out and grabbed her wrist, pulling her back.

"I think someone's around back," Eden said, her green eyes glinting with suspicion at Archie's sudden change of heart. "He's just trying to distract us. Come on."

Backing toward the stairs, Veronica heard the unmistakable click of a gun being cocked. It was a sound she'd heard many times at the firing range with her mother. She looked up to see Archie holding a heavy black pistol toward her. Her eyes followed the muzzle as it jumped and shook in his hand.

"Get off my property, now."

The old man's voice was cold, and Veronica had no doubt he would fire the weapon without remorse. But as she stood transfixed by fear, a shadowy figure loomed up behind Archie. A wide face moved forward into the light, and Veronica looked past Archie into Boyd Faraday's cruel eyes.

"What's going on here, father?"

Boyd's voice stunned the old man, who spun around to face his son. Boyd reached out and plucked the weapon from his hand.

"They're looking for you, Junior," Archie croaked, recoiling as Boyd turned and pointed the gun at Veronica.

"You couldn't keep your nose out of it, could you, *weather girl*?"

Frozen with fear, Veronica tried to shake her head, tried to speak. But she couldn't move. Her mother had been right. She should have been more careful. She should have listened. Now she would end up suffering a terrible death just like her mother had always warned her.

But as Boyd lifted the pistol, Archie grabbed his arm, pulling down hard. The gunshot was followed by an explosion of shards and splinters from the wooden banister next to Veronica.

The deafening noise released Veronica from her paralysis just as a hand wrapped around her wrist and yanked her toward the side of the house and pulled her toward the backyard. Veronica could see Eden's blonde hair ahead of her, although her face was hidden in the shadows under the big oak trees in the yard.

Bursting out into the backyard, Eden pointed to a small guest house nestled in the corner of the overgrown garden. She turned fierce eyes on Veronica and squeezed her hand.

"He must be keeping Sabrina in there," Eden gasped.

"Let's...go get...her," Veronica replied, trying to catch her breath.

Rushing forward, Veronica was surprised to find the door unlocked. Thrusting it open, she pulled Eden in behind her and slammed the door shut. She reached up and slid the big deadbolt into place just as Boyd's heavy fist smashed against the thick wood.

"We've got to find Sabrina," Veronica whispered, backing away from the door. "Then we can find a way past him."

As Boyd pounded on the front door, Eden turned on the light in the little bathroom revealing faded wallpaper and an empty shower stall. Veronica tried the door leading to the bedroom, but it was locked.

Boyd's curses echoed through the house as he kicked at the front door. Suddenly the shouts and the banging stopped. Eden and Veronica huddled together outside the bedroom. In the silence, they could hear moans coming from inside.

"Sabrina?" Veronica shouted, her heart thumping hard. "We're here for you, Sabrina. We're going to help you."

Eden crawled toward the front door, keeping away from the window. She gestured silently to a metal hook by the door. A single key dangled from it. Eden grabbed the key with a trembling hand and scurried back to Veronica. They didn't speak as Eden slid the key in the lock and turned. Sabrina was curled up on the floor like a small child, her face swollen, and her blonde hair matted with blood.

As Sabrina lifted her head to stare at Veronica and Eden, an avalanche of glass shattered down onto the floor behind them. Boyd burst through the remnants of the window, teeth bared and the gun still in hand. Aiming the gun at Veronica, he stepped close enough for her to smell the rancid odor of the sweat and blood that coated his shirt.

"You bastard," she snarled. "Look what you've done to her!"

Hurling herself forward, Veronica crashed into Boyd's arm, knocking the gun to the floor and causing the stocky man to stumble back and hit his head against a heavy wooden sideboard. He moaned and tried to sit up while Veronica scrambled after the gun. She didn't hesitate to aim and fire. The gun clicked harmlessly in her hand.

There was a moment of stunned silence as Veronica looked helplessly at the empty weapon. Then the faint sound of sirens approaching in the distance filled the room. Boyd staggered to his feet as Eden tried to move past him toward Sabrina. Grabbing Eden around her waist, he tackled her to the ground.

He looked up just as Veronica disappeared out the front door. With a terrible yell, Boyd wrenched himself off the floor and raced after her, his face red and wild, his legs pumping at full speed.

She'd made it all the way to the driveway when he caught up to her. Wrapping a thick arm around her waist and cupping an iron hand over her mouth, Boyd forced Veronica toward the big black Mercedes. She struggled, pushing against the car's doorframe until he raised a heavy fist and brought it down hard on her arm. She screamed soundlessly against his palm as he bundled her in and tied her hands behind her back.

As the bright blue Prius turned onto the driveway, Boyd slipped into the Mercedes' driver's seat and started the silent engine. Veronica struggled to sit up. She could see a car approaching through the front windshield. Three men stepped out and approached the house as Boyd slipped the car into drive and revved the engine.

CHAPTER FORTY-THREE

B arker didn't see the big black Mercedes start to move until it was racing toward them. He felt time slow down to a heavy crawl, watching in slow motion as the sedan barreled forward, its big tires sending streams of gravel and debris flying into the air like confetti. He noticed the sun glinting off the grill just as rough hands shoved him off his feet. He landed safely on the ground a yard away.

"Frankie!"

Leo Steele's shout brought Barker out of his daze. He sat up and looked back at the spot where he'd just been standing. Faint burn marks showed the path the car had taken.

His eyes moved to the other side of the driveway and he saw Frankie splayed on the ground.

Leo was already kneeling next to him as Barker ran up.

"Is he...okay?" Barker asked, joining Leo by Frankie's side.

His partner looked peaceful. Barker could have imagined he was only sleeping if his leg hadn't been twisted at an unnatural angle.

"He's out cold," Leo said, "But he's still breathing."

Pulling out his phone, Leo thumbed in 911 and waited. Within seconds he was giving the operator directions to Faraday Manor.

As soon as he'd disconnected the call, Leo ran to the red Jeep and opened the door. Duke jumped out with a frenzied bark, scrambling toward the backyard just as Eden appeared around the corner of the house.

She ran to Duke and grabbed him in a fierce hug, then quickly turned to Leo.

"Call for an ambulance, Leo. Sabrina West is in the guesthouse. She's hurt, but she's still alive. She needs help."

Barker took out his phone.

"I've got this one!" he called out to Leo, who had pulled Eden into a bear hug. "I'll tell them to send two units."

Eden looked over in confusion and saw Barker kneeling on the ground next to Frankie.

"What happened to him?" Eden asked.

A frown creased her forehead as she looked around the yard and down the driveway.

"Some idiot in a black Mercedes tried to run over us." Barker shook his head as if unable to believe his own words. "The car sped out of here going a hundred miles an hour."

Terror filled Eden's face as she turned back to Leo.

"You mean the police didn't catch Boyd? I heard the sirens...I thought they'd gotten him." She stared up at Leo with frantic eyes. "And where's Veronica? She ran out and he chased her..."

Barker pushed himself back to his feet. He was beginning to realize the situation was even worse than what he'd thought.

"Eden, what did Boyd say? Do you know where he's going?"

But Eden was staring down the driveway. A black Dodge Charger had just turned in. They all watched as the car approached.

Barker could see that Vanzinger was driving and Jankowski was riding shotgun. The two big men stepped out with wary expressions, their hands resting on their holsters as they surveyed the area.

"Nessa sent us out here to question Boyd Faraday," Vanzinger said. "Then we heard two emergency calls for this address."

"Yes, we found Sabrina West. She's alive but injured," Eden said, her voice strained. "And poor Frankie was hit by Boyd Faraday. He...he's taken Veronica Lee and driven away in his father's car."

Jotting down a description of the Mercedes, along with descriptions of Boyd and Veronica, Vanzinger jumped back in the Dodge to radio in an APB.

"What about Archie?" Vanzinger asked, looking up at the empty windows of the big house. "Is he aware of all this?"

Eden's eyes narrowed as she spoke, her anger palpable.

"He tried to tell us Boyd wasn't here. When we wanted to look around he pulled a gun on us."

"Archie Faraday threatened you?" Leo asked, his voice hard. "I want to see him try that with me."

Holding on to Leo with a tight grip, Eden shook her head.

"We don't have time for that now. We have to find Veronica before it's too late. And we need to let Nessa know what's happened."

"Where is Nessa by the way?" Barker asked Vanzinger. "I thought she'd have come here with you guys."

Vanzinger shook his head.

"She said she wanted to see if Boyd was at the Channel Ten station. She was planning to wait there for him."

"And maybe that's where he's headed." Barker suddenly had a bad feeling that Boyd Faraday wasn't going to just drive away into the sunset.

Even if he had taken another victim, Boyd would know that his cover had been blown. He could never come home, and he'd be a wanted man, always on the run. Barker knew there was nothing more dangerous than a man with nothing left to lose.

"I think I know where Boyd is headed."

Barker turned to Vanzinger and Jankowski.

"I can't leave Frankie here like this, but you two should get to Channel Ten as soon as you can. You need to find Boyd and stop him. The little shit's not going to go quietly."

An awful certainty settled into Barker's mind.

If Boyd's going down, he'll take as many people with him as possible.

"Now go!" Barker shouted at Jankowski and Vanzinger.

He knew without a doubt that Nessa and everyone else at the Channel Ten station were in terrible danger.

CHAPTER FORTY-FOUR

Nessa sat in Hunter Hadley's office looking out through the glass wall that separated him from his crew. It felt strange to be so close and yet so removed from the activity around them. Looking over at the station manager she wondered if the wall made him feel safe. Perhaps it offered an illusion that he was somehow shielded from the depressing news that he and his crew covered every day.

"Why are you so determined to talk to Boyd?" Hunter asked. "Yesterday *I* was your number one suspect in the Willow Bay Stalker case. Has Boyd done something to win my title?"

His flippant tone irritated her. One of his reporters was missing, and his ex-girlfriend was dead. The whole town was in crisis mode. It seemed to her he'd show a little more concern.

"What if he is?" Nessa asked. "What if someone on your crew pointed the finger at Boyd? Would that surprise you?"

"Are you serious?"

She raised her eyebrows at his obvious incredulity

"Why would that be so hard to believe?" Nessa asked.

She knew that people often failed to see the warning signs in coworkers, neighbors, or even family members who turned out to be criminals, but Hunter was a reporter. He should be trained to notice these things.

"Actually, it wouldn't be hard for me to believe at all," Hunter said. "You can never tell what people are capable of."

"How long have you known Boyd Faraday, Mr. Hadley?"

Hunter leaned back in his chair and sighed.

"Call me Hunter. And, I've known Boyd since I was little. We kind of grew up together. Of course, back then he went by Junior."

"And does *Junior* usually ignore your call?"

She was getting impatient and it showed.

Hunter picked up his phone and tapped in a number.

"Okay, fine. I'll try to call him again now."

He held the phone to his ear, listening. Seconds later he put it down again and sighed.

Nessa offered him a tight smile.

"No luck?"

Shaking his head, he stood and paced to the glass wall, looking out at his crew. He ran a hand through his uncombed curls.

"Are you seriously thinking Boyd's the Stalker?"

"I'm deadly serious, Mr. Hadley," Nessa replied, her voice grim. "Sabrina West is missing; two women have been beaten; two other women are dead. The man who attacked these women is full of hate and rage. He takes that rage out on innocent women. Does that sound like Boyd to you?"

Hunter turned to Nessa. She saw a shadow pass over his face.

"That woman whose picture you showed me the last time. The one that had been killed years ago?"

Nessa's pulse quickened at his words.

"You mean Celeste Reed?"

Hunter nodded, his hands tightening into fists as he spoke.

"I've seen her before. At first, I couldn't think where, but then after you left I started to have these flashes...I could see her face..."

Leaning forward in her chair, Nessa noticed that Hunter had started to breathe faster, and his body was tense. She thought back to his arrest record and the notes the case worker had written in his file.

PTSD Diagnosis. Experienced flashbacks leading up to the offense. Exhibits memory lapse and dissociative reactions to current environment.

Was his effort to remember triggering some type of panic attack? Could he even become violent if she pushed too hard?

"Celeste Reed came to see me a few weeks before she was killed," Hunter said slowly. "She asked me to talk to Boyd. She said he always talked about me and that he'd listen to me. She wanted me to convince him to leave her alone. She was scared of him."

Clearing his throat, Hunter dropped his eyes.

"She couldn't have known, but I wasn't in any shape to help her. I'd been having flashbacks. That was just after I'd been arrested."

It was Nessa's turn to look away. She felt guilty at having checked his medical records. It seemed intrusive and unfair.

"I was having a bad...*episode*. I was in the street and I...I caused a disturbance. I pushed some people...I yelled. The police were called."

He left out the details and Nessa didn't blame him. She'd read all about it anyway. He'd told the responding officers that there were dead bodies everywhere. That all the girls had died because of him. He'd been arrested and subjected to a mental health evaluation.

"Anyway, at that time in my life, I couldn't help myself, much less save Celeste. But I remember her fear, and I wonder now if Boyd-"

The sound of a phone ringing interrupted his words. It took Nessa another two rings to realize that Eden's phone was in her pocket and that someone was calling. She dug out the phone to see Pete Barker's name on the display.

"That you, Barker?"

"Nessa...listen to me. Boyd Faraday is the Stalker. He was the one that abducted Sabrina West, but we've got her back. He's on the run in his father's black Mercedes sedan. He's taken Veronica Lee as a hostage."

Nessa's head spun as she listened to Barker's breathless voice.

"Barker, where are you?"

"Just listen, Nessa," Barker growled. "He's headed toward the Channel Ten station. He's most likely armed. Vanzinger and Jankowski are on their way to you now, but they're at least five minutes behind him."

Sirens blared on Barker's end and his voice sounded far away.

"Listen, the ambulance is here for Frankie. I've gotta go. Take care of yourself, Nessa."

"What's wrong with Frankie?" Nessa shouted, but Barker was already gone.

She shoved Eden's phone back in her pocket. Fear and fury hardened her voice as she saw that Hunter was staring out the window as if in a daze.

"Looks like your buddy, Boyd, had Sabrina all along," Nessa fumed. "He's abducted Veronica Lee and is heading this way."

Hunter didn't respond. Nessa crossed to the window and followed his gaze. A big black Mercedes was speeding down Townsend Road. They watched as the car skidded into the Channel Ten lot and raced toward the entrance. Nessa regained her senses in time to run into the newsroom and yell to the crew.

"Get down everybody...Boyd Faraday has a weapon and-"

But it was too late. Boyd stood at the door, a gun in one hand and a small backpack in the other. He waved the gun and Veronica Lee stepped inside.

"Nobody move!" Boyd shouted, his face flushed and sweaty. "There's a grenade in this bag that will explode on impact. It's strong enough to take out everyone in this newsroom."

Everyone in the room froze, including Nessa.

"What do you want, Junior?" Hunter called out. "Why are you doing this?"

Nessa flicked her eyes toward Hunter, not daring to move her head until she had a better handle on the situation. His face was red and sweaty, and he looked angry, but not out of control. At least not yet.

"Don't call me that!" Boyd roared. "I'm the Willow Bay Stalker now, and I deserve some fucking respect!"

Spittle flew from Boyd's mouth as he screamed the words.

Lifting the gun toward Hunter, he motioned toward the studio beyond the glass wall.

"We're going to produce a special report tonight," Boyd muttered, looking toward Veronica. "And you, little weather girl, are going to finally get the chance you've been dying for. Now move!"

But Veronica was in shock, her green eyes staring blankly ahead. When she didn't respond to Boyd's command, he raised the gun as if to strike her, and Hunter called out in a deep, commanding voice.

"Veronica, honey, you've got to move. Go on into the studio. It's time for you to give your report.

Blinking over at him, Veronica nodded and began inching toward the studio on trembling legs.

"Hurry up!" Boyd shouted, looking over his shoulder at the entrance. "I'm not going to let anybody screw this up for me."

As Boyd forced Veronica forward, Nessa kept her eyes trained on the backpack, hoping that he'd been bluffing about the grenade. But there was definitely something in the bag, and from her position, she couldn't rule out the possibility that he actually did have a device that would explode on impact.

Once Veronica entered the studio, Boyd shoved her in front of the green screen and turned back to the crew in the newsroom.

"Everybody else get on the ground," Boyd shouted, holding up the gun. "If I see anybody moving I'll use this."

But his attention had turned to the big studio cameras, and he hung the backpack on a hook before stepping behind the camera closest to the door. Nessa inhaled sharply as she noted how carefully he handled the bag as if there was something inside that he didn't want to break.

The screens in the newsroom lit up, and Nessa could see Veronica standing in the studio, transfixed by the bright lights and the knowledge that her death was going to be broadcast to everyone in Channel Ten's viewing area.

"Okay, Hunter, you and that cop get in here," Boyd demanded. "I want the whole town to hear my story, and I don't want anybody trying to end it before I'm ready."

Nessa looked desperately toward Hunter, who held up a hand, motioning for her to wait. He stepped into the studio and faced Boyd, blocking his view through the door.

"What are you planning to broadcast?"

"The truth," Boyd spit out. "I'm going to tell everybody out there that I've been lied to and mistreated my whole damn life. And then I'm gonna take my revenge."

Stepping further into the room, Hunter dropped his voice to a more intimate level.

"I don't blame you for being upset, Boyd," Hunter told him, shaking his head. "With the way your father treated you...and your mother running out. I'd be pretty mad, too."

"You don't know the half of it, pretty boy," Boyd sneered. "You've had women falling all over you your whole life. What have I had? Even my own mother wouldn't stick around. Even she lied to me. But now she'll know what she did. After this...she'll know it was all her fault."

Edging toward Veronica, Hunter looked over at Boyd with a pained expression. He pointed to a clip-on microphone used by the news anchors.

"Why let Veronica tell your story, Boyd? You're the one they'll want to hear anyway. People want the truth. Isn't that what you want? To tell it like it is?"

Nessa suddenly realized what Hunter was trying to do. He was giving her time to clear out the crew. He was stalling for time until backup arrived. Moving stealthily, Nessa began to shepherd the crew together until they were all huddled by the door.

"When I give the signal, slip through the door single file," she whispered. "Be as quiet as you can."

A woman in the huddle began to cry.

"But what if he sees us?" she whimpered. "What if he shoots?"

"Just don't let him hear you," Nessa whispered back, slipping up toward the studio door again.

She looked into the studio just in time to see Boyd grab the little mic and clip it on his collar. Nessa's stomach lurched as she saw the dried blood on his hands.

He moved in front of the camera quickly, wrapping a thick arm around Veronica's neck and pointing the gun at her temple.

"Okay, Hunter, you talked me into it. Take me live or I'll put a bullet through her brain."

Nodding solemnly, Hunter flipped several switches on the console and stepped behind the center camera. Nessa saw the countdown clock begin. Five, four, three, two, one. The screens in the newsroom lit up, all showing Boyd's sweaty face. Nessa signaled to the crew to leave, and she held her breath as they quickly filed out.

"This story is for my mother, Luella Faraday," Boyd said, staring straight into the lens. "Of course, she may go by a different name now, but she knows who she is, and she knows what she's done. This whole mess is her fault. Her and every other lying woman that I ever knew. They all caused this to happen, and they all deserved everything they got."

"But why kill Veronica?" Hunter asked, stepping out from behind the bulky studio camera. "What has she done? She's never lied to you, has she? She's just an innocent girl."

"That just makes it even sweeter," Boyd said, but his voice wavered and the grip around Veronica's neck loosened. "Cause she'll never get the chance to hurt anyone. And you know what they say...love hurts....it really hurts."

"You don't have to do this, Boyd." Hunter's voice was soft and soothing. "You don't have to ruin your life because of what your mother or any other woman has done. I'll get you help. Just lay down the gun, Boyd. Let me help you."

Nessa kept her eyes on the screen. She saw a flicker of doubt in Boyd's eyes. He lowered the gun just an inch or two, but it was enough. Hunter lunged at Boyd, grabbing his hand and forcing the gun toward the ground.

Nessa heard the door slam open behind her. Vanzinger and Jankowski bolted past her into the little studio, quickly wrestling Boyd into submission. She hurried past them to Veronica's side, snapping at Hunter to turn off the cameras.

"You think I want my kids seeing this?"

Hunter shook his head and glared down at Boyd.

"We aren't live, Nessa," he said. "We never were. You think I'd let this animal do any more damage to our town? I think we've all been through enough."

Looking toward the backpack, Hunter walked over and slowly lifted it up and off the hook.

"Hunter, you wait now. Let's call in someone who knows about explosives," Nessa said, watching with growing panic as he turned to go. "You're gonna get us all killed!"

But Hunter wasn't listening. He was moving quickly toward the door. Nessa turned to Vanzinger, who was snapping cuffs around Boyd's wrists.

"You know something about explosives, don't you, Vanzinger?"

"I'm in the Guard, Nessa, not on the bomb squad," he said, moving down to secure Boyd's feet with several thick zip ties.

"Fine, then I'll stop him."

But as she ran after Hunter, she realized no one was going to stop him. He was on a mission, and everyone else would have to get out of the way. Flinging open the door, she saw the nervous crew gathered around a police cruiser. Andy Ford had set up a perimeter and it looked like Dave Eddings had already begun to take statements.

"Move back!" Nessa screamed as Hunter made his way through the parking lot. "Stay behind the cruiser."

She watched with worried eyes as Hunter continued past the paved lot. He squinted out into the bright sunshine of the perfect Spring afternoon and flung the backpack as far as he could into the open pasture beyond. The thunderous explosion caused the station windows to rattle as Nessa recoiled and looked away.

She looked back to see the dust settling over a small crater in the grass. A blue Prius pulled into the lot. Nessa was surprised to see Eden and Leo step out. She jogged over to greet them.

"We got Boyd, and Veronica's safe," she told them before they could ask. "Where's Barker?"

"He's at the hospital with Frankie," Eden said. "The paramedics said he likely had a broken leg and a concussion, but they didn't seem too worried."

Digging into her pocket, Nessa pulled out Eden's phone. Her eyes noted the time as she handed it over, and she grimaced, angry that Boyd Faraday had managed to ruin something else.

"It's after two," Nessa said. "I'm sorry to have to break the news, but you all missed your own wedding."

CHAPTER FORTY-FIVE

Winston jumped down from the windowsill and landed lightly on the ground at Veronica's feet. She bent to pick him up just as Ling Lee appeared in the doorway with a steaming mug of tea on a tray. Her mother's smile disappeared as she caught sight of the big tabby cat in her daughter's arms.

"All that hair," she grumbled as she set the tray on the bedside table. "I'll be vacuuming constantly."

"He's very clean, Ma." Veronica dropped her head to nuzzle Winston's soft fur. "And he makes me feel...safe."

Sighing in resignation, Ling perched on Veronica's bed and studied her daughter's new pet. Nessa Ainsley had brought the big orange cat by the house a few days after Boyd had been arrested. She'd explained that Winston had also had a rough time and thought maybe the two of them could help each other heal.

Ling Lee hadn't been pleased, but she'd seen her daughter smiling for the first time since she'd been rescued, and she hadn't had the heart to turn the cat away.

Veronica turned to her closet and began searching through the rack of clothes, trying to ignore her mother's worried gaze. She'd been living back at home for two weeks, and her mother had been treating her like a sick child. As much as she appreciated Ling's support, the constant hovering was starting to annoy her.

"Are you sure you're ready to go back to work?" Ling asked.

"Yes, Ma, I'm sure."

She pulled out a simple black dress and a white, capped-sleeve jacket. She turned to see Ling studying the outfit with curious eyes.

"Now that Hunter Hadley has saved your life, are you still telling me that you're not interested in him?"

Veronica scoffed, but her cheeks flushed pink.

"Yeah, he's a real knight in shining armor, Ma," she said, hiding her face as she searched for her black pumps at the bottom of the closet. "Unfortunately, his armor is already a bit tarnished."

Finding only one of the shoes, Veronica looked up to see a disapproving look on her mother's face.

"I thought I was the one that was supposed to be judgmental," Ling said, cocking her head. "Has this whole experience changed you that much?"

Veronica shrugged, but she felt the sting of her mother's criticism.

"Well, Hunter Hadley is a complicated man," she murmured as she retrieved the missing shoe from under the bed. "And complicated men don't fit into my future plans."

Hearing a car door slam in the driveway below, Veronica looked out the window and winced.

"And here's someone else that doesn't fit in with my new plan."

Ling joined her at the window. They watched Sabrina West walk up the path to the front door. They didn't move until the doorbell rang, but Veronica knew she couldn't avoid Sabrina forever. She swung open the door, startled to see Sabrina looking healthy and cheerful. There was no outward sign that she'd been badly beaten only weeks before.

Sabrina noticed Veronica's shocked face and smiled.

"Make-up is a wonderful thing." She adjusted her jacket nervously and cleared her throat. "Look, I can't stay long. I really just came to say goodbye."

"Good-bye? Where are you..."

"Willow Bay is too small," Sabrina said, looking back toward her car as if she were impatient to leave. "I'm moving to Miami. There are more opportunities there and...well, I need a city as big as my dreams. You know what I mean?"

Veronica nodded, but she could hear the fear behind Sabrina's rehearsed words. The truth hung awkwardly in the air between them. Sabrina was running away, and Veronica couldn't blame her. The town was full of memories, and a new place might help them fade.

"I hope you find what you're looking for," Veronica said, leaning in for a hug.

"You, too, Ronnie." Sabrina's blue eyes were damp as she held Veronica's gaze. "You're a good reporter. Don't ever doubt it."

A lump formed suddenly in Veronica's throat and she swallowed hard as she watched Sabrina walk back to her car. It had the feeling of an ending. Not an end to their friendship so much as an end to an era. She was no longer a college student, and no longer Sabrina West's sidekick. The thought was both scary and thrilling.

I guess it's time to find out who I'm gonna be next.

* * *

The Channel Ten station looked exactly the same as always when Veronica's red Jeep pulled into the parking lot. She hadn't been back since the day Boyd had forced her inside at gunpoint, and she'd imagined that it would look different after everything that had happened. But it appeared that nothing had changed.

"Except me," she whispered into the mild morning air as she climbed out of the Jeep. "I'm not the same girl."

She stopped to look over at the pasture beyond the lot. The grass had already started to grow back over the crater left by the grenade.

Soon there would be nothing to remind any of them of what Boyd Faraday had done, or what he'd taken from her.

"You coming inside?"

Hunter Hadley stood in the doorway. Perhaps he'd seen her pull in. Maybe he'd even been waiting for her. Her mother's voice spoke in her mind, prompting a hot flush of embarrassment.

"Now that Hunter Hadley has saved your life, are you still telling me that you're not interested in him?"

Slipping past Hunter without making eye contact, Veronica crossed to her little desk and dropped her bag on the floor beside it. She felt Hunter hovering behind her, but she kept her eyes on the desk. She needed to prepare for the noon weather report, and there were loads of emails to catch up on.

"Tenley Frost isn't due back from maternity leave for a few more months," Hunter said. "And apparently Sabrina has skipped town, so I need to hire a new reporter."

Veronica froze as hope stirred inside her. What was Hunter saying? Was he about to offer her the job?

"So, I was hoping you might know someone who would be a good fit for the job. I mean, I'd appreciate any recommendations. That is if you know of a reporter that can handle it. It's a demanding job."

Anger flooded through Veronica as she listened to him ramble on. Bolting out of her chair, she turned on Hunter with fierce green eyes.

"Hell, yes, I know a reporter. She's a real go-getter who would be perfect for the job. Someone who'll bust her ass for this little station without all the usual drama and..."

The outrage in her voice faded as Hunter started to grin.

"I was hoping you'd say that."

He waited for another beat as Veronica caught her breath.

"So, I guess that means you're our new investigative reporter."

Smiling up at him with poorly concealed glee, Veronica nodded. She sat back at her desk and began collecting her mail and personal items.

"What are you doing?" Hunter asked, watching her with amusement.

"I'm moving to the investigative reporter's desk," she said. "The new weather reporter will need this one."

Hunter paused and thought for a minute.

"I've got another question for you."

Veronica raised her eyebrows.

"You know of anyone looking for a job as a weather girl?"

Grinning at her look of surprise, Hunter walked toward his office. He went in but left his door open. Veronica watched him for a few seconds, then went back to switching desks. It looked like some things at the station had changed after all.

Opening her email, Veronica skimmed through the messages, knowing that she'd need to come up with a good story for her first assignment. She might be able to resurrect the piece she'd written on the search for a chief of police, but she'd have to find out the current status first.

And then there had to be a good story behind Boyd Faraday's crime spree. She even had a great hook. Who wouldn't want to read the real story behind the capture of the Willow Bay Stalker as told by someone who lived through it?

Opening a blank document on her computer, Veronica felt a thrill of excitement as she began to write her story.

CHAPTER FORTY-SIX

Hunter watched through the glass wall as Veronica began to type, smiling to himself at the memory of her earlier outburst. She'd changed since he'd first hired her in. She was starting to believe in herself, and that, combined with her talent for telling a story and her natural on-screen presence, would be an unbeatable combination.

Leaning back in his chair, he realized that something about the hunger in her eyes reminded him of his younger self. He'd wanted to be an investigative reporter ever since he'd been a boy watching reports on the evening news about the Gulf War in Iraq. He'd marveled at the men who seemed immune to the fighting and chaos. Brave men who wore helmets and crouched behind buildings as missiles flew past, and who never seemed to be afraid.

Of course, he'd made the mistake of believing the job would be full of adventure and excitement, and at first, it had been. He'd traveled the world working for an international news agency before landing a contract to cover the Middle East just as the Arab Spring exploded. He'd covered stories from Turkey to Syria to Iraq. Suddenly he was living his dream, but it had turned out to be a nightmare.

Hunter shook his head, not wanting to ruin his rare good mood with thoughts that would surely drag him back into the darkness. It took him a minute to realize that something was different. He was remembering, but he wasn't shaking and his head wasn't foggy.

He could see the little road clearly in his mind, and the girls standing outside of the school. They carried books and were laughing. Then the teacher he'd been interviewing had called out in a frightened voice. There was a blast, and he was flying backward.

He'd been bruised and battered, and his left arm had been broken in three places, but he'd been okay.

The little girls that had waited outside, and the teacher he had persuaded to give him an interview, were not. They lay scattered in the street around him. Blood and body parts and dirt and stone.

It was a scene out of hell, and it had seared his soul. The screams woke him up at night, and the voice in his head always asked the same questions, but there were never any answers.

If I hadn't been there that day...if I hadn't insisted on the interview, would they still have died? Or was it my fault? Is their blood on my hands?

Hunter looked at his hands and flexed them. Ever since he'd thrown Boyd's backpack away, and the grenade had exploded harmlessly in the green grass of the pasture, he'd felt lighter. The anxiety and guilt had receded.

Reggie Horn had told him he needed to make peace with what had happened, and that he wouldn't be able to overcome his trauma until he did. Maybe she'd been right. Perhaps throwing away Boyd's backpack and preventing another tragedy from happening had been his way of making peace with the past.

The phone on his desk buzzed, bringing his attention back to the office. He frowned at the number on the display. His source inside the courthouse was calling. Something big must be happening.

* * *

The mayor's office was quiet when Hunter entered. His father sat at his desk writing on a steno notepad with a ballpoint pen. He looked up with a smile and threw down the pen.

"There's the hero," he called out, jumping up from the desk. "I've been wondering when you'd make it by to see your old man."

Looking at the steno pad, Hunter could see his father had been writing a speech. The election would be coming up in the Fall and his father would want to be ready. His eyes moved to the snifter of brandy on the desk. It wasn't even lunchtime yet.

"You have a computer, Dad. Why don't you use it instead of handwriting all that?"

The mayor sniffed indignantly.

"I can't think using that thing. I'm so busy trying to figure out which button to push I can't remember what I was trying to write."

Hunter felt a stab of pity for his aging father. Getting older wasn't easy, and things were about to get even harder for his old man. He was suddenly tempted to let the police break the news.

Sighing, Hunter decided to just get it over with.

"There's something you need to know."

The mayor stiffened at the solemn words.

"What've you done this time, Hunter?"

"You need to be asking what Archie Faraday has done," Hunter said, refusing to let his father get under his skin. "The police have uncovered old bones on the Faraday property and I'm about to break the story. I thought you'd want to know."

"What do you mean by old?" Mayor Hadley asked. "You mean like prehistoric bones, or–"

"I mean like the bones of someone who was murdered and left in a shallow grave," Hunter snapped, frowning at his father in amazed disbelief.

The man was obviously in a state of denial, and he had lived that way for a long time. It was time for him to finally accept the truth.

"Initial findings show that the bones have been in the ground for over twenty years," Hunter said. "The crime scene techs have already run a DNA analysis and they came up with a match. Someone that was reported missing over twenty years ago."

"But Boyd would have been just a child back then."

"That's right," Hunter said. "Boyd didn't kill her."

Shaking his head, the mayor returned to his seat.

"Her? Who...I don't understand what you're saying."

But Hunter could see that was a lie. His father knew exactly what he was saying. He just didn't want it to be true.

"The DNA analysis shows the bones belong to Luella Faraday. Her parents had reported her missing apparently, although no one in town got the news."

"But...Archie always said Luella ran out on him and Junior. He was devastated. Maybe someone else did this terrible thing. A stranger."

Hunter put both hands on the desk and leaned toward his father.

"She was buried in Archie's backyard with a bullet in her head. A bullet that came from the gun Archie had in his home when his son was arrested."

"Why haven't I been told about any of this?" the mayor demanded. "I should have been informed."

Raising his eyebrows, Hunter shrugged and turned to the door.

"You'll have to ask the chief of police about that. I just wanted to break the news to you before you heard it from anyone else."

He put a hand on the doorknob, then hesitated. He wouldn't be back anytime soon; he should say what needed to be said now.

"Too many people have gotten hurt in Willow Bay because nobody would stand up to the bullies and crooks running this town. But you should know that's all about to change, and anyone who resists isn't going to be reelected as Mayor."

Closing the door behind him, Hunter walked out into the sunshine of a perfect Spring day, free from the shadows at last.

CHAPTER FORTY-SEVEN

Nessa had never seen Mayor Hadley looking so down. His face was haggard and even his red power tie had lost its sheen. And the news she was about to deliver wouldn't make him feel any better. She should have already told him about the investigation into Archie Faraday but seeing they were such close friends, it had been a potential conflict of interest. Now that the decision had been made, there was no way around it.

"Mayor Hadley, I'm sorry to be the bearer of bad news, but Archie Faraday has been arrested. We've charged him with the murder of his late wife, Luella Faraday."

"Luella skipped town on her family twenty years ago," the mayor muttered, his bloodshot eyes resting on Nessa with contempt. "And now all of a sudden we're all supposed to believe she was there in Archie's back garden all along?"

Dropping her eyes to the empty snifter on Hadley's desk, Nessa didn't try to argue. She crossed to the door and opened it. Riley Odell sat on the loveseat in the outer office.

"Ms. Odell? I think I'm going to need you to explain the situation to the mayor. He's having a hard time understanding the charges we've filed against Archie Faraday."

Riley stood and straightened her jacket, giving Nessa a wry smile.

"Well, let me see what I can do to explain."

Striding into the office, Riley approached the mayor's desk and stood across from him wearing a stern expression. Nessa assumed it was the same one she wore in court when cross-examining particularly difficult witnesses.

"We have enough physical and circumstantial evidence to convict Archibald Faraday twice, Mr. Mayor," Riley said in a hard voice. "A bullet shot from a gun he still owns was found lodged in his wife's shattered skull in a shallow grave in his garden. He never reported her missing and never bothered looking for her."

Mayor Hadley crossed his arms over his chest and raised his chin. Nessa braced herself for another angry outburst, but then he sighed and shook his head sadly.

"Well, if that's your decision, then you have my support, Ms. Odell. Make sure you let the state attorney know that."

"Oh, I definitely will, Mayor Hadley. I've already explained that you made the decision to appoint Nessa as the new chief of police and he was quite happy to hear it."

Stiffening in his chair, the mayor frowned.

"You told him that Nessa is the new chief of police?"

"Yes, I did," Riley agreed.

"And he was...happy about it?"

"Yes, he was," Riley said. "He wasn't looking forward to calling for another federal investigation into Willow Bay. We like to keep things at a state or local level whenever possible."

The mayor nodded eagerly.

"Oh, I do, too, Ms. Odell. That's definitely my preference."

"Then it's all settled," Riley said. "We've got a new chief of police, and Archie Faraday will be tried for first-degree murder."

Mayor Hadley looked stunned as Nessa followed Riley out of the office. They exited City Hall and stood in the courtyard.

"You did a good job catching Boyd Faraday and his father," Riley said, her eyes shining with approval. "I'm not sure anyone has ever

304

prosecuted a father and his son for first-degree murder at the same time, but for separate crimes. It'll be the highpoint of my career."

Nessa shook her head and rolled her eyes.

"We do tend to make things a little difficult for ourselves around here. But maybe you'll be a good influence on this town."

"Well, hopefully during the next election the citizens of Willow Bay will decide it's time for new leadership," Riley said, lowering her voice. "Perhaps it's not my place to say it, but Mayor Hadley and his brandy need to go."

Grinning over at the prosecutor, Nessa didn't argue. She wouldn't badmouth her boss in public, but she couldn't stop others from doing so, could she?

"By the way," Riley said, "there's a rumor going around that Detectives Ingram and Ortiz were eating lunch in the Blue-Ribbon Diner when your call for back-up at Channel Ten came over the radio. The waitress said they ordered pie and coffee before responding."

"Yeah, I've got my hands full with those two detectives," Nessa said, her grin fading. "They better shape up or they'll find themselves back in uniform."

She'd heard the pie and coffee rumor, too, and she hadn't decided yet what she was going to do about it. She'd already had to reprimand Ortiz for sharing confidential information with the press. One more strike against him and she'd be forced to suspend him or demote him back to patrol.

Luckily Jankowski was back on the job, although his grief over Gabby's death and his breakup with Iris had made him a bear to work with, and Vanzinger was already complaining about his mood swings. Of course, her new detective had brought along his own baggage. She turned to look at Riley.

"And speaking of detectives," Nessa said, a wicked gleam lighting up her eyes, "what's the deal with you and Detective Vanzinger?"

Looking away, Riley bit her lip and sighed.

"I wish I knew," she finally said. "I interned at a law office in Willow Bay when I was still in college. Tucker had just gotten promoted to detective when we met. We just...clicked. At least I thought so. Then one day he left town. Told me to forget about him. Let's just say it took me a while to get over him."

"From what I can tell, I don't think he ever did get over you," Nessa said, remembering the look of longing in Vanzinger's eyes when he'd watched Riley walk away. "And you do know why he had to leave, don't you?"

Tucking a dark, glossy strand of hair behind her ear, Riley held up a dismissive hand.

"It doesn't matter. That was a long time ago and I'm a different person now. The girl that fell in love with Tucker Vanzinger doesn't exist anymore."

"Right, and I'm a size six," Nessa said with an arched eyebrow, not willing to give up so easily. "Chief Kramer and Detective Reinhardt were dirty; they ran Vanzinger out of town when he wouldn't play along. They threatened him. I wouldn't doubt that they had threatened to hurt you, too, if they knew you guys were seeing each other."

Noting the shock on Riley's face, Nessa plowed on.

"Vanzinger disappeared for years, but when Jankowski needed him, he came back to help. After everything he's done in the last few months, he's redeemed himself in my book."

Riley had closed her eyes against Nessa's onslaught.

"Okay, I'll shut up now," Nessa said. "It's just that he's a good cop and we don't seem to get many of those around here."

Feeling her phone buzzing in her pocket, Nessa grabbed it, suddenly worried about the time.

How long had she been talking to Riley? But she still had time to get home and get changed before she and Jerry needed to leave. She gave Riley one last meaningful look.

"He's still single you know. He never did find anyone else."

"I thought you said you were going to shut up now," Riley shot back. But as Nessa left, she noticed that Riley was smiling.

CHAPTER FORTY-EIGHT

B arker called up the stairs to Taylor again, then checked his watch. They still had twenty minutes until they needed to leave, but he was getting nervous. There was no way he was going to show up late for the big surprise. Not after everything that had happened before, and not when Reggie Horn would be there, too.

As he dropped his phone and car keys into his pocket, Barker was relieved to hear a loud knock at the door. Frankie stood on the doorstep leaning on an aluminum crutch. As Barker opened the door Frankie waved a piece of paper over his head.

"Mr. Delancey finally came through with the payment," he said, hobbling through the door. "And he even added a bonus since I got hurt on the job."

"I'll bet he did," Barker muttered, taking the check and holding it up to the light. "He's probably scared we'll sue him."

Circling Barker, Frankie let out a low whistle.

"Nice jacket, man," Frankie said, his eyes wide. "Where did you get that? You look like fucking James Bond."

"Watch your mouth," Barker warned. "Taylor's upstairs."

Barker straightened the lapels of his jacket, glad that he'd gotten one that fit his slimmer frame.

"Leo took me to his tailor," Barker explained, turning around to show off the jacket from every angle. "The whole suit has been tailored to my exact measurements."

"It looks great, man. I'm gonna have to get me one of those."

Frankie stared down at his own baggy suit as Barker called up the stairs again to Taylor.

"Taylor, we're leaving in ten minutes with or without you!"

There was no response from upstairs.

"Charming, man," Frankie said. "Give her a fucking break."

"I said to watch your mouth, Frankie," Barker snapped. "How is Bella doing by the way?"

Frankie crutched further into the room and lowered himself onto the sofa. He looked up at Barker and shrugged before taking out a stick of gum and sticking it into his mouth.

"She and Ian are doing pretty good from what I could see." Frankie chewed loudly as he spoke. "Although they were both shocked that Boyd was the guy who attacked her. Ian said he's known the dumbass since they were kids."

"Maybe that's why he did it," Barker said. "Maybe Boyd chose Bella because he knew she was cheating on his friend."

Frankie frowned and scratched at his chin.

"Yeah, I guess. Boyd knew all the rich kids. They all grew up to be big shots while he was just a regular guy. Maybe that pissed him off."

Looking at his watch again, Barker wondered if they'd ever come up with a logical explanation for what Boyd had done.

The Stalker had tried to tell Nessa and Hunter Hadley that he'd been mistreated and lied to. That he was getting revenge on his mother and every other woman who had lied to him. But then, maybe that was just a convenient excuse. Plenty of men had lost a mother or been lied to by a girlfriend. It didn't mean they had a free pass to go around killing people.

"I stopped by and checked on Olympia Glass, too," Frankie said. "I figured she might have known Boyd as well, but she didn't. My guess is that Boyd knew Milo."

"Olympia Glass, huh." Barker narrowed his eyes. "What else did the lovely Ms. Glass have to say?"

Struggling to get his crutches in the right position to stand up, Frankie tried to act casual. He scratched at his chin again and shrugged.

"She didn't say much really, but she's gone through some hard times. I think she was screwing around with that jerk Milo because she didn't want to get too close to anyone, you know what I mean?"

It just sounded like more excuses to Barker, but something in the way Frankie talked about Olympia made him hold his tongue. Who was he to judge anyway?

"Olympia's a strong woman," Frankie said as if Barker had tried to deny it. "And she's trying to get past the mistakes she's made."

Barker nodded, but he didn't respond. He gave Frankie time to talk. He'd learn more that way.

"We all make mistakes, man." Frankie looked down at his new pair of sneakers. "But that douche bag Milo's out of the picture now, so that's something."

"Well, it certainly makes it convenient for you," Barker said, unable to hold back any longer. "Cause somebody has a crush."

A flush of color spread over Frankie's face, but he didn't bother to deny it. Instead, he pointed to Barker's expertly tailored jacket and smirked.

"Looks like I'm not the only one, man. Love is in the air."

Barker glared at Frankie then looked up the stairs. Taylor stood on the top step wearing a pale green dress and strappy white sandals. Her long, dark hair had been brushed into a high ponytail.

"Who's in love?" Taylor asked, her bright blue eyes twinkling.

"Frankie is," Barker responded quickly, suddenly terrified that Taylor would suspect he had feelings for Reggie.

Taylor raised her eyebrows in mock surprise.

"Oh, I thought you were talking about your crush on Dr. Horn."

"I think she's on to you, partner!" Frankie slapped Barker on the back and shook his hand. "And it looks like you just got the green light to ask Dr. Horn if she's interested in your old ass, too."

Pulling Taylor in for a hug, Barker felt a pang of guilt in his gut. How could he ever be with anyone other than Caroline? It was wrong. He couldn't ask Taylor to watch him dating another woman while her mother was six feet under at Sacred Heart Cemetery.

Taylor put a soft hand on Barker's chin and turned his flushed face toward her. She stared at him with Caroline's blue eyes.

"It's time for you to be happy again, Dad. Mom would want that for you. *I* want that for you."

Blinking hard, Barker grabbed his keys off the rack and opened the door. Motioning for Frankie to hop through the door first, Barker waited for Taylor to walk through, then closed the door behind them, inhaling deeply as he walked into the cool evening air.

"Hurry up you two," he said, feeling a heady sense of anticipation for whatever lay ahead. "We have a party to get to."

CHAPTER FORTY-NINE

L eo clicked *send* and logged out of his computer. It was Friday night and he was more than ready to go home. He'd spent a long week filing the paperwork to overturn Seth Reed's murder conviction, and he needed a break from the grisly evidence he'd had to present in order to prove that Boyd Faraday had been the man who had beaten Celeste Reed to death. With any luck, Seth Reed would be a free man within the next few weeks.

As he gathered the files and papers he wanted to review over the weekend, Leo heard Pat Monahan moving around in the reception area. Frowning, he stood and opened his door.

"Pat, what are you doing here after five on a Friday afternoon?"

The paralegal finished the sentence she'd been typing and looked up with a distracted smile.

"Is it that late?" she asked, turning to look up at the big clock on the wall. "I guess I lost track of the time working on this filing."

She bent her head over the keyboard again and Leo stared at her cap of gray curls with concern. Pat wasn't the type to lose track of time. She lived by the clock and spent a great deal of effort trying to make him do the same. Could she be having memory problems? She wasn't getting any younger after all.

Walking back into his office, Leo wondered if Pat had anyone to check on her and make sure she was taking care of herself. She wasn't married and she didn't have children.

Just like me.

The thought popped into his head before he could stop himself. He knew it wasn't the same. He had Eden. And Hope and Devon. Even though the wedding hadn't turned out the way they'd expected, they still had each other. And of course, eventually, there would be a wedding. But after their last fiasco, they had needed a little time to recover. Or at least, Eden had needed time.

Remembering how eager he'd been to have a family he could call his own, Leo allowed himself a minute to sulk in private. He'd been looking forward to having someone to list as next-of-kin again.

Pat had been the only person he'd listed as an emergency contact in many years. He knew Eden would still be his contact going forward, wedding or no wedding, but it wouldn't be quite as exciting if he couldn't write *wife* in the relationship field.

Leo studied a framed picture of Eden and Duke on his desk. It was the picture she'd given him as a Christmas present on the night he proposed. He picked up the frame next to it. It was his new favorite.

In the picture, he stood next to Eden. Hope and Devon stood in front of them, and Duke sat at attention on the ground at Eden's feet. They looked like a real family. He ran a big finger over the glass.

Each of them had been shattered by loss in the past, but somehow they'd picked up the pieces. They'd managed to put together a new picture of what their family looked like, and somehow it all worked. He was finally part of a family again. A wedding certificate wouldn't change that, would it?

His thoughts were interrupted by a harsh knock on the outer door. Leo stood and walked out to the lobby just in time to see Jankowski and Vanzinger barge in.

"I'm sorry to have to do it this way, Leo, but you need to come with us," Jankowski growled, guiding Leo toward the door. "We have a warrant. We'll need to take you downtown for questioning. If you don't make a fuss I won't put on the cuffs."

"This is insane," Leo said, turning back to Pat in a panic. "Check the warrant, Pat. See what it says."

Grabbing the warrant from Vanzinger's hand, Pat put on her glasses and held it up to the light.

"It's true, Leo," Pat said, folding the warrant and handing it back to Vanzinger. "I think you'll have to go downtown."

Leading Leo toward a black Dodge Charger, Vanzinger opened the back door and waited for Leo to slide in. He shut the door then climbed in the front as Jankowski got into the driver's seat.

"Tell me what this is all about," Leo demanded, feeling the car start to move underneath him.

"I'm sure we'll get this all cleared up quickly," Vanzinger soothed.

Leo sat back against the seat. Obviously, a mistake had been made, and he'd have to talk with Nessa Ainsley and Riley Odell. He was sure the two women would explain what was going on. And once they'd realized they'd made a mistake he would be free to go home.

But the Charger raced past the police station without slowing down and without turning in.

"Where are we going?" he asked, looking out the window as the city flew by.

"We told you. We're going downtown for questioning," Jankowski said, grinning back at Leo. "And when we get there, your answer better be *I do*."

CHAPTER FIFTY

The Mercy Harbor administration building seemed deserted as Eden shut off her computer and gathered her purse and car keys. Shutting off the lights in her office, Eden pushed her way out into the hall. Reggie's office was dark, and Eden frowned, wondering why Reggie hadn't said goodbye before leaving.

Maybe she has a hot date. It is Friday night after all.

The hall was dim, and Eden's pulse quickened as she walked toward the elevator. It had been two weeks since the police had dragged Boyd Faraday off to jail, but she was still a little jumpy. Especially after Nessa had called with the news that Archie Faraday had been arrested for murdering his wife. Eden couldn't believe the crotchety old man had put a bullet in Luella Faraday's head.

I guess you can never really know what anyone is truly capable of.

Refusing to let her nerves take over, Eden pressed the *Down* button and pulled out her phone. No text from the kids or Leo. They were all probably busy wrapping up their Friday afternoons. They'd have plenty of time to spend together once they'd all made it home. And maybe she'd ask Leo to stop and get a take-out curry and a nice bottle of cabernet.

The elevator door slid open, and Eden was surprised to see Edgar, the head security guard at Riverview Tower. The old man looked surprised to see her as well. He waited until she stepped in, then cleared his throat.

"I was just coming up to speak to you, Ms. Winthrop," he said, fidgeting with the radio on his belt. "I think there's something downstairs you need to see."

"Can it wait until Monday, Edgar? I was hoping to get an early start on my weekend."

Edgar looked uncomfortable. He hitched up his pants and sighed.

"I think you're gonna wanna see this tonight."

As the elevator reached the ground floor, Edgar put out a hand and ushered her toward the building's grand conference hall. It was a part of the building reserved for special events, and she rarely had a reason to visit the richly decorated event space.

"In here, ma'am," Edgar said, knocking softly on a small door across from the elaborate entrance to the Riverwalk Ballroom.

The door swung open, and Eden gasped to see Duke sitting on a rug in front of a floor-length mirror.

"Duke?" Eden turned puzzled eyes on Edgar, but he just smiled and motioned for her to step inside.

"Congratulations," he said, breaking into a warm smile before he turned and walked back toward the lobby.

Rushing forward, Eden crouched by Duke and inspected his golden fur. He appeared to be all right, but why was he here? She looked around, realizing it was some type of dressing room. A magnificent cheval mirror stood in the corner, and soft lights illuminated an elegant dressing table and chair.

"Hello, Aunt Eden," a soft voice said behind her.

She whipped around, startled by Hope's sudden appearance.

"What in the world..."

But then she couldn't speak as she saw Hope standing in the beautiful blue silk dress they'd selected for the wedding. Eden had never had the chance to see her niece in the dress, and the sight took her breath away.

"You look so gorgeous...so grown up," Eden said, stepping forward to take her hand. "What is all this?"

She looked around the room, gasping when she saw a dress rack with a Bridal Bliss garment bag hanging on it.

"I wanted you to have your wedding, Aunt Eden. After the last one was ruined, I knew you'd be too worried to plan another one, because you'd think that one would go wrong, too."

Eden opened her mouth to protest, then closed it. Hope was right. Even thinking about rescheduling the wedding had made her anxiety rise. She'd been scared that something might happen to ruin it again.

"Is this what you've been doing on the computer all the time?" Eden asked. "Were you setting this up?"

Wincing at the question, Hope shook her head.

"Not really," she admitted. "I mean, it was my idea and everything, but Barb and Reggie did most of the planning."

Eden nodded, swallowing her disappointment. She'd hoped there was a simple explanation for Hope's recent behavior.

"You've seemed so preoccupied lately, Hope. I've been worried."

"I'm sorry, Aunt Eden. I shouldn't have worried you. But I knew you were busy planning the wedding, and I didn't want the petition and the campaign to get in the way, and then after Boyd Faraday was arrested, you were so upset, and..."

Eden frowned and put her hands on Hope's shoulders. She stared into the blue eyes that were so like Mercy's.

"Are you saying you're the one that organized the Nessa for chief petition? And all the signs and stuff around town?"

Nodding slowly, Hope dropped her eyes.

"I'm sorry I didn't tell you. Are you mad at me, Aunt Eden?"

Eden pulled Hope in for a hug, laughing with relief and joy.

"Of course, I'm not mad at you, honey. I'm proud of you." She leaned back and looked into Hope's eyes. "So proud of the young woman you've become. And your mom would be, too."

317

Duke barked as the door swung open and Devon peeked in.

"I'm supposed to take Duke to get ready," he said, looking uncomfortable in a jacket and tie.

"Did you know about all this, Devon?" Eden asked, reaching out to ruffle her nephew's neatly combed hair.

"No...they never tell me anything," he said, leading Duke out of the room.

The door had barely closed behind Devon when Reggie and Barb pushed through. They were both dressed in their wedding finery and their arms were full of flowers.

"We've got the bouquets," Reggie said, giving Eden a hug. "Do you need help getting your dress on?"

"No, but if I do, I've got Hope to help me."

Barb unzipped the garment bag and pulled out the lovely white gown Eden had feared she'd never get a chance to wear. Hanging it on the rack, Barb opened the box with Eden's white satin shoes.

"I think I brought everything," Barb said, already holding a tissue and dabbing at her eyes as she looked at the gown.

"We'll leave you to get ready, then." Reggie pulled Barb toward the door. "But don't take too long. Leo will be waiting for you in the ballroom at six o'clock sharp."

The words sent a thrill through Eden. She was going to marry Leo Steele. Tonight. It seemed almost too good to be true. After everything she'd been through, after everything they'd been through together. It was finally going to happen.

Minutes later Eden stood in front of the mirror admiring her white satin dress and pumps. Hope stood behind her.

"You're not quite ready, Aunt Eden," Hope said with a smile. "Something's definitely missing."

Eden bit her lip, studying her reflection, trying to figure out what she had forgotten.

"Well, your dress is new," Hope said, "but you still need something old and borrowed and blue."

Eden looked down as Hope slid a delicate bracelet onto her wrist. She gasped as she saw the aquamarine stones.

"I think this checks the other boxes," Hope said. "It's old and blue, and you can't keep it...I'm just letting you borrow it."

Eden stared at her niece, then dropped her eyes again to her wrist. It was the bracelet Mercy had gotten from their father when she was a teenager. The one Eden had passed on to Hope on her last birthday.

"Mom would have wanted you to wear this," Hope said, her voice a whisper. "She'd want to be with you on your big day."

"She *is* with me, honey, and with you and Devon." Eden forced herself not to cry. "She's always with us. She always will be."

Eden took Hope's hand.

"Now, I think I'm ready. Let's go to the ball."

* * *

Leo stood in front of the big picture window that faced the river. The sun was starting to set behind him when Eden stepped through the door into the Riverwalk Ballroom, her white gown luminous in the light of the candles that glowed all around. The happy faces in the room were a blur as she looked toward him. A soft nuzzle on her hand made her look down. Duke stood beside her. In place of his collar, he wore a white satin bowtie.

"Are you going to walk me down the aisle, boy?"

Duke blinked up at her as if he understood, and they watched as Hope began to walk down the aisle with a bouquet in her hand. Seconds later they followed Hope into the room and were greeted by a round of applause.

Eden felt her heart swell in her chest until she was sure it would burst. How had she gotten to this perfect moment, walking toward a man who was perfect for her?

Everyone stood as she moved through the room, and she began to recognize the faces of people she knew from throughout Willow Bay. Mercy Harbor staff, neighbors, and friends, even her old history teacher Ms. Lee and Veronica. It looked like the whole town had been invited.

She saw Nessa Ainsley standing next to her husband, his arm around her waist and her head resting on his shoulder. Jankowski and Vanzinger grinned at her from their seats next to Frankie Dawson, who winked as she passed by.

As she neared the front of the room, Eden noticed that Reggie stood next to a pleased-looking Barker on one side of the front row while Barb stood on the other side holding a box of tissues.

Nathan Rush, immaculate in a formal black suit, stood beside Barb wearing a wide smile. Eden met his eyes, hoping he knew how much it meant to her that he had flown all the way across the country again to be there.

Hope turned and gave Eden a tight hug, before stepping to the side. Devon stood next to Leo, handsome in his little suit and tie.

"I'm the best man," he whispered, as Eden bent to hug him.

"You sure are," she whispered back before he stepped away.

Taking Leo's hand, Eden felt warm contentment settle over her. She was right where she was supposed to be. Standing with the man she loved, in front of her family, her friends, and her town.

They faced Pat Monahan, who gave Eden a mischievous smile as she opened her notes. Leo's longtime paralegal had been like family to him for years, and when Eden found out she was also a notary, she'd insisted that Pat officiate at their wedding.

"We're here tonight to celebrate the wedding of Leo Steele and Eden Winthrop, who have somehow managed to find each other in this difficult and challenging world."

Leo gripped Eden's hand tighter as Pat continued.

"What a joy it is to witness their happiness as they pledge their undying love and commitment with a ring and a kiss."

And as the sun set over the river, and the long day came to an end, Eden realized that her new life with Leo had officially begun.

Start the Next Series Now...

Want to read more about Willow Bay? Ready to find out what some of your favorite characters are up to? Then start the new Veronica Lee Thriller spin-off series now with:

<u>Her Last Summer: A Veronica Lee Thriller, Book One</u>
by Melinda Woodhall

And don't forget to sign up for the Melinda Woodhall Newsletter to receive bonus scenes and insider details at <u>www.melindawoodhall.com/newsletter</u>

ACKNOWLEDGEMENTS

I SET OUT TO WRITE THIS BOOK in the middle of my children's summer break and didn't finish it until the school year was in full, chaotic swing. It's always a challenge to find enough time to write, and I owe a debt of gratitude to Giles, my incredibly supportive, loving husband who made sure I got the time and space I needed to finish this book on schedule.

I'm always amazed at the support and encouragement I get from my five wonderful children, Michael, Joey, Linda, Owen, and Juliet. I am truly blessed to have their constant love in my life.

Much love and thanks are also due to my extended family, including Melissa Romero, Leopoldo Romero, Melanie Arvin Kutz, David Woodhall, and Tessa Woodhall.

My journey as a writer started with my mother's encouragement. Her kind spirit and love of reading remain with me as I continue the adventure. For that, I am truly grateful.

If you enjoyed this book, please

Leave a review for Girls Who Lie

ABOUT THE AUTHOR

Melinda Woodhall is the author of the page-turning *Mercy Harbor Thriller* series. After leaving a career in corporate software sales to focus on writing, Melinda now spends her time writing romantic thrillers and police procedurals. She also writes women's contemporary fiction as M.M. Arvin.

When she's not writing, Melinda can be found reading, gardening, chauffeuring her children around town, and updating her vegetarian lifestyle website. Melinda is a native Floridian and the proud mother of five children. She lives with her family in Orlando.

Visit Melinda's website at www.melindawoodhall.com

Other books by Melinda Woodhall

The River Girls
Girl Eight
Catch the Girl
Girls Who Lie
Her Last Summer
Her Final Fall
Her Winter of Darkness
Her Silent Spring
Her Day to Die

Made in the USA
Middletown, DE
06 May 2024

53954071R00194